# Wild Cowboy Country

ERIN MARSH

Published by Sourcebooks Casablanca, an imprint of Sourcebooks
P.O. Box 4410, Naperville, Illinois 60567-4410
(630) 961-3900
sourcebooks.com

Printed and bound in Canada.
MBP 10 9 8 7 6 5 4 3 2 1

*For my grandparents, who took me on family vacations to national parks and taught me to love our country's ecological diversity.*

# Chapter 1

Sending gravel spraying in all directions, Lacey Montgomery swung her ancient Jeep Cherokee next to the massive pickup before putting her vehicle in Park. Yanking off her seat belt, she jumped out to glare at the giant decal stretching from the truck's four-door cab to the end of its extended bed. No one—not even someone as myopic as a mole—could miss the advertisement for Valhalla Beef. Only a city slicker like Clay Stevens would be so tacky and self-absorbed as to emblazon the entire side of his F-350 with the name of his ranch.

When Lacey had decided to stop by the wolf den on her day off work as a ranger for Rocky Ridge National Park, she hadn't expected to see the greenhorn's vehicle at one of the backcountry trailheads. Although Clay owned one of the largest and oldest spreads in Sagebrush Flats, he had a reputation for enjoying creature comforts over riding his land. His ranch hands claimed he spent more time poring over spreadsheets in his air-conditioned office than checking fences. They always joked down at the Prairie Dog Café that you could take the boy out of New York but not the New York out of the boy.

Lacey agreed. Clay may have gotten a fancy degree in ranch management, but he had the heart of a Wall Street stockbroker…and, if he was anything like his daddy, a corrupt one. All he cared about was profit. He was so worried about taking a loss that he kept trying to organize the local ranchers against the national park's wolf reintroduction program.

Unlike a lot of towns, Sagebrush Flats welcomed the return of the majestic animals. Lacey supposed she might have had a part in that. Her whole life, the sleek canine hunters had fascinated her. She'd never forget the time her father and she had backpacked overnight in Yellowstone and had spied a pack playing with their pups. Lacey had been twelve, and she'd stared through her dad's binoculars for more than half an hour as she watched the little dark-brown fluffs roll and tussle. She'd quite simply fallen in love with the fascinating species.

Lacey had become an expert on wolves and would talk to anyone who would listen about the benefits of bringing the apex predator back. Since her mom owned and operated the town's main restaurant, she'd had a pretty large audience. Slowly, she'd won over every last rancher—even the surliest, crankiest ones. Until Clay. Ever since he'd inherited his maternal grandfather's land, he'd tried to stir up animosity, complaining at town hall meetings and at the local watering hole that the wolves were killing calves and pestering the cattle and that they had no business being allowed to run wild.

Although Clay had never shot or even tried to kill a wolf, she didn't trust the son of the man who'd bilked most of Sagebrush's residents out of their life savings with his pyramid scheme. It concerned her to see the New Yorker's vehicle parked near the best path to the national park's most popular den, especially since he didn't seem like the type to take recreational hikes.

Grabbing her walkie-talkie from her glove compartment, Lacey set off at a brisk pace. She didn't have the rest of her park ranger gear today, but she always carried the radio since cell phone reception could be spotty. Normally when she wasn't officially working, she took her time moving through the scrub, letting her senses steep in the tangy smell of pinyon pine and the quiet rustle of life in the arid wilderness. Wolves might be her primary passion, but as an ecologist, she loved the land from the tiniest form of fungi to the impressive grizzly bear. She'd originally planned to take a leisurely walk, snapping photos for a ranger presentation she gave at the lodge before swinging by to check on the pack of Mexican wolves. For the past few years, the subspecies of gray wolves, which were also called lobos, had made an abandoned bear den their nursery. Since it was late April, Lacey kept checking the area for activity, and she couldn't resist coming, even on her day off.

Turning from the main path, she headed deeper into the brush, trying to move as quietly as possible. Although the pack usually patrolled an occupied den, they typically fled at the sound of humans. Lacey was careful not to get too close and risk the lobos relocating their young.

As she approached the site, her body stilled as anger shot through her. In the distance, she heard the unmistakable sounds of teenage boys—drunk ones given their slurred, overly loud conversation. Park visitors shouldn't be off-trail, especially in this area. Aside from the wolves' presence, cryptobiotic soil crust grew here. Although the mixture of algae, bacteria, lichens, and fungi looked like black, dry dirt clumps, it formed an important part of the ecosystem, preventing erosion and improving water absorption. Once crushed under human feet, the delicate colony could take more than two centuries to grow back. Lacey knew how to avoid stepping on it, but most people would overlook the vegetation. Even if they did notice the dark patches, they wouldn't understand their importance.

Lacey's anger only grew when she detected a whiff of smoke. Although this spring was relatively wet, the teens weren't in a designated campground. And Lacey didn't have a lot of faith that a group of drunk adolescents would build a proper fire ring, even if they ended up being locals. Reaching for her walkie-talkie, she radioed in to the main ranger station.

"You know you're not scheduled to be in today." Kylie Lambert's voice came crackling through the speaker.

"I wanted to check on the wolf den," Lacey said between huffs as she scrambled up a steep grade.

Kylie chuckled. "You know you're allowed to take a day off."

"Nature doesn't," Lacey quipped.

Kylie groaned in response. "I *knew* you'd say that."

Lacey didn't comment. It was, after all, her favorite expression, and she didn't have time for small talk. "It's a good thing I came. Somebody built a campfire off-trail near Coyote Rock. From the sounds of it, I think it's drunk teenagers—maybe four or five."

"Lacey, you're not a commissioned law officer. You're an ecologist. Let me send Paul to handle it. He's out by Pinyon Pine Basin."

Reaching the top of a ridge, Lacey half slid down the other side. She could see the smoke now, and it looked like it came from near the burrow. "That's still half an hour away. It's just kids fooling around, so I can handle it."

Breathing hard, she reached another crest. Her heart squeezed in panic as she caught sight of the troublemakers. The four adolescents had built their illegal campsite right on top of the wolf den. The structure was old, having been dug and abandoned by a bear years ago. She didn't know how stable the roof would be, especially in this arid climate. The whole area had been carved by an ancient, long-dried-up arroyo and was prone to collapse. The tallest of the teens stood near the edge of the old bank to capture a selfie. Like the other boys, he wore a hoodie, making it difficult to identify him, especially given the distance between Lacey and the trespassers. As the teenager snapped a picture, his left foot sent a cascade of rocks tumbling below. He moved to more stable ground, but the mini rockslide must have amused him. Experimentally, he tramped on the ground. Lacey cried out in warning, but the boys didn't hear her over the noise they were making. The kid's hiking boot struck, sending a chunk of dirt and rock thudding downward. His friends decided to join him, and all four began stomping.

Not wanting the teenagers to cause more damage, Lacey raced toward them, shouting for them to stop. Finally noticing her, the kids scattered. Unfortunately, the rapid movement caused more debris to fall. From her vantage point on the ridge, Lacey spotted the mama lobo dart from the burrow, a baby in her mouth.

"Walk carefully!" Lacey yelled. "There's a wolf den below you with pups inside. You need to cautiously back away from the edge. Don't trigger a bigger landslide!"

The shortest of the boys listened, but the rest bounded away like mountain goats, causing more dirt to break off and hurtle downward.

"Shit!" the remaining boy cried out. "Are there really baby wolves down there?"

Lacey ignored him as she scanned the landscape for the mama lobo. The canines were shier creatures than many humans realized, and she only hoped that the combination of the shouting and landslides hadn't driven the mother away.

"What should I do?" the teenager asked.

"Just slowly retreat." Lacey forced her voice to remain calm as she scanned for the female lobo. She had no way of knowing how long the wolf would stay away or how many pups were in the den.

Making her decision, she climbed into the ancient creek bed. Glancing around, she saw no movement other than the slip and slide of more rocks. Resolutely, she pulled out her flashlight and placed it between her teeth. If any pups were inside, she needed to get them out now.

They weren't just any gray wolves but the more critically endangered subspecies.

"Hey," the boy called, his voice high and a little wobbly from panic. "Are you crazy? Crawling in there would be fucking insane. You could get hurt, like seriously hurt!"

Lacey didn't think it was appropriate for a ranger to respond with "No shit, Sherlock," so she simply shrugged off her backpack. "The pups can't stay in there."

Cautiously, she entered the narrow passage. As she moved deeper into the old bear-dug den, she tried not to brush against the sides. They were already crumbling, and she didn't want to bring the roof down. Her light shone on four babies. Tucking two under her jacket, she scuttled back down the tunnel.

To her surprise, she found the teenager waiting outside. Catching her first good glimpse of his face, she felt recognition slam into her. The presence of Clay Stevens's truck suddenly made sense. The adolescent was his uncle's mini-me with golden-blond hair and blue-green eyes. He'd arrived in Sagebrush sometime last summer and had a reputation for being as mean as a rattler and just as dangerous. But that description didn't match the worried boy standing before her. He could've run like the others, but he'd stayed to help.

"Here. Take these two." Lacey thrust the two pups into the boy's arms.

"You trust me to do that?"

The utter shock in the kid's voice surprised Lacey. She

honestly didn't have much of a choice other than to let the adolescent help, but she didn't point that out.

"Yes."

He carefully accepted the two bundles. "They're so small."

"Yes," Lacey said curtly. "They're only a day or two old."

"They look like sausages." Despite the less-than-flattering observation, Lacey could hear the awe in the boy's voice. Evidently, he didn't share his uncle's distaste for the species. "Will they be all right?"

"Yes. Hopefully, we'll be able to quickly reunite them with their mother," Lacey said.

He bent over the pups, his guilt apparent. "Hey, little guys, sorry about accidentally destroying your home."

"Watch over them," Lacey instructed as she started to turn toward the den's entrance.

"Where are you going?"

"Back for their siblings," Lacey said. "Keep them warm until I get back."

"I will." The boy still kept his focus on the pups. He spoke his next words so softly Lacey almost didn't catch them. "It's no fun being cold when you're little."

At the hint of sadness in the teenager's voice, she swiveled abruptly and headed back to the den. As an interpretive ranger, she loved interacting with children, especially the younger ones. She enjoyed their enthusiasm and wonder. Their questions never bothered her, no matter how repetitive or simplistic.

But she didn't like to become emotionally close with the young locals. Because when she did, they reminded her of her little brother. And although this particular boy had blue eyes and golden locks instead of Jesse's fawn-brown gaze and chestnut hair, he radiated the same masked pain. It was so faint Lacey doubted most people would even detect it. But she did. And the similarity to her sibling's hidden hurt pierced through all the walls Lacey had constructed around her heart.

Forcibly burying her memories of Jesse, Lacey focused on navigating the narrow passage. She'd just grabbed the last two squirming wolves when she heard the ominous *whoosh* of falling dirt. Using her body, she shielded the baby lobos the best she could. She'd just started to hand them to the teenager when more debris slammed into her back. Then a rock cracked against her skull. The world flashed a brilliant white… and then nothing.

---

Clay was going to kill Zach.

His fourteen-year-old nephew had stolen his truck. Clay hadn't discovered it missing until he'd gone to make a trip into town. It hadn't taken Clay long to track Zach's location, or at least the location of Zach's phone using the app he'd downloaded. Unfortunately, this wasn't the first time the kid had decided to go joyriding. Clay now kept his keys locked up, but evidently Zach must have learned how to hotwire. The kid couldn't bother with doing homework, but when it came to troublemaking, he had no difficulty researching a new "skill."

One of the ranch hands had dropped Clay off at the Rocky Ridge trailhead closest to where the map had shown Zach's position. Sure enough, Clay's F-350 had been parked in the gravel lot. Clay had debated about just climbing inside, driving off, and leaving Zach stranded. His grandfather—the old hard-ass—would've done it. But Clay couldn't bring himself to abandon his nephew. Zach had put up with adults doing stuff like that his whole life…and not because any of them meant to teach him a lesson. No, they'd just been too fucked up on drugs to remember they had a son.

When Clay had agreed to take Zach last summer, he'd promised to give the teen a stable home. He could tell by the kid's expression that he hadn't believed Clay, and he didn't blame his nephew. When he had been in the boy's position, he hadn't trusted his grandfather either… although the old man had phrased it less politely. His exact words were: *This summer, you'll answer directly to me. Not a maid. Not a shrink. Not a school director. Not anyone else your parents hire to do their own damn job in rearing you. I won't put up with your crap, and I won't be soft on you.*

Although Clay had borrowed a few of his grandfather's tough love lessons this past year, he knew the old man would still accuse him of coddling the boy. Maybe it was because Zach would look at him with those blue-green eyes of his, and Clay would see a flash of the older brother he'd idolized before drugs had claimed him.

And there was another reason Clay went easier on Zach. A decade later and Clay was still trying to win his grandfather's approval, even though the old man had been in the ground for more than three years. It didn't help that Clay's foreman kept telling him how much his grandfather would've hated Clay's use of technology. Seeking affirmation from a dead man was a hell of a way to live, and Clay didn't want Zach thinking he always had to prove himself.

Which was why Clay found himself trudging through a barren wasteland, searching for his nephew. He'd used the GPS on the kid's phone to locate him. The idiot had gone off-trail, and Clay had a good idea why. The Stevens family always attracted the wrong sort of company, and Zach was no exception. He'd immediately fallen in with Sagebrush Flats's brand of hoodlums. They drank, took joyrides, went cow tipping, and caused all sorts of headaches for the locals. But they knew this country, this land. Zach didn't. He wouldn't last a minute drunk in the arid backcountry.

Clay cared about the kid. He didn't want him hurt and alone. He also didn't want to see him sent to a juvenile detention center, which was where he'd been headed before Clay had agreed to be his guardian. Getting into trouble on federal land could send Zach into lockup. And Clay didn't think it would scare Zach straight—not with the Stevens contrariness running through him. Prison had only introduced Clay's brother to harder drugs and shadier criminal connections.

The staccato ring of Clay's phone broke his reverie. Seeing Zach's number, he immediately answered. "Where the hell are you?"

The phone crackled. No surprise. It was a miracle either of them had reception. Although he couldn't make out Zach's words, the high note of panic in his voice slammed into Clay with the force of a charging longhorn. In the past year, he'd heard his nephew angry, defiant, sullen, and sarcastic. He'd never heard him scared.

"Need…your…help."

At Zach's plea, Clay's heart jumped like a bull with his testicles in a cinch. His nephew went out of his way to prove he didn't require any assistance, especially from Clay.

Picking up his pace, Clay spoke into the phone. "I'm already on my way, Zach."

"Should…I…move?" Zach's words were barely audible over the static.

"No, stay put. I've got your GPS coordinates."

"No…her."

Worry thudded through Clay. What trouble had Zach gotten into now? Clay broke into a run. He wasn't the soccer star his brother had been, but he kept in shape. His ranch hands complained that Clay stayed behind a desk all day, but it was far from the truth. Technology would never replace blood and sweat, at least not on a spread like his. It wouldn't matter, though, if he slept and ate in the saddle. He would always be the pampered screwup from New York whose daddy had swindled the whole town.

Breathing hard, he crested a hill and skidded to a stop. His nephew, with tears streaking down his face, was frantically digging at a pile of dirt and rocks. Clay skidded into the basin, sending dust flying.

His nephew looked up and wiped his nose against his sleeve. "She was trying to save the wolf pups. I didn't know they were in there. I swear. I'm sorry."

Clay didn't think he'd ever heard Zach speak this much. The boy had perfected the monosyllabic answer. After months of wishing for one, just one conversation with his nephew, Clay had no idea how to respond. He made a shitty role model for a kid, but unfortunately, he was all Zach had.

"Why don't you start at the beginning?" Clay suggested as he scanned the dirt mound. He was afraid to start moving anything before he understood exactly how this had happened.

"Me and—" His nephew stopped himself. Even now, the kid stuck to the bro code. As much as it irritated Clay, he had to give the kid credit. He didn't rat out his friends. Clay's father had squealed louder than a hog in a greased-pig contest when his pyramid scheme had crumbled.

"My friends," Zach continued, "and I camped on top of a wolf den and caused it to collapse. A lady spotted our fire and yelled for us to move, but it was too late. She went inside the cave to save the pups, and she'd just rescued the last two when the whole thing fell. I managed to dig out the little guys. They seem okay, but I haven't reached the woman yet. When I've called out to her, she's moaned in response. I swear we didn't mean for anyone to get hurt."

Every organ inside Clay shriveled up. "Was she petite with long chestnut hair and brown eyes? All energy?"

"Yeah," Zach said.

Clay closed his eyes for the briefest of moments. Ah, hell. If his nephew had just injured the town's darling, Lacey Montgomery, no one could protect him or Clay from the rain of hellfire that would fall on both their heads.

A low groan emanated from the rock pile, and it was the most beautiful sound Clay had ever heard. Zach grabbed his arm—the first time the kid had voluntarily touched him. "Did you hear that? We've got to get her out!"

Clay clasped his nephew's shoulder before Zach could launch himself at the mound. "We need to be careful. I don't want more rocks falling."

"Crap!" Zach said. "I didn't think of that."

"Did you call 911 or the park services?" Clay asked as he inspected the dirt pile.

Zach nodded as he rubbed his hands up and down his upper arms. The kid did that a lot when he was upset and he thought no one was watching. Clay hadn't let on that he knew about the habit.

"How far out are they?" Clay crouched lower, tilting his head. Most of the tunnel lay in the hillside, and he couldn't judge its structural soundness.

"Twenty to thirty minutes."

Another groan, louder now. Clay crouched down on

the ground. He didn't know if she could hear him, but just in case, he said, "Hey, we're going to get you out of there as soon as we can."

No response. Instead, he heard the last thing he wanted: the shifting and settling of more dirt. Fuck.

"What do we do?" Zach asked, his teenage voice cracking with panic.

"We get her out now." Clay began to move the rocks and dirt from the top first. He worked as quickly as he could without upsetting the delicate balance. Sweat dripped between his shoulder blades, and not just from exertion. This was worse than turning a breeched calf.

For once, Zach listened. He helped only when Clay asked, and he didn't protest at the heavy job. The kid had character after all—that, Clay had never doubted. He just didn't know how to get through all the surly layers the kid had wrapped around himself. Not that Clay would have a chance much longer to form a connection with Zach. The kid was so deep in trouble, Clay had no idea how to pull him out of it. After this stunt, the boy was no doubt headed straight to juvenile detention.

---

The suffocating haze hit as Lacey slowly regained consciousness. A fog had settled over her mind like a thick, overly warm blanket. Her eyes flew open, but darkness greeted her. Now panicked, she began to thrash. The movement caused a spinning sensation, and she gasped.

Clawing at the dirt, she tried to stop her fall, until she realized she wasn't tumbling anywhere. Only her brain was spiraling in an unstoppable whirl.

"Easy there," a voice said. Calm. Solid. It was a voice a man would use to steady a skittish horse. Normally, the tone would only rile Lacey, but the competency soothed her.

"My nephew and I are working to free you," her faceless rescuer continued.

Memories came back in flashes. The reckless teenagers. The falling rocks. The lobo pups.

"Wolves..." she managed weakly. She would have said more, but her energy had ebbed. The buzzing in her head had grown more insistent—like swarms of angry bees and hornets. She felt herself slipping back into unconsciousness, but she fought against it.

"Zach already dug them out. All four are happily snuggled in his jacket," the voice promised. A crack of light appeared. Then another. It hurt, but Lacey didn't close her eyes against it. Sunlight meant hope.

"I'm going to move you now," the voice said. "I'd rather wait for a ranger, but there's enough of the rock pile left that it could collapse again."

"Okay," Lacey murmured. She was having trouble thinking. Her thoughts flashed in and out of her brain like fireflies. She'd barely begin to process them before they vanished.

Strong arms wrapped around her. Gently, slowly, her rescuer lifted her, turning her cautiously in his arms. Despite his carefulness, her stomach pitched dangerously.

She lifted a shaking hand to her lips and pressed it there. Her head ached and throbbed. Forcing her eyes opened, she stared at the man who'd pulled her from the rubble.

He stood directly in front of the afternoon sun. Light washed over him, illuminating his wavy blond hair like a halo. His blue-green eyes stared down at her, worried. A small line appeared above the bridge of his nose, marring the otherwise perfection of his face. Faint golden stubble glistened over high cheekbones balanced by a strong jaw. Something jingled in the back of Lacey's mind. A warning, maybe. But her brain was too exhausted to listen.

She reached for that male beauty, her hand resting against the man's temple. His skin felt warm, his five-o'clock shadow scratchy against her fingertips. A peaceful sensation—both delightful and calming—whispered through her. Her lips curled into a smile, and his aquamarine eyes widened.

"My angel," she whispered.

Then as pricks of gray and black dots scattered over her vision, she frowned. Something didn't feel quite right about that. Her hand fell limply away, but even as his image blurred, she focused on him.

"No," she breathed, "not angel. Devil. Handsome devil."

Then she collapsed back into the churning sea of black and gray, letting its inky waves take her under.

---

Next to him, Clay heard his nephew snicker. Clay shot him a dirty look, but that didn't dampen the boy's amusement. Instead, he only sniggered harder. "I think she had it right the second time."

"Har har," Clay replied drily. "Since I'm helping save your ass and hers, you might want to reconsider."

Zach responded with a shit-eating grin, which Clay supposed was an improvement over his normal scowls. Since they'd successfully pulled Lacey from the collapsed tunnel, the kid had gone practically giddy with relief.

Clay wished he had the same reaction, but all he could feel was the memory of Lacey's soft hand against his face, her touch both innocent and searing. It was as if she'd branded him, his skin remembering the shape of her surprisingly delicate fingers as they'd cupped his cheek.

Eager to put the woman down, Clay glanced around the barren landscape dotted only with pinyon pines, sagebrush, and a few other hardy plants. He glanced at his nephew. "Is there anything at the campsite we could use for padding so she's not lying on the ground?"

His nephew's smirk vanished. Without further comment, Zach gingerly climbed back to the illegal fire circle to collect the sleeping bags. The teenager clearly moved as fast as he could without triggering another landslide. When he returned, he bent to arrange the material into a semblance of a bed.

"Do you think she'll be okay?" Zach asked as he concentrated on the task.

Clay nodded, not quite able to glance away from

Lacey. "Yeah, kid, I do. She took a hard hit to her head, but she seemed lucid enough."

Zach snorted as he tested the nest of sleeping bags, pushing down to confirm he'd created enough cushion without making it lumpy. "She called you an angel."

"Momentary lapse in judgment," Clay responded, trying to ignore the alien softness creeping through his heart at the memory. No one had ever looked at Clay quite like that. With wonder. Sure, he'd inspired his share of appreciative glances, but he'd never been regarded as some kind of hero before. And hell if it hadn't done something to him.

But Lacey had recognized him quickly enough despite her obvious confusion. It hadn't taken long for her eyes to narrow into a more familiar look. He'd seen it on the faces of his teachers, the good folks of Sagebrush Flats, his own parents, and the women he hooked up with. Being called a devil wasn't new. He was used to being the bad boy—even if he hadn't really been one in years. But he felt… something, maybe even a slight twinge of loss, when Lacey's expression changed from gratitude to irritation. Which was all sorts of fucked up. He didn't even *like* the woman.

"I think you can lay her down now," Zach said, finally finishing fiddling with the sleeping bags. Clay hadn't missed how carefully his nephew had arranged the makeshift bed. The kid was definitely feeling guilty about his role in Lacey's injury.

Clay bent and slowly lowered Lacey onto the nest

of material. She instinctually burrowed into the pile of sleeping bags. Straightening, he stood back and shoved his hand into his hair, knocking his cowboy hat backward. He'd never noticed how petite Lacey Montgomery really was. Of course, it was probably because she normally was as angry as a wet street cat in his presence—all snarls and unsheathed claws. Her energy and fire made her seem larger than her five-foot-three frame.

And that wasn't all Clay had overlooked. She had surprisingly delicate, pixie-like features: Cupid's-bow mouth, perfectly arched eyebrows, and a slightly upturned nose with a smattering of freckles across the bridge. The faint brown specks dusted her cheekbones too. She had a girl-next-door appeal—not his usual type. He'd always gone for the bombshell—perfectly applied makeup, clothes that looked tailored to their form, and heels a mile high.

None of that was fresh-scrubbed Lacey Montgomery. Hell, he didn't even know if Lacey bothered with cosmetics. He'd never seen her in anything but jeans or her dark-green ranger's uniform. She always scraped her chestnut locks into a no-nonsense ponytail, which fit with her intensity. Whenever she got particularly pissed off, her hair seemed to bounce in sympathetic outrage.

But Lacey was still now. And even though Clay knew she was a capable woman, he couldn't stop an odd rush of tenderness. It wasn't just because she looked fragile lying on the ground or that he'd just pulled her from a collapsed tunnel. It was how she'd reached for him, touched him.

No one had ever seen him as a protector, and hell if a part of him didn't like the role. Not that he'd ever admit it.

"I think the baby wolves are going to be okay," Zach said. His adrenaline was apparently still making him unusually chatty. "The two pups that were in her hands when the tunnel collapsed got a little banged up, but they seem okay."

Clay glanced over at the adorable bundle of sleeping wolves. Oblivious to the danger they'd just survived, they slumbered peacefully together on Zach's gray hoodie.

"Good," Clay said. He might not want to see the apex predators running free on his property, but it didn't mean he wanted them to suffer. They belonged in zoos, especially this subspecies. Mexican wolves weren't native to the area but to the south of Sagebrush Flats. Yes, they were more critically endangered than other gray wolves, but they didn't belong here, no matter what Lacey Montgomery thought.

Before Clay could answer, he heard the tread of footsteps and the slide of rocks and pebbles. Turning, he saw a male ranger quickly make his way down the hillside. The guy skidded a few feet to the bottom. His expression flattened as he scanned the scene. Out of the corner of his eye, Clay saw his nephew rub his upper arms. At least the kid had some respect for the trouble he was in...for once. Clay fought his own wave of uneasiness as he straightened to face the newcomer.

"We managed to get Ranger Montgomery out of the collapsed tunnel." Clay kept his hands against his thighs and spoke in a relaxed tone. He had no idea how much the federal police officer knew, but the man's expression had turned especially stony when he'd caught sight of him. Zach probably hadn't been speaking too clearly when he'd called the station, and Clay didn't know how great the connection had been. Regardless, the situation didn't look good for either Clay or Zach. They were two Stevenses surrounded by an unconscious national park ranger and rescued pups. Yeah, they were screwed.

# Chapter 2

"THAT'S NOT ME," ZACH SHOUTED, SPRINGING FROM his seat in the interrogation room. The teen had spent most of the interview slumped in his chair, his arms crossed, his face closed off. If his eyes hadn't been open, Clay might have started to wonder if the kid had fallen asleep. But as soon as Officer McPherson had shown them a photo of a teenager slipping beer under his sweatshirt at a local convenience store, Zach had bobbed to attention faster than a prairie dog spotting a hawk circling overhead.

He swung his gaze toward Clay, his blue eyes beseeching. "I *swear* that isn't me." Zach might be sullen and difficult, but he never lied. If he'd done it, he'd be staring down at the ground, his eyes blank blue pools of stubborn defiance.

Officer McPherson stabbed his finger at the tall, lanky teenager in the photo. "That's your hoodie, isn't it? According to the park police, it matches the description of what you were wearing that day."

"It's a *gray* hoodie." Clay said as he exchanged a look with Zach's public defender, Marisol Lopez. Hell, probably every teenage boy in town owned one.

"Yes. The same color your nephew was wearing when he harassed an endangered species in a national park."

Marisol leaned forward in her seat. "With all due

respect, what happened in Rocky Ridge National Park is not part of your jurisdiction, Officer McPherson."

"Yes, but an underage minor stealing alcohol in town is." The policeman tapped the grainy photo with undisguised glee.

Clay wondered how much effort the man had expended to track down the image. There weren't too many stores in Sagebrush Flats that sold beer, but there were enough to make the task hard. But with the town's low criminal activity, the force had time on its hands, and the officer nursed a personal grudge against the Stevens family. He'd lost big in Clay's father's investment scheme. Clay had overheard the man complain that he would have retired five years ago if he hadn't been swindled.

"That's not me!" Zach protested again.

Clay settled back into the uncomfortable plastic chair. He needed to appear calm even if he felt like a heifer trapped in a box canyon during a stampede. "All you have is a photo of a kid in a nondescript gray hoodie. You can't see the teen's face."

Officer McPherson's smile dropped into an unyielding line. "This was taken three hours before the attack on the wolf pups. The alcohol being stolen is the same as what showed up at the scene. When your nephew was arrested by the park police, he was wearing an outfit identical to the shoplifter's. Now, if Zach could give us another name..."

Marisol turned toward the teenager. "You should tell the officer who else was with you. We've talked about this."

"I'm not a narc." Zach shifted his gaze toward the ground as he squeaked the tip of his sneaker against the floor.

"He's not coming up with names because he's the one who stole the six-pack," Officer McPherson continued. "All evidence points toward him being the culprit."

Clay studied the photograph, focusing on the height of the boy. His nephew was just now starting to hit his growth spurt. He'd probably end up being tall like Clay, but he still had a lot of growing left. The teenager in the picture towered over the shelves surrounding him.

"That kid doesn't even fit Zach's build," Clay said, and Marisol grabbed the grainy snapshot to look closer.

"Mr. Stevens is right." Marisol pushed the image in Officer McPherson's direction.

He narrowed his eyes. He didn't seem convinced. "I'm going to investigate further. The stolen cans don't account for all the beer at the campsite."

"This is speculation," Marisol said. "And, again, out of your jurisdiction."

The officer swung his eyes on Clay, his expression hard. "How did those kids get their hands on so much beer? It's almost like an adult purchased some for them."

Clay stilled. Aw hell, now *he* was under scrutiny? "I wouldn't know."

"Funny that your truck was there, and you never reported it stolen. I'm figuring either you chauffeured the kids there or Zach drove it, which means he was driving as a minor without a license on roads under *my* jurisdiction."

"Do you have any evidence, Officer?" Marisol asked crisply.

"I'm still working on it." McPherson's voice was as hard and unyielding as quartz. "But I'll find something. He's a Stevens, after all."

---

"But I *want* to return to work!" Lacey protested as she rested her head against the cool surface of her refrigerator. She'd learned over the past few days that the cold helped her low-grade headaches. In addition to the dull pain, her head felt like it was encased in gelatin.

"Lacey," her supervisor said in a calm voice, "you suffered a brain injury."

"My CT scan came back clear," Lacey protested.

"But you *were* diagnosed with a concussion," her boss, Mary, pointed out.

"I can work through it," Lacey said quickly.

"I've had a brain injury myself. You need rest. Your job is physically demanding, and there's a lot of stimuli involved that could aggravate your symptoms."

"I don't want to be cooped up in my house." Lacey needed the outdoors. Needed to smell the tangy scent of sagebrush and pine. Needed to feel the fresh air against her skin and the warm spring sun beating down on her back. Needed to hear the sharp, loud cry of the Steller's jay. The wilderness, with all its harshness, healed her. Time and time again, she'd found solace in its untamed beauty.

"Have you tried stepping outside?" Mary asked.

"Of course," Lacey said, her voice waspish. Except with a certain wolf-hating man, she was generally even-tempered, but the dizziness made her cranky. Her boss, luckily, did not appear fazed by Lacey's tone.

"How does it feel to step into the sunlight?"

Like she was sinking into a vat of Vaseline, but Lacey chose to keep that particular observation to herself.

"Lacey, you haven't taken a vacation since you started working here," Mary continued. "It is okay to take more than a day off. We need you healthy for the high season this summer."

"But—" Lacey began.

"I'm not asking you. This is an order. We can't have a ranger out on the trails who is suffering from a concussion. If something were to happen, do you really want us expending resources to rescue you?"

"No," Lacey said reluctantly as she opened the freezer door and pulled out an ice pack.

"You'll recover faster if you allow yourself time to rest."

But Lacey didn't like to rest. She preferred staying active. If she didn't…well, there were reasons she never stayed still for long. Demons couldn't catch her if she ran fast enough and hard enough.

"How long is my enforced 'relaxation' going to be?"

"We'll see what your doctor has to say."

"You're not going to give me any other choice, are you?"

"Nope."

Lacey sighed. "Fine."

"And Lacey?" Mary's voice was gentle but firm. "I mean it. If we catch you at Rocky Ridge, I'm going to extend your medical leave."

Lacey wanted to protest more but realized the futility. Mumbling out an "okay," she hung up the phone and left the kitchen. With a sigh, she collapsed onto the beat-up couch that had been her grandparents'. As she sunk into the cushions, she arranged the ice pack over her eyes. Although she hated to admit it, lying down felt good. Really good.

---

"You suck."

Clay glanced over at his sullen nephew. The kid had his arms crossed as he scowled at the road stretching before them. The temporary camaraderie they'd experienced while rescuing Lacey and the wolves had long since vanished. Ever since Zach had been released by law enforcement into Clay's custody, the boy had brooded. Clay kept reminding himself that the teen was scared... and he should be. He was facing a buttload of charges. Marisol was pretty convinced the state wouldn't have enough evidence to build a case, but the district attorney's office certainly had enough to proceed to trial. Hell, even Clay was a witness.

"Zach, your actions caused Ms. Montgomery to be trapped in a cave-in. You owe her an apology."

His nephew jerked his head to the right so that he faced away from Clay. "I didn't make her go into that hole."

Clay suppressed a sigh. He might not be the most intuitive person, but even he recognized that the incident bothered Zach. The boy seemed more defensive than defiant.

"Zach, you know your actions triggered the whole event."

Silence. The boy didn't say anything as he traced his finger along the passenger-side door. Clay didn't push him. He honestly didn't know how to communicate with the kid, and anything he said seemed to make things worse.

"Ms. Lopez doesn't think we should talk to Ms. Montgomery," Zach said finally, his voice surly.

"That might make legal sense," Clay agreed, "but this is the decent thing to do. And it's not like she's suing us."

*Yet.* After all, the Montgomerys had every reason to squeeze money from them. Trent Stevens's pyramid scheme had nearly destroyed Lacey's family. Her dad had suffered a fatal heart attack when he'd discovered he'd lost his entire savings in the scam. Folks said Lacey's younger brother never recovered from his father's death. The previously quiet and studious teenager had sought increasingly dangerous stunts until dying in a car crash caused by his reckless driving.

Unfortunately, Clay didn't have a lot of cash to spare. His grandfather's ranch hadn't been doing great before the old man's death. Although Clay had cut waste by keeping better track of supplies, he pumped all the profits into his plans to turn the ranch into a specialty beef business. He wanted to make Valhalla Beef as famous as Kobe.

"You're an asshat."

"I'm well aware of that," Clay said.

Zach turned in his direction long enough to shoot him a killer glare before he returned to staring morosely out the window. Clay wondered if he'd been this bad as a teen. When the answer came to him, a side of his mouth quirked up. No, Clay had been worse and for far less reason than Zach. No wonder Clay's parents had sent him to military school and then to his maternal grandfather's. He'd been an irritating SOB.

"What are you smiling at?"

Clay turned to find his nephew watching him once again. He didn't drop his lopsided grin. Instead, he shrugged as he turned into Lacey's driveway. "Nothing."

The petite ranger lived fairly close to his ranch in a small bungalow on her uncle's spread. Since it was more than a mile from the main compound, it was a rather desolate place, especially for a single person. He would have thought the bouncy woman would have chosen to live closer to town, but he supposed this was nearer to her work. Her backyard practically abutted the national park. He was surprised she didn't live inside Rocky Ridge, but the area didn't have too many facilities aside from a small lodge.

When Clay parked, he was relieved when his nephew climbed from the truck without another fight. Yeah, he might have shut the door a little hard, but at least Clay wasn't going to have to drag him out by his collar and frog-march him up the sidewalk.

Clay rang the doorbell once. As they waited, Zach mumbled quietly, "I still think this is a bad idea."

"Just put on a smile," Clay said quietly. Zach didn't, but he dropped the scowl. Without it, his fear became more apparent. Cautiously, Clay laid his hand on the boy's shoulder. To his surprise, his nephew didn't shake him off. Instead, he sighed and straightened a little as the door began to swing open.

Lacey stood in front of them, and for once, she didn't look like a bubbly Girl Scout. If Clay hadn't known about her head injury, he would've thought her hungover. Clumps of hair had come loose from her normally tight ponytail. The color had leached from her face, making her brown freckles stand out even more. Her eyes were narrowed, but it seemed more of a reflex against the sunlight than in irritation over their visit.

Clay found himself taking a step toward her. He didn't know what he expected to accomplish. She just looked so miserable, and a part of him wanted to help. At his movement, her gaze swung toward his, and she shot him a look someone would give a rattler. He immediately froze. After all, he knew how folks in Sagebrush Flats took care of unwanted reptiles.

Clay cleared his throat. "Zach and I came to apologize and to see how you are doing."

Some of the anger cleared from Lacey's eyes. "I'm

fine." She paused. "I should thank you. Paul said you dug me out yourself."

Clay nodded. She sounded sincere enough, but he noticed she didn't invite them inside. If they'd been anyone else, she would've. Folks were generally friendly in these parts.

"We're sorry you were put in that situation."

"The wolf pups?" Zach's question came suddenly, without warning. To Clay's surprise, his nephew's voice cracked a little. Both he and Lacey swiveled in the teenager's direction. The young man's features looked drawn, his lips pressed into a tight line. Zach was no longer masking his guilt. It dawned on Clay that the kid had dreaded learning the animals' fate. The boy cared. Deeply. Clay hadn't suspected that, but he should've. After all, he'd been a master at hiding his own emotions under layers of douchebaggery.

Lacey must have also detected Zach's desperation. Her entire face softened. "Two of the pups have already been reunited with their mother and sibling. The pack has moved them all to a new den in Rocky Ridge."

"What about the other two pups? I didn't kill 'em, did I?" At the fear in Zach's voice, Clay gently squeezed the boy's shoulder. He didn't know how else to comfort him.

Lacey shook her head. "They suffered some minor injuries to their legs and needed medical care. They're at the Sagebrush Zoo and are doing well all things considered. They will probably stay at the animal park permanently since they likely won't be able to return to the wild."

Zach's shoulders slumped in relief. He gazed at Lacey, his blue eyes surprisingly vulnerable. His aloofness had momentarily melted away, exposing a flood of juvenile insecurities. "I screwed up. I'm so sorry."

To Clay's surprise, Lacey didn't lash out at Zach. The woman was so protective of her wolves that Clay hadn't known how she'd react to their visit. He'd only known that apologizing was the right thing to do. His grandfather would've made him do the same, and Zach had to start accepting responsibility for his mistakes. Just as importantly, he needed to know Clay would support him through the cleanup process.

The whole thing made Clay think of the time he'd stolen a horse from his grandfather in an attempt to run away. He'd hated waking when the ranch hands did, and he'd sworn the old man made him do the worst jobs. Back then, he didn't know a damn thing about riding. The mare had spooked at the creek crossing, throwing Clay. He'd busted his shoulder on a rock and bruised an ankle. His grandfather had collected the bay and left Clay to hobble back on his own. He'd still had to finish his chores when he'd returned. But his grandfather had stayed up until Clay went to bed. No matter what stunt Clay had pulled that season, the old man had never sent him packing. He'd even invited Clay back the next summer and every one after that.

"I believed you when you said you didn't know the wolves were there," Lacey told Zach.

The teenager's blue-green eyes widened slightly. Like

Clay, the kid wasn't used to people giving him the benefit of the doubt. "You did?"

"But your behavior was still reckless," Lacey spoke softly, her voice factual and not accusing. She'd entered ranger mode. "The campfire alone could have caused untold damage and not just to the park's animal residents. A desert ecosystem is surprisingly fragile."

Zach ducked his head. To Clay's surprise, he didn't talk back, which was his usual MO. "It was dumb of us."

A gentle smile touched Lacey's lips, and something cinched inside Clay near the vicinity of his heart. When she wasn't railing at him, the woman exuded a soft warmth that wrapped around a man's soul like a flannel blanket fresh from the dryer. It wasn't hard to see why the whole town championed her. Even Zach didn't appear immune to her wholesome charm.

"It was very dangerous," Lacey agreed. "Hopefully, you'll be more careful next time you're in the national park."

"So the wolves are really going to be okay? Even the two who were stuck in the tunnel with you? You're not just telling me that 'cause I'm fourteen?"

"I talk to the zoo director every day about the lobos. They're still under medical care, but the veterinarian says they're getting stronger."

"Is there anything I can do to help?" Zach blurted out. Even he appeared surprised by his offer. The teen typically avoided everything but trouble.

Lacey recovered first. She paused, clearly considering. "I could talk with Bowie Wilson, who runs the animal park. He's always looking for volunteers. I don't know how much you could assist with the pups, but there's plenty of other work. Anything you could do around the zoo would give Bowie more time to care for the wolves."

Zach swung his eyes toward Clay. He looked belligerent again. "Would you let me?"

Although Clay didn't turn, he felt Lacey's accusing gaze burn into the side of his face. Her gentle warmth had been replaced by thinly veiled fury. This was the Lacey he knew. Of course, she assumed the worst. Sure, he made Zach work on the ranch. It was good for him. But he hadn't taken the teen in for free labor, and he didn't demand much. Schoolwork came first, and if Zach would show an interest in anything other than deviant behavior, Clay would be the first to encourage him. But now, that may no longer be possible.

"Zach, I have no problem with you helping out at the zoo, but—"

"Oh please," Lacey interjected.

This time, Clay did swing in her direction. Her topaz eyes glowed with righteous outrage, and he forced his own temper to calm. Zach was in enough trouble without Clay antagonizing a park ranger in a screaming match.

"Do you really despise the wolves so much—"

"I don't," Clay said simply. "I may not want them killing my livestock, but I'd be more than happy to see Zach clean up the mess he made by volunteering at the zoo. The fact is, ma'am, this whole thing is out of my control. Right now, it looks like Zach might be spending at least the spring and summer in juvenile detention. We're on our way back from a meeting with the Sagebrush police."

Clay watched as the golden fire in Lacey's eyes banked. Understanding took its place and then swift confusion. "Everything happened on federal property. Why is the local force involved?"

"They're curious how my truck got to the trailhead, and there's a video of a kid lifting alcohol from the convenience store. Zach says it's not him, and both the public defender and I agree the teen in the footage is too tall."

Lacey's chestnut-brown eyebrows drew down. "There was an older, lankier boy there that night. He was the one who actually caused the landslide."

Clay glanced over at his nephew. He hadn't known that. Zach didn't look at either adult. He kept studying the ground as he rubbed his upper arms.

"Who was the other boy?" Lacey asked Zach.

He didn't glance up at the question. Instead, he scuffed his sneakers in the dirt next to the sidewalk. "I won't narc on my friends," Zach said.

"Are you sure you want people like that to be your friends?" Lacey asked.

Zach jerked his chin up, his blue eyes fierce. He reminded Clay of his brother back when Greg had played soccer. Greg used to look like that during the last quarter of a game. He wouldn't let anyone stop him from scoring one more goal.

"They're my *friends*."

Lacey studied him, her brown eyes not expressive

for once. Finally, she bobbed her head and winced at the action.

"We've been here too long," Clay said. "It looks like you should lie down."

Lacey visibly bristled. He swore even her limp, half-undone ponytail quivered in sympathetic outrage. "I'm fine."

"All right," he said easily, "but we'll stop pestering you. Thanks for accepting our apology." Clay tipped his grandfather's Stetson and turned to walk down the path. Zach trailed after him.

"Clay Stevens?"

He turned, halfway to his truck. Lacey looked torn, which surprised him. Until then, he would've doubted her capacity to second-guess herself. The woman had the single-mindedness of a charging bull.

"Yes, ma'am?"

"Can I talk to you for a second? Without Zach?"

Clay glanced down at his nephew. "Can you wait for me in the truck?"

He thought he might have seen a glimpse of unease in Zach's face, but the kid just shrugged. "Yeah. Whatever."

Clay jogged back to the stoop. Lacey didn't speak until Zach had climbed into the cab and loudly shut the door.

"How bad does it look for him?"

Clay resisted the urge to look in his nephew's direction. He'd hated when adults had talked about him behind his back, and Zach was no different. The kid had to know he was the topic of discussion, but staring at him would be like sticking the teen with a cattle prod.

"Not good," Clay said.

"Why did you get custody of your nephew in the first place?"

Clay took off his hat and ran his hand through his curls. "Is there a point to these questions, ma'am?"

Lacey's answer came swiftly. "Yes."

"And that would be?" He sure as hell wasn't going to give Sagebrush Flats any more reason to distrust Zach or provide folks with more fodder to gossip about his family.

"Whether it's worth it to stick my neck out for the both of you."

Her tone grated. He'd done nothing wrong, yet he found himself constantly on the defensive in this town. "Is Little Red Riding Hood going to call off the witch hunt?"

The ire in her topaz eyes sparked, bringing out the gold undertone. She obviously hated that nickname, which is why he used it so often. He hadn't learned much from his old man, but he'd picked up the technique of how to rile an opponent. Angry people make mistakes, and mistakes make them easy to manipulate.

"It isn't exactly a witch hunt since your nephew did break several laws."

"Fair point," Clay conceded, "but what I can't see is why you'd help us."

"Because Zach didn't run when he had the chance. He stayed to help the pups and then me. All his other friends fled. If he'd left too, I never would've been able to identify him. It seems unfair that he might be sent to juvenile detention for ultimately doing the right thing."

Clay rubbed the bridge of his nose. She seemed sincere. He might not like the woman, but he never doubted her honesty. She didn't try to mold the truth; she just believed she held all the truth. Although Clay didn't agree with her opinion on wolf reintroduction, the woman wielded a lot of power in town, and she worked for the national park. If anyone could help Zach, it would be her.

"I'm the best guardian they could find," Clay relented. "I'd prefer this not being told all over town, but my brother got into drugs after a knee injury his senior year of high school. He met his girlfriend, Zach's mother, at a party hosted by one of his dealers. Zach bounced between them and his maternal grandmother in Ohio, who was also on some pretty strong stuff. He got in trouble for vandalism, and I agreed to be his guardian last year."

To Clay's surprise, Lacey's expression didn't change. She only nodded solemnly...almost academically. Clay resisted the urge to shift uncomfortably. He didn't talk about his family much, and it was odd having Lacey listen like he was telling her about animal migration patterns. Yet her clinical approach didn't make him feel as raw as he normally did when thinking about his brother.

"I mean my next question honestly. Do you think heading to juvenile detention would scare him straight?"

Clay shoved his hat back down on his head. "It would force him further down the path he's on, and if he goes much further, I'm not sure I can steer him off it."

---

Lacey stood on her small front porch as she watched Clay's truck disappear in a cloud of dust. His visit had left her with a lot to think about...and right now, her mind didn't appreciate complex thoughts. Problems—even simple ones like selecting a premade dinner from the freezer—caused the dizziness to intensify.

Part of her—heck, most of her—warned her not to get involved. Her boss was right. She needed rest, and dealing with Zach Stevens's issues would require more energy than she currently possessed.

But she couldn't push the memory of the teen's blue eyes from her mind. Jesse's had been brown, but both boys had been lost. Maybe Zach's contained a different kind of desolation, but Lacey couldn't help but respond to the plea for help. The teen might have buried his vulnerability under a tough-guy attitude a mile deep, but Lacey knew how to detect hidden pain.

To her surprise, Clay seemed to care about his nephew. She hadn't expected that. He wanted to help the kid, but he couldn't if Zach ended up in juvie. And for once, she agreed with Clay. Being locked up wouldn't save the troubled teenager...but working with animals could. She'd seen how his dead eyes blazed to life at the mention of working at the animal park.

Slowly, Lacey walked into the house, her thoughts still on Zach and the wolf pups. She'd worked at the Sagebrush Zoo during college and knew both the present and former owners well. She'd loved working so closely with the animals and sometimes missed the personal interactions. Ecologists were trained to observe, not to meddle.

But Lacey had held the small wolf pups...she'd felt their warm bodies snuggling against hers. The two caught in the cave-in would never return to the national park. Their care required too much human interaction, and their injuries could impact their ability to survive. But they could thrive in a zoo...and their offspring could be fostered by wild parents and successfully integrated into a wolf pack. For a subspecies on the brink, every member counted...even the smallest, weakest ones.

If Lacey was going to be forced to take a vacation, she might as well start by finding ways to pass the time. Nothing relaxed her more than working with baby animals. Even hiking in Rocky Ridge didn't induce the same amount of endorphins.

Lacey reached for her cell phone as she eased onto the couch. Closing her eyes, she settled her head onto the pillow and covered herself with the blanket her great-aunt had knitted for her. She might as well get comfortable. After all, she had several calls to make.

---

Clay sat dumbfounded across from Marisol Lopez. "So Zach will be able to stay in Sagebrush? With me?"

Marisol nodded. "Provided he completes the requirements of the diversion program, yes. In addition to his community service at the zoo after school and on weekends, he'll need to attend educational classes regarding his behavior and write a statement about the impact of his actions, especially upon Ms. Montgomery, the wolves, and the national park." She swung her gaze toward Zach. "Do you think you can do that?"

Zach bobbed his head immediately. The teen was smart enough not to look sullen for once. Although he hadn't said anything during the ride to the public defender's, he'd rubbed his upper arms for most of the trip. He'd been worried, and now Marisol was offering him an unexpected chance.

"I don't know how to thank you," Clay said. "Whatever you said to work out this deal, we appreciate it."

Marisol smiled. "As much as I'd like to say this was all due to my legal skills, Lacey Montgomery started the process. It's unusual for the district attorney's office to agree to a diversion program, but Lacey convinced her superiors at the national park and also spoke with the federal prosecutor. She stopped by the police station and identified the boy stealing beer at the gas station as the one who originally triggered the cave-in—not Zach."

"So we don't have to worry about any charges from the authorities here in Sagebrush?"

Marisol shook her head. "No. I talked with the state prosecutor, and she agrees there isn't enough evidence for a case." The public defender turned her attention to Clay's nephew. "You are a very fortunate young man. The diversion program isn't a chance most kids in your situation get."

"So my community service will be at the zoo?" Zach asked. Clay could tell his nephew was trying to keep his voice neutral, but he could hear the relief and excitement rippling beneath the surface.

"Yes," Marisol said. "That was Lacey's idea too. The national park doesn't need as much help this time of the year, and she thought it would be good for you to work directly with the injured wolves."

Surprise flared through Clay. Lacey had mentioned sticking her neck out for them, but he'd never expected this. Maybe, just maybe, he'd misjudged her.

---

"Won't Ms. Montgomery get pissed if we keep swinging by her house?" Zach asked from the passenger seat as Clay pulled onto the dirt road leading to Lacey's bungalow. This time, the kid didn't seem quite as morose at the prospect of visiting her, but he wasn't thrilled either.

"Zach, the woman just saved your butt," Clay said. "We owe her a thank-you."

"Couldn't I just text her?"

Clay shot his nephew a dry look. "I think she deserves something a little more personal. Don't you?"

Zach gave a noncommittal shrug.

Clay suppressed a sigh as he added, "We're also doing this face-to-face for your benefit."

Zach arched an eyebrow. "My benefit? Do you think I have some sort of crush on her or something?" As he spoke the words, Zach's mouth quirked into a smirk. "Hey, that's it! *You're* crushing on the ranger."

Unbidden, an image of Lacey popped into Clay's mind. Like she did in real life, she crackled with energy, the gold highlights in her brown eyes sparkling. For one mad moment, Clay wondered what it would be like if that focus turned on him...not in anger but in something else entirely. Something more fun and definitely more dangerous.

"I am sooo right," Zach said gleefully. Clay tried his best quelling look. As usual, it did nothing. Zach snickered. Loudly.

"No," Clay said firmly, "we are not here because I'm infatuated with Lacey. We're here because you need to start taking responsibility. That's why I made you apologize, and it's the same reason why you should thank her. She had no obligation to vouch for you."

"Suuure," Zach said, but he seemed a little more sober than before.

"Just try to take this seriously, okay?" Clay asked as he parked the truck in front of Lacey's. There were two pickups outside in addition to her Jeep. Clearly, she had company. He debated about turning his F-350 around, but he wanted Zach to learn this lesson. It might even be better if he had an audience.

Clay climbed from his vehicle. Zach followed more slowly. When they reached the porch, Clay stepped back, forcing Zach to take the lead. With a beleaguered sigh, the teenager rang the bell. Clay could hear muffled male voices inside along with Lacey's more bubbly tones. Footsteps sounded, and then the door opened to reveal Lacey.

"My uncle said we needed to thank you," Zach said without ceremony.

Clay barely prevented a groan as he stepped forward. "What my nephew means to say is that we're sorry we bothered you, but we want to let you know how much we appreciate what you did for Zach."

"At least they're showing gratitude," a gravelly voice said from inside Lacey's bungalow.

Clay stiffened. Although he'd only talked to Buck Montgomery once or twice, the old cowboy had a distinctive way of speaking. It reminded Clay of a thunderclap... an angry, carefully controlled thunderclap.

Lacey gave them a weak smile. "Why don't you guys step inside? My grandfather is here along with his friend Stanley."

Great. Just what they needed. Although Clay wasn't aware of Stanley losing any money on the pyramid scheme, the other old-timer had a glare that could slice a man in half.

Zach shot Clay a morose look, but Clay gestured for his nephew to step inside. As soon as they entered the foyer, the inquisition began.

"So you're the young man who's caused the big ruckus," Stanley said.

Lacey massaged her forehead. "Stanley, be nice. Zach came here to thank me, not to be scrutinized."

Zach rubbed his upper arms, causing his jacket to bunch around his biceps. The situation clearly made him uncomfortable. Clay didn't blame him. Why the hell hadn't he turned the truck around when he'd spotted the other vehicles?

"We're very grateful for Lacey's support," Clay said stiffly.

Buck harrumphed. "Never thought I'd live to see the day when a Montgomery bailed out a Stevens."

To Clay's surprise, Lacey's brown eyes flashed with something that looked very close to indignant anger. "Neither Clay nor Zach was involved in Trent Stevens's investment scheme. They should be judged by their own actions, not those of another man."

At Lacey's impassioned words, Clay swallowed. Hard. He'd given up hope of hearing something like that from a resident of Sagebrush Flats. He certainly hadn't expected its favorite daughter—the one most hurt by his dad's crime—to speak those words.

Emotion rushed through Clay. It wasn't relief or even vindication. It felt good, though, and maybe even a little freeing. And damn if he wasn't starting to see why the town worshiped Lacey Montgomery.

She turned in his nephew's direction. "Zach made a very poor choice, but he didn't run away when he had the chance. He stayed to rescue me and the wolves." She whirled back toward her grandfather. "Don't you always say a man isn't measured by his mistakes but what he does about them?"

Buck harrumphed again, but he didn't argue. This time. It wasn't hard to detect the doubt rolling off him.

Zach shifted again. He lifted his chin in Lacey's direction, surprise transforming his normally sullen face. He hadn't expected Lacey to champion him either, and Clay wondered how many adults had ever defended him or really tried to understand why he acted the way he did. Maybe this conversation wouldn't be as disastrous as Clay had feared a minute ago. But that didn't mean it still couldn't all go to hell. The situation was as delicate as a vat of nitroglycerin. One wrong bump, and it would detonate.

"We just came to show our appreciation for what you did for us," Clay said. "Now that we've thanked you, we should probably go."

Buck started to speak, but Lacey quelled him with a deadly glare. Then with a pleasant expression, she turned back to Clay and Zach, her ponytail swinging. "You're welcome. But, Zach, if you really want to thank me, stay out of trouble. Okay?"

To Clay's shock, Zach didn't protest or even glance away with his lips pursed as if he'd eaten something nasty. Instead, he jerked his head quickly in acknowledgment. Lacey Montgomery definitely had a gift when it came to charming people.

Clay was just about to turn to leave when she brushed her fingers against his arm. The gentle touch sent electric shock waves coursing through him. Unfortunately, the entire room also seemed stunned by the gesture. He could feel protective defensiveness radiating from both Buck and Stanley.

"Can you wait for me on the porch?" she asked. "There's something I need to talk to you about."

He bobbed his head and then quickly shepherded Zach from the room before everything simultaneously imploded and exploded. As soon as Lacey shut the door behind them, Zach headed to the truck. When he climbed inside, he slammed the door with a resounding bang. He clearly hadn't appreciated the visit. Clay didn't blame him. He wanted nothing more than to hightail it out of here, but Lacey had asked him to stay, and he owed her.

He'd just shoved his hands into the pockets of his jeans and moved to the porch rail when he heard the voices. Glancing over, he grimaced when he spotted the gap between the bungalow's front door and its frame. The door must have popped back open after Lacey closed it. Buck's voice drifted through the opening as clear as a jay's call. "I hope you're right about the Stevens kid."

Stanley added, "He's already caused a whole heap of trouble, and with his family background, I'd say we're in for a whole lot more."

"I don't think I'm wrong about Zach," Lacey said firmly.

"Lacey, you've always had too kind a heart," her grandfather said.

"Have I been wrong about anything I've championed before?" Lacey asked.

"But he's a Stevens," Stanley protested.

"He's a fourteen-year-old boy who needs more people to believe in him," Lacey countered. "He's going to prove you both wrong. Just wait and see."

Clay heard footsteps coming, and he realized he'd be caught eavesdropping. It had started accidentally, but unlike with Zach, Lacey always expected the worst from him. He started to retreat, but he wasn't quick enough. When she noticed the cracked door, she arched an eyebrow, her expression full of challenge.

"Hear anything interesting?" Lacey's voice cut like a corded rope being pulled by an irate steer. But for once, her tone didn't want to make him buck back.

"Yeah, I did," he said. "Thanks for believing in Zach. I thought I was the only one."

Given their usual animosity, the fight fled from her with surprising quickness. She tilted her head and focused on him.

His gaze fixed on her lips...her very plump, very kissable, very enticing lips. He was so absorbed by her face he almost missed her question.

"How is Zach going to get to the zoo? Will you send one of your ranch hands?"

Clay blinked as the non sequitur jarred him from his inappropriate thoughts. Focusing on answering her, he wondered if she meant to test his commitment to his nephew. "I'll take him."

"Don't you have a spread to manage?"

"I'll make the time. My grandfather did the same for me."

Surprise flitted across her face. She sucked in her bottom lip, and Clay's whole body jerked in response. Hell, the woman had no idea how sexy she looked with her teeth rubbing against her skin. Clay wanted to reach out and cup her face with his hand, which didn't make sense. He wasn't the tender type, especially around Lacey.

She patted him on the forearm, and once again, her hand felt like a cattle brand. Shock made the streaks of gold in her irises glint brightly, and he knew the searing blaze had touched her too. She didn't pull back though. Instead, the molten flecks in her eyes cooled into shimmering ice crystals. Her lips curled in a clear challenge, and he felt his muscles stiffen for an entirely different reason than attraction. As a kid, he'd never been able to walk away from a dare. He'd matured, but evidently not when it came to a certain topaz-eyed pixie.

"Then I guess you're going to be my ride."

"Your ride?" Clay repeated. When she smiled at his confusion, he cursed his instinctual reaction. She knew she had the upper hand, and he'd practically gifted it to her.

"I'm volunteering at the zoo too, and I need a way to get there. My head is currently messed up due to your nephew and his friends, and I can't keep bothering my grandfather for lifts. He's got more to do than haul me around."

"I guess I don't have a choice." It wasn't the most gentlemanly response, but he hated being maneuvered like a young, foolish calf.

"No," Lacey said with a slight smile, "I guess you don't."

---

In the nursery at the Sagebrush Zoo, Sylvia, the capybara, snuggled her newest charges. She loved all the orphans she'd watched over through the years, but these two wolf pups seemed extra special. With white bandages wrapped around their little paws, the tiny lobos spent most of their time sleeping, but Sylvia didn't mind. She enjoyed the feel of their small bodies tucked against hers as she listened to their gentle breathing. Capybaras were social animals, and she relished the company of other critters.

When she was a young pup, she'd lived in a house with a small yard, and her old owner would yell at her for chewing on the furniture and baseboards. Now, she had a lovely pond to soak in, plenty of toys to sink her large front teeth into, and scads of companions. But she liked nothing more than cuddling with the zoo's new orphans. She also received plenty of pats from the elderly veterinarian, the owner of the zoo, and his wife, along with their eldest daughter, Abby. The teenage girl gave the best scratches. Sylvia hadn't interacted much with the new human twins. They tended to pull Sylvia's fur, which she didn't mind. After all, she was used to baby animals tugging on her. The bipeds, however, didn't want the youngsters bothering her, so they didn't let them too close.

Sylvia sighed as she settled her large head on the nest of blankets keeping her and the wolf pups warm. She sensed a change was about to occur in her little herd, and she was never wrong about these types of things.

# Chapter 3

"What do you mean you've never been to the Sagebrush Zoo?" Lacey asked two days later as she swiveled to regard Clay. He might wear a cowboy hat and a Western shirt, but the man still exuded a city slicker vibe. True, he was handsome. Although Lacey hated to admit it, there were times her heart caught when she saw him... even when he made her angrier than a coyote with a mouth full of porcupine quills. But his handsome face was part of his problem. He was too perfect, too clean-cut. The sun had tanned Clay's skin, but it looked like he'd achieved the golden hue lounging on a beach in the Hamptons rather than from riding his land. He didn't even have a small scar to offset his masculine beauty. With his high cheekbones and even features, he always seemed like he was about to star in an underwear ad, the kind shot in black and white where everyone wore the same sexy pout.

And he had a body that went well with jeans and tailored cotton shirts. The simple materials showcased his muscles...and he had plenty of them. Lacey hadn't wanted to look... Well, she hadn't thought it *wise* to look, but Clay's physique just attracted attention. Despite its undeniable deliciousness, it was the build of a model, not of a rancher. He might inspire fantasies, but he didn't inspire confidence...at least not in Sagebrush Flats.

Yet Lacey had glimpsed something when he'd shown

up twice on her porch with his nephew in tow. The preppy outsider might have more depths than she'd expected, and maybe, just maybe, part of her felt intrigued. She didn't appreciate the feeling. Since her brother's death, she'd avoided any potential emotional quagmires, and getting into a relationship with Sagebrush's Big Bad Wolf would be like diving headfirst into quicksand.

Clay shrugged as he pulled into a parking space. "I never saw the need to visit the zoo, I guess."

"It's a Sagebrush Flats institution. Haven't you lived here for more than a decade?"

A wry smile twisted Clay's sculpted lips, and he looked like he was posing for a pretentious perfume ad. "If you haven't noticed, I'm not exactly welcome at Sagebrush Flats institutions."

Although Clay didn't sound accusatory, that didn't stop a small twinge of guilt. Lacey's mother owned the most popular eating establishment in town. Although no one had ever actually refused Clay service, Lacey knew the waitstaff went out of their way to make him feel uncomfortable. They just might wait a little too long to take his order, his food might arrive a tad bit cold, and his pie might be slightly smooshed.

Although Lacey didn't like the man's policy on wolves, she was starting to wonder if the town treated him too harshly. He'd been a teenager when his father's investment scheme had collapsed like an ecosystem with dried-up aquifers. Like she'd told her grandfather and Stanley yesterday, it wasn't fair to hold him or Zach responsible.

"I'm sorry about that," Lacey told him quietly.

Surprise flashed first in his aquamarine eyes, and then a genuine warmth spread through them. Lacey had never visited the Caribbean, but she imagined the waters looked like his irises...clear blue-green and utterly inviting. Although Lacey had always preferred hiking to swimming, something about the cerulean color made her want to take a nice, long dip. The emerald undertone darkened, and Lacey felt a tug deep inside. As if entranced, she leaned forward. Her lips parted involuntarily. Clay sucked in his breath.

"Are we actually going to get out of the truck sometime today," Zach asked in a bored voice, "or are you two just going to stare at each other?"

With a gasp, Lacey jerked back in her seat. It almost felt like she'd been submerged underwater. Sucking in air, she blamed her head injury. For the past few days, fuzziness had distracted her, making it hard to concentrate. It made some sense she'd gotten caught in the undertow of Clay's sea-toned gaze...at least that was what she was telling herself.

"Have you toured the zoo?" Lacey asked Zach, her voice a little too chipper.

He didn't say anything about her overly bright tone, but he gave her the suspicious look that teenagers had perfected. "Isn't it for little kids?"

"Zoos are for everyone."

"I'm surprised you like animal parks," Clay said as he unbuckled his seat belt. "I thought you were the type who believed all animals should run free." His tone was a mixture of genuine curiosity and hidden challenge.

Since Lacey didn't have the bandwidth for an argument today, she focused on his honest question.

"As an ecologist, I'd obviously like to see all animals in their natural habitat, but I realize it's not always possible," Lacey said as she climbed out of the truck. "Properly run zoos like Sagebrush's help preserve the genetic integrity of a species. The Mexican gray wolf was extinct in the wild, and the captive breeding populations allowed us to bring them back."

"But they aren't native to this area," Clay said, and Lacey felt her temper rise. They'd had this argument numerous times.

"Gray wolves are, and Rocky Ridge isn't too far north of the subspecies historic range."

"But—"

"Hi, guys." Bowie Wilson's voice broke into their conversation. Lacey turned to see the zoo director strolling up to them. He had a broad smile on his handsome face. Even before he'd married Lacey's distant cousin, Katie, she'd always considered him a de facto older brother. Back when she'd worked at the zoo, she'd reported to Bowie, and she'd never had a better boss. If anyone loved animals more than she, it was Bowie.

Clay's mouth stretched into a welcoming grin. In the past, Lacey had considered it smarmy. Folks said he had his dad's obsequious charm. But now Lacey had begun to wonder if she'd detected a surprising trustworthiness at his core.

Clay started to extend his hand, but Lacey noticed that

he hesitated as if he wasn't sure of his reception. When Bowie lifted his own, Lacey spotted the tiniest flicker of relief flash over Clay's face. It struck her that a lot of folks in Sagebrush wouldn't be so welcoming.

"Thanks for agreeing to take on my nephew," Clay said.

The teenager made a disgusted sound. "He gets free labor. Like it's a big deal for him."

"Zach!" Clay made his voice sharp with warning.

Bowie, however, didn't appear fazed by the bad attitude. Instead, he gave Zach a genuine smile, his gray eyes warm. "We're always happy for more help. Lacey said you were a natural with the wolf pups."

Zach shot her a startled glance. Like his uncle, he seemed surprised by any support. Lacey gave him an encouraging smile, but it only seemed to make him more uncomfortable. He focused his eyes on the ground as he scuffed at the gravel with his shoe. "Am I going to spend all my time here shoveling shit?"

Instead of being offended, Bowie laughed. "Well, there will be some of that, but we'll try to give you interesting jobs too. Why don't we start with a tour? You can meet some of our residents."

Zach appeared torn between preserving his aloofness and giving in to his curiosity. To Lacey's surprise, he swung his gaze toward her again. For some reason, the kid actually listened to her, but then people normally did. Her mother said she'd been born with the gift of putting others at ease. Working at her mother's restaurant had only improved her people skills. As a ranger, her talent helped her hold the audience's attention when she led walks or gave talks. Aside from observing wildlife, her favorite part of her job was hosting fireside chats for the young guests. But she didn't get involved in their lives. Not like this.

"Bowie is a great guide," Lacey said. "He started working at the zoo when he was a little older than you."

"My first job was cleaning up graffiti—my own handiwork." Bowie directed his broad grin at Zach, clearly trying to put the teenager at ease.

Shock chased the sullenness from Zach's face, and he looked younger. "*You* tagged this place?"

"Yep, right after I got kicked out by my foster parents on my eighteenth birthday. Lou Warrenton and his wife took me in."

Zach's face clouded again. "I'm not looking for a home."

Bowie chuckled. "Understood. With twin babies in residence, the house is a little tight at the moment, but we still have plenty of jobs at the zoo. Come on. Let's go meet your charges."

"My charges?" Zach asked as the two of them began to walk away.

"You're going to be helping take care of them," Bowie said as they disappeared around the corner, "so they'll be yours in a way."

As soon as his nephew was definitely out of earshot, Clay cleared his throat. "Thanks for setting this all up—and not just for getting Zach out of juvie. Working here will be good for him. I didn't realize Bowie Wilson had a similar background."

Lacey nodded. "His parents were drug addicts too. His mom died of an overdose. I was just a kid when it happened, but I remember folks gossiping about it at the café. They'd quit talking when they noticed me, but I think the sudden stop in conversation is why I remember it so vividly."

Clay stared off at one of the distant rock formations. "That's how Zach's mom died. He's the one who found her. His father, my brother, is still alive, but I'm not sure for how long."

"I'm sorry. Addiction is a terrible disease."

Clay shifted back in her direction. This time, his eyes appeared more blue than green as he focused on her face with surprising intensity. When he spoke, his voice was solemn and a tad gravelly. "Thanks."

Lacey cocked her head at his unexpected response, so he continued. "For calling it a disease."

"That's what it is," Lacey said.

One side of his mouth quirked up ruefully. "Not everyone sees it that way."

Before Lacey could say more, Clay cleared his throat in an attempt to change the subject. "You're good with him."

"Zach?"

Clay nodded sharply. "I've been trying to break through his sullen exterior for a year, and you're the first to get him to stop scowling for a nanosecond. It doesn't sound like much, but it is for Zach."

His observation made her feel itchier than an ill-fitting wool sweater. "Folks say I have a way with people."

Clay made a short, harsh sound that sounded like half a chuckle. "Yeah. Well, your powers of persuasion typically don't work on me, but this time, I guess we're on the same side."

An unexpected sense of camaraderie slipped through Lacey. "I guess you're right."

An awkward quiet fell over them next, and their gazes drifted apart. Lacey concentrated on a clump of dying sagebrush. Clay was the first to break the silence.

"I better get back to the ranch."

Lacey looked back up just as he began to move toward his truck. She only caught his profile, but he looked so lost in that brief moment...maybe even more than his nephew.

"Wait." The word escaped Lacey's mouth before she could think better.

Clay turned expectantly in her direction. "Yes?"

"Would you like a tour of the zoo?" My goodness, where had that suggestion come from? "In high school and college, I worked here during the summers."

Clay's sculpted lips formed a slow, sexy grin. The flecks of green in his eyes deepened. "I'd like that. A lot."

A warm wave of desire crashed over Lacey. It felt as good and as surprisingly welcome as the ocean spray on a hot day. Worse, she didn't feel even a hint of trepidation, which paradoxically triggered a sense of worry. After all, a woman shouldn't approach uncharted waters without some sense of hesitancy, especially those known to turn stormy.

---

There was something about Lacey's brown gaze that wrapped around Clay like a Pendleton camp blanket on a cold winter's night. It felt as if he'd found a place of refuge after being stuck in a relentless blizzard. And for a guy who'd never really had a home, the sensation was intoxicating.

Clay wanted to reach forward and seize the feeling. His fingers twitched as he imagined the silky glide of her hair. Would her lips taste as velvety and inviting as they looked? How deep would the warm heat of her body sink into his skin if she nestled against him?

He started to lift his hand, but the welcoming glow in her eyes banked as the gold streaks hardened into crystals again. To hide his gesture, he pretended to scratch an itch on his other arm. Lacey stepped back, her expression polite but nothing more.

"We'll start with Lulubelle," Lacey said as if he should recognize the name. "Her pen is the closest to the entrance, and she's the unofficial greeter."

"Lulubelle?" Clay asked.

"You haven't heard of her? She's an internet star."

"My time on the computer is spent updating spreadsheets and researching beef market trends."

"You really are focused on the business side of ranching," Lacey said, and it didn't sound like a compliment. Clay should be accustomed to the criticism, but her tone irked.

"I run an operation that's subject to constant,

unpredictable change." Clay forcibly kept his tone light despite his burgeoning annoyance. "It keeps not only me but all my ranch hands employed. I'm also responsible for the herd, the horses, the farm dog, and all the other animals on my spread. So yes, I review charts and data to cut waste, make better predictions, and keep the whole damn thing from folding."

To Clay's surprise, a responding anger didn't blaze in Lacey's eyes like it normally did when they argued. Instead, she regarded him steadily. "I didn't realize you were so passionate about ranching."

That. That surprised him. "How many heated fights have we had about your wolves killing my calves?"

"I thought you just liked being ornery."

Clay felt like he'd been thrown from a horse. Even the air whooshed out of him. He'd been engaged in a public debate with the woman for more than four years, and she thought he'd done it because of sheer stubbornness? Hell, Sagebrush Flats really did view him as the spawn of the devil.

Lacey shook her head, a wry smile touching her lips. "You know, we've been shouting at each other for years, but I don't think we've ever actually *heard* each other."

Something jiggled loose inside him, and he felt his own mouth quirk up at the corners. He wouldn't say he and Lacey were anywhere close to reaching a permanent accord, but it felt good to concede a truce...even if just for the morning.

"You might just be right," Clay said, his voice sounding

thick to his own ears. Before he could say anything more, a rumbling sound broke into their conversation. He glanced over his shoulder to discover two giant, liquid-brown eyes staring back at him.

Lacey immediately walked over to the camel and began rubbing her neck. "Clay, meet Lulubelle. Lulubelle, meet Clay."

The animal gave him a silly smile, and he swore she inclined her massive head in his direction.

"Pleased to make your acquaintance."

Lulubelle loudly sniffed the air, her nostrils flaring. Imploringly, she swung back toward Lacey and began to snuffle her shoulder. Lacey laughed, the sound bright and easy. "I'm sorry, but I don't have any treats today."

Undeterred, the camel began to chew on her ponytail.

"Hey," Lacey protested. "I need that, and I prefer my hair free of saliva."

Lulubelle shifted in Clay's direction and gazed at him mournfully. Despite her massive size, she reminded him of a heifer. And he'd always been partial to herd animals despite being a loner himself.

"Sorry, Lulubelle, I don't have anything either. I'll try to bring one the next time I drop Zach off."

Lulubelle brayed. At the sound, a little head poked out from a lean-to structure that provided shade for the animals. A smaller, knobby-legged camel picked its way over to the fence. At the sight of Lulubelle's gangly offspring, amusement bubbled up in Clay. He couldn't help it. The juvenile just radiated a goofy cheerfulness.

"And who's this little guy?" Clay asked.

"Girl," Lacey corrected. "Her name is Savannah, and she was born about a year ago."

The teenage calf bounced over, her brown eyes eager. Without hesitation, she thrust her nose over the fence, trying to reach their pockets for food. Just then, a larger camel swaggered out of the partial shed. He rumbled a greeting as he lumbered in their direction.

"And last but not least is Hank. He's Savannah's father and Lulubelle's soul mate."

"I don't think camels have soul mates," Clay said.

Hank chose that moment to snort in Clay's hair. Lacey patted the male on his neck. "You tell him, Hank."

Clay retreated a step. Gingerly, he touched the top of his head. Yup. It was wet. He should've worn his hat, although then the camel might have eaten it...or sneezed on it too. His hair was at least easier to wash than his grandfather's Stetson. "All right, you guys win. So why are Hank and Lulubelle each other's destiny?"

Lacey reached over and stroked the female. "The poor girl was lonely. The llamas were bullying her—"

"Seriously?"

"Yep." Lacey used her thumb to point to the herd of llamas chewing hay on the other half of the corral. "They are very hierarchal, and when one of them had a cria—that's a baby llama—they started picking on Lulubelle, who lived with them at the time."

"Which caused her to show signs of depression from the isolation?" Clay guessed. The story was actually starting to make sense. One of his cows wouldn't react too well if the entire herd ostracized her.

"Exactly. Bowie and his now wife organized a fund-raiser to help the zoo get the money to find her a partner. Hence Hank here. The rest is history."

"Ah," Clay said.

"Isn't camel romance the best?"

"If you say so," Clay said dryly, but he couldn't prevent his amusement.

"Admit it. You think it's kind of sweet." Lacey lightly bumped him with her shoulder.

"Okay. Maybe a little."

They shared a smile then, and it felt good...maybe too good. Devils didn't date town darlings...at least not squeaky-clean ones like Lacey Montgomery.

---

"And here are three of my favorite zoo residents," Lacey told Clay as they approached the next enclosure. "Larry, Curly, and Moe."

Clay rested his elbows against the outer fence rail as he gazed into the exhibit. Lacey watched as he scanned the concrete waterslides and large pool. When his eyes lit on the furry inhabitants, she was surprised at the fond amusement that spread over his handsome features.

"River otters."

"Yep," Lacey said as Curly scurried up a slope. His long body sashayed back and forth as he maneuvered over the artificial rocks. When he reached the top, he slipped into the water and shot down the slide headfirst. Reaching the pool below, he transformed into a dark-brown torpedo zipping through the water. As soon as he neared a wall, he curled into a ball and flipped around as perfectly as an Olympic gold medalist. Slowing his pace, he stuck his little brown head above the water to watch her and Clay as he slowly paddled in their direction.

"I've spotted otters a few times playing in the large creek that runs through the ranch," Clay said. "One day, I spent half an hour watching them."

Now that surprised Lacey. Clay must have felt her shock, because one side of his mouth lifted wryly, even though he hadn't turned his attention from Curly. "I don't hate animals, you know. They're how I make my living."

"I never doubted that you cared for your herd."

"Sure you did," Clay said, his voice surprisingly matter-of-fact without any trace of bite. "Folks think my cows and steers are just numbers in a column for me and that my horses are simply a status symbol."

An uncomfortable feeling snaked through Lacey. She prided herself on her open-mindedness, but she wondered if she might have judged Clay too perfunctorily. They'd been adversaries for almost half a decade, but she really knew nothing about the man except for what she'd learned from town gossip.

"What are they to you?"

The question appeared to surprise Clay. He turned from watching Curly dive down into the pool. His blue eyes had darkened, giving him an almost studious appearance. He looked like an Ivy League professor instead of a frat boy.

"Responsibility. A connection...to the land...to my past...to my heritage. They're the lifeblood of the ranch."

A grudging respect slipped through Lacey. "Careful or I might think you buy into the whole romantic cowboy mythos."

"Who says I don't?"

Curly distracted Lacey from responding. Apparently bored with swimming, he emerged from the water. Standing on the bank, he shook himself off, sending droplets of water everywhere. After two more shakes for good measure, he bounded over to where his brothers were sunning themselves on a rock. Disregarding their slumber, he pounced. His siblings didn't seem to mind their sleep being disturbed. Instead of snarling or hissing at Curly, the other two immediately began to play. The trio formed a furry ball of wiggling tails and flailing short legs.

"This is why I ended up staring at the otters during my lunch break instead of reading my book."

Okay. That image also jarred with her internal one of Clay. She imagined him scarfing down a sandwich while staring at a computer or enjoying a meal with potential commercial buyers at the nearest country club.

"I *do* ride my land. My dad was the Wall Street banker, not me."

Lacey felt her cheeks grow pink as she realized how close he'd come to echoing her thoughts. But his insight shouldn't have startled her. After all, the town made it very clear how they viewed him, and Clay—for all his failings, true or imagined—appeared to be an intelligent man.

"Do you often read by the creek?"

"If I can," Clay said. "I make an effort to carve myself a little time at least once a week in the summer months. It keeps me balanced."

A glimpse of Clay stretched out on a rock near the water popped into Lacey's mind. He even wore cowboy boots and a Stetson. Surprisingly, this time, the idea didn't feel odd but right…maybe too right. She might… just might have pictured herself there too. In a sundress. Which didn't make any sense. She was a jeans-and-T-shirt kind of gal, and if she were going to put effort into dressing up, it wouldn't be for a picnic with Clay. Even if it would be awfully easy for him to slip one of the spaghetti straps off her shoulder as he leaned forward to kiss her…

A splash from the otters jerked Lacey from her all-too-inappropriate fantasy. The return to reality was so sudden, it felt like the water had actually doused her. Before she could think better, she emitted a tiny gasp. Clay shot her an odd look, but he luckily continued talking.

"And that's when I saw the trumpeter swans."

"Trumpeter swans!" Lacey said a tad too enthusiastically, even for her.

"Uh, yeah." Clay's gaze sharpened as he studied her. "Are you getting dizzy again?"

"Dizzy?" The question came out as a squeak.

"From your head injury."

Oh, yeah, *that* light-headedness. Lacey nodded. Her current foggy state explained a lot, including the wayward image of Clay and her on the riverbank, his lips descending…

"Are you sure they weren't tundra swans?" Lacey asked in a rush. "They're much more common. Trumpeters are still pretty rare in this area."

"Positive. Some tundra swans were also on the water, so I was able to see the differences."

"They're pretty hard to tell apart," Lacey said.

"Not when you have a telephoto zoom lens and you get pictures for comparison."

"*You* take wildlife photography?"

Clay lifted his shoulders and dropped them, the motion casual…almost too much so. It struck Lacey that her tone had bothered him—not irritated but bothered. Did Clay Stevens actually care about her opinion of him? He always seemed so impervious, but then again, they'd never spoken outside of arguing about wolves.

"I dabble in it," Clay said. "I picked it up as a teen when I got bored on the ranch. My dad liked expensive gadgets, even if he never used them. It wasn't hard to swipe a camera from my parents' empty house near the ski resort."

"Why didn't you just ask to borrow it?"

He didn't answer right away. Instead, he rubbed his thumb over the rough wood of the railing. When he spoke, his voice sounded different…remote and shut off. "My relationship with my parents is complicated. There wasn't a lot of trust between us, and they probably would have thought I'd either break it or pawn it."

The faintest hint of desolation lurked in his voice, and a twinge of pain squeezed Lacey's heart. If she'd known him better, she would have reached out and patted his arm. But they were only now on speaking terms, and she didn't know if he'd appreciate any gesture of comfort.

"Oh," she said instead, the word rather inadequate, but she didn't have a better one. She'd always imagined him as a spoiled rich kid. And maybe he had been. But that didn't mean he'd had it easy.

Her own parents had just scraped by. Only recently had the Prairie Dog Café started to bring in a nice profit. But she'd had a happy childhood…until her dad's heart attack.

"Look at those three chase each other." Clay pointed toward the otters. It was a clear attempt to maneuver the conversation away from him, and Lacey didn't fight it. She didn't want to get close to the man, didn't want to learn about his past, didn't want to feel a connection. She liked living alone. It hurt less.

The mustelids were romping in and out of the water. Sometimes Curly was in the lead, and sometimes Moe or Larry headed the pack. They moved with utter abandon and pure energy. People often compared their personalities to friendly, exuberant dogs, and Lacey could see why. Even adults like these three loved to play.

"They never stop, do they?" Lacey asked.

"I love how their hindquarters move."

She laughed. "I know. They look like furry inchworms with their rumps in the air when they run fast."

Larry shot into the pool, and his brothers dived after him. Curly climbed out first with Moe close behind. He pounced, and the two curved around each other, forming a momentary hoop as they spiraled together.

"I wish I had my camera," Clay said.

"You could bring it next time when you drop Zach and me off," Lacey offered. "I know Bowie won't mind, especially if you post a couple pictures on the zoo's website."

"I might just do that," Clay said. "Otters are certainly easier to capture on film here than on my ranch."

"It's a shame these guys aren't still in the wild."

Clay glanced over at her. "They weren't born in captivity?"

"No," Lacey said. "They're actually from Rocky Ridge. A backpacker found them and thought their mother had abandoned them. Unfortunately, instead of telling a ranger about their location, he decided to gather them in his backpack and take them to the visitor's center. They were so dehydrated from the journey, they needed serious medical intervention. It was either hand-rear them or euthanize them. I knew that Bowie had lost his otters to old age and had a great exhibit, so they came here."

"They seem happy."

Lacey nodded. "They do. Speaking of rescues, do you want to see the wolves?"

Clay grinned. "You're not afraid I'll put a curse on them?"

Lacey felt an unexpected smile drift over her lips. She never would've thought the two of them could joke when it came to wolves. She sobered and shook her head. "I want to thank you again for rescuing the pups and me."

"The biggest thanks you could've given me is when you defended Zach, fought for him even," Clay said. "I don't think anyone has ever done that, except for me. Although he didn't say much when we stopped by the second time, it meant a lot to him...and to me too."

His tone softened on the last bit, and Lacey swore she heard a twinge of vulnerability not too different from his nephew's. It dawned on her that he'd lived his entire adult life in a town that despised him and his family. She wondered for a moment why he hadn't left, but the answer was surprisingly simple. The land. That was why they all stayed, even during the difficult times before Sagebrush had become a growing tourist destination. Perhaps he possessed more of his ancestors' blood than she'd realized.

"What's that?" Clay asked as they passed a rather spartan exhibit. Although the Sagebrush Zoo was relatively small, Bowie put a lot of detail and effort into each enclosure. Not only did the animals have plenty of room, but they could explore rock formations, vegetation, log structures, and water features. In contrast, this particular home had steep concrete walls, two shelters, and small enrichment toys.

"This would be the home of the honey badgers."

"Sagebrush has honey badgers?" Clay asked. "The animal that doesn't give a shit?"

"I take it you've watched the video," Lacey said, mildly surprised he knew about the species. Most people mistook them for actual badgers. The long weasel-like mustelid actually came from Africa and had a reputation for its bad temper and ferocity.

"Hey, any creature that can take a cobra bite, pass out, and then wake up to eat the snake has my respect."

"They're incredibly smart too," Lacey said. "Bowie has tried everything to keep the male and female from escaping, which is why their exhibit looks like it does. The honey badgers have even used mud to build escape ramps."

Clay whistled. "And I thought it was tough to keep cows contained."

Lacey laughed. "At least when the honey badgers escape, they don't leave the zoo's grounds. Sometimes you can catch a glimpse of Fluffy—that's the male—but I've heard you only see the female, Honey, when she wants you to. At least that was until she had her kit. Little Scamp likes to make noise, and he's still at the stage where he follows her everywhere. Bowie says it's a lot easier to keep track of her now."

"How long ago did you say you worked here, Ms. Encyclopedia?"

Lacey didn't mind his gentle teasing. She knew she nerded out when it came to animals, but she didn't care. "I keep up via their website and animal cams. Bowie and his wife, Katie, have been making an effort the past couple years to improve their outreach."

"I heard she's a PR whiz. I approached her about helping me with a Valhalla Beef campaign, but she turned me down. She said her schedule was full. I guess her new business is doing well."

It was, but Lacey was pretty sure that wasn't why her distant cousin had turned down the work. She wouldn't have wanted to offend Lacey's family by helping a Stevens. "I can put in a good word for you if you're still interested."

Clay's eyes sharpened, the blue turning more crystalline as the green flecks faded into the background. "I'm surprised you'd want to do anything to promote my business."

"As long as you're not trying to kill the wolf reintroduction program, I have no problem with Valhalla Beef or you."

"Even after what my dad did to yours?" Clay asked.

He spoke the question gently, but it still sliced. It hurt...oh gosh, did it *hurt*, to talk about her father and brother or to even think of them. She should have expected Clay's question. After all, their shared history hovered at the edges of any conversation between the two of them. But despite the specter of past tragedy, they'd never verbally acknowledged it. It had just hung there, festering.

"I don't see your father standing in front of me," Lacey said. "It's just you."

---

Clay glanced over at the woman cradling the squeaking wolf pup. Lacey was making cooing sounds, her voice high and soft. Affection radiated from her. It wasn't meant for him, but he wanted to bask in it anyway.

*I don't see your father standing in front of me. It's just you.*

The words had sunk so deep they'd reached his very core. For that moment—that one brief moment—she hadn't judged him. He didn't know if anyone had ever done that before. Not even his parents. He'd been an inconvenience since his conception. Neither of them had planned for another child. His father had his perfect carbon copy in Greg, and his mother hadn't wanted to deal with the effort of re-toning her body after his birth. Nannies and teachers all received prior warnings about his bad behavior. His grandfather had regarded him as the rebellious teen in need of reform. Even long after Clay had given up his wild ways, the old man had never completely trusted him. Clay had sensed that the lifelong cowboy had never stopped expecting him to get tired of the hard work and hightail it back to New York.

Something had changed between Lacey and him today. He'd watched her charm people time and time again. He'd thought himself immune. He was good at calling people out on their bullshit. But that was the thing. He no longer thought Lacey full of crap. Yeah, he still disagreed with her wolf introduction program, but he no longer found her sweetness an act. Lacey had a solid piece of goodness inside her that somehow hadn't broken under the pressures of life. She was as rare as a red diamond and just as mesmerizing.

"Do you want to hold one?" Lou, the elderly former

owner of the zoo and its current veterinarian, asked. Clay started. At first, he thought the man was talking about gemstones and then realized he meant the wolf pup.

"Uh, are you sure I won't hurt him?" Clay glanced down at the small tube of fur. The little animal looked so tiny, so vulnerable, lying next to the zoo's capybara. The brown, kidney-shaped rodent had a knack for mothering the animal park's orphans. Even Clay had heard about the unconventional nursemaid when she'd appeared on *Good Morning America*.

Lacey glanced over, her eyes as warm as a cup of hot chocolate on a snowy day. "Lou will make sure you take good care of the pup."

"You just want me to fall in love with the little guys." Clay reached down with one gloved finger and stroked the wolf's back. Both he and Lacey had donned medical gloves before handling the lobos to prevent them from accidentally spreading disease to the baby animals.

"Maybe," she admitted.

"They're cute, but so are my calves," Clay said, but he let Lou show him how to properly support the pup's belly. The vet's lined face was soft with affection for the little critter, and he watched closely as Clay carefully accepted the furry bundle. The small wolf instantly snuggled into Clay, trying to burrow between the buttons of his shirt. He would never admit it, but he was instantly smitten.

"Whoa there," he said as he felt the tiny, cold nose brush against his skin. The pup began to squeak and wiggle. Despite the fact that the wolf's eyes hadn't opened, his black muzzle twitched back and forth in an endless quest for milk. One of his back legs had been splinted, but his front paws stretched wide as he voiced his demands for food.

"I've been around enough calves to know this little guy is hungry," Clay said.

"Did you just compare a wolf to a *cow*?" Lacey asked.

"A baby mammal is a baby mammal."

"He's not completely wrong," Lou said, his voice laced with amusement.

"See," Clay said proudly, "the vet agrees with me."

Lacey did not seem impressed. "I think you've just insulted the entire *Canis lupus* species."

"What's wrong with being compared to a calf?" Clay asked, feigning insult. He heard a bark of suppressed laughter from Lou.

"Well, for starters, bovines are not the most...well, intelligent of species—"

"So you're an intellectual snob then?"

"I never said that," Lacey said, clearly flustered. She scrunched her slightly upturned nose, reminding Clay of a befuddled pixie.

"A food-chain elitist then. If they're not predators with razor-sharp minds and teeth, screw 'em. Herbivores just aren't worth your attention—the poor schlubs munching their way through grass and clover."

Lacey opened her mouth to dispute him but dissolved into laughter instead. Beside her, Lou joined in. Disturbed by the mirth, the pup in her arms began to squirm. Both humans instantly quieted for the animal's sake, and Lacey brushed a soothing hand over the upset wolf.

"I like this man," Lou pronounced as he gave Clay a friendly wink. "I've never heard anyone outtalk our girl when it comes to animals."

Lacey ignored Lou's observation as she turned to Clay. "Since you correctly diagnosed the little guy's hunger, do you want to give him milk?"

Although Clay had helped bottle-feed calves rejected by their mothers, he'd never administered formula to a creature this small. Despite his reservations toward the species, Lacey's offer appealed to him. "Do you mind?" he asked Lou.

"No," the eighty-year-old said, his eyes twinkling, "but I think Lacey might be playing a trick on you."

"How so?"

"Before they get their bottle, we help them go to the bathroom."

Now that momentarily stopped Clay. "They don't poop on their own?"

"A lot of species don't at this stage," Lacey quickly explained, obviously eager to defend her beloved wolves. "Panda bears are another—"

"Yes, but they only eat plants, and we all know your opinion on creatures who prefer leafy things." Clay would have said more, but the wolf in his arms began to squeak in earnest. He turned his attention back to the little guy. "Okay. I get it. No more jokes until you're fed."

Lacey rose and indicated with her head for him to

follow. "Come this way. The paper towels are over here, if you're still willing to give it a try."

"I work on a ranch. I'm used to dealing with all kinds of crap."

Clay followed Lacey over to the counter. She showed him how to gently massage the pup's lower abdomen. It didn't take long for the little wolf's instincts to kick in. Getting the bottle in the animal's mouth, though, turned out to be more difficult.

"He's really clamping his gums together," Clay said. The dark-gray bundle of fur wiggled in his hands, the squeaks increasing in volume. Although the wolf's pinkish-gray paws paddled in the air in his quest for nourishment, he seemed to have no interest in the rubber nipple.

"He's just overeager," Lou said. "Try to get him to suck on your finger first."

"Makes sense," Clay said. He'd had more than one baby calf try to suckle his hand. He'd always found it adorable, not that he'd ever confess his thoughts to his ranch hands. A word like *adorable* wouldn't do his reputation any favors.

He managed to work his gloved index finger between the wolf's strong jaws. Although the pup's mouth didn't exert the same amount of pressure as a baby cow's, there was enough strength in his bite to remind Clay that one day, this tiny speck would grow into a lethal predator. Clay could admire that, even appreciate it...as long as the animal wasn't killing his vulnerable livestock.

With his past experience bottle-feeding cows, he

didn't have a problem switching out his finger for the rubber nipple. It was strange, though, holding a lobo in his arms. Orphaned calves normally stood at the edge of the pen, their heads eagerly sticking through the fence rails to reach the bottle. Even as a know-it-all teenager, Clay had never minded the chore, not that he'd told his grandfather. Clay suspected that the old man had known though. He'd made the task part of Clay's daily routine, and it had ultimately taught him to love the ranch.

He was afraid feeding the wolf might have the same effect. A man couldn't help but feel some sense of duty toward a creature he'd helped raise. But for a rancher, it was a bond hardened with the practicality of running a business. Folks on the outside had trouble understanding it. Clay had too the first summer, but he'd learned…or more accurately he'd slowly absorbed the lesson into his DNA.

The wolf continued to make high-pitched noises as he hungrily sucked down the contents of the bottle. He drank fast, the formula disappearing quickly. When the little guy finished, Lou carefully recorded how much he'd eaten.

"The pups are regularly weighed too," Lacey explained. "It's one of the best ways to check their health, especially when they're this small."

"He has high energy," Lou said, his tone warm as he regarded the wolf. "Considering his rough start, he's pretty strong. It's still good we're closely monitoring the pups. You made the right call bringing them here, Lacey."

"What about the other one?" Clay tilted his head in the direction of the lobo still snuggled against Lacey.

"His injuries were more extensive," Lou said. "We were worried about him, but his appetite is good, and he's gaining weight. So far, we haven't detected any signs of infection."

"Unfortunately, by the time we could reunite them with their mother," Lacey said, "they will have been handled too much by humans. They'll be important to the captive breeding population though."

"Bowie is applying for grants to support a program here. Other zoos have successfully started packs that include siblings of the same sex, so we're hoping we can keep both boys," Lou explained.

Clay wasn't sure how he felt about that news. He didn't want to see the subspecies die off, but he didn't want them loose on his land either. They were magnificent creatures. He'd never deny it. Last summer, he'd spotted a few loping through his pasture. Since they hadn't been bothering his herd, he'd just watched them through the lens of his camera. They'd fascinated him, not that he'd tell Lacey. The woman was too good at swaying people to reveal a vulnerability like that. He had a duty to his livestock and to his business.

Driving Lacey to and from the zoo every day was going to complicate his life more than he'd realized. Until yesterday, she'd been his enemy. It had been easy to dismiss her along with the reintroduction program. Now, he found himself drawn to her. And for a couple of brief moments, she'd looked at him like he wasn't the Big Bad Wolf in their story. Her brief acceptance had felt tantalizingly good, and he wanted more of it...even if it wasn't necessarily wise for him or for his ranch.

---

Every day brought new bipeds to the zoo. They annoyed Scamp's mother and father, but the throng of humans amused the juvenile honey badger. He especially enjoyed the wee ones who made high-pitched sounds. Sometimes they would drop food near his exhibit, which Scamp and his mother would eat on their evening outings.

But today had brought a different type of visitor. The humans had arrived when the zoo was normally quiet and right around the time Scamp and his mother usually went exploring. First the zookeeper had passed by the enclosure with the scowling Blue-Eyed One. The frowning biped had interested Scamp immensely. Something about his look reminded Scamp of himself. He was also smaller than the other male humans, not fully grown, also just like Scamp.

Later, more new bipeds had leaned over the rail and peered into Scamp's territory. They'd chattered to each other, but they had merely bored Scamp. Adult humans were almost as dull as mature honey badgers.

Now the young biped was back and alone. He was staring morosely down at the dirt. Scamp stuck his head out of the burrow he still shared with his mother. She chittered, but he ignored her. As he lifted his chin to get a better look, the Blue-Eyed One's gaze fell on him. The human's lips turned up for a moment.

"Hey there, you must be one of the honey badgers. I've watched videos about you guys. You're pretty badass."

Scamp cocked his head even though the sounds the human made were meaningless. The biped's voice was higher pitched than the other male humans' but lower than the females'.

The Blue-Eyed One's mouth flattened again. He looked exactly how Scamp felt when his mother scolded him for trying to leave the enclosure on his own.

"I heard you guys escape a lot." The biped continued making noise. "I can't blame you. It looks boring down there. I know what it's liked to feel trapped. I'm stuck here too."

The human let out a huge, gusty sigh. Unlike his stream of chatter, this expression Scamp understood. In fact, he'd made it plenty of times himself. The boy leaned his forearms on the railing and rested his chin on his hands as he stared glumly at Scamp.

The honey badger's lips curled up to show his teeth. The Blue-Eyed One needed excitement just as much as he did. Scamp had finally found a worthy playmate.

---

Lacey watched as Clay carefully brought the baby wolf to his shoulder to burp the lobo. He didn't quite have the technique down, which didn't surprise her. But his general ease around animals did. Most ranchers knew how to bottle-feed their livestock, but she hadn't expected Clay's proficiency.

"Just rub along the pup's rib cage and belly," Lacey instructed. "If that doesn't work, then you can try gentle pats."

Clay took her instructions seriously. Murmuring softly, he gazed at the animal. His chin practically touched the wolf's muzzle, and his eyes had turned the same blue-green as the Aegean Sea when it met the white beaches of Greece. Watching Clay's eyes change was like taking a trip through the world's oceans, and Lacey found herself drawn along with the current.

She couldn't think of a sexier image than a muscular man going all gooey-eyed over a tiny pup. The animal's minuscule pink tongue lolled out as the lobo basked in Clay's attention. Lacey didn't blame the little guy. She didn't even like Clay Stevens, but if he ever looked at her like that, she might very well pant too.

A faint belch emerged from the wolf, and a slow, devastating smile spread over Clay's face. A peculiar soaring sensation swept through Lacey. Annoyed with herself, she tried to suppress the bubble of elation. She hadn't acted this silly over a guy since her teenage years, and she couldn't think of a more inappropriate match.

The wolf pup yawned, his mouth a bright flash of pink against his grayish-brown fur. When fully grown, the lobo would be smaller than the more common gray wolf and sport reddish-brown and black hues in his coat.

"I think he's ready for a nap."

"Lay him next to Sylvia." Lou gestured to the capybara.

"You're fortunate she's so good with orphaned animals," Lacey said quietly. "It sure beats regulating their body temperature artificially."

Lou nodded. "When not using an incubator, I found putting rice in an old cotton sock and heating it in the microwave worked best, but Sylvia is a natural snuggler."

Lacey swore the rodent looked up at the compliment and gave them a serene smile. Then again, given the shape of the capybara's head, she always looked like she was grinning, especially from the side profile.

The pups instantly snuggled against Sylvia's warmth. They looked so small against the older animal's reddish-brown fur. One of the lobos emitted a contented sound. He moved his small chin as he sought the most comfortable position. His rounded ears stood out on the sides of his head, almost like a teddy bear's. They would grow longer and pointier, but now they were as tiny as the rest of the pup.

"You did well, Papa Wolf," Lacey teased as Clay stared down at the sleeping duo. She reached over to pat his arm. As soon as her fingertips brushed against his bicep, she realized her mistake. The thin cotton of his shirt did little to shield her from his warmth. The heat seemed to turn into electricity as it zipped along her nerves. A shiver threatened, but she suppressed it. She didn't want either Clay or Lou to witness her reaction.

Clay turned in her direction, his eyes now Mediterranean blue. Oh, she wanted to sink into their depths, but she didn't dare. She jerked her hand back, and she could sense that Clay felt her withdrawal. He didn't react to it though. Instead, he gave her an easy grin.

"I'm not sure what I think about the nickname, but it sure beats being the Big Bad Wolf."

A guilty feeling snaked through her. "Oh. You know about that one."

He shrugged. "I've never heard it directly, but given the circumstances, I figured it's been tossed around."

"Anytime you want to drop by and give an orphaned animal a bottle is fine by me," Lou said. Although the veterinarian had always possessed a welcoming personality, Lacey could tell by his voice he meant his words. He approved of Clay Stevens. Clearly, the man's ease around animals had won over Lou, and maybe, just maybe, Clay had started to impress Lacey too.

"Well, with Zach working here for the spring and summer, I might just take you up on that," Clay said as he offered his hand to Lou. "I better head back to the ranch now. It's calving season, and there's a lot of work to be done."

Lou nodded. Although he had never opened a practice in Sagebrush Flats, he'd often pitched in when the local vet was away and a rancher needed help. He'd grown up here too and knew the rhythm and rigors of ranching.

"I'll walk you to the parking lot," Lacey volunteered without thinking. She didn't know why. It wasn't as if the zoo was extremely large. Clay could easily find his way back. Yet something felt incomplete, like his visit wasn't quite finished yet.

They strolled next to each other in surprisingly

companionable silence. Unbidden, a memory of her father played in Lacey's mind. Both of them had loved hiking, and sometimes they'd cover a mile without speaking. *When a long stretch of quiet feels as comfortable as a conversation, you know you've found a lifelong friend.* Her dad had always been coming up with sayings like that one. Lacey didn't often think of them anymore. Even after all these years, it still hurt too much. But she did try to live her life by his lessons.

When they reached Clay's truck, he turned in her direction. The afternoon light caught his hair, changing it from burnished to spun gold. If it weren't for his truck's obnoxious Valhalla Beef insignia, he'd look like he was posing for a Ford advertisement.

He paused, and Lacey could hear his intake of air. The moment seemed charged. Lacey swore an undercurrent of electricity crackled. She'd come, she realized, for this.

"Would you like to visit Valhalla to see how I run things?"

Lacey should say no. She didn't like entanglements, and Clay's offer promised plenty. Her family wouldn't appreciate her getting close to a Stevens. And Clay and she had fundamentally different views. It was like trying to make the edge of a square and circle match up. Yet despite all that, she swore she felt a connection sizzling between them. But anyone who worked in an arid environment knew how dangerous a wayward spark could be.

She started to say no. Clay knew. His muscles stiffened almost imperceptibly, preparing for the rejection.

She studied him then as he stood against his massive truck with its huge decal. He should have looked arrogant in his Western shirt and expensive cowboy boots. But he didn't. He looked like a man who was trying hard, maybe even too hard, to fit into a world that didn't want him. And Lacey had always been a sucker for a stray.

"I'll come."

A slow, triumphant smile slid over Clay's mouth, making him look even more gorgeous. Lacey's heart squeezed at the sight.

"Does tomorrow morning work for you?"

"Sure."

"I'll pick you up at ten o'clock."

Clay climbed into his vehicle and gave her a wave as he pulled out. She stood there for a few more seconds, hoping she hadn't just made a very bad mistake.

# Chapter 4

Clay surreptitiously glanced over at Lacey as they approached the ranch complex. He felt nervous, bringing her here. He'd had potential commercial buyers and federal and state inspectors tour the facility, but he'd never invited anyone for a personal visit. His mother wasn't interested. His father was still serving time in jail. And no one knew where his brother was. Clay had severed his New York connections years ago. His old friends had done nothing but party, and after what had happened to Greg, he'd wanted free of that lifestyle. Even if Clay had wanted to rebuild some of his former contacts, his dad had also scammed their East Coast social network. The Stevens name was even more hated in the Big Apple than in Sagebrush.

"You know, I've never been here before," Lacey said as she stepped from the truck and scanned the cluster of buildings. "It's good land."

Clay nodded. His maternal ancestors had established the ranch after feeling overcrowded in the East. The isolation of Sagebrush Flats had suited them. He supposed they'd felt protected in their oasis surrounded by semiarid flat lands that turned into a network of box canyons to the north. When he sat near the creek and listened to the wind move through the aspens, he could see why they'd thought they'd found their own little paradise.

"I'm fortunate," Clay said.

He watched as Lacey's eyes skimmed over the horse barn. It was a massive, old structure and too big for a modern ranch. Nowadays, ranchers used four-wheelers and side-by-sides instead of horses. Since he was in the process of reducing his herd as part of his goal to produce one-hundred-percent grass-fed beef, he also needed less storage. But Clay hadn't had the heart to change the old barn. His people had built it by hand more than a century before. Instead, he'd converted some of the old stalls into office space. He'd torn down the more recently constructed outbuildings but kept any with historic value. They'd fit well with his stage-two plans for the ranch.

"The barn is gorgeous," Lacey said. "You've kept it well maintained."

Clay nodded. "The roof inside is amazing. They would have had to bring the lumber from up north."

Lacey turned to scan the rest of the property. He waited for her eyes to fall on the ranch's most unique feature. Her reaction didn't disappoint. Her lips parted slightly as she caught sight of the famed Frasier Mansion. "It really does look like a miniature English manor house."

"My great-great-grandmother refused to leave England to marry a no-good American from Scottish stock unless my great-great-grandfather built her one," Clay said.

"So the local legends are true?" Lacey asked.

"After my grandfather's death, I went through the boxes and trunks in the attic. I found the letters my ancestors had exchanged around the turn of the twentieth century.

Sure enough, Great-Great-Grandma Elinor demanded that Great-Great-Grandpa Robert send her a photograph of the house before she was willing to accept his offer of marriage."

"You're joking."

"Nope. I ended up framing her letter and sticking it on the wall."

Lacey burst into laughter. "She must have been a pistol. How'd they meet?"

"Robert's father was a proud man, and he wanted his son to go on a grand tour like aristocrats did. Elinor met Robert at a local dance when he was traveling through the English countryside. She came from impoverished gentry. I think her father was a baron or something, but he supposedly had a bunch of gambling debts. Good ole Elinor probably married Robert for his money rather than for love. It's an unfortunate family tradition."

"Well, *he* must have been in love to build her this. Bricks wouldn't have been cheap back in those days, especially out here."

"The ranch was doing good then," Clay said. "The house is difficult to maintain though. It's more than a hundred years old, and the plumbing sucks. I got it rewired about a year ago. It cost a fortune. It was mostly knob and tube, and there's places where you can still see the old gas fixtures."

Lacey shot him a decidedly worried look. "You're not going to tear it down, are you? It's a piece of Sagebrush's history!"

Clay was surprised by the fond smile that crept over his lips. Hell, when had he begun to find Lacey's campaigning spirit endearing?

"Don't tell me your conservation efforts extend to crumbly old houses and not just vicious meat-eaters."

The mulish expression on Lacey's face told him she'd have his house declared a historic landmark before she'd let him touch one brick. She crossed her arms. "History deserves saving too."

"We may just agree on that point."

She'd already opened her mouth to rebut his statement, but his capitulation left her momentarily at a loss. Her jaw worked for a moment, and the transformation from outrage to mollification was comical. She looked like a confused pixie again, and for one mad moment, Clay wanted to stoop down and kiss her.

He didn't, but he didn't like how close he'd come.

"So you're not going to tear it down?" Lacey finally asked.

Clay shook his head. "The house might be a pain in the butt, but I don't want to be the person who destroys what my ancestors built. The whole point is to save the ranch. I'd rather not start with dismantling it."

"How many bedrooms does it have?" Lacey asked.

"Ten."

She whistled. "That's enough for a small hotel."

Nervousness crept through Clay. This was his chance. He would need the town's support to start the second phase of saving the ranch. If he could just convince the town's favorite daughter to champion his cause, it was as good as won. "Well, that's part of the plan."

"What plan?" Lacey asked, her voice instantly on guard. "Are you thinking of opening a boutique hotel?"

"Not exactly," Clay said. "More of a wedding venue. Between the house and the barn, I think we could have something really special."

Lacey gave the cluster of buildings a more critical look. "It is picturesque here. The property has a different feel than most ranches in this area."

"The creek would be a great place for photography. I'm thinking about building a gazebo down by the water. I'd like to renovate the bedrooms in the house in case some of the wedding party wants to stay onsite."

"What does your foreman think?"

Clay felt his mouth twist at the mention of Pete Thompson. The man had never liked him, and the feeling had only worsened when his grandfather's will had been read. Thompson's family had been foremen on the ranch for most of its existence, and when Clay's mom had moved East with her husband, Thompson had become Clay's grandfather's de facto son. The man had been convinced he'd inherit the estate instead of a useless city slicker.

"I alluded to the idea once or twice. Thompson wasn't thrilled." *Only a shit-brained idiot would think of turning a working ranch into a prissy wedding venue.* True, Clay had only said he'd read an article about the trend, but he doubted Thompson would have softened his words even if Clay had admitted to seriously considering the idea. If it weren't for the fact that Clay was certain he'd lose all his ranch hands, he would have fired Pete. But Pete was an institution, and although he didn't approve of Clay, he was still a damn good foreman. Nobody knew the land better than him, including Clay.

"Yeah, Uncle Pete is pretty old school," Lacey said.

Clay barely suppressed a groan. When he spoke, he tried to keep his voice light. "So you're related to Thompson too?"

His exasperation must have shown in his voice, though, because Lacey shot him an amused grin. "No, it's an honorific like with Uncle Stanley. Since my grandfather's property borders yours, my family was always close to Uncle Pete. Even though Grandpa lives in town now, he still sees him at least once a week. Plus Uncle Pete is a regular at the Prairie Dog Café."

"Is it confusing trying to figure out all your family relations and connections in town?"

"Sometimes," Lacey admitted. "Jesse used to say we needed a flowchart." At the mention of her brother, sadness washed over her face as quickly as a flash flood. A deep silence descended—one of those quiets that threatened to consume a person. Clay recognized it. He felt the same thing when he thought about his own sibling, who was lost to opioids instead of to death. He started to reach for Lacey, but before his fingers could brush her arms, his dog Ace bounded up. Lacey's face instantly brightened at the sight of the muscular beast barreling toward them. Despite Ace's rough start in life, his face was always stretched in permanent doggy joy. He'd had a few teeth pulled, so his tongue lolled out, making him appear even sillier.

"Who is this?" Lacey crouched to greet sixty-five pounds of wiggling canine. Her voice sounded a little too cheerful, as if she was overcompensating for the earlier darkness. Clay didn't mention it. Instead, he bent down next to her and the dog.

"Ace. He's a pit bull–Lab mix. He might have some mastiff in him too. But he is one hundred percent love."

"I can see that," Lacey said as she received sloppy dog kisses on her face. She didn't pull away like a lot of folks did. Ace was built to intimidate, and he'd been forced to fight by his previous owners. When Clay had met him at the pound near the city, he hadn't been able to resist Ace's soulful eyes. The poor guy had lived at the rescue center for a long time. Although the volunteers had healed him physically, he needed open air and space. He'd first learned to trust Clay and then to enjoy life. Despite his past, he was nothing but an old softie who loved following Clay around.

"He seems to like you," he told Lacey.

"And I like him too," she replied, speaking in the silly tone people used around animals and babies, her focus entirely on Ace's adoring face. As she scratched behind his ears, the dog soaked up the attention. His mouth opened in a blissful grin, his tongue lolling out even further with each excited pant.

"Aren't you a handsome boy?"

Ace responded with a lick from her chin to her hairline. She giggled at the onslaught. Some people wouldn't appreciate Ace's massive jaws and teeth so close to their face, but this was a woman who loved wolves.

"How old is he?"

"About seven, we think. He was rescued from a dog-fighting ring when he was two. I adopted him when he was four."

He could see the surprise in Lacey's eyes, and it bugged him a little. But this was what today was about. He needed her to see that he cared for the animals under his responsibility, that he worked the land, *and* that he belonged in Sagebrush.

"I have a lot of plans for the ranch," Clay said. "But they're not going to succeed if I don't have local support."

Lacey looked up from petting Ace. "What are they?"

"How do you feel about a horse ride over some of my property?"

---

Fleur, the rescued cougar, twitched her long tail as she watched the newcomer from her vantage point on the high rocks in her enclosure. Her sister, Tonks, lay in the sun, her legs stretched out to the side as she slept. Although Fleur also appreciated the warm rays as winter moved into spring, she had more important things to do than snooze. Hand-reared by humans, she found the bipeds fascinating.

Lately, the Black-Haired One had begun erecting a new enclosure. Even more intriguing, an adolescent human had begun to help him. Only two years old herself, Fleur found youthful bipeds the most fascinating. She was particularly fond of the Black-Haired One's eldest daughter, the Gray-Eyed One. Most of the animals were.

Fleur's ears perked as she heard the crunch of talons on gravel. She *knew* that sound. Her sister began to stir. She rose gracefully and crouched down into a stretch. Her jaws opened, revealing sharp canines and a pink tongue. She plopped her hindquarters on the ground and made a show of grooming her front paw, but Fleur had roughhoused with her sibling enough to recognize her act. Tonks was only pretending to be distracted. She'd sensed the same noise as Fleur.

The juvenile honey badger, Scamp, was making his way to their enclosure. The little weasel loved tunneling into their home. Fleur found his antics rather diverting. Although the humans provided them with rubber balls, food hanging from trees, and ropes to tug on, it was simply not the same as chasing a real animal.

To Fleur's surprise, Scamp did not enter their exhibit. Instead, he scurried straight toward the new biped. The human, who Fleur decided to call the Blue-Eyed One, did not notice. He was too busy digging. Scamp then tried chittering, but even that did not draw the teenager's attention. The human wore odd things in his ears, which seemed to be interfering with his hearing. Fleur watched with interest as Scamp's gaze focused on the white wire attached to something in the boy's pocket. It ran all the way up to the white discs in the biped's ears. When the Blue-Eyed One reached for a tool on the ground, Scamp rose on his hind legs and caught the white wire in his teeth. The biped let out a howl, and Scamp dashed away.

"Hey! Come back here! Those earbuds are mine!"

Fleur relaxed her muscles as the teenager dashed after the honey badger. Her sister sighed and settled back down in the sun. Scamp had found a new playmate, and the chase was on.

---

"You're in the process of introducing holistic land management to your ranch?" Lacey repeated. She thought she saw Clay's jaw tighten, but she couldn't hide her surprise. She'd heard Uncle Pete grumble about *that Stevens boy* trying to use book learning to run a real ranch. She'd thought he meant spreadsheets and graphs. She hadn't expected Clay to bring her to the edge of a wetland he was rehabilitating.

"I didn't just take ranch management courses in college, Lacey. I double-majored in that and ecology."

She stared at him in disbelief. They shared a *degree*? "Neither of those disciplines is easy."

He shrugged and bent to pet Ace, who'd trailed after them. "I needed to keep busy, especially back then. When I was a kid, I got bored easily, and that's when I got into trouble. I knew college was full of parties. After what happened to my brother, I was over that crap, so I made sure I didn't have time for them."

"You're not at all like I thought," Lacey admitted as a swell of respect for Clay swept through her like a rising river.

Clay gave a tight nod as he straightened. "I was hoping to convince you of that today. I thought you might be receptive to my plans."

"I still can't believe the Frasier ranch has a ciénega or that you're working to restore it. This is beyond incredible."

Lacey and Clay had dismounted from their horses to walk along the marshy ground. The midmorning sun glinted off pools of low-lying water, and a fresh earthy scent filled the air as the breeze rustled the grasses growing out of the swampy dirt. The twill of northern leopard frogs resonated across the land. Lacey even caught a glimpse of one of the spotted amphibians as it dove for cover behind a clump of alkali sacaton plants. Unfortunately, Ace noticed too. With a bark, he took off running. His movement startled a white-tailed kite that flew straight into the air. When the majestic hawk reached the right altitude, it spread its dark wings, its white body a bright streak in the cloudless sky. It swooped near the red cliffs surrounding the peaceful canyon.

"The land here was always a little wet and slightly spongy," Clay explained. "When I learned about ciénegas in college, I thought this might have been an alkaline marshland. I asked my grandfather, and he remembered his own grandfather mentioning draining a swamp in his youth. So I went up in the attic and rummaged through my ancestor's old journals, and sure enough, there was talk about water bubbling up from the ground."

"How did I not know about this?" Excitement zipped through Lacey. Ciénegas were alkaline marshlands unique to the American Southwest that used to dot the landscape, bringing much-needed water and life to the arid environment. But misuse, misunderstanding, and mismanagement had caused them to dry up. Very few untouched ones remained, and their usefulness was just beginning to be understood. A large ciénega so close to the national park would be invaluable. The wetland would offer shelter to so many animals, from beavers and muskrats to the spiny soft-shelled turtle and the belted kingfisher.

Clay's mouth twisted in frustration laced with bitterness. "I guess Uncle Pete didn't tell you about *that Stevens boy's damn swamp*."

"Your ranch hands don't approve?"

Clay removed his cowboy hat to scratch his head. Perspiration had caused a couple of locks to curl against his forehead, and Lacey found herself battling the urge to smooth them back. Her fingers even twitched.

"No." Clay ran his hands through his hair, causing several strands to stick up.

Lacey's nerves stood at attention. She told herself to focus on his words. This conversation was important. Surprisingly important. If more ranchers considered reintroducing wetlands to their property, it could help alleviate the endless droughts plaguing the Southwest.

"They think I'm crazy trying to improve a 'muck patch in the desert.' My grandfather thought the same."

"I assume that's a direct quote."

"Yes, ma'am."

"But it's a natural feature," Lacey said. "You're not building new ones, just restoring an existing one."

"It's not how my grandfather ranched or his father or his father's father or his father's grandfather. I caught a lot of hell from Pete when I closed up the old diversion ditches."

"But this is Sagebrush Flats! We're one of the few ranching communities openly embracing wolf reintroduction. You're talking about water. Water! This land needs more of it. You don't have to be an ecologist to know the West's aquifers are in trouble."

Lacey halted her tirade when she spotted Clay watching her with a bemused expression on his face. Disbelief crept through her. He looked…affectionate? Toward her? An unexpected warmth flooded Lacey. Surely, she'd misinterpreted his look.

"Lacey, you could talk the town into collectively relocating to the International Space Station. But I'm not you. My ranch hands aren't happy when I ask them to build dams in the creek or to loosen up ground and then use the rocks we excavate to make patterns to trap the soil. As Thompson says, 'Moving dirt isn't ranching.'"

Realization sunk into her. Maybe she *had* misread his expression. "You need my help."

"Support would be a better word," Clay corrected as they headed back toward their horses.

"With your own ranch hands?"

He winced a little at her question as he climbed into the saddle. "They might not like the work we're doing on the ciénegas, but I'm still the boss. But if I'm going to build the Valhalla Beef brand and transform the ranch into a wedding venue, I need to stop being blackballed by the community."

"You're not blackballed," Lacey protested as she mounted the mare Clay had lent her.

He pressed his heels into his gelding's sides as he directed the horse back to a knoll overlooking the creek running through the property. He gave a whistle before answering. Ace loped up to them, and Clay kept their pace slow enough that the dog could easily follow.

"I'd read about programs where high school students help restore ciénegas. But when I called Sagebrush High, they weren't interested in a project involving a Stevens."

"It's a lot of work for a teacher to set up something like that. Maybe no one was available."

"True, but folks won't collaborate with me even if it benefits them. I already told you Katie Wilson turned down the opportunity to design some ads and help me put together an online video. She said her schedule was too full."

"Maybe it really was," Lacey said, although even she doubted that. Katie was doing great as a freelancer, but she'd normally jump to put together an ad campaign for someone local.

"She's your cousin."

"Second or third." Lacey wished the slight buzzing in

her head would stop. Horseback riding with a brain injury was turning out to be challenging. She wondered if Clay noticed her discomfort, because he pulled his horse up short as they reached a knoll overlooking the creek cutting through the land. Cottonwoods and aspens grew alongside it, their leaves rustling in the air. Clay's ancestors had chosen a beautiful spot. They'd settled at the headwaters, which would make Clay's plans for restoring the ciénega easier since he wouldn't have to fight for water rights.

Ace glanced at the creek and then swiveled his large head back in Clay's direction. His ears were perked in excitement, his brown eyes liquid pools of longing. Clay made a motion with his hand, and the dog let off a stream of happy barks as he raced into the water, the spray glistening in the sunlight.

As the canine splashed happily in the eddies, Clay leaned forward in the saddle, his eyes focused on his dog as he spoke. "And then there's June Winters. She doesn't currently offer burgers, but I told her the tourists would go crazy for one-hundred-percent grass-fed beef. She seemed interested until I told her I wanted her to market them as Valhalla Beef. She gave me her best 'poor little chickadee' smile and told me they wouldn't sell."

"'Poor little chickadee' smile?"

Clay tilted his head, made his blue eyes soft and gooey, and plastered on the world's most placating smile. He looked like a caricature of June Winters and her sunny southern charm. A surprised laugh bubbled out of Lacey, but Clay didn't appear amused.

"I want to build a specialty beef business, so I'm not sending my herd to be fattened at feed lots. If I can build a brand, I can sell each heifer for more. Then I can decrease the herd and rotate the fields, which means better grassland, more biodiversity, and less water use. But to do all that, I need a local market, but nobody's buying. Even the national park won't touch me. They all know you and your mom."

Lacey would have never suspected she and Clay Stevens would agree on anything, but his long-term goals for his spread were an ecologist's dream. Between the ciénega and better land management, he would bring back habitat for many local animals, including the black-footed ferrets that the Sagebrush Zoo was currently breeding for release.

"I want to see your plans."

"Okay," Clay said congenially as if she'd just told him she'd like tea instead of coffee rather than asking him to share his business model. She would have expected Clay to balk at handing over details of his proposed improvements to his own property. As much as she got along with her uncle, she doubted even he'd appreciate her reviewing his strategy for the family ranch.

"Just like that, okay?" Lacey asked, a little surprised.

"I might not agree with you regarding the wolves, but you're a damn good ecologist. Why the hell would I turn down your expertise?"

"You don't exactly like me."

Clay's eyes warmed to a tropical blue-green. "I wouldn't go that far. In fact—"

"Stevens!" The sharp voice cracked into the moment, shattering it. Both Lacey and Clay turned to see his foreman barreling toward them in a four-wheeler. Dust sprayed from the tires as he skidded to a stop. The raw-boned fifty-year-old jumped off the vehicle and marched up the hill. When his eyes fell on Lacey, they widened first in shock before they narrowed.

"What are you doing out here, Lacey?" The man attempted to modulate his voice to sound pleasant, but he couldn't completely smooth over the underlying terseness.

"I was just showing her the ranch," Clay said, his voice stiff. He didn't sound defensive, but it also wasn't a tone a boss would usually take with an employee challenging his control. It was more the sound of a man dealing with a professional adversary.

Uncle Pete's lips tightened, but he didn't question Lacey any further. Instead, he turned his hard eyes on Clay. "There's been a wolf sighting."

Clay's entire body went rigid. "Where?"

"Tim Forrester said he spotted them leaving his property and heading toward the north pasture."

Clay swore. He turned toward Lacey. The green flecks had all but vanished from his eyes, leaving a clear blue behind. This was a man steeled for action. He didn't look so much like a predator as he did a defender, ready to stand guard over those under his protection.

"That's where the calves and their mothers are," he explained to her. "It's the farthest from Rocky Ridge."

"I've already sent Hawkins and Stewart that direction, but I thought you'd want to know." Uncle Pete's eyes slid toward hers, and she swore she saw a challenging glint. "Considering your low opinion of wolves."

Ignoring his foreman's last comment, Clay turned his horse toward the north. He gave a sharp whistle, and Ace loped up the hillside, his tongue happily lolling to the side. Clay jerked his head in the dog's direction as he addressed Pete. "Take him and Lacey to the main complex. I don't want him tangling with a wolf."

"I'm coming with you," Lacey said.

Clay shot her a glance. The fire in his eyes almost blasted her back. "I'm not going to shoot one of your Mexican gray wolves. They're a protected species. I know the law. I'm just going to help scare them off."

"And I'm an expert on wolf behavior, and it's odd for them to be active this time of day," Lacey said calmly, although he wasn't completely wrong about one of her reasons for tagging along. She was beginning to realize Clay's appreciation for wildlife, but he was still a man protecting his livelihood. "I can help you safely chase the lobos from your property. This is a good opportunity for me to document their behavior."

"Suit yourself." Clay pressed his heels into his mount's sides and took off at a gallop.

Lacey followed. Her parents might have owned a diner in town, but she'd spent enough time on the Montgomery family ranch that she knew how to ride. It surprised her how well Clay did. He sat easy in the saddle. The leisurely ride out to the ciénega and the creek had been difficult with her concussion, but this fast jaunt triggered an uncomfortable pressure in her head.

Still, she didn't stop. Clay and his men had a duty to the cattle. Hers was to the wolves. They needed a champion on their side.

Luckily, the horse was sure-footed and knew the land as it followed Clay's gelding. Finally, when Lacey thought she'd have to slack her pace, they reached the back pasture. Ignoring her symptoms, Lacey gazed over the sheltered land stretching along the creek. She couldn't spot anything moving in the grass except the cows and Clay's men. The two ranch hands were staring down at the ground, and Clay rode straight toward them.

"Any wolves?"

The taller cowboy shook his head. "Not that we can see. The herd seems content. Found a couple tracks though."

Clay dismounted and crouched down. While the men focused on the paw prints, Lacey slowly got off her horse, using the saddle to steady herself. Fortunately, the mare wasn't skittish.

When she turned, she found the men still analyzing the dirt by the creek bank. Walking toward the trio, she lowered herself to the ground to get a better look at the tracks.

"What do you think?" Clay asked her.

Still feeling off-balance from the horse ride, she had difficulty concentrating on the impressions in the mud.

The outlines seemed blurry...and not because the tracks had been smudged. Lately, she'd experienced a similar problem when trying to read.

She tried to blink and refocus, but it didn't work. She swore she noticed something unusual about the paw prints, but she couldn't be certain.

"Lacey?"

Clay sounded worried. His boots appeared in her peripheral vision. She started to stand, but she swayed just a little. She pulled in a calming breath. His hand rested on her left shoulder, and she concentrated on that. Even through the cotton fabric of her T-shirt, his fingers felt strong, reassuringly so.

---

Clay didn't like Lacey's pallor. The freckles dusting her nose stood in stark contrast to her milky-white skin.

"Is she okay?" Carter Hawkins asked a little nervously. He was the youngest of Clay's ranch hands. Although the guy knew his way around cows, his social skills were occasionally lacking. He was a loner and clearly didn't relish the idea of being stuck with a sick person.

"I'm fine," Lacey said, but her voice didn't contain its normal perkiness.

"Stewart, can you get my canteen?" Clay asked. "Lacey might need water."

Joe Stewart nodded. He was in his early fifties. Although he'd worked for Clay's grandfather too, he didn't give Clay as much resistance as the rest of the old guard did. It didn't take Stewart long to retrieve the flask. Clay took it and handed it to Lacey.

To his surprise, when she shifted to sip from the container, she leaned against him. The trust in the gesture shocked him. He didn't want to admit how good her slight weight felt. Clay yearned to snake his arms around her and pull her even closer. He didn't dare though. The woman clearly wasn't feeling well. The last thing she needed was for him to take advantage. Plus, even if Hawkins and Stewart weren't the most talkative sorts, they wouldn't be able to resist gossiping about their boss embracing the town sweetheart.

Lacey tipped her head back, letting it rest against his shoulder. "I'm sorry," she said so quietly Clay almost didn't hear her despite their proximity. "I feel a little off-kilter after the ride."

*Shit.* Clay might just be getting to know the real Lacey Montgomery, but she didn't seem like a woman who'd willingly show any weakness. She must be feeling pretty ill to confess this. And he understood the need to hide vulnerabilities. He glanced up at his ranch hands. Clay would have preferred to look for the pack himself, but both men were meticulous. He trusted them to do the job. So did his foreman.

"Stewart. Hawkins. Keep looking for the wolves. Radio if you see any. I'm going to stay here with Lacey. I'll take her back to Frasier Mansion."

The men appeared visibly relieved. They jerked their

heads in acknowledgment before climbing back on their side-by-sides. Chances were they wouldn't see any lobos. The sound of the motors would drive off the notoriously skittish canines. Either way, the herd would be safe.

As the men sped away, Clay glanced down at Lacey, who was gingerly sipping water. Sweat had dampened her skin and plastered a few tendrils of hair to her forehead.

His brother had gotten a couple of concussions playing soccer, and Clay recognized the symptoms. After all, he'd been the one hanging out with Greg while his parents went to yet another social event.

"Are you light-headed?" Clay asked gently.

Lacey glanced at him. "Yeah."

"Headache?"

She started to nod and then winced. "I might have the beginnings of one. How did you know?"

"My brother was a soccer star, and his team was uber competitive—a lot of headshots, lots of collisions. It was before the serious implications of brain injuries were widely understood, so Greg just played through the pain. His reaction was about the same as yours," Clay explained.

"It's not fun."

"Do you want an aspirin? I have some in my saddlebag."

She raised a single chestnut-brown eyebrow. "You ride prepared."

He shrugged. "I started carrying it when my grandfather had his first chest pains. A couple of my ranch hands are older, so I keep some on hand."

"You and your grandfather were close?"

Clay moved away from Lacey and busied himself with finding the medicine. "I looked up to the old man." His grandfather's feelings toward him had been a lot more complicated. Hell, Clay was more surprised than Pete that he, rather than the foreman, had inherited the ranch.

"Here." Clay handed her the tablets. "Hopefully this will help dull the pain for the ride back."

"Thanks," she said before downing the pills. "You don't happen to have some Coke or ginger ale in there?"

"Nope," Clay said. "Midnight's a tough horse, but even he'd balk at hauling a soda machine."

Lacey chuckled and then sobered. "Thanks for taking care of me. I know this is your busy season, and you have more to do than babysit me out in a pasture."

"Hell, it's always busy season on a ranch," Clay said, "but I can spare a few moments. It's a good chance for me to check on the herd."

The cattle had long ago stopped showing interest in them. They'd moved downriver a little way. The babies stayed close by their mothers' sides. As they got older, they'd explore more. Clay loved the stage when the calves romped with one another and worked on their bucking skills. Today, the scene was more peaceful than playful, the quiet only occasionally punctured by the lowing of the cows. As always, sitting still and watching his livestock on his own land triggered an elemental satisfaction deep inside Clay.

He returned his attention to Lacey. Although he thought he spotted some pink returning to her cheeks, she still looked a little peaked.

"Have you seen a doctor?" It probably wasn't his place to ask, but the question had slipped out before he'd had a chance to think. She just looked so small and lost sitting in the red dirt beside clumps of big bluestem grass that his protective instincts had taken over.

"Sort of," she admitted.

"What does that mean?"

"I saw my local GP here in Sagebrush, and he recommended I see a specialist in the city," she said.

"Have you made an appointment?"

Silence and then a small "no."

"Let me guess, you're one of those stubborn types who doesn't like to go to the doctor."

"I was hoping it would go away on its own, and I don't feel up to driving that far. I could ask my mom, but she hates being away from the Prairie Dog. My grandfather could take me, but I've already been asking him to chauffeur me to the store. At this stage in his life, I should be helping him, not the other way around."

"I could drive you." Once again, the words fell from Clay's lips before he'd thought them through.

Her head bobbed up. "Really? It would take at least half a day."

"My nephew was partly responsible for your injury. It's the least I can do," Clay explained, even though he would have offered anyway. He felt drawn to Lacey, and he couldn't seem to stop himself from wanting to spend more time with her. It was odd, this feeling of connection. He'd never been close, really close, to another person except for Greg. His old friendships had been shallow ones, and he'd lived as a loner in Sagebrush Flats.

"I'm not sure—"

"Do you want me to tell your mom or grandfather about today?"

She had enough energy to glare at him. "You wouldn't dare."

"You need a push."

"What makes you think they'd even listen to you?"

"Because they care about *you* more than they dislike *me*."

Lacey didn't argue. She just sighed in patent resignation. "Fine. I'll call and make an appointment. You're sure you're okay with driving me?"

"Well, I won't go so far as to say it would be my *pleasure*," he said with exaggerated slowness until he added seriously, "but no, I don't mind."

She poked him in the shoulder, and he smiled down at her. Arguing with him had definitely brought some life back to her face. The golden gleam had returned to her topaz eyes, and her skin didn't appear as ghost-white as before.

"Do you think you're up for a ride?"

She groaned. "It's too far to walk, isn't it?"

"In your condition, probably," Clay said.

"I'm normally great on a horse, but it feels like the scenery is rushing at me, ready to zip right through me."

"You could ride back with me," Clay offered softly, not wanting to spook her. To his surprise, she didn't reject his words outright, so he continued. "I can tie Luna to

Midnight, and you can sit behind me. That way, you can close your eyes if you want. I'll keep Midnight to a baby trot."

"The classic damsel in distress?"

"Not quite," Clay said. "Aren't I the big bad dragon you're trying to slay?"

Lacey's grin still seemed a little weak, but it was real. "I'm the girl who loves wolves. If I ever met a dragon, I wouldn't want to kill it."

"I stand corrected," Clay said. "I guess I'm the black knight then. I played hooky the day they handed out the shining armor."

---

Clay may have been right about not being a classic hero, but holding him sure felt good. He possessed a solidness that helped steady Lacey's swirling world. He was lean enough that she had no trouble holding onto his waist but broad enough that he oozed masculine strength. He even smelled good as she rested her head against his cotton shirt. The detergent he used had a clean, crisp fragrance, and even the faint odor of sweat didn't bother her. She much preferred it to woody-smelling colognes. There was something honest about Clay Stevens's scent.

She hadn't intended to press herself against his muscular back. At first, she'd sat stiffly, keeping a good inch between them. But then he'd urged Midnight into a gentle baby trot, and she'd had no choice but to slump against

Clay. When her arms had curled around his abdomen, his body had felt too incredible to let go.

The pseudo embrace sent an undeniable thrill sizzling through her. She felt as alive as the desert after a surprise rain. Eddies of excitement whirled through her, filling her with potential energy despite her earlier symptoms. She knew she'd crash on her couch as soon as she returned to her bungalow. But now...now she felt charged.

Deep down, she recognized that she should fight against the dangerous emotions brewing inside her, but she'd spent her strength battling the mental fog. All her fight had drained away. So she clung to Clay, keeping her eyes closed against the scenery rushing by and simply basking in the electric glow his nearness triggered.

When Midnight slowed to a stop, part of her felt relieved they'd reached the ranch complex. The arduous ride was over. But another part of her didn't want to release Clay.

"I remember some of my brother's concussions made him sensitive to light," Clay said. "Would it be better if we dismounted in the barn?"

"Probably," Lacey admitted.

When Lacey opened her eyes, the shadows protected her. Although the pungent odor of horses, cattle, and straw seemed stronger than usual, she found comfort in it. She'd loved spending time on her family's ranch. The livestock had fascinated her as a small child. Her grandfather and her uncle had hoped she'd join the family operation, but her heart had always belonged to wild animals.

Clay dismounted first and then turned to regard her. "I know you're a skilled rider, but you still look a little pale. Do you want help down?"

Although she felt much better than she had out in the pasture, she didn't want to push herself again. "It might be a good idea."

As she slid off the horse, Clay's strong hands wrapped around her sides as he guided and steadied her. The warmth of his fingers seemed to seep inside her and pool in her stomach. Excitement flickered. Her feet hit the wooden floorboards with a muffled thump. She instinctually turned in the circle of his arms. The spark flared into an inferno as she stared into his blue-green eyes. Their brilliant color seemed to glow in the relative darkness of the barn. She must have knocked off his cowboy hat during her descent from Midnight, and his blond hair stood in clumps. This time, she didn't resist. She reached up and smoothed down one of the unruly strands. Clay sucked in his breath. The sound galvanized Lacey. She brushed through the lock hanging over his forehead, her fingertips grazing his temple. Clay's hand flexed on her middle.

Lacey's world tilted wildly and *not* from her concussion. Instinctually, she cupped Clay's cheek, his golden stubble pricking her skin. His eyes darkened. They no longer looked like the sea but a dark jungle pool…full of beckoning mystery.

"Lacey?" Her name sounded decadent on his lips, and she could hear the question, the invitation. She didn't answer with words. She placed her other hand on his face and drew him down toward her. He didn't hesitate. His lips captured hers, soft, certain, devastating. Sweet liquid fire shot straight to her toes. Then sensation erupted throughout her body. This was the kind of kiss a woman dreamed about when she climbed into her bed alone on a winter's night. It was the kind of kiss Lacey didn't believe existed until now...the kind of kiss that changed a person.

Her hands tangled in the softness of Clay's hair. His hands pressed against the small of her back, drawing her against the hardness of his chest. They weren't a perfect fit. He needed to bend into the embrace, but that didn't take away from its rightness. Normally, first kisses were awkward—two people learning each other's preferences. This wasn't. Lacey sank into it and allowed the riot of emotions to parade through her. Clay groaned, the sound reverberating along Lacey's nerve endings, making her shiver. His hands moved then, heading downward. They'd just skimmed the belt of her jeans when she heard the loud tread of boots behind them.

"LACEY DIANE MONTGOMERY."

The use of her full name cracked the bliss surrounding Lacey. Reality jolted through her with such force that her head began to pound again. She and Clay sprang apart, moving faster than two startled jackrabbits. They turned in unison to find Pete Thompson silhouetted in the open barn door.

Growing up as the town darling meant everyone thought they had a say in her personal life. Lacey had more "grandmothers" trying to set her up with nice young men. When she inevitably broke down and agreed to go on the date, practically every male resident over forty gave the hapless guy a speech about polishing his shotgun. Pete was no exception. He might not have a rifle on him, but his expression indicated that if he did, he'd be pointing it straight at his boss. He'd watched Lacey toddle around the Montgomery ranch and then zoom through childhood at the Prairie Dog Café. Like the rest of Sagebrush Flats, he felt a kinship toward her.

"I heard hoofbeats," Pete said, his voice sharper than a new razor blade. "I thought you might have returned. Did you see any wolves?"

"No," Clay said just as stiffly, "just some tracks. Hawkins and Stewart are checking the rest of the property."

"Why is Luna tied up behind Midnight?" Pete asked, his voice like a razor. "Did she turn up lame?"

"I'm afraid that's my fault," Lacey said gently, trying to defuse the situation before one of the men exploded. "I hit my head a few days ago, and I wasn't feeling too well. Clay and I rode back together."

Her explanation didn't mollify Pete. Instead, it incited him further. His gray eyes turned the color of wet slate as he clenched his fists. He even took a subtle step in Clay's direction before he stopped himself. The dismissive loathing in Pete's face would get most foremen fired, but his family had worked at Valhalla for almost a century. If Clay let him go, he'd face the wrath of the town...and his own ranch hands.

"Typical Stevens." Pete's words were so low that Lacey was fairly certain she and Clay weren't supposed to hear them. Unfortunately, Pete's anger had caused him to misjudge the volume. Clay's shoulders snapped to attention, and the tension in the barn crackled worse than an electric fence at full voltage.

"What was that, Pete?" Clay asked, his voice a challenge.

Pete's jaw worked as if he were literally chewing his words. He wanted to speak so badly that his neck muscles coiled. A warning sensation whispered through Lacey like a dry wind. She hated drama, and now she found herself at its epicenter.

"If you have something to say," Clay said coolly, "say it."

"You're a bastard." The words exploded from Pete, but not in a fiery fashion. It was more like built-up steam—slow and scalding. "Seducing a woman after she got knocked on the head."

Anger shot through Lacey as swiftly as a striking Mojave rattler. Typically, Lacey was a calm person. After Jesse's death, she didn't trust strong emotions. She preferred to keep her passions for protecting wildlife. In the past, Clay was one of the few people who managed to break her self-imposed calm. But Pete's comment blazed through her control.

"I might have bumped my head, but I am perfectly capable of knowing what I want. Clay did not take advantage of me. I'm the one who initiated the kiss, and I knew what I was doing."

Pete swung his body toward her. "Did you?"

"Thompson..." Clay's voice held a warning to it.

"What do you think it's going to do to your mama when she finds out you're with *him*? His daddy destroyed this town. Almost all of us had money tied up in that damn company. We all got hurt, but none as badly as your family."

The fight in Lacey dried up faster than a shallow arroyo during a bad drought. Horror rushed in to fill the void. She stepped back from the force of it. She felt Clay's hand on her shoulder. Gentle. Reassuring. Comforting.

She shook him off. Too many feelings clashed inside her, forming an ugly, vicious ball. She'd felt like this only a couple of times before. After her father's death...after Jesse's.

For years, no one in Sagebrush Flats had even alluded to her family's tragedy in front of her. She hadn't expected Uncle Pete's accusation. Even if she had anticipated his words, she couldn't have prepared herself for the maelstrom of emotions. They bombarded her. Her head ached again, and the mental murkiness deepened. With her concussion, she was ill-equipped to deal with the added pain and guilt. Tears sprang to her eyes.

She would not cry. She would *not*. But if she stayed here, she would.

She stalked from the barn. Her shoulder brushed against Pete Thompson's arm. It was accidental, but part of her felt good when he stepped back. Let him move for her. He had no business kicking up the past like a wolf trying to cover its scat.

She stepped into the light. It hurt, but staying in the barn would cause more than just physical agony. She walked straight toward an ash tree. Resting her hand against its trunk, she stared down at the ground.

Pete wasn't wrong. Her mother wouldn't approve of her daughter getting tangled with a Stevens...nor would her grandfather. Lacey didn't want to stir up turmoil in her family. They'd endured enough. She was the bright spot. The one who gave them hope. How could she destroy that?

"Lacey?" Clay's voice was soft and concerned. He had a nice deep one—the kind that could wrap around a woman's heart if she wasn't careful. She wondered inanely for a moment why she hadn't noticed before. It was a silly observation given the raw anguish coursing through her, but her brain had had trouble focusing lately.

"I'm sorry about what Pete said," Clay told her. "He was mad at me. You shouldn't have gotten caught in the crosshairs."

"I want to go home."

"Okay."

Clay walked Lacey back to his truck, and they rode to her bungalow in silence. They said their goodbyes quickly. Lacey sensed Clay wanted to talk more, but he didn't. He waited in his truck as she trudged up her walk and opened her door. She shuffled inside and collapsed on her couch. Luckily, she didn't have to wait long until the oblivion of sleep claimed her.

# Chapter 5

"I HEAR YOU'RE FOOLING AROUND WITH MY GRAND-daughter."

With a fifty-pound bag of powdered milk replacer over his shoulder, Clay turned at the sound of Buck Montgomery's voice. Hell, couldn't a man even shop at the local feedstore without getting accosted about his love life?

Clay was tempted...sorely tempted to tell the older man to go to hell. He didn't for several reasons. One, the ex-rancher had always reminded him a bit of his own grandfather. For another, the man had more of a right to complain than Pete Thompson. Third, he didn't think Lacey would appreciate his response. She also didn't deserve rumors flying around town either.

"I invited Lacey to my ranch to get her opinion on improving the water levels on the property," Clay said evenly.

"I may be old, but I'm no fool." Buck Montgomery was still a tall man. Despite his age, he retained an aura of strength. With his creased, leathery face permanently bronzed by the sun, he had the look of a man who made his living working outdoors. No one would ever mistake him for a businessman, even if he wore a suit instead of his standard jeans and Western shirt. He was someone Clay respected, even if the feeling was far from mutual.

"I never thought you were one," Clay said.

"My granddaughter's a smart girl."

"Agreed. That's why I sought her opinion."

Buck glared at him. He held a bundle of rope in his hand, and Clay knew the man was itching to hog-tie him with it. "Your daddy was good at flattery too."

"He was a con man," Clay said simply. Buck's golden-brown eyes—the same color as Lacey's—widened in surprise. Clay waited a beat before adding, "I'm not."

Buck frowned. "I heard you dropped my granddaughter off at the zoo today and the day before."

"That would be right."

"Doesn't sound like a man who's just after advice on ecology."

"Lacey wants to take care of the wolf pups, and I go right past her house every day when I drive my nephew to the zoo for his community service. She asked me to give her a lift. I agreed. That's all."

Except it wasn't. Not for him. Not anymore. Not after that kiss.

He'd never experienced anything like it. After she'd left, explosive energy had coursed through him. He'd ended up riding the fences, but instead of taking in the scenery, he'd seen *her* with eyes half-lidded as she pulled him closer. Their embrace had felt incredible. He'd wanted that kiss. She hadn't needed to guide him toward her.

Then, when her soft lips had touched his... He'd stopped thinking entirely. Nothing could have prepared him for the buoyant rush of pleasure. It had swept away any rational thought, leaving him with nothing but sensation. He'd never tasted a high like it, not even during his wild drunken party days. And it hadn't been an artificial happiness either. She'd made him feel good down to the molecular level. Unlike all the desires he used to chase, she wasn't bad for him. Quite the opposite. A woman like Lacey Montgomery wouldn't go easy on her man. She'd push and she'd prod until he was the best version of himself. That might scare some, but not Clay. He wasn't afraid of making himself better. Not anymore.

But even if Lacey may be right for him, he was all wrong for her. Pete Thompson was at least correct on that point. His foreman had chosen a piss-poor way to interrupt their kiss. He could've banged the door or done a million other things that would've alerted them to his presence without embarrassing Lacey. And then he'd gone and attacked her. His words had struck Lacey hard, and hell, they'd bothered Clay too.

Any relationship between Lacey and him would feel like a betrayal to her family. He'd be a reminder of old pains, and his presence would create new hurts. He'd create friction between her and her mother and grandfather and even the town. And Clay didn't want that…as much as he was beginning to want Lacey Montgomery. But there was one thing he'd become good at through the years, and that was denying his cravings.

"I don't trust the word of a Stevens," Lacey's grandfather said.

Clay felt his lips form into a humorless smile. "No, I wouldn't expect you would."

"You stay away from her."

He should, but he couldn't completely. He'd promised to drive her to the zoo and to the doctor appointments in the city. Those things were good for Lacey, and he wouldn't renege. "I'll keep my distance in the way that matters."

Lacey's grandfather's chest expanded, and even his thick mustache seemed to shake with indignation. "What the hell is that supposed to mean?"

"I have obligations toward your granddaughter, so I can't avoid her altogether. You may see me driving her around town, but that's it."

"I want you to leave her alone. I can take her wherever she wants to go. Hasn't your family caused ours enough trouble?"

The words slammed into Clay harder than a physical blow. He'd been thinking the exact same thing, which he supposed was what made them so impactful. He couldn't escape his father's legacy. Not here in Sagebrush Flats at least. From time to time, he'd thought about moving. He could sell his spread and buy a smaller, greener one far away. But he had roots in this dry land. And ironically, Sagebrush was the only place he felt that he fit—the town's attitude be damned.

"If Lacey asks me to stop, then I will," Clay said. "That's all I can promise, other than I have no intention of hurting her."

Buck didn't move as red suffused his weathered face. For a moment, Clay thought Lacey's grandfather might take a swing at him. The old rancher's hands slowly clenched into fists. Clay braced himself for the blow. He didn't want to embarrass the elderly man by ducking. He'd let him get in a punch. Buck had probably been yearning to hit a Stevens for years, and Clay was the only adult member of the clan around.

"You're a bastard," Buck repeated.

"So everyone in this town likes to claim."

Buck's flush spread to his neck as he opened and closed his fingers. Clay probably shouldn't have made the verbal swipe, but it wasn't easy being the town's favorite punching bag. Sometimes, he needed to get a jab in too. Buck made a disgusted sound in the back of his throat. He threw up his hands and stalked down the aisle. The old cowboy might not be as steady on his feet as he'd once been, but he still made a hell of an exit.

For a moment, Clay didn't move. He stood under the bright fluorescent lights. Vaguely, he noticed the milk supplement growing heavy on his shoulder.

He had problems, and not just those caused by a pocket-sized dynamo with chestnut-brown hair and pixie-like features. He was fairly certain Lacey hadn't told her grandfather about their kiss. Hell, she was probably doing everything she could to scrub it from her mind. Which meant Pete Thompson had called Buck Montgomery. Firing Pete would cause him a shitload of trouble, but keeping him around seemed to be doing the same. The man's thinly veiled hostility had started to seep out. Clay himself was seething over Thompson's attack on Lacey.

Every time Clay thought of Lacey's pale, horrified face, a fresh surge of anger thrummed through him. He'd wanted to terminate Pete on the spot, but he hadn't. Long ago, he'd learned a white-hot temper only caused problems. When he made a decision regarding Pete, it would need to be carefully considered.

Another shopper appeared, startling Clay from his thoughts. Evidently, it was neighbor day at the feedstore. Tim Forrester walked in his direction. He held a box of bullets, which didn't surprise Clay. The guy liked his target practice. Clay often heard gunshots coming from Tim's spread. Tim had purchased the land only a few years back, so he didn't have any animosity toward Clay. Forrester wasn't exactly friendly though. He was polite, but he was the kind of man who liked to put some distance between himself and others. Like Clay, he hailed from back East, and Clay figured he'd moved West to get away from people.

Clay didn't think much of the man's son, not that he'd ever admit that to Tim. Linus was three years ahead of Zach in school, but the two had become close friends. Linus had a tendency to drag Zach into stupid pranks like turning the sprinklers on during football practice, and Clay wouldn't be surprised if the older teen had masterminded the illegal campout at Rocky Ridge. He was the right height for the kid in the security footage stealing alcohol, but since Zach wasn't willing to talk, Clay had no proof of who else was involved.

"I just saw Buck Montgomery storm out of here," Tim said.

Clay grunted. Of course, Forrester would pick this moment to become chatty.

"You two fighting over Lacey's wolves?" Tim was the only other person who called the park's canines that, and even he only used the appellation around Clay. He got the impression Tim wasn't too happy about the pack's presence either, but the rancher publicly supported them. Unlike Clay, he didn't seem willing to risk the town's wrath.

"Something like that," Clay said.

"Did you catch them on your land this morning?"

Clay shook his head. "No. Two of my ranch hands went looking but came up with nothing. We did spot tracks near the pasture where the cows and the calves are."

Tim whistled sharply. "It would be a damn shame if you lost some of your herd again."

Clay nodded. "Thanks for the heads-up."

"No problem," Tim said. "I've been seeing them more and more on my land."

"Shit," Clay said. "I hadn't noticed any uptick. I'll have to ask my guys if they have."

"That might be a good idea."

As Clay turned to head to the checkout counter, the clerk's cheerful smile flattened into an emotionless line. Although the staff at the local establishments stopped short of being downright rude to him, they weren't welcoming either. Clay just gave the older woman a cheerful smile. He'd become immune to everyone's reaction.

By the time he'd left the store, he'd already pushed the

encounter with the saleswoman from his mind, but he hadn't the ones with Lacey's grandfather or Tim Forrester. Maybe it was a good thing the past made a future with Lacey impossible. If the wolf pack was expanding its territory, his professional world was about to collide with hers once again. He had a duty to the ranch, and he couldn't allow any nascent romantic feelings to get in the way.

---

The footsteps in the hall to the zoo's nursery woke Lacey. When she'd arrived at the animal park mid-Saturday afternoon, she hadn't felt well. The stiff, stilted ride with Clay and his nephew hadn't helped her head, nor had the overhead lights in the nursery. Lou had noticed her paleness and ordered her to lie down. Luckily, Bowie had set up an air mattress in an adjacent room since he needed to stay with the wolves overnight.

Feeling better after her nap, she swung her feet off the low-lying bed and headed to the door. When she pushed it open, she saw Zach coming down the hall. He had a smudge of dirt on his face, which didn't surprise Lacey. In addition to cleaning the animal stalls, Zach was also helping prepare a new wolf enclosure, though the pups would stay in the nursery for a while longer. The zoo had a lot of room to expand, and Bowie was meticulous about the homes he created for his charges. The large, carefully considered habitats were one of the reasons Lacey sent him animals that could no longer survive in the wild. Despite being a relatively small operation, the animal park provided excellent care.

"Hi," she called to Zach.

The teenager jerked his chin in her direction, but he didn't quite meet her eyes. If Lacey hadn't spent time with him, she would've thought him sullen. Now, she was wondering if he wasn't just shy around adults.

"Are you done for the day?"

Zach shook his head. "Bowie said I've been such a big help with the wolf exhibit that I could take a break and help with the pups before I dig more fencepost holes."

Lacey hid a smile. Bowie was smart to make one of the chores look like a treat. He'd probably sensed the teenager's love for animals. Babysitting the wolves was a great way to encourage it, and Zach needed a focus other than causing trouble.

"I'm headed that direction myself."

Zach dipped his chin again. They fell into silence as they walked the short distance to the nursery. When they opened the door, one of the pups lifted his head from the capybara's flank, while the other remained asleep. The alert lobo's big blue eyes looked bright against his grayish-brown fluff. His tiny mouth opened next, showing a flash of pink tongue as he squeaked in a clear demand for food. Abby glanced up from her position in the corner of the room where she was working on her homework. She gave a little wave, which Lacey returned. Zach didn't seem to notice the other teenager as he sucked in his breath excitedly, his gaze riveted to the young canine.

"His eyes are open!" Surprise had chased away Zach's protective layer of surliness. The smile on his face made him appear younger…or maybe it just made him look his age. A toughness clung to the teen that typically made him seem a lot older than his fourteen years.

"Yes," Lacey said, "but he can't see very well yet." Still, she couldn't help but share Zach's excitement.

"I didn't know wolves had blue eyes." Zach had lowered his voice to a whisper, his awe apparent.

"They'll change to goldish-brown as they age," Lacey said.

"Really? That's kind of fucking awesome."

"At this point, I should probably tell you to watch your language," Lacey said.

A small grin touched Zach's features. "Yeah. Probably."

The wolf began to squeak as he pulled himself forward on his front legs in clear pursuit of milk. It wouldn't be much longer before the little guy could stand. His movements woke his brother, who also began to whine.

"Would you like to feed them?" Abby, Bowie's daughter, asked. Her voice was soft and hesitant, but it still made Zach jump. He obviously had been too distracted by the pups to notice Abby.

She must have picked up on his surprise because she added shyly, "I'm Abby. I'm a year behind you in school."

"Oh, yeah," Zach mumbled. "I've seen you around. You work here too?"

"My dad's Mr. Wilson, so I help out a lot. We live in the house right next to the zoo."

"That's pretty lit," Zach said, which Lacey figured meant "cool." Although she worked with kids as a park ranger, she had trouble keeping up with the changing slang.

"It is," Abby said, her gray eyes brightening. "If you want, I can show you how to mix up the formula."

Zach swung his gaze toward Lacey. "Can I?"

Lacey nodded. The kid was trying to hide his interest, but she could sense his excitement. She wondered how much of his cavalier attitude came from true teenage disinterest and how much sprung from his desire to protect himself.

The teenagers moved over to the counter, and Lacey stayed back. She didn't want to hover. It was good for Zach to have an adult put a little faith in him, and Abby would get the formula right. She'd grown up caring for animals, and Lou never would have left her alone with the pups if he didn't trust her.

Abby showed Zach how to test the temperature of the formula on his wrist, and he listened intently. He was clearly trying, Lacey realized. She was glad he didn't resent being forced to work here. With his love for animals, he reminded Lacey of her younger self despite the fact that she'd been an outgoing overachiever. But when her world had disintegrated, volunteering at the zoo had given her a stronghold.

The teens headed over to the wolves. They sat cross-legged on the floor as each lifted a squirming pup. The wolves began to squeak louder, realizing food was nearby. They padded the air in excitement, their long bodies wiggling like fuzzy caterpillars.

"Keep their bellies flat and don't tip their heads back too far," Abby instructed. "If you do, the formula could get into their lungs."

"Do they eat any meat?" Zach asked after double-checking his hold on the squirming lobo. The little guy eagerly latched onto the bottle.

"Not yet," Abby said.

"Their first teeth should appear in a week or so," Lacey explained. "Once that happens, we can introduce strained meat into their diet."

Zach's face screwed up as he pondered this. "How does it get ground up in the wild?"

Lacey and Abby exchanged a look. The thirteen-year-old answered, "You know how a mama bird feeds a baby bird?"

Zach screwed up his face. "They eat regurgitated food? Gross!" Then he looked down at the wolf greedily sucking on the bottle. "The stuff you're going to get will practically be gourmet in comparison, little buddy."

The pup stared up at the boy as the lobo noisily drank. Although the animal wouldn't be able to make out Zach's features, the kid didn't know that. He gazed down at the tiny ball of fluff with unmistakable affection. Unfortunately, as he did so, he changed the bottle's angle. Lacey was about to correct him, but Abby was faster. She reached over and gently nudged the glass container to the right position.

"Thanks," Zach said, but Lacey could see the flags of color on his cheeks. He hadn't liked making a mistake in front of the other teenager.

"No problem," Abby said. "It can be tricky until you get the hang of it. You're doing better than some of the adult volunteers."

Zach dipped his head, but Lacey could tell the comment pleased him. She wondered how often he'd received encouragement growing up with addicts. Although she didn't doubt Clay praised the boy, it would be hard to undo years of neglect. Plus compliments always meant more coming from a peer, especially one of the opposite sex.

"What are their names?" Zach asked.

"They just have numbers right now," Abby said. "The Mexican Gray Wolf Survival Species Plan assigns them to help with the breeding program."

"That sucks not having an actual name."

"We'll give them one," Abby said quickly as she turned toward Lacey. "We were actually waiting for you, Ms. Montgomery. Dad thought you might want to name the pups since you saved them."

"You know," Lacey said slowly, "Zach helped with the rescue. If it's okay, I'd like to transfer my naming rights over to him."

Zach swung his gaze in her direction. His aquamarine eyes were comically wide with surprise. "Seriously? You'd let me do that after I..." He trailed off and shot Abby a glance. Obviously, he didn't want to admit in front of her that he'd endangered the wolves in the first place. He took a breath and concluded with "after I messed up."

Lacey nodded. "You're the one who stuck around to help save them. I'd say that qualifies you."

Zach switched his attention to Abby. When he spoke, his words tumbled out in a rush. "Are you sure you don't mind? This being your dad's zoo and all."

"Nope." Abby gave him a little smile. His excitement was infectious. Lacey felt a tug on her lips too.

"What do you think, little guy?" Zach asked as he carefully lifted the wolf to stare into the pup's vibrant blue eyes. "What would be a good name for you?"

The wolf yawned, showing off toothless pink gums.

Zach chuckled. "I don't think 'Sleepy' would be a good one. That's a dwarf's name, not a predator's. You need something more badass."

Abby's grin broadened at the swear word, and Lacey wondered if she should correct Zach's language. Bowie wouldn't appreciate his daughter learning how to cuss, but then she'd probably heard worse in school. In the end, Lacey decided she didn't want to interrupt the moment. For the first time since she'd met the teen, Zach seemed comfortable, and Lacey didn't want to ruin that.

"Fang?" Zach offered. The puppy yawned again, and Zach stroked the animal's soft fur with one finger. "Too obvious, huh?"

The lobo's little pink tongue flicked out to capture a droplet of milk on his muzzle.

"The history of wolves goes way back," Zach continued, his focus still on the animal, "so maybe you should have an old name. How 'bout Theseus? He was tough. He even killed the Minotaur and found his way out of the labyrinth, just like you had to escape the cave where you were born."

The lobo settled his tiny chin on Zach's forearm. The pup heaved a huge sigh as he pressed his eyes closed.

Zach brushed his hand over the animal's neck. "You like that one, don't you?"

"Do you read Greek mythology?" Abby asked.

Zach jerked at the question. Lacey realized he'd momentarily forgotten Abby's and her presence. Baby animals had a tendency to make people do that. Zach's face immediately reddened. "Yeah. There's a lot of fighting and shit."

It didn't surprise Lacey that Abby knew about Greek heroes. The girl read everything. Her habit had started when she was very small. When Lacey had volunteered at the zoo, Abby had been a toddler. If she wasn't pointing at the animals, she was waddling up to an adult with a book in her hand in a clear demand for a story.

Lacey hadn't expected Zach to start spouting ancient stories though. She would have thought he'd name the lobos after video game characters. Lacey could sense that the boy's knowledge embarrassed him, but she couldn't help but ask, "How did you learn about them?"

Zach shifted uncomfortably. Theseus peeped, so the teen settled, his fingers buried in the pup's fur. "My dad gave me an anthology of Greek myths during one of his visits. It was my fifth birthday."

That was an odd gift for a five-year-old. Clearly, Abby felt so as well. She bit her lip as she stroked the other wolf and finally said in a tentative tone, "My dad always bought me books for my birthday too."

Zach's gaze slid toward hers and then back to

Theseus. He traced his fingertips lightly down the animal's spine.

"Yeah, my dad didn't normally. I think it was what he could shoplift the easiest. The book was probably part of a sidewalk sale or something. It would've been too big for him to smuggle from the store. It wasn't really for little kids, but it had good illustrations. I liked looking at them before I could understand most of the words."

At his explanation, Lacey's heart broke a little, and she suspected Abby's did too. Zach had probably revealed more than he'd intended. Lacey could clearly see a blond five-year-old balancing a massive anthology on his lap as he pored over one of his tenuous connections to his absentee father. No wonder Greek mythology fascinated him.

"Well, I think Theseus is a perfect name," Lacey said. "He did emerge from a labyrinth of sorts."

"And he likes it." Abby reached over to pet the pup's fur. Lacey noticed that the girl was careful to avoid Zach's fingers.

A cautious smile broke over the boy's face. "I think so too. He went to sleep when I said it. That means he's comfortable with it, right?"

"Absolutely," Abby said. "Wolves are very sensitive. I love all animals, but canines are my favorite. They're the most in tune with people."

"My uncle has a dog named Ace," Zach said. "He's huge but really friendly."

"So what's this little guy's name?" Abby asked, gently lifting the other pup. The lobo's eyes were half-lidded, but he hadn't quite fallen asleep yet.

"Should I give him a Greek name too?"

Abby nodded solemnly. "Most definitely. You can't let him feel left out."

"Perseus was always my favorite."

It struck Lacey how many Greek heroes grew up without their fathers under rough circumstances. Zach probably saw a bit of himself in the ancient warriors.

"Who was he?" Abby asked.

"The one who slew Medusa with the snake hair."

"Oh," Abby said. "I don't remember the good guys. I'm better with the monsters."

"Most people are," Zach said softly, and Lacey wondered how many modern monsters the boy had faced.

Abby adjusted the pup in her arms and stared down at his sleepy face. "Do you approve, Perseus?" The wolf exhaled contentedly, his little torso expanding with the effort. Abby giggled. "I think you picked the right ones."

Zach's shy grin touched Lacey's heart. In his smile, she could see his confidence battling against a lifetime of insecurity. He didn't need saving so much as he needed a platform where he could shine. She wondered if his uncle fully understood that. Maybe Clay was trying too hard to change his nephew instead of working to build up his existing character.

Lacey sat in the corner of the room as the two teenagers chatted with the wolf pups sleeping in their laps. Letting her eyes flutter shut, she allowed herself to zone out. Clay was right. She did need to make an appointment with a neurologist. She didn't feel right, and overall, her symptoms weren't improving on their own. Luckily, just closing her eyes and disengaging for a few minutes gave her a little boost.

About half an hour later, Abby excused herself to go do homework. Lacey picked herself off the floor and headed over to Zach. He was quiet as he watched the wolf in his lap.

"How are you keeping up with school with working here every evening and on the weekends?" Lacey asked.

Zach lifted his shoulders and let them drop. "I've never been a good student."

"That surprises me."

Zach's head whipped up. "Seriously? Me? You think someone like me would get As?"

"I don't see why not," Lacey said. "You're smart and hard-working."

"That's not me."

"Hasn't anyone ever told you that before?"

Zach gave her a look that informed her that he seriously doubted her intelligence. It was another expression teenagers had perfected for centuries, and Zach was no exception. Luckily, she had plenty of experience dealing with exasperated adolescents being dragged by their families on outdoor vacations when they just wanted to spend their summer playing computer games and watching YouTube.

"I'm sure your uncle has said something similar."

Zach rolled his eyes. "Yeah," he said and then deepened his voice. "*Zach, you're too smart for this.*"

"He's probably right," Lacey said gently. She expected

him to glare, but he kept petting the wolf pup. She wondered what expectations he had for himself. "Did you ever think about working with animals when you grow up?"

"You mean be a rancher like my uncle?" Zach asked. "That's not really my thing."

"What is your thing?"

Silence. The teenager kept his gaze trained on Theseus, and Lacey had her answer. He didn't have plans for the future. At fourteen, he shouldn't have his life planned out, but he should have some vague desires of what adulthood might hold.

"I didn't necessarily mean ranching," Lacey said. "There are a lot of careers out there that involve working with critters. There's mine. I'm an ecologist at the national park. Bowie is another good example, and so is Lou."

"Yeah, right. Me, a vet."

"You have a natural affinity with wildlife," Lacey told him. "I wouldn't say it if I didn't mean it."

Quiet descended. Lacey sensed Zach was at least considering her words. She stopped pushing. She couldn't expect a breakthrough in one conversation. But she'd planted a seed she hoped would blossom into a dream, because every kid needed one.

To her surprise, it was Zach who broke the stillness. "Did you and my uncle have another fight?"

His insight startled Lacey. "I'm not sure I understand your question."

"You guys seemed weird in the truck today. I mean, you always seem weird. But you were, I don't know, weirder."

"And you say you're not smart," Lacey muttered under her breath.

Unfortunately, Zach heard her. His face broke into a triumphant smile. "So I *was* right."

"Did anyone ever tell you that your hearing is better than a greater wax moth's?"

Zach screwed up his face. "Uh, no. Is that a good thing?"

Lacey laughed. "They're supposed to have the best audition out of all animals."

"Audition means hearing?"

Lacey nodded.

"What do they loo—" Zach shook his head in the middle of his sentence. "Hey, you're trying to distract me!"

"That could be the plan," Lacey said.

"But that's *my* trick," Zach said, giving her a look of newfound respect, "and you almost got me."

"I'm a professional when it comes to distractions." She'd had to be for her mother after the deaths of her father and brother.

"So am I, but your technique is subtler."

"I don't like drama," Lacey said. "Simpler is easier."

The teenager shrugged. "I don't know. Sometimes you have to create a little trouble to avoid bigger shit."

"Language, Zach. Language."

"So are you and my uncle fighting about the wolf pack again? I heard there were some on his property."

It didn't escape Lacey's notice that Zach referred to the ranch as only Clay's instead of using the pronoun *our* like most kids would when describing where they lived. It told Lacey that either Zach didn't consider Valhalla his home…or he expected Clay would kick him out sooner or later. She decided not to touch the issue for now.

"Are you trying to distract me from your swearing?"

"Not really," Zach said. "I'm just trying to get the conversation back to where I want it."

Lacey sighed, realizing Zach wouldn't give up easily. "Your uncle and I aren't currently arguing over the lobos. The situation between us is complicated."

"Because of what my grandfather did to this town?"

"You know about it?" Lacey asked. Zach would have been fairly young at the time of the scandal. She didn't know how much his family had shielded him from his grandfather's arrest and subsequent imprisonment.

"A little. Your grandfather mentioned it the other day at your house, and I'd heard other shit—" Zach broke off at her sharp look and started over. "I'd heard *stuff* growing up, but I didn't know he'd screwed over an entire town until I moved here. It didn't take me long to figure it out. Kids kept picking fights, and the teachers didn't give a sh—crap and blamed me. Which I guess wasn't too different from my old school, but they seemed smug about it. Uncle Clay doesn't get punched in the face, but you can tell everybody wants to slug him."

"I'm sorry about that, Zach. That isn't fair to you or your uncle."

Again, Zach lifted his shoulders and let them drop. He'd returned his attention back to the lobo in his lap.

"When your whole family's been in and out of prison, you get used to it."

Lacey didn't know exactly why Zach had chosen to open up to her. He seemed like a bivalve mollusk, keeping his shell tightly shut and sealing off his hurts with a multitude of protective layers. But the teen needed someone, and from the little Clay had said, she didn't think Zach confided in his uncle. The boy was smart enough to realize Lacey had saved him from a long stint in juvenile detention. Whatever the reason, she knew she couldn't follow through with her natural instincts and push him away. He deserved to find an adult he could trust. If he chose her, she wouldn't abandon him.

"How much did your family lose in my grandfather's con?" Zach asked quietly, his attention still focused on the wolf in his arms.

Lacey paused, unsure of how much she should burden the teenager with the old, unhealed hurts.

Zach looked up, his blue eyes dark. "You can tell me the truth. It's funny when adults try to protect me when I've seen shit most of them never will."

The kid had voluntarily revealed himself to her. She wouldn't insult him by not doing the same. "My family owns the Prairie Dog Café."

"Yeah, I know it. I've been there once or twice. People kinda looked at me funny, so I stopped going. I asked Clay about it, and he said it was probably best if I didn't go there anymore. He wasn't real clear, but he mumbled something about my grandfather."

"Years ago, your grandparents owned a big house close to the ski resort. They'd fly in during the winter for a couple weeks, but they mostly lived in New York."

"Yeah, they were loaded. My grandmother still is. She married some wealthy guy when my grandfather went to jail. She doesn't want anything to do with me. My other grandmother is poor, like really poor. After her house got foreclosed on, we kept getting evicted from our rentals."

"How did your parents meet?"

"Some party in New York. My mom ran away from home to be a model. She found more drugs instead. When she got knocked up with me, we lived in shitty apartments in New York for a while. Then when my dad went to jail for the first time, she moved back to Ohio."

"That must have been hard for you."

Zach's mouth twitched, but he didn't comment. Instead, he changed the subject. "So what shit did my grandfather pull?"

"Stuff," Lacey corrected gently.

"Huh?"

"What *stuff* did he pull."

Zach rolled his eyes, and he said with an exaggerated tone, "Okay, what *stuff* did he pull?"

"He and his wife never spent much time in town during their visits, but suddenly, he became a fixture. He frequented the Prairie Dog a lot. My dad was thinking about expanding our operations. He'd grown up on a ranch next to your uncle's, and he thought maybe our family could run a chuckwagon-style restaurant in the summers. But he didn't have a lot of capital, and he didn't like the idea of taking out a loan since he needed to educate my brother and me. So when Trent Stevens started talking about a sure investment that could double or triple in value, my dad listened."

Zach's eyes widened. "Crap. How much did he invest?"

"All of my parents' savings. Trent didn't give him a lot of time to think, so my dad didn't check with my mom. When the pyramid scheme collapsed, we were the hardest hit in Sagebrush. We lost everything but the Prairie Dog, and back then, we didn't even know if we'd manage to hold onto it."

Zach winced. "I'm sorry."

"It's not your fault," Lacey said. "I don't want you to feel bad, but you wanted the truth, and since you've faced some of the fallout, I think you deserve to know."

"How did your dad handle it? Did your mom get real mad at him?"

Lacey paused. This was the hard part. "My dad died of a heart attack right after he received the news."

Zach's eyes widened. "Fuck."

"Word choice."

"You can't tell me that doesn't warrant a fuck."

It did, but she wouldn't concede that point. She gave the teenager a hard stare.

He sighed and said, "That had to suck for your family."

"It was a difficult time," Lacey said. Zach's words might not be poetic, but they were heartfelt.

"So that's why things are off between you and my uncle?"

"Not exactly," Lacey said. "Like I said, I don't blame you or your uncle for your past."

Triumphant understanding zapped across Zach's face. "But your family does. You're fu—freaking Romeo and Juliet."

Lacey knew she shouldn't encourage the reference to star-crossed lovers, but she couldn't stop the soft smile stretching across her face. "Zach, I think you're more well read than you let on."

"Everyone knows that reference. It's not like I said Tristan and Isolde." He gave her a cocky teenage grin. Unlike when he'd mentioned Greek mythology, the second literary reference hadn't been a mistake. He wanted her to know she'd been right about his intelligence, but he wasn't completely ready to admit it aloud.

"Okay. You're right. Our families are a bit like the Montagues and the Capulets." Lacey didn't want to tell the kid he was more accurate than he knew with his references to the Bard's tragedies. Their families' intertwined past *did* contain one other death. But she didn't want to dump her brother's increasingly risky behavior and fatal accident on an already vulnerable fourteen-year-old.

"But you're not angry at me?" Zach asked. He said the words quietly. Although she'd already made the point clear, she knew he wanted reassurance.

"No, Zach, not at all."

Clay didn't deserve being coupled to his father's crimes either, but in the opinion of her mother and grandfather, he was just another link welded to the Stevens family chain—a chain that had choked and nearly suffocated the town of Sagebrush Flats. And even without that unbreakable connection, she doubted a relationship between the two of them would work.

True, Clay cared about his land. He might even have a soft spot for birds and smaller mammals. But he'd never understand, never accept, her love for wolves. And how could she ever form a lasting relationship with a man who actively fought against her life's work?

---

Scamp would've chittered happily as the Blue-Eyed One chased him, but his mouth was full of a shiny, slippery substance. The silvery flash had first attracted Scamp's attention as he'd watched the Blue-Eyed One shovel pieces of bread and a hunk of meat into his mouth. The unopened bag had sat beside the biped on the bench where he'd been taking a break from digging fence holes. Scamp had seized the opportunity. He'd given the object one quick shake to attract notice before he'd scurried away. He'd selected wisely. Although hard to grip, the material crunched most delightfully.

"Hey, that's part of my dinner!"

Scamp ignored the human's distressed cry. He could hear the Blue-Eyed One's footsteps pound behind him. For a biped, he could run fast. Not quick enough to catch Scamp, but speedy enough to make things interesting.

Scamp rounded a corner and saw the young female

human walking toward the llama shed. Although the Gray-Eyed One brought him honey-covered larvae, she did not interest him as much as the juvenile male. She did not have enough honey badger in her, but the Blue-Eyed One…he had plenty.

Scamp darted between her legs. She gasped and bent down to catch him, but her fingers didn't even scrape against his fur. He would have made a sound of triumph, but he didn't want to risk losing his prize. He continued his forward dash until he heard new sounds…the clatter of spraying gravel, a high-pitched squeal, and a lower *ooof*.

Turning, Scamp spotted the Blue-Eyed One doubled over the Gray-Eyed One. His arms were wrapped around her middle in a clear attempt to prevent himself from knocking her to the ground. When they both managed to retain their balance, they straightened. The Gray-Eyed One was giggling, but the Blue-Eyed One's face had turned an interesting shade of red. Scamp tilted his head. He had not known a biped's skin could change colors.

"Are you okay?" The sounds the Blue-Eyed One made had a huffy quality and a higher pitch than normal. "I'm sorry I almost took you out. I was chasing Scamp."

The female biped responded with chatter of her own. "I know. He zipped right under me."

"You're not hurt? I slammed into you pretty hard." The biped didn't take as many gulps of air when he spoke, but his voice still seemed off. It reminded Scamp of how his mother chittered when she had trouble locating him or when he was about to take a dangerous tumble.

"You caught me before my head hit the ground. I'm good." The female's lips curled up, and Scamp could see her white teeth. They were not sharp like a honey badger's. The sight did not impress Scamp, but the dark pink in the Blue-Eyed One's face had spread to his neck.

"Um, uh, I better try to catch him." The male rubbed his upper arms. Scamp had never seen a human do that.

"I'll help."

"Okay."

Both bipeds charged after him. Scamp felt a thrill. This would be fun. As he dashed forward, he looked over his shoulder and saw the Blue-Eyed One glance at the Gray-Eyed One when her head was turned. Something in his expression caused Scamp to slow his pace. When the male dove in his direction, Scamp didn't dart out of his grasp. Oh, he wriggled his body and twisted his neck, but he didn't jerk out of the Blue-Eyed One's hands.

"Wow!" The female made an excited chitter, her gray eyes bright. "I don't think anyone's ever caught Scamp before."

The Blue-Eyed One's chest puffed out against Scamp. The young male talked a little longer to the female before he carried Scamp back to the enclosure. Before he released him, he made a low, quiet sound. "Thanks, buddy."

# Chapter 6

"You don't look well, sweetie," Lacey's mom said as they walked through the zoo two weeks later. "You're pale, and the skin around your eyes is pinched like you're in pain."

Lacey's head did ache a little from the bright sun…not that she would admit it. Her mother worried. A lot. Lacey didn't blame her. After all, she'd lost half her family in less than six soul-crushing months. They'd clung to each other for support during the aftermath of the tragedy. Although Lacey had been daddy's little girl, she'd always had a great relationship with her mother too. When they'd only had each other, they'd grown closer…but also further apart. Lacey had learned then to hide things from her mother. Not big things. Just small things that would upset her. Like getting a ride from her teenage friends instead of being chauffeured by a parent. Or hiking by herself in Rocky Ridge. Or hiding the extent of her current headaches.

"I'm fine, Mom," Lacey said.

"I think you should see a doctor."

Just then, Lulubelle, the camel, came tripping over to see them. As always, she thrust her neck over the fence, eager for a pat. When Lacey's mom didn't respond immediately, the animal peeled back her large lips and made raspberry sounds.

Lacey's mom laughed, bright and easy. A bystander

wouldn't know how hard-earned the sound was. There'd been a stretch when Lacey had worried her mother would never again find a steady, solid happiness. But both of them had found their peace. Lacey's was Rocky Ridge and the wolf pack. Her mom's was the Prairie Dog Café and her customers.

"Okay, okay," Peggy Montgomery said to Lulubelle as she reached up and petted her. "I can take a hint."

The camel made a satisfied rumble. At the sound, little Savannah poked her head out of the shed Bowie had recently built when he'd separated the camels from the llamas. Seeing her mother receive attention, the calf galloped over, a smaller version of Lulubelle.

"Yes, I see you there," Lacey's mom said. "You are a cutie. We need to name a dish after you too." Over the past few years, the Prairie Dog Café and the zoo had participated in several successful cross-promotions. As part of the collaboration, Bowie's wife, Katie, had redesigned the menu to feature the zoo's various residents. The restaurant's meatloaf with haystack onions had always been a favorite with the locals, but when Katie had placed Lulubelle's picture by the item, it had become extremely popular with the tourists as well.

"What do you think, Lacey?" her mom asked as she petted Savannah. "Should I feature this little peanut's baby picture on the children's or dessert menu?"

With her mom's attention focused on the half-grown calf, Lacey rubbed her temples. "Maybe you could name a milkshake after her?"

"Oooh, that's a good..." Her mom trailed off as she lifted her eyes in Lacey's direction. Lacey's fingers froze mid-massage.

"Honey, what is wrong? And don't try distracting me. You've got a headache. That makes three already this week."

Actually, she'd had one on and off for two weeks straight. "It's just so bright today, Mom. That's all."

"Lacey Diane Montgomery, do I need to call a specialist myself? I am not above making an appointment for you."

Lacey didn't doubt that for a moment. Her mom was a natural-born manager. Her dad had loved to cook, and her mother had run the business end of the restaurant. He'd always teased her, calling her Mrs. Bossy Pants. She would pretend to swat him, but she'd never succeeded in hiding her smile.

"I have an appointment with a specialist scheduled for later today," Lacey finally admitted. They'd reached the point where her mother would worry more if Lacey didn't tell her.

The news did not mollify Peggy. Her cornflower-blue eyes narrowed. "In the city?"

"Yep," Lacey said. "Dr. Peyton referred me to a clinic with a focus on brain injuries."

Her mom crossed her arms. "How are you getting there?"

This was the even harder part. "I have my ways."

Her mother was a petite woman. Lacey had inherited

Peggy's height, or rather lack of it, but she'd grown slightly taller than her mom. The couple extra inches didn't matter though. Peggy knew how to appear bigger than a towering grizzly standing on its hind legs. She didn't even need to straighten her shoulders. It was all personality.

"Do not play coy with me, young lady. You didn't even feel up to driving to the zoo. Is your grandfather taking you?"

Lacey couldn't help it. She shifted guiltily. At twenty-seven, she still had no immunity against her mother's *look*.

"Lacey..."

The warning note in her mother's voice jarred the words from Lacey's lips. "Grandpa hates waiting rooms and hospitals. It'll be a marathon too. I have an appointment with a neuropsychologist and a neuro-ophthalmologist who treats concussion patients. They were good enough to schedule everything at once since I live so far away." She hoped if she tossed enough balls of information at her mother, Peggy would be too focused on juggling them to keep grilling Lacey. She also didn't mention she'd need to stay overnight in the city since the appointment with the eye doctor was a day later. No sense in alerting her mother to the fact that she'd be sleeping in the same hotel as Clay Stevens or that they'd be spending two days together.

"What is a neuropsy..." Her mother trailed off. "You're trying to distract me. Who is taking you? Why are you being so evasive?"

"Mom, don't you want to see the baby wolves?"

"Lacey, I'm onto all of your little tricks. Is Katie going with you? Is that why you came to the zoo early today instead of with those horrible Stevenses? I still don't understand why you insist on volunteering at the same time as that hoodlum who caused your brain injury."

"Mom," Lacey said quietly. "We talked about this. You've got enough to do at the Prairie Dog without playing limo driver."

Her mother snorted. "My secondhand clunker is hardly a limousine, and I can rearrange the schedule. I do own the restaurant."

"Mom, Clay has to drive past my house to drop off his nephew. It is a waste of gas not to join them."

"I don't trust that man. He's no good. You can see it in his eyes. His father's were the same fickle blue. You can't put your faith in someone whose eyes change so easily. I told your father..."

Pain caused Peggy's face to momentarily crumple. Time had tempered its rawness but not its power. Lacey knew too well. Both her mother and she could go along for days, weeks even, without feeling the razor-sharp slice of loss. But then, unexpectedly, it would strike, sure and deep. And for Peggy, mentioning the Stevens family was like stabbing a well-honed knife through her carefully constructed tranquility.

Lacey wanted to tell her mother that Clay wasn't his father, but intellectually, her mom already knew that. It was her heart that couldn't accept it. So Lacey just said, "I know, Mom. I know."

Her mother ran her tongue over her teeth twice. She swallowed. Hard. Then the muscles around her mouth tightened before relaxing into a placid expression. "Well, enough about *that Stevens boy*. How are you..." Realization flooded her mother's face. She tilted her head, her lips slightly parted in horror. "Surely, you're not letting *him* take you into town."

There was no avoiding the whole truth now. "Clay owes me. Like you said, his nephew did help cause all this."

"*I* should be taking you," her mother said.

"You have a business to run, and you hate hospitals as much as Grandpa, maybe even more. Clay is just my chauffeur. We're barely going to talk to each other—same as when he gives me a lift to the zoo." That, at least, was true. They'd barely chatted since the aborted kiss. Zach sprawled in the back with his headphones while she and Clay sat in stony silence with the radio playing country music.

"I didn't want to bring this up, but your grandfather said Pete Thompson called him a few weeks ago. Evidently, he caught you kissing *that Stevens boy* in his barn."

"Mo-om," Lacey said.

Her mother held up her hand. "I know. I know. You're twenty-seven years old. You have a right to your privacy and your love life, which is why I didn't say anything until now. But *him*? He's a con artist, Lacey. You need to be careful. People like him know how to take a person's good sense and twist it into a pretzel. Don't get entangled with that man."

"I'm not going to," Lacey said. "Pete Thompson was

just letting his imagination get the better of him. Clay had taken me riding to show me some ideas he had for improving water retention on his property. I got dizzy, and he was helping me dismount when Uncle Pete walked in. That's all."

It wasn't exactly the whole truth, but Lacey didn't want to worry her mother. Besides, nothing was going to happen between Clay and her.

"Pete is an excitable person. I always wondered how he managed to get along with Clay's grandfather. Now John Frasier was a reserved individual, nothing like his jet-setting daughter. She was too much like her mother. I have no idea why John married a socialite from back East, although I suppose I really shouldn't be surprised. The men in that family never marry local girls. I suppose Clay will be no different. It's not as if any woman from Sagebrush would give him the time of day. He may be handsome, but we Western girls can recognize a rattler when we see one."

And with all the biology classes Lacey had taken, she shouldn't have trouble identifying one. But lately, she'd begun to wonder if the town had put Clay in the wrong taxonomy entirely.

"Why don't we see the baby wolves?" Lacey asked, hoping to end this increasingly awkward conversation. Her mom nodded. As soon as they began to walk away from the camels, Savannah gave a rumbling sound of protest. Lacey laughed and patted the calf on her fuzzy head. "You're turning into a bigger people person than your mama."

Savannah sighed heavily.

Lacey gave her one last rub. "Don't worry. I'll be back tomorrow."

"Do you ever miss your old job at the zoo?" her mother asked as they turned in the direction of the nursery.

"A little," Lacey admitted. "It's nice to be able to interact so closely with the animals, but there's nothing like watching them in their natural habitat."

"You and your father always did like the outdoors." Her mother's expression had turned wistful—the pain still present but with a bittersweetness tempering it. Lacey patted her mother's shoulder. Peggy reached up and briefly touched her hand, giving it a light squeeze. In silence, they walked into the maintenance building. When Lacey pushed open the door to the nursery, she caught sight of her distant cousin standing in front of her camera perched on a tripod. Katie lifted her head, shaking her curly, red hair from her eyes. She waved Lacey inside but signaled her to stay quiet. Passing on the message to her mom by pressing her finger against her lips, Lacey softly padded into the room with Peggy close on her heels.

They stood next to Katie, their backs against the wall, as the pups practiced walking. Most wolves would be fairly steady on their feet by now and getting ready to start exploring outside the den. Unfortunately, Theseus's and Perseus's injuries from the cave-in had put the two behind their siblings in the wild. Perseus's leg remained bandaged. Although he'd probably walk with an uneven gait, Lou was fairly confident they'd saved the limb. And canines in zoos adapted remarkably well to a weakened or even a missing leg. Theseus had healed faster, but his movements remained a little unsure for his age.

Despite their difficulties, the pups managed to climb clumsily over each other. Theseus tugged playfully at Perseus's left ear. The little guy emitted a sound between a growl and a squeak. Even with his bad leg, he wiggled out from under his brother and scrambled to get on top. This time, it was Theseus who got a light chomp on the loose skin at the back of his neck. Happy, high-pitched squeals filled the room, and a smile stretched across Lacey's face. No wonder Katie had hushed them. She filmed the zoo's promotional videos, and the public would melt at the adorable sounds. Lacey knew she was enjoying watching the lobos, even if following their jerky movements made her head feel more woozy than usual.

The pups' energy began to flag. Perseus let out a small yawn. Clearly sensing that the little lobos needed a rest, the capybara rose on her stubby legs and lumbered over to the duo. With her large snout, Sylvia gently nudged them over to their nest of blankets. Perseus immediately snuggled against her, but Theseus took more time than his brother to settle. Eventually, his jaws opened to reveal his pink mouth and tongue. Closing them again, he licked the inside of his lips before resting his tiny chin on the capybara's haunch. After that, all three animals quickly fell asleep.

Katie turned off her camera and turned to greet them with a warm smile. When she spoke, she kept her voice low. "Sorry about hushing you."

"Oh, don't worry about it, sweetie." Lacey's mom

waved away her concern. "That was a perfect moment. I'm glad we didn't ruin it."

"They're so much more active today," Lacey whispered as the three of them crept quietly from the room. The nursery had a large picture window in the hallway, which allowed them to observe the animals without interrupting their slumber.

Katie nodded. "I love this baby animal stage. Little Sorcha, our polar bear cub, is getting so big now."

"The wolves will grow quicker than she did," Lacey explained to her mom. "It won't be long before their ears perk up and they start looking more like juveniles."

Katie's expression turned wistful. "I'm going to miss their floppy ears. They make the puppies look rumpled and *sooo* squeezable. Bowie says I'm worse than Abby when it comes to cuddling the zoo babies. With my own twins crawling, I don't get as much snuggle time as I used to."

Lacey laughed and patted her friend's shoulder. "At least you get to interact with the animals in the zoo. I love my career, but sometimes it's hard to be an observer when a critter is struggling. But my job is to watch over the entire ecosystem, not just one of its members."

"You do realize you can't control entire environments," her mom said in the tone mothers always use when imparting wisdom.

Lacey resisted the urge to roll her eyes. "I know that."

"Do you?" her mother asked lightly. "Ever since you were a little girl, you felt personally responsible if something went wrong. I swear it was growing up at the Prairie Dog. Life doesn't always run like a restaurant."

"Mom, you're wasting your talents at the café. You should be writing internet memes instead," Lacey said.

Her mother turned to Katie. "Do you see what I have to put up with?"

Katie raised both her hands, her chocolate-brown eyes as wide as a startled mule deer's. "I am staying out of this."

"Wait until your twins get older," her mom said sagely. "Then you'll take my side."

Katie gave a theatrical moan. "They're already growing up too fast. Ever since they figured out how to roll, they're everywhere at once. As soon as I disentangle one from a near disaster, the other one finds a way to make the most innocuous object become a potential death trap. I swear I've babyproofed the house at least eight times."

"Anytime you need a babysitter, you can call Aunt Peg here," Lacey's mother said. "Although I'm not sure if your mom would appreciate someone else horning in on her territory."

Katie laughed, sending her red curls bouncing. "She is over the moon since the twins arrived. My dad too."

"I don't blame them. You and Bowie make exceptionally sweet babies."

Lacey studied her mom. Although she'd never pressured Lacey to start a family, the woman simply loved kids. Whenever a baby was brought to the Prairie Dog, her mom would stop whatever she was doing and come out to greet the little bundle. She'd make funny faces and sounds until the child smiled, and the locals would always quip that Lacey needed to give her grandbabies. But she didn't know if she ever would. Oh, she enjoyed watching newborns sleeping in their parents' arms, but having one would mean opening her heart to hurt. And she didn't want that. She'd stick to watching over the wildlife at Rocky Ridge instead.

---

Clay pulled his truck into the underground parking garage and glanced over at his sleeping passenger. Neither he nor Lacey had spoken much on the long drive into the city. During the last half, she'd closed her eyes and drifted to sleep.

It was strangely intimate, sitting next to her and listening to her measured breathing. Each soft inhale drew him toward her. He yearned to pull her against him and feel the weight of her head against his shoulder. He imagined a different drive. One where they were going on an adventure instead of heading to the doctor. Maybe they'd go north to the Grand Tetons and Yellowstone. They could hike together. He'd bring his camera and capture Lacey in the wilderness she loved. She'd be laughing, her lips parted ever so slightly. After he found the perfect shot, he'd gather her into his arms and kiss her. And there, away from the ranch, away from Sagebrush Flats, away from everything, they could simply be two people learning about each other.

"Lacey," Clay called gently, not wanting to startle her. His thoughts had deepened his voice, making it husky even to his own ears. At the sound of her name, Lacey gave a little half smile and snuggled deeper into the passenger seat. He cleared his throat and spoke louder. "Lacey." This time, her lips dipped into a frown. With an annoyed snort he found unbearably cute, she shifted away from him, her eyes still tightly closed.

Gently, he brushed his hand against her shoulder, keeping his touch light. Her eyes fluttered open. Sleep had made her irises richer, the gold melting into a warmer brown. Dark and inviting, her gaze latched onto his. Her hand reached up next and settled against his cheek, her fingers pleasantly hot against his skin. He sucked in his breath, his heart kicking like a donkey. Hell, he wanted to lean forward and take what she sleepily offered. But he didn't. Because a fully awake Lacey wouldn't want to kiss him again. But he might…just might…have leaned into her hand for a second before he pulled back and gave her one of his most brilliant smiles.

"We're here."

She blinked, some of the bleariness clearing. With a yawn, she stretched in the seat, the movement pulling the knit fabric of her sweater tight over her breasts. Clay glanced away. Hell, what was it about Lacey that turned him into a damn teenager?

"So, um, it looks like we've got time to kill before your appointment today. Traffic was lighter than I thought."

"Do you want to walk around before we head inside?" Lacey asked.

"Are you up for that?"

Lacey shrugged. "It's better than sitting in a waiting room. I don't know which I hate more: hospitals or being cooped up."

No, he couldn't imagine Lacey patiently sitting at a doctor's office or anywhere. Even with her brain injury slowing her down, she was constantly in motion.

"We drove past a nice shopping district and a little park that's fairly close to the garage," Clay said as he climbed from the cab.

"Sounds good." Lacey lifted her arms above her head again and bent her neck from side to side as they walked toward the elevator. "I should stretch my legs anyway."

When they reached ground level, Clay opened the building's exit door for Lacey. As soon as she walked into the sunshine, he noticed her wince at the bright light. Without thinking, he reached for his cowboy hat and settled it on her head. Pushing the brim back to adjust for her smaller head size, she glanced at him in surprise. He gave a sheepish smile. "I thought some shade might help."

"It does," she said. "Did anyone ever tell you that you are an observant man?"

Clay managed a short laugh. "People seem more inclined to point out my shortcomings, but I make a habit of paying attention to my surroundings. You need to focus on the details when you run a ranch."

"Thanks again for accompanying me to my doctor appointments."

Clay shrugged. "Like I've said before, this is partially my nephew's fault. I figure I owe you."

"But you could've just dropped me off today and picked me up tomorrow. You didn't need to stay the whole time."

Clay grinned broadly to hide his discomfort with her praise. "Maybe I just like waiting rooms."

Her lips parted in a deep belly laugh, the kind shared between close friends or family members. The sound bubbled through him like an underground spring, making him feel buoyant. Lacey shook her head. "Nobody likes sitting in doctors' offices."

"I don't know. They've got magazines, a TV, and, if you're lucky, free coffee."

"I think you might be mixing them up with fancy car repair shops."

"Now those are the gold standard of waiting rooms. In fact, I've spent entire days in one."

"I just bet you have," Lacey said before she sobered. "In all seriousness, thank you. I didn't want to drag my family with me, and I'm glad I'm not doing this alone."

"Even if you are with a Stevens." As soon as Clay said the words, he wished he hadn't. Lacey's face immediately went stony, and their fragile camaraderie shriveled up like a dead sego lily under the desert sun. But maybe it was a good thing. Neither of them could afford to get chummy. Their family histories would always lie between them, and it wasn't good for them to lose sight of that.

"So," Lacey said brightly, maybe too brightly, "your nephew is okay with you being gone overnight?"

Clay snorted, allowing her to change the subject. "He's

thrilled. I'm glad Bowie agreed he can stay at the zoo and watch over the wolf pups. I could've asked one of the ranch hands to keep an eye on him, but he's legendary for sneaking out."

"Bowie will keep a close watch," Lacey said, "and I don't think Zach would abandon Perseus and Theseus. He won't admit it, but he's got a soft spot for them."

Clay glanced over at Lacey, studying her. "How do you do it?"

"Do what?"

"Get everyone to like you, including my nephew," he said. "I've been trying for more than a year to get close to him—nothing works."

"I think he's afraid."

"Of me?" Clay asked, unable to stop the kernel of hurt from sprouting. He'd thought they'd moved beyond Lacey seeing him as the Big Bad Wolf.

"Not precisely," Lacey said slowly as she clearly considered her next words. "Deep down, he's worried you'll leave him. From what I can tell, your brother would flit in and out of his life."

Clay understood that fear too well. Hell, he'd felt abandoned when addiction had stolen his formerly self-possessed sibling, and Greg had only been his older brother, not a parent.

"And every time his mom or grandma got too high to remember his existence, he'd lose them all over again," he added.

"I'm not a blood relation, nor am I his guardian." Lacey

gently laid her hand on his sleeve. "Zach realizes I'm just passing through his life, so he knows there's no risk of forming expectations that could leave him crushed."

The heat from Lacey's fingertips penetrated Clay's cotton shirt, the warmth spreading through him like a bright-orange sunrise over the red-sandstone rocks. The understanding in her simple touch caused the next words to spill from him. "He's so much like me, you would think I'd know how to reach him."

Lacey blinked, her topaz eyes huge. "You two are alike?"

*Shit.* He hadn't meant to reveal anything about his own past. In response to her question, he gave the best nonchalant shrug he could manage. "My brother and I were pretty close growing up. He was six years older than me, and our parents weren't around too much. When he got hooked on opioids after a sports injury, I lost him too."

Lacey stopped walking, forcing him to do the same. She reached for him. Her hand lay softly on his arm, the gesture meant to comfort, not to restrain, but it ensnared him anyway. No one had touched him like this for years, to offer simple human compassion. He had vague memories of Greg soothing him after he'd woken from a nightmare, but that had been years and years ago.

Lacey studied him, and he felt like a damn wolf pup... or a piece of particularly interesting fungus. She was trying to figure him out like an ecosystem, and he wasn't sure if he liked it. But he didn't pull away. Didn't shake her off. Instead, he allowed the inspection.

To his surprise, she didn't push further. In fact, she changed the subject. "Is there a bookstore around here?"

"Pardon?"

"A bookstore," she repeated. "This looks like an area that might have an independent one."

"Uh, maybe," Clay said as he scanned the tree-lined street filled with neat storefronts built in the Italianate style that populated a lot of Western towns. "Do you want to get something to read during the appointments?"

Lacey shook her head. "You should pick up a book on Greek mythology for Zach."

Clay waited a beat for the punch line, but she regarded him seriously, her eyes as big and solemn as a boreal owl's.

"You're not joking, are you?"

"No. Your nephew likes to read."

"Zach, the kid who never does his homework and bails on school every chance he gets? That nephew?"

"Yup," Lacey said. "He's fascinated by ancient myths. Your brother gave him a book on Greek heroes when he was just five, and he's been obsessed with them ever since."

Clay shook his head, trying to make sense of the conversation. Although Greg had gotten mostly As and Bs, he'd never been particularly academic. He'd lived for soccer. If Greg would've bought his son any reading material, it would have been about sports. "Why'd my brother choose that?"

Once again, Lacey took her time before she said carefully, "Zach thinks it's what your brother could shoplift from a sidewalk sale."

"Ah." Sadness crept through Clay...at what his brother had become, at what Zach had faced, at the entire frustrating situation. It wasn't hard to see why his nephew would've clung to anything his father had given him.

"He's smart," Lacey said. "Part of him is embarrassed by his intelligence, but mostly I think he's yearning for someone to recognize it."

Clay jerked his chin as he thought about her words. He'd been messed up too when he'd arrived at his grandfather's ranch. He'd loved nothing better than challenging authority, but it had been an attention-seeking defiance. He'd wanted someone to see him, value him. And his grandfather had. His tough love had contained an element of respect. His grandfather expected him to learn ranching and finish his chores, no matter how difficult or dirty they were. And he hadn't let Clay weasel out of responsibility. In trying to recreate his grandfather's lessons for Zach, maybe Clay was too focused on his own teenage experiences instead of taking the time to understand his nephew.

"I'll see about finding a bookstore." Clay reached into his pocket and pulled out his phone. Sure enough, he located one just a couple of blocks away. "There's one within walking distance."

"All right then. Let's go." She smiled—wide and brilliant and full of life and hope. He wanted to grab onto some of that joy, so he extended his hand without thinking. For a moment, she stared down at it. Just when he was about to withdraw, she reached out and wrapped her fingers around his. A heady sensation whipped through him. The gesture was supposed to be simple, and Clay supposed that in some ways, it was. There was something honest and wholesome about a couple walking hand in hand down the street. It was as welcoming and satisfying as a big slice of warm apple pie on a crisp fall day.

Lacey's knuckles brushed against his jeans, and he glanced down at her. She was a remarkable woman, so full of passion for the causes she cared about. But even with all her outward energy, she was observant. He supposed her job called on her to be both. Whatever the reason for her powers of perception, he was grateful for them. He needed an outsider's view on his relationship with Zach. He certainly hadn't been making much progress alone. And he didn't know too many people who could've gotten his nephew to open up. Lacey had a way of drawing people to her, like a spring of cool, fresh water in an otherwise dry, dusty desert.

Hell, even he, her only opposition, found his fingers entwined in hers. All because he wanted a bit of her goodness in his life. For once, they weren't enemies fighting over the wolf program. Their families' past didn't matter in this city. No one knew them. Here, they were just two people, strolling down the street, giving each other a little comfort.

---

Perseus was *not* pleased. Despite his most plaintive cries, his brother was getting fed first! Although Perseus generally liked the Blue-Eyed One, he did *not* appreciate being overlooked. True, his brother may have started complaining first, but Perseus did not care. He could *smell* the milk. It made him think of how delightful the sweet substance tasted and how it warmed his little belly...a little belly that was now rumbling in anticipation.

He opened his mouth and tried to make a loud demand. A rather impressive squeak came out. This pleased him, even if it did not have the desired result of a bottle being placed in his mouth. Perseus tried again. The sound sort of caught in his throat, making it longer and more drawn out. Something about making the noise seemed right, natural. But it seemed like he should be doing something more, something impressive. Perseus tried again. And again. He forgot about his hunger pains. He'd just loosened his jaw for a third time when a hand gently caught him around the middle. His big noise came out in a disappointing squawk.

"I hear you. I hear you," the Blue-Eyed One said. "Your bottle is ready."

Perseus smelled the delicious formula again. Noise-making forgotten, he clamped his lips around the rubber nipple and suckled. Excited by the taste, he paddled his paws. The Blue-Eyed One chuckled. Perseus liked the sound. It made him feel safe.

"It's a good thing you're still so little or you could do some serious damage with those claws. You have a good shredding motion."

Perseus's stomach began to feel wonderfully full. He

loved the sensation. When he finished his bottle, the human laid him down next to his brother and the nice warm rodent. Perseus enjoyed snuggling against her. It made him happy and content. Even her huge sighs relaxed him. They seemed to whoosh through him too, making everything settle inside him. They were a pack—Perseus, his brother, Sylvia, and their human caretakers.

Just then, the Blue-Eyed One sat down across from him. He opened a paper-filled object on his lap and began to emit a steady stream of noise as his eyes slowly scanned back and forth. Perseus's eyes had almost drifted closed when he spotted a white-and-black creature entering the room. The newcomer stared at the biped for a moment before he too curled into a ball. It seemed he also liked the rise and fall of the human's voice. A few moments later, the Blue-Eyed One paused, his gaze landing on the interloper for the first time. The human looked startled, but then he gave a nod and returned to making the calming noises. Cocooned in comfort, Perseus faded into sleep.

---

Waves of light-headedness crashed into Lacey. It didn't help that a band of pressure dug into the left side of her head. It wasn't a particularly severe headache, but she'd had it since they'd left the bookstore. The fluorescent lights and rows and rows of paperbacks crammed into a tight space had triggered a dull ache. The pain had only worsened while she was in the waiting room at the doctor's office. Now, all she wanted was a soft bed and soothing blackness.

"You're really pale," Clay said as they rode the hotel elevator to their floor.

Lacey responded with a weak smile, not wanting to complain.

"Maybe we shouldn't go out for dinner," Clay said. "I can bring some food to your room. And I swear that's not a line."

She laughed softly. "I didn't take it as one. Your suggestion sounds perfect. Thank you."

"Okay," Clay said as the elevator door opened, and they both stepped out into the hallway. "I'll just drop your bag off at your room first, and then I'll find us some grub."

"All right, cowboy."

At her comment, Clay's sculptured lips spread into a wide grin. A flicker of excitement started in her belly and then roared through her like a swollen river during a flash flood. When Clay spoke, his voice was husky and as smooth as top-shelf liquor. It was a voice a woman could get drunk on. "You know, that's the first time someone's called me that. I kind of like it."

If his reaction was going to be like this every time she called him *cowboy*, Lacey kind of liked it too. Clay's eyes darkened into a blue-green as rich and as stunning as a Yellowstone hot spring. Lacey sucked in her breath as he leaned closer. The memory of their last kiss flickered to life, and she could almost feel his warm lips against hers. Her eyelids had just started to flutter downward when

Clay pulled back. Her momentary sense of rejection fled when she saw the deep blue hue of his irises. He wanted the kiss too.

"Get some rest," he told her gruffly. He gave her a half smile before he opened her door and laid her bag on one of the beds. Handing her the room key, he turned and headed back down the hallway. As soon as he disappeared around the corner, the air whooshed from Lacey...and so did the welcome sense of excitement.

She didn't even bother turning on the lights when she entered the room. She just strolled over to the nearest bed and collapsed. Despite the solid mattress under her, the world seemed off-kilter. To her horror, tears of frustration stung the backs of her eyes. She wanted to cry out and pound her fists against the pillows, but she'd learned long ago that railing against the unchangeable accomplished nothing.

Sleep, unfortunately, evaded her. She would've turned on the TV, but she knew from past experience that its glow would only increase her symptoms. Finally, she heard a knock. Climbing from the bed, she walked over to the peephole. She saw Clay standing there with a large paper bag in one hand and a six-pack of ginger ale in the other. When she opened the door, he lifted the cans and gave her a devastating smile. "I feel like a G-rated version of a college student on spring break, but this stuff might settle your stomach."

"How'd you know I was a little nauseated?" She'd purposely kept herself from grousing.

"My brother's concussions gave him a sour stomach. Ginger tea works too."

She reached for one of the cans. As soon as her fingers closed around the cool aluminum, she had a sudden urge to press the chilled surface against her throbbing head. Sending Clay a sideways glance, she decided he wouldn't judge her, and she gave in to temptation. He laughed, the sound warm. "Not exactly what I intended, but hey, that works too."

Lacey realized she didn't want to be alone in the dark. She wanted companionship. More specifically, she wanted Clay. She shuffled a few steps into the hotel room, giving him space to enter. "Why don't you come in? We can eat together."

"Are you sure you're up to it? You don't need to feel obligated. I'm fine eating alone."

Lacey would've nodded, but she was beginning to train herself not to. Instead, she said, "I'd like the company, as long as you're okay eating in low light."

"Works for me."

She padded into the room and opened the drapes halfway. Natural light always seemed better than artificial, and luckily the sun had started its retreat below the horizon. Clay laid the food on the small table, and she moved the desk chair over.

As they ate, she began to feel better. Slowly, the pressures of the day receded along with the worst of her symptoms. The food gave her energy...and so did Clay's presence.

The hotel room only had a small desk pushed against

the wall, which forced her and Clay to crowd next to each other. His thigh pressed against hers, sending a welcome warmth through her body along with a whisper of anticipation. Trying her best to ignore the giddiness his closeness triggered, she tried to think of an innocuous discussion to distract her and asked him about his plans for the ranch.

Placing his burger down, he leaned back in his chair. Lacey tried not to notice how the movement caused the cotton of his shirt to pull over his muscles. She purposely shifted her focus to his words. "We've used controlled burns to get rid of the woody plants and invasive species. Some of the natural grasses are returning."

"Have you tried transplanting?" This was a good conversation. Safe. Scientific. And decidedly *not* romantic.

"Some. I planted alkali sacaton plants," Clay said.

"Not a bad choice," Lacey said between bites of fries. "Since the native animals don't typically eat it, that'll leave more for your cattle."

"I'm trying to introduce ellisiana prickly pear."

Intrigued, Lacey straightened as he mentioned the spineless variety of the cactus. She'd read about ranchers, especially in Texas and New Mexico, using the nopal for fodder. Unfortunately, her response caused her body to brush against his, causing an altogether different interest to ripple through her. Ignoring it, she resolutely stuck to their conversation. "Are you planning for the cows to graze on it?"

Lacey thought Clay stiffened at their unexpected contact, but his gaze remained studiously glued to their food. “The ranch hands aren’t happy with me, but we’re currently scorching the needles off the prickly pear plants already growing in the pastures. I can’t feed the cacti exclusively to the cows because of the risk of pear balls in their digestive tract, but it’s a pretty good source of nutrients and water.”

Respect for Clay thundered through Lacey. Even after touring his ranch, she hadn’t realized how innovative he’d become. She didn’t know another rancher in Sagebrush Flats so willing to work with the environment instead of fighting against it and trying to mold it into their ideal of a perfect grazing ground.

“Have you considered nonlethal methods to control the wolves?” Lacey almost hated destroying their peaceful accord with the question, but it seemed like the perfect opportunity.

Thankfully, Clay didn’t bristle. “I’ve considered getting some dogs to stay with the cattle. Hell, I’ve even toyed with the idea of a guard llama.”

Not many people knew the seemingly docile herd animal actually made a good protector and would fiercely defend animals it had bonded with against predators. They’d even been known to kick a coyote to death to protect sheep. “A llama wouldn’t be able to take on a pack of canines or fend off a mountain lion,” Lacey said. “Dogs are a better choice. The strategy works best if you also have a human guard watching the herd at night, so when the dogs raise the alarm, your ranch hand can help chase off the wolves.”

"What type of breed would you recommend?"

"If you're willing to import dogs, the USDA did a study and found the best choices aren't the ones American ranchers typically use but the Kengal from Turkey, the Transmontano mastiff from Portugal, and the Karakachan from Bulgaria. I can get you more information about the dogs and their breeders if you're interested. There are some U.S. breeders of Karakachans."

Clay reached for his burger again. "I wouldn't mind learning more about them."

Pleased he seemed so receptive, Lacey tried another suggestion. "Have you thought about fladry fencing—the kind with strips of material attached to a string? It's one of the more inexpensive solutions."

"Don't wolves just become desensitized to them?"

"Maybe it would help if you used them strategically, like during calving."

"That's an idea." Clay placed his food back down, his arm brushing against hers.

Her stubborn desire for him fluttered again, demanding release. She noticed him shift away from her as if he was battling the same reaction. Sucking in her breath, Lacey redirected her thoughts back to their discussion.

"There's also a herding technique where you apply less pressure on the cattle and allow them to huddle together organically without forcing them into a formation. It helps them move together naturally during a wolf attack, similar to how buffalo respond."

Clay snorted. "Try telling Pete Thompson he's

rounding up cows wrong. I'm going to have enough pushback this spring and summer when we increase the number of dams on my property. The creek bed cut pretty deep over the years, so we have a lot of work to do."

"What do you think about reintroducing beavers? I could put you in touch with some conservation groups."

Surprise flooded Clay's face. "You'd do that?"

"Of course," she said. "You're serious about restoring the ciénegas, and it would benefit Rocky Ridge. Have you looked into any grants?"

Clay nodded. "I received one last year."

"The local paper should've done a story on it."

Clay's mouth twisted. "They weren't interested."

"They should've been."

"Well, they were until they asked for my name," Clay said. "Since my idea for doing a project with the local high school didn't pan out, I've considered reaching out to some colleges to see if they have any interest."

Lacey tapped her finger on the table as she thought. "One of my old professors is an expert in wetlands in the Southwest. If you talked to her, she or one of her grad students might be interested."

"Really?" Clay's whole face lit up. "That would be terrific."

Their eyes locked, and the warm camaraderie finally flared into something more. Something hot. Something intense. Something unstoppable.

Lacey swallowed. Hard. She'd never felt want like this before. Despite everything pushing them apart, she couldn't deny that a primal force kept pulling them back together. His eyes looked like hot springs again and not just because of the brilliant aquamarine color. This time, she could practically see steam rising from them. She sucked in her breath, and she watched as his searing gaze slipped to her lips. Her body stilled. Right here, right now, no one could stop them.

Just as she started to lean forward, he gave a little jerk, like someone who'd caught themselves nodding off. He cleared his throat, the sound low and gravelly. It rumbled through Lacey, leaving want in its wake. But it looked like Clay wouldn't be satisfying her craving. His eyes had already started to cool into a lighter blue.

"I should get going. I was just finishing eating anyway," Clay said, his voice matter-of-fact. It was the type of tone she suspected he used when assigning a task to his ranch hands. It was obvious he wanted to put some distance between them by keeping things businesslike. Given their history, it was the sensible choice. But Lacey didn't want practical right now. She wanted the fantasy.

Her desire must have shown on her face, because Clay's sculpted lips twisted wryly. "You're tired, and you've had a long day. Our timing is off today."

A humorless laugh escaped her lips. "Our timing is so off, we might as well live in different epochs."

His chuckle was real as he stood up. Bunching up his food wrapper, he tossed it into the empty bag that had held the food. "I'll take the garbage when I leave. Greasy smells used to bug the hell out of my brother."

"It's like I've got a superpowered sniffer," Lacey said. "When I was a kid, I thought it would be cool if I had ability to detect scents like a wolf. Now, I'm very glad I don't."

Clay laughed again as he gathered up her napkin. "That wouldn't be my first choice for a superpower."

"What would you pick?"

He paused, thinking for a moment. "Honestly, understanding what makes each person tick."

"That's an odd one."

He lifted one shoulder and let it drop. "You have it to a degree, and so does June Winters. You two make friends without even thinking about it. Look at how you convinced a town full of ranchers to embrace wolves. And you've gotten further with my nephew in a month than I have in a year."

Lacey opened her mouth, closed it, and then opened it again. "I...I don't know what to say. I've never thought about it that way. I grew up at the Prairie Dog Café, so I guess Sagebrush is just like one big family to me."

"It's more than that. Do you get kids to participate in your ranger talks?"

"Well, yes, it's part of my job."

"Engaging children on summer vacation isn't easy, Lacey. You have a knack with people. It's amazing how you can bring them over to your way of thinking."

A little sliver of doubt crept through her along with a glimmer of hurt. Were they back to retreading old ground about her wolf project? "Do you think I'm manipulative?"

The shock on his face doused her suspicions.

"Hell, not that. It's something I admire about you, even when you're arguing against me. Maybe I was even a little envious before I got to know you. I've never figured out the trick. When I was a kid, I used to pull stupid shit to get people to laugh. But once I stopped being the class clown, I didn't have another way to connect with others."

Lacey wanted to reach out and touch him, but for an entirely different reason than before. She didn't think he fully grasped how much he'd just revealed. He'd meant to reassure her, but in doing so, he'd exposed his own vulnerabilities. She knew the exact moment he realized it too.

His cheek muscles tightened, and he straightened his shoulders. "Well," he said gruffly, "I've stayed long enough. Get some rest, Lacey."

He turned to leave, and the room suddenly felt like a dark, yawning hole. She didn't want to be alone, and Clay had a wonderfully grounding presence. And she had no trouble detecting the loneliness rolling off him too.

"Don't go. Please stay."

---

Clay paused at the door. He yearned to turn around. But he didn't. Instead, he stood in the small alcove, staring unseeingly at the evacuation route sign. "I'm not sure if that would be smart."

Getting involved with Lacey Montgomery was a bad idea for both of them. Right now, she wasn't thinking clearly, so he needed to for both of them. And since he had little willpower when it came to resisting temptation, he avoided it altogether.

"You're right," she admitted in a soft voice. "But I'm not talking about starting something, Clay. I…I just don't want to be alone."

His hand froze on the door handle. He didn't like the slight quiver he heard in her voice. He was used to Lacey Montgomery being indomitable. This was the woman who'd crawled into an unstable den to save a litter of wolf pups.

"Lacey," he said softly, his voice a warning to both of them.

"You make me forget about my light-headedness."

Ah, hell. He was going to cave.

"Please."

He turned back around. "I'm still not sure about this." Although he couldn't make out her face in the dim light, he sensed that she wore a smile.

"To be honest, neither am I. But I *know* I need this right now."

He heaved out a sigh, dropped the remains of their supper in the garbage can by the door, and made his way back to her. "So you just want to sit in the dark and talk?"

"Could…" She paused, her tone hesitant. When she spoke again, her voice was firmer. "Could you hold me?"

His heart slammed against his chest with the force of a landslide. It had been hard enough sitting pressed against her as they ate dinner. Every damn time one of them shifted, a spike of want had pierced him. He'd never experienced that much need just by being next to a woman. He couldn't imagine how he'd feel if he wrapped his arms around her. "That could be dangerous."

This time, he was close enough to see the sweet curl of her lips. "Maybe I've always liked a little bit of danger. My passion is working with apex predators, after all."

He snorted. "Lacey, I was the king of bad situations. Believe me. You have nothing on me."

"Then sitting in the dark while holding me and talking shouldn't faze you."

She was dead wrong. The idea would've scared the shit out of him if he didn't find it so damn appealing. And that was the problem. He'd always craved things that would only end up bringing him trouble.

"There isn't a couch in the room," he pointed out, "and it would get pretty uncomfortable in the armchair."

"There's the bed."

Her quiet words rushed through him like a monsoon. When he spoke, he couldn't keep a rough skeptical quality from his voice. "And nothing's going to happen?"

"Nothing but talking and maybe sleeping."

He wanted this woman with an intensity that defied reason. Doing what she asked would amount to sweet torture. But he couldn't walk away.

"Are you sure this will make you feel better?"

"Pretty sure." Her confidence had returned, and he liked the slight cocky note.

"If it doesn't work, you'll let me know, and I'll go back to my own room."

"Okay."

"And neither of us is going to try to seduce the other."

She emitted an uncharacteristic giggle, the sound bright and downright intoxicating. "You sound like a hero in a historical romance."

He was not nearly as amused. "Right now, I feel like one minus the britches."

"I can't even imagine wearing a corset with a concussion."

An image of Lacey in boudoir clothing popped into his mind. Even though he'd only seen her in T-shirts and jeans and her ranger's uniform, he had no trouble imagining her in a tightly laced red top. The outfit would lift her breasts, and he'd...

Not think about it. At all.

"Let's not talk about undergarments."

Her chuckle turned into a full-blown belly laugh that helped dissipate some of the lust coiling through him. "Now you really sound like you're in a Regency novel."

This time, he ignored her comment. He didn't need more sexy images of her burning into his brain. "Well, if we're going to do this, let's."

"It's not like we're climbing into a raft and running class-five rapids. We're just going to have a conversation in the dark." She sat on the edge of the king-size bed and carefully lay back.

"Lacey, there will never be smooth waters between us."

She sobered a little. "Point taken."

He carefully stretched out on the big mattress, keeping his distance from Lacey. It didn't work. She sidled up to him and tucked her small frame against his. It felt good. Too damn good. He gritted his teeth. This evening was going to be hell and heaven all rolled up together until he couldn't tell where one ended and the other began.

They snuggled in silence as Clay tried to quiet his body's natural reaction to her presence. He forced his thoughts back to their earlier conversation about his ranch. He was so busy concentrating on the work he needed to do to change the water flow on his property that he almost missed her soft words.

"It's funny. Sitting with the lights out."

Her words had a solemn quality that cut through his brainstorming. Sensing she was about to impart something important, Clay shifted in her direction.

"In what way?"

"I used to hate the dark." The statement was made quietly, almost like that of a parishioner ready to make a startling confession. "After my father and brother died, I slept with my bedside lamp on even when I went to college. It drove my roommates nuts until I finally got a single room my junior year."

"It makes sense. You'd been through a lot." Clay reached for her hand. As soon as his fingers brushed her skin, she immediately turned her palm and pressed it tightly against his. A burst of warmth surrounded his heart, and he yearned to pull Lacey even closer.

Her next words sounded hollow and sad. "I was afraid the blackness would swallow me whole like it did my brother."

Lacey's pain sliced through Clay. His father had caused so much damage. How many families had he ripped apart in his quest for more money, more power? And Lacey? Lacey was brightness. She shouldn't be worried about shadows. His dad and his scheming had done that. And for what? A fancy yacht that his sons trashed during parties? Several massive houses that never became homes? A garage full of fancy sports cars no one ever drove?

"Right before my brother's junior year in high school, he messed up his leg playing soccer. It wasn't even a real game. He'd just been fooling around with some of his buddies. It took several surgeries, but Greg was going to play again. Just like our dad did. But by his senior year, he was hooked on painkillers. He injured his leg in the second game. Sports career over—just like that. Before college. So that's when the parties started for him...and me."

"How old were you?" Lacey asked.

"Twelve."

Lacey straightened as she studied him. He had no idea how much she could observe in the dim light. He hoped not much. But he could make out her features well enough in the glow coming from the crack in the curtain. He could see her shock in the way she held her chin. But it was the sadness in her eyes that gripped him.

"How old were the other kids?"

"About my brother's age or older."

"He never should've taken you." Lacey's voice vibrated with outrage. He'd heard the tone countless times before.

But it had always been directed at him like a sword, not in his defense.

Clay lifted his shoulders and dropped them. "I wasn't exactly an innocent baby brother. I'd already been kicked out of three private schools by then. If Greg hadn't taken me to those parties, I would've found them myself. Hell, it wasn't even the first drink I had. I was already stealing top-shelf alcohol from my parents. Greg was the one who used to shout at me about it. My parents didn't even notice, except the one time my friends and I got caught at school with a six-pack."

"What did they do then?"

"Told me I was an annoying disappointment and shipped me off to a military academy. Mom had just returned from a spa in Europe, so she was irked that all the drama had interfered with her newfound inner peace. Dad had to cancel important meetings, so he wasn't happy either."

"I always thought your family had a glamorous life," Lacey said softly.

Clay barked out a humorless laugh as he thought about their old wealth. His parents had liked flash and plenty of it. "We did. It just happened to be an empty one. I get what you mean about the darkness. I wish I'd just turned on a light to chase it away like you did. Instead, I picked pranks, parties, and pissing off my parents to fill the void."

"How did you end up at your grandfather's ranch?"

"I got kicked out of my second military school. Greg had dropped out of college by then and was on a downward spiral. Even Zach's birth hadn't stopped it. Everybody idolized Greg, so my parents figured they had to do something drastic with me. Hell, that's not even right. They saw me as a lost cause and had run out of other ways to get rid of me."

Lacey's grip on Clay's fingers tightened, and even amid all the old pain, his need for her hummed through him.

"It was that bad?"

Her quiet question about his past caused his throat to seize up. Hell, why was he telling Lacey all this? But he couldn't stop. Sitting quietly in the dark was making his past bubble up and spew over. Maybe because she was hurting too.

"Yeah," he answered and let the word hang there.

"My family was tight-knit until—"

"Mine."

Lacey did not respond to his simple response, but she didn't deny it either. Clay knew she couldn't. That was why he'd spoken up—so she didn't have to. They both knew the truth, and ignoring it for years had only caused it to fester.

"We went hiking a lot, which wasn't easy with the hours the restaurant takes to run. My parents made it work though. The customers at the Prairie Dog were also like a big extended family. I had so many 'grandparents' growing up. I couldn't get away with anything because someone would inevitably tell Mom. My brother sometimes resented it, but I didn't. I loved it. I loved feeling part of something. And then my dad died...and my brother, and it just got hard, caring so much, loving so much. It hurts too much to lose someone."

Clay heard the raw pain in her voice. This time, he didn't ignore the need simmering between them. He pulled her close and pressed a kiss to her temple. "Part of me prays I'll hear from my brother, and the other half dreads it. Because every time I talk to him, I lose him a little bit more."

"You used to be close?"

"Extremely. My first strong memory is of him holding me. I'd fallen after trying to climb a new sculpture my mom bought. I had the wind knocked out of me, and I thought I was dying. Greg held my hand until I could breathe again, and then we went into the kitchen and ate an entire carton of ice cream. It probably wasn't the smartest thing to do, but hell, it tasted good."

"My brother and I used to steal freshly baked cookies. Jesse would distract Dad, and I'd poach them. It drove Dad nuts, especially when we did it at the café."

"Greg and I would make giant forts out of sheets and blankets. Once or twice, we managed to cover a whole floor of our big-ass house. It would take us days or even weeks to build one."

"Your parents didn't make you tear it down?"

"Naw. They were probably out of town. I don't really remember where they were. They weren't around much. Greg said he saw them more when he was little."

"What was your grandfather like?" Lacey asked as she burrowed closer to him. Clay responded by giving her a squeeze. Although desire still whispered through him, it had quieted into something slow and steady. Lacey sighed, and he watched as her eyes drifted shut.

"He was completely different from my parents," Clay said. "I have no idea how he ended up raising someone like my mom. I don't think they knew either. Honestly, my mom was probably just as much a rebel as I was, except once she got married, she did it by shopping on Rodeo Drive and in Vienna. My grandfather never approved of my parents' lifestyle, even before my dad's arrest. He thought I was a spoiled punk, but he gave me a chance to change. Hell, he believed I *could* change, and that made all the difference."

"What did you think of living on the ranch?"

Clay closed his own eyes as he shifted both their bodies so he could lean against the headboard. It felt so right holding her like this. Giving in to the quiet warmth, he allowed the memories to wash over him. "I hated it at first. The house Mom and Dad owned in Sagebrush Flats near the ski resort was my least favorite. All I saw was a bunch of red rocks and dust. My grandfather seemed like a bitter old caricature from a bad Western. And it was boring in Sagebrush. No clubs. No fancy restaurants. No sporting events. No wild parties."

"Since you're still here, I take it your opinion changed."

"Hell yes. I fell in love with the place. I can't tell you how or even exactly when. I know it happened the first summer here. I finally realized it when I was out in the back pasture with my grandfather rounding up the cattle.

I looked up and really saw the land for the first time. This...this swell came over me. Pride, I guess. The ranch had been part of my family for generations, and here I was doing the same damn thing they'd done, and I didn't suck at it. I knew I was doing a good job 'cause my grandfather had grunted at me in approval instead of riding my ass like he normally did. And then there was the beautiful vista. It wasn't dry like I'd thought. There were vegetation and the sounds of life. I could hear the babble from the creek and the call of a jay."

When Lacey spoke, Clay could hear a sleepy smile in her voice. "You sound like a Sagebrushian."

A little trickle of frustration flowed through him. "I *am* a Sagebrushian."

Lacey moved her head to his chest. "Yep," she said, "sounds like the heart of a Sagebrushian."

All his muscles uncoiled. Carefully, he reached up and gently stroked her hair. Her breathing grew steadier and shallower. When he spoke, he kept his voice low. "So we have a different heartbeat from the rest of the world?"

"Uh-huh." Lacey gave a little wiggle. Her words had grown faint at the edges, and he could tell she was seconds from falling asleep. "I like holding you. The world doesn't spin so much."

A second later, Clay heard a soft snore. A grin touched his lips as he kept lightly running his fingers through her smooth locks. He opened both eyes as he stared down at her. Unfortunately, the light through the crack in the curtains had grown dimmer. He could no longer make out her individual features, but he could still see the outline of her form curled against his. And just like the day he'd first really looked at the red cliffs surrounding him, he felt a rush roar through him, settling in his chest.

# Chapter 7

"Are you sure you're up to this? I can just pick up Zach. We don't need to walk through the zoo. I can get pictures of the animals another time."

Lacey had no trouble detecting the worry in Clay's voice as she unbuckled her seat belt. In all honesty, she didn't know the answer to his question. She felt as wrung out as a washrag at her mother's café. The past two days had been grueling. Unfortunately, she'd have to return to the city next week for therapy. The whole thing made her want to hike to the most remote part of Rocky Ridge and let out a bloodcurdling scream.

"I need this." If she couldn't lose herself in the wilderness, watching animals would soothe her.

"Okay," Clay said simply as he grabbed his camera and climbed from the truck. He walked around to the other side and opened the door.

She gave him a pointed look. "I'm not so weak I can't get out of a vehicle without assistance."

"Humor me, Lacey. If you start to feel woozy, I want to be by your side."

And there it was. That unstoppable gush of emotion. It had been building all day like warm bathwater filling a tub, and she wanted to take a soak in it. A nice, long one.

She'd slept in Clay's arms the entire night. She'd woken up with her body wedged against his, her head still resting on his chest. And for the first time since her injury, she didn't feel so adrift. But it wasn't just his physical presence that anchored her.

Something had changed last night. They'd formed a bond. She could sense it even now. This connection. It was both comforting and frightening. She could detect his worry and concern for her...and his affection. When he'd awoken seconds after her, his eyes had been a bottomless blue-green, making her think of a secluded lagoon. And every time his gaze fell on her, the rich hue returned.

She wondered what he saw in her expression, because she felt pulled toward him. She hadn't expected his story to resonate with her. But it had. He'd suffered loss too... different yet somehow the same. And her heart ached for him, that lonely boy growing up in beautiful emptiness. In the past, she would've used those same two words to describe him...an impossibly handsome man with seemingly nothing substantial inside. She'd been wrong. She'd known it for weeks. But even then, she hadn't realized their shared similarities. They both loved Sagebrush and its harsh, unforgiving beauty. They'd found peace in the red cliffs. And somewhere in the vastness of the desert, when they'd felt utterly lost, each of them had discovered a sense of belonging.

Today, Clay hadn't left her side once. Oh, he hadn't gone back to the examination room when the nurse called her name, but he'd stuck around in the waiting area. She'd told him he could head outside and go to a coffee shop or some other place more pleasant. After all, she could always text him. But he'd stayed, this man who'd taken in his nephew when no other family member would.

Now they walked together through the empty zoo. It was after five o'clock in the afternoon, and the place had closed for the day. Clay started down the shortest path to the main building, but Lacey grabbed his arm. "Let's go the long way around so you can take more pictures." He studied her, so she added, "The fresh air will do me good, and I'd like to see more of the animals."

"Which ones?"

Lacey didn't need any time to consider her answer. "The bears—little Sorcha and Frida."

"Sorcha's the polar bear, right?"

"Yep," Lacey said. "She's about a year old now. Her exhibit is right next to the old grizzly bear's. They get along so well that Bowie actually built a connection between the two enclosures. It's a little unorthodox, but it works. He's hoping he can get a male polar bear for Sorcha soon and an orphaned grizzly cub next year. I've let some of my contacts at the national parks and fish and wildlife commission know."

Clay smiled. "When you're on medical leave, you're supposed to, you know, *rest*."

"Huh. What is that word again, *rest*?"

"Oh, that thing you do when you get off your feet and lie down."

"Lying in the dark gets boring very quickly."

"I didn't find last night dull at all."

The husky timbre in Clay's voice resonated through

Lacey. She tried but couldn't quite manage to suppress a little shiver. He noticed immediately and slung his arm around her shoulders, pulling her against his side. Her nerve endings instantly flickered to life, sending zings of energy skipping through her.

"Neither did I," she whispered, surprised at how husky her voice sounded. She didn't *do* throaty. She did clear and precise.

A decidedly wolfish smile spread across Clay's mouth, and a dimple appeared in his cheek. Yup. The man definitely looked like an underwear model.

"Maybe you just need me in your bed."

Hot electricity crackled through her. She watched as Clay's eyes lit with a responding flare. He'd meant the words innocently, but once spoken, neither of them had taken them that way. Kinetic energy transformed into magnetic as they leaned toward each other. Their lips met, hungry, needy, and maybe just a little desperate. She clung to him, wanting him closer, yearning for what she'd been denying herself. His tongue plunged into her mouth as he crushed her against his chest. His embrace wasn't rough, but it was powerful. She swore even the air hummed around them.

The kiss deepened further. His hand slid up her back to cradle her head, the edge of his palm resting against the sensitive skin of her neck. Another chill skittered down her spine. More desire detonated like a string of carefully laid explosives. Her defenses softened, she arched into him, trying to bring him nearer, their height difference frustrating her.

Clay groaned, and the sound reverberated through her like the echo of rushing rapids bouncing off the walls of a narrow slot canyon. "Damn, Lacey, you're going to kill me."

Setting his camera bag down, Clay hoisted her into the air. She immediately wrapped her legs around his torso as he gripped her butt. When she placed her hands around the back of his neck, she knocked off his cowboy hat. Neither of them cared as it fell to the ground. With better access, she plundered his mouth, pouring all her pent-up longing into the kiss. He made a low sound, and she absolutely loved it. His lips moved just as fiercely. It should have been messy and sloppy. It wasn't. It was every hot fantasy played out in real time.

"We should stop," Clay said, his voice hoarse.

"I know," Lacey whispered back.

But their mouths met again, and they kept on kissing... until the chittering. The very loud, very disruptive staccato chittering. They both froze, their lips still together, their gazes locked. Clay glanced away first. When his eyes widened into deep blue-green pools, Lacey turned her head too. A honey badger stood in the middle of the path. He was on the smaller side, so she guessed he was the baby, Scamp. The little mustelid watched them intently, his head cocked to one side. He seemed more curious than his rascally parents. He wasn't quite a year old, which meant that his mother, Honey, was probably close by, most likely hiding in the bushes. She had a reputation for only being seen when she wanted to play a game of chase.

"Is that a honey badger?" Clay asked softly as he lowered her to the ground.

She moved to his side to study the animal. "Yup. I think he's the kit."

"Will he attack?" Clay looked decidedly uncomfortable. "I hear they go after—"

"A male's private area," Lacey finished. "That just may be lions and other large predators."

Clay gave her a sideways glance. "If you haven't noticed, Miss Ecologist, humans are major predators."

She laughed and patted his shoulder. "Point taken, but the zoo's honey badgers don't bite humans. Generally."

"I don't know if I like that qualification."

"Don't worry. Fluffy, the male, was properly provoked the only time he used his teeth on a person. The man he chomped down on was an escaped convict trying to shoot Bowie."

"I remember reading about that in the paper."

The words struck Lacey. More than anything else Clay had stated, it showed how isolated he was. The assault at the zoo had spread around town faster than butter on a pancake hot from the griddle. The local paper only came out weekly. Days would have passed before Clay had learned what everyone was gossiping about. With a story that big in Sagebrush, he should've found out within a couple of hours.

She stepped closer, ready to draw him to her once again. That was when she heard it. Running footsteps. She jerked back just as Zach's voice filled the air.

"There you are, you little weasel." Although his word choice was harsh, affection lined his normally surly voice. The teenager rounded the corner, his attention fixed on the juvenile honey badger.

Scamp gave a muffled cry, his mouth full of Clay's cowboy hat. As quickly as a striking golden eagle, he darted under Clay's feet, still carrying the Stetson. Zach drew up short, obviously catching sight of them for the first time. His blue eyes, so much like his uncle's, darkened in surprise before a glint of understanding grew in them. A knowing smirk spread over his face. Self-consciously, Lacey looked down. Her jacket was bunched up at an odd angle from being pressed against Clay. Quickly, she yanked to straighten it.

Clay cleared his throat. "We just got back from the city. Lacey wanted to see Sorcha."

"Suuure," Zach said. "That's why your hair is sticking up and a honey badger currently has your hat."

Clay gave his nephew a level look. Lacey was surprised that he managed to resist smoothing down his locks. "What are you doing out here?"

"My job. I'm the best at catching Scamp." On the surface, Zach sounded defiant, but Lacey could detect an underlying thread of pride. Luckily, so did his uncle.

"It doesn't look like it's easy. I'd take lassoing a bull over wrangling one of those fur tubes with teeth."

Zach grinned. "The fur tubes grow on you, and Scamp acts tougher than he is. He's more scrappy than mean."

"If you say so," Clay said. "I'd appreciate if you could

get my hat back. It's my favorite, and I'd rather not see it turned into a honey badger chew toy."

Zach responded with a mock salute. He started to dash away, but right before he disappeared, he pivoted and gave them a cheese-eating grin. "Have fun, kids. You know, 'visiting Sorcha.'" Then he was gone.

Clay glanced over at Lacey, his expression tight. "I don't think Zach will tell anyone, but I never know with him."

Lacey nodded, and she hated herself for it. Although getting caught with mussed clothes wasn't ideal, she shouldn't care if the whole town knew about her and Clay. She was used to her business being spread like manure during spring planting, and Clay was a good man. People had been rooting for her to find someone special for years. Unfortunately, her heart might have settled on the very person they'd been cussing out for just as long.

Clay grabbed his camera again, and they walked in silence, keeping a good foot between them. It was as if they both knew if they came any closer, they'd end up in each other's arms. She'd never felt this pull toward another human being. It wasn't just sexual either. She'd confided things to him that she'd never told anyone, not even her mother or grandfather. She just kept coming back to the same word to describe what she felt around him: connected. It was like a fiber optic cable ran between them, sending messages at the speed of light.

At the sound of their feet crunching on gravel, Sorcha lifted her furry white head from the ball she'd been nosing. Lacey had only managed to visit the animal park a couple of times when Sorcha was a young cub, but she'd followed the youngster's growth on the zoo's web page. The little tyke had fascinated the whole town when she'd arrived from Alaska—a small, compact bundle with shining black eyes and a delightful personality. Now, more than twelve months later, Sorcha had the gangly build of a teenager. She reminded Lacey of a juvenile dog. Not quite a puppy but still filled with energy and emphatic joy.

Sorcha snuffled the air and then snorted. Lying with her head on a rock, Frida, the zoo's elderly grizzly, shifted in her sleep. Sorcha observed Lacey and Clay for a moment, her eyes shining with curiosity. When they did nothing but stand and watch her, the bear quickly grew bored. She turned her attention back to her big rubber ball. She batted it with her paw, tracking it with her eyes as it bounced on the fake rock facade, her snout bobbing in rhythm. She lumbered after it, giving it another whack. This time, it landed in the bears' pool with a huge splat. The spray of water caused Sorcha to crouch low, anticipation shining in her eyes. Lacey wondered if the splash had triggered the polar bear's seal-hunting instincts.

Sorcha plunged into the water, straight toward her toy. Grabbing it with her front claws, she turned onto her back. As she floated, she tussled with the ball. The black pads on her feet flashed in the air as even her back legs got in on the action.

"Shit, they are powerful animals." Clay's voice was tinged with awe as he lifted his camera to take a shot.

Lacey nodded. "Sorcha isn't even full grown. She still

has a few more inches to grow, and she'll pack on a lot of muscle."

"I've never seen a polar bear in person before."

That surprised Lacey. "Really? You grew up near New York City. There are so many excellent zoos there."

"My dad was always working, and zoos weren't my mom's thing. Too many smells and not enough of the kind of people she wanted to impress."

Sorcha chose that moment to flip over. Standing in the pool now, she had more leverage over the ball. Seizing it, she gave it a ferocious toss. It flew through the air and landed with a plop, right on top of the sleeping Frida. Clay's camera clicked as the elderly bear roared, her massive jaws gaping open as she leaped to her feet. Lacey didn't think she'd seen the old gal move that fast in years. The startled bruin swiveled her head. Her rheumy gaze focused on the offending toy. With one giant sweep of her paw, she swatted it away. Then, with a satisfied rumble, Frida lay back down. She wiggled her massive rear as she tried to get comfortable on her rock. When she did, she exhaled, her fur rippling from the effort.

Oblivious to the irritation she'd caused Frida, Sorcha emerged from the water. She paused only long enough to shake off. She did it so vigorously that droplets even landed on Lacey and Clay despite the large moat and concrete barrier separating zoo visitors from the enclosure. Sorcha gave one last good shimmy before she pounced on her ball.

"I didn't know bears were so playful," Clay said quietly

as he took more shots. “Sorcha almost reminds me of a river otter.”

“Play is important for mammals,” Lacey said. “In the wild, Sorcha would still be with her mother, learning how to hunt and survive on the ice floes.”

The polar bear pushed the ball back into the water. As Sorcha jumped in after it, Lacey wished she could feel the animal’s happiness. Normally, nothing elevated Lacey’s spirits like watching a critter enjoy itself, but she felt an unexpected hollowness. Now that she and Clay had returned to Sagebrush Flats, all the things between them had begun to weigh down their connection, threatening to sever it. But Lacey didn’t want to lose it…even if keeping it meant accepting a risk to her heart.

Taking a deep breath, her gaze still focused on Sorcha, she asked, “What now?”

From the corner of her eye, she saw Clay start and then slowly put down his camera. He clearly hadn’t anticipated the question, but he still knew what she meant. When he spoke, his voice sounded heavy, dragged down by the same weariness she felt. “I don’t know.”

“Everyone in town would tell us to walk away from each other.”

Clay snorted, the sound bitter. “They’d tell you to run. Me, they’d chase off with a shotgun.”

“I don’t want to listen to them anymore.”

Clay stiffened. “What are you saying, Lace?”

She smiled softly at the nickname and turned in his direction. “Lace. I like it.”

Clay's face remained stoic as his eyes searched hers. The green had faded again, making them a clearer blue. He wanted an answer. Needed it. She didn't blame him. She wanted one too. Only there wasn't an easy one. She took a steadying breath. "I'm willing to take a chance, Clay. On us. I think there's something here. Something that could be good if we don't let the weeds of the past choke it out."

The emerald flecks in his eyes returned, giving them a warmer glow. He reached out and gently tucked a strand of her hair behind her ear. "I'd like that. A lot. But are you ready for what happens when everyone finds out you're with the town's Big Bad Wolf?"

Lacey felt her lips twist, both at the nickname and at the reminder of how her family would react. "I'm sorry I used to call you that."

He shrugged. "It fits how everyone sees me. And they are going to find out. Even if we try to keep this a secret, if it goes on long enough, people will know. And they're not going to like it."

Lacey straightened her shoulders with more confidence than she felt. Reaching up, she laid her fingers over his. "Well, I've always had a talent at convincing the town to accept the presence of wolves."

A real smile stretched over Clay's face. "You may have a more difficult time selling Sagebrush Flats on this particular subspecies."

For the first time, a sense of hope curled through Lacey along with a bubble of excitement. "It'll be good for me to have a challenge. We'll see how sharp my skills at persuasion really are."

His lips dropped back into a serious expression. "Are you sure you're up to this, Lace?"

She nodded.

"What's the plan then? How are we going to do this? Do you want to keep our relationship under wraps as long as we can?"

Part of her wanted to nod. It would be easier, so much easier to hide. But she couldn't do that to Clay. He didn't deserve to be treated like a dirty little secret any more than he deserved the town's wrath for a crime his father had orchestrated.

"What do you want, Clay? If you say the word, I'll walk hand in hand with you down Main Street on a Friday night, as long as I can tell my mother and grandfather first."

At her words, Clay visibly swallowed. His hands reached up to frame her face. He looked so earnest that it caused a wonderful ache deep inside Lacey's heart.

"You don't know how much those words mean to me, but I'm not going to ask you to do that. Let's keep what we have private, at least for now."

This time, Lacey reached up to touch his cheek. His skin felt warm, a contrast to the chill in the evening air. "You wouldn't resent it?"

"Discretion makes the most sense given our unique situation," Clay said. "Think of us as a new ecosystem that needs protecting before we let onlookers stomp all over us."

A spurt of surprised laughter burst from her. If she'd

had any doubts about embarking on a relationship with this man, those words washed any misgivings away.

"I bet you say that to all the girls," she teased.

He leaned closer and whispered, "Only the ones with ecology degrees. I know how to play to my audience."

She arched a teasing brow. "Well, you were an ecology major too. I'm sure you know plenty of us."

"But I've only kissed one of you," he said, his voice husky, his eyes a luxurious blue-green that brought to mind warm tropic waters.

"Hmm." Lacey pulled him close. "Is that so?"

Their lips met, gently, tenderly, slowly. Joy, bright and frothy, bubbled inside Lacey. She'd never savored a kiss like this, letting it seep into her. Bliss saturated every nerve ending. She had no idea the last time she'd felt so marvelous, so alive. It was like being part of a brilliant sunrise over the desert wilderness. All warm hues and glorious light.

When they broke apart, they just stared at each other for a moment with silly, giddy smiles on their faces. They heard a grunt, and they turned to find the polar bear watching them curiously. The elderly grizzly gave a large snore, and her back paw twitched.

"Do you think Sorcha will tell?" Clay whispered near Lacey's ear.

She laughed. "Only Frida would, and she's asleep."

Clay reached for her hand, rubbing his thumb along the back of it. "I'm racking my brain trying to figure out when I can see you again with no one noticing."

Lacey leaned her head against his shoulder as she watched Sorcha return to playing with her ball. "I wish we could spend the night together."

He squeezed her fingers. When he spoke, his voice sounded as rich as one of the banana cream pies the Prairie Dog sold. "So do I, but I can't dump Zach on Bowie for a second night in a row, and something tells me my nephew might notice if I didn't drop you off at your house."

"My bungalow isn't too far from your place," Lacey pointed out. "I could drive that far and meet you on your lunch hour."

Clay shook his head. "Someone would recognize your Jeep and wonder what you were doing at Valhalla in the middle of the day."

Lacey sighed. "Nobody ever mentions how logistically difficult secret relationships are. They should come with warning labels."

Clay barked out a chuckle. He turned and pressed a kiss against her temple. "We'll figure something out, Lace."

---

"Zach?" Clay said just as his nephew was about to head up the old wooden staircase to his room in the finished attic. Clay had lived there when he'd stayed with his grandfather, and he thought the boy might enjoy the relative independence of having a floor to himself.

The teenager reluctantly paused, his hand on the knob at the bottom of the banister. "Yeah? What?"

"Here." Clay felt awkward as he thrust out a plastic bag containing the book on Greek mythology and another on Western wildlife that Lacey had helped him pick out.

Zach didn't move. He just eyed the parcel suspiciously. "What is it?"

"A gift."

"It's not my birthday."

"I know. That isn't for a few months yet."

Surprise flared in Zach's blue eyes before he expertly masked the emotion. And damn if the boy's shock that his uncle had remembered his birthday didn't cause a twinge inside Clay. Clay's own parents had forgotten his birthday, but Greg never had...at least not until the drugs.

"Are you trying to buy my silence 'cause I caught you making out with Ms. Montgomery?"

Clay tamped down on the flare of anger. Zach wanted to push him away. He needed to stop letting him succeed. Keeping his voice casual, he said, "What you saw was us standing on the path staring at the honey badger. And no. This gift was purchased with you in mind when I was in the city. Lacey helped me pick it out."

The mention of Lacey piqued Zach's interest enough that he lifted his foot from the first step and pivoted in Clay's direction. "If she helped, then it might not be totally lame."

"You know you probably shouldn't insult the person trying to give you a present."

Zach nonchalantly shrugged, but he did reach for the bag. When he pulled out the book on Greek mythology, he froze. His sullen expression dropped, and he looked young and vulnerable…and even more like his father.

"She told you," Zach said quietly, and Clay wondered if he'd made a mistake in getting him something similar to what Greg had.

"I'm not trying to replace him," Clay said quickly. "I know I'm not your father."

Zach snorted then—the sound should've been too harsh and too jaded to come from a teenager. "I never really had a dad to replace." Zach lifted the book. "Thanks though. For this. Ms. Montgomery wasn't wrong. I do like this shit."

Clay almost let him turn around. Almost let him walk away. That would be the easy thing to do. But evidently tonight, Clay had decided to stop taking the simple path. Perhaps he was still riding on the high from the kiss he'd shared with Lacey. She made him believe in possibilities again. Maybe even for the first time.

"I lost him too."

That brought up Zach short. He turned. "Greg?"

Clay nodded. "Even though he's only six years older, he was more of a parent to me than my own."

Zach's face screwed up in confusion. "We are talking about the same guy here. The one who can't stay out of prison or rehab for more than a couple months."

"He wasn't like that before he became addicted to painkillers," Clay said. He should've told Zach this earlier, but talking about his brother hurt too much. Speaking about Greg with Lacey had paved the way for this conversation.

This time, though, Clay wasn't sitting in the dark. He was standing right under the entryway light, all his pain on glaring display.

"What was he like?" Zach asked and then shook his head harshly. "Maybe I shouldn't know."

"He was the kind of person who walked into a room and people immediately liked him. Whatever he tried, he excelled at. He got solid grades and led his high school soccer team to the state championship three years in a row."

Zach snorted. "I'm nothing like him then. At least, the non-messed-up version of him."

"No," Clay said, "you're like me."

"You?" Zach asked in disbelief. "The guy who has his shit together? The cowboy who runs a ranch?"

His nephew thought *he* had *his* shit together? Then again, in comparison to the other adults in Zach's life, he probably did. "I came as an unexpected and unpleasant surprise to my parents. They did their best to ignore my existence, so I acted out. I skateboarded in the house, hit my dad's monogrammed golf balls into the lake, and cut up my mom's silk dresses to 'make' a hot-air balloon. They sent me to boarding school after boarding school. I was the class clown, so I ended up in a military academy. I just increased the level of my pranks from cracking jokes during class to helping the rival team steal our own mascot. After the second cadet school kicked me out, I came here, and my grandfather—your great-grandfather—was the first person who didn't toss my ass out when I tried to pull shit on his ranch. And I changed. I became who I am now."

For the first time since their conversation had started, Zach looked away. He scuffed his shoe against the terra-cotta tile floor before rubbing his upper arms. Clay's words had unsettled his nephew, but for the first time, Clay realized that might not be all bad. The teenager wasn't used to adults standing by him and paying attention. Unlike most people, Zach needed to be pushed into a comfort zone, not out of one.

"I'm not going anywhere, Zach. And for as long as you want, my door—my home—is open to you."

Zach lifted his chin. "Why? Because of Greg?"

"No," Clay shook his head. "Because of you."

"I've been a jackass."

"So was I, once."

Zach considered this for a moment. "What's the other book you got me?"

"It's on local wildlife. I've been impressed by the work you're doing at the zoo, and I thought you might like it."

Zach shifted again, but at least he didn't start kicking aimlessly at the floor. When he spoke, he sounded half-defiant. "Once my community service ends, I was thinking about volunteering at the animal park or getting a job if Mr. Wilson will hire me."

"Okay."

Surprise flared again in the teen's eyes. "You're okay with me working more there and not at the ranch?"

"I wouldn't mind if you started helping out around

here, especially in the summer, but I didn't invite you to live here because I wanted a hired hand. You're family, and if you have an interest in zoology, you should explore it."

"Oh," Zach said. The kid had clearly been spoiling for a fight.

"If you want, on a Sunday, we can ride out to the river. I can show you where I've spotted otters before."

"Maybe," Zach said.

Considering the responses he'd received in the past from his nephew, Clay took the equivocation as progress. Zach turned to leave. He'd only reached the second step, though, when he turned back in Clay's direction.

"I won't tell anyone, by the way."

It took Clay a moment to realize Zach was talking about his kiss with Lacey. "Thanks."

"I like her," Zach said simply. "She's pretty awesome for an adult."

"She'd appreciate that."

Zach paused. "You're less grumpy with her around. You should have her over."

"Things are complicated with our family histories."

The teenager gave him a meaningful look, indicating that once again, he questioned Clay's intelligence. "Like I said, I'm not talking."

---

Clay headed through the zoo's main gate, his camera in hand. He was here to pick up his nephew and Lacey, and he hoped he'd find her alone in the nursery. After his conversation with Zach last night, he'd made up his mind to ask her to join the two of them for dinner. It would be dark by the time they arrived at the ranch. Luckily, Clay's grandfather had added a connecting garage to the old mansion. Evidently, his grandmother hadn't liked the cold or scraping snow off her car. Although she'd died long before Clay was born, the old rancher must have loved her to build something that he would've considered an unnecessary extravagance. But whatever the reason, it was handy for Clay now.

He'd debated about calling Lacey, but he'd hoped to invite her in person. He certainly hadn't wanted to spring it on her when he'd driven her to the zoo. Zach had been in the cab, so he'd figured he'd wait until later. If Lacey wasn't alone with the wolf cubs, then he'd just ask her to show him more of the animal park. He'd even brought along his camera as cover.

Opening the door to the maintenance building, Clay immediately heard Lacey's voice. It was higher pitched and sweeter than normal, and excited yips followed. Walking down the corridor, he felt a smile playing at the corners of his lips. From the sounds of it, Lacey was playing with the wolf pups. No one could miss the affection in her tone as she asked, "Who's a mighty hunter? Are you practicing your pouncing? Did you get it? Is it dead now?"

When he entered the nursery, he found Lacey on the floor with a rope toy. One of the pups pulled on it, shaking his head furiously, while the other bit down on a plushie.

The little tykes had grown since he'd last seen them. Their ears no longer flopped against their heads, but the tips still curled over, giving them an adorable look that was both sleepy and perky at the same time. Their blue eyes were bright and alert.

They were definitely cute. He couldn't deny that. Even given his history with the predator, he still wanted to get down and join their play. He'd never had a chance to interact with puppies. All the ranch dogs had been adult rescues, and his parents hadn't liked animals in the house. When Lacey glanced in his direction, the brown in her topaz eyes stood out, making them seem softer than usual. "Hi, Clay."

"Teaching them how to be killers, are you?" He kept his voice teasing so she didn't take his words the wrong way.

She laughed and ruffled the nearest wolf's fluffy fur. The pup rolled over and used his disproportionately large paws to bat at Lacey's fingers. "This is a rare luxury. Normally, I only observe the lobos with binoculars. Even when I visit the wolf rescue and rehabilitation center, I can't get this close."

Clay crouched down beside her. "They're just dogs with sharper teeth, aren't they?"

She paused and then said very lightly, "Are you changing your mind?"

"Lace, just because I have a soft spot for canines doesn't mean I want them killing my calves. I would feel the same about a pack of wild dogs—more so since they tend to kill just for pleasure. But I am glad you and Zach saved these two little guys."

Lacey was silent for a moment, absorbing this. When she spoke, her voice was soft but serious. "I'm going to keep trying to change your mind."

"I know," Clay said simply. "You wouldn't be you if you didn't. I offer no promises other than I'll listen to you make your case without biting off your head."

"Well, I suppose that's an improvement." The tips of her lips curled slightly, and he wanted to bend down and capture her amusement. Kissing Lacey had become his favorite pastime. But before he could act, she tossed one of the plushies into his lap. A wolf pup immediately followed, his warm little body squirming over Clay's knees as the lobo tried to reach the stuffed chipmunk.

He squeaked the toy and dragged it across his thigh. The wolf clumsily lurched forward. The pup was just beginning to hone his skills. With a string of enthusiastic squeaks, he attempted to pounce, but his back paws gave him trouble.

"That's Perseus," Lacey said. "I'm playing with Theseus."

"Pretty impressive names," Clay said.

"They are all Zach's doing. Abby let him perform the honors since he helped save them."

Clay pushed the toy in Perseus's direction. The little dude managed to sink his sharp puppy teeth into the fake fur. A happy trill followed. The pup gave the toy a vicious shake.

"Speaking of Zach," Clay said slowly as he reached for the plushie, "he and I had an interesting talk last night."

Lacey looked up from her game of tug-of-war with Theseus. "Did it go well?"

"Actually, yeah." Clay wiggled the chipmunk in Perseus's mouth. The wolf went wild. Using his three good legs, he tugged hard.

"We may have had a minor breakthrough," Clay continued. "We still have a long way to go, but it's a start."

"I'm glad." Lacey reached over and gave his free hand a squeeze.

Before she could withdraw it, he turned his palm over and laced their fingers together. "We also talked about us."

"Us? As in you and me?" Lacey's voice squeaked slightly, which he found adorable. He leaned over and brushed a kiss against her cheek.

"Yep. That would be the right us," he confirmed. "I didn't say much, but Zach promised he'd keep our secret…and he told me to invite you over. So I'm taking his advice. Would you like to join my nephew and me for dinner? I've got an attached garage, so none of the ranch hands should see you."

"Sounds like a plan," Lacey said.

"Good," Clay said and then did what he'd wanted to do since he'd entered the nursery…he captured her soft lips with his. Her mouth instantly opened, welcoming him. He deepened the kiss, loving the way she went pliant against him. He'd never tasted anything so addictive as Lacey Montgomery. Something about her got into his bloodstream and circulated through his body, bringing waves of pleasure. She made a soft sound in the back of her throat, and his desire spiked. He swore his muscles even trembled from the force of his need. With a groan, he yanked away from her. Someone could walk in on them at any moment, especially with his senses swamped by her nearness. She made a sound of protest, and he leaned his forehead against hers.

"Tonight," he whispered, not sure if he was giving her or himself a promise. "We'll have tonight." As soon as the words left his lips, he felt like some modern-day Romeo. But Lacey and he were star-crossed lovers, after all. He just hoped their relationship didn't spell doom.

---

"That was delicious chili," Lacey said as she put her spoon down. They were eating in the roomy kitchen Clay said his grandmother had insisted on adding to the back of the house. Unlike the rest of the stately old home with its high ceilings and impressive moldings and plasterwork, this room felt more akin to the style of Sagebrush Flats. The cabinets had been stained a warm hue that enhanced the natural grain. The same wood framed the large picture window above the sink and countertops. Pots and pans hung from the exposed beams in the ceiling, and what looked to be vintage turquoise Fiestaware lined the plate rack on the wall. Instead of a kitchen island, an old-fashioned table sat in the middle of the terra-cotta-tiled floor.

Clay shrugged as he rose from the table to carry dishes to the sink. Ace got up from his spot on the floor to pad after him. He looked up at the plates with soulful brown eyes. Clay pulled a treat off the counter and handed it to him instead. “When you’ve lived alone as long as I have, you find a specialty.”

Zach reached over and popped the last piece of garlic bread into his mouth. “Clay’s cooking doesn’t totally suck. It’s better than the guy who makes dinner for the ranch hands.”

“Hmm,” Lacey said. “Since you’re the master of the understatement, that sounds like high praise.”

Zach lifted both his shoulders and then dropped them.

Lacey leaned forward, resting her elbows on the table as she regarded both Stevenses. “Did you know that you two have the exact same shrug?”

The two men exchanged a startled glance. Clearly, they hadn’t. She wondered what other similarities they’d failed to notice. Zach not only looked like a younger clone of his uncle, they had the same mannerisms too. Even now, they’d turned in each other’s direction as if connected by a rope.

“Gross. Don’t tell me I’m going to age into *him*.” Zach jerked his thumb in his uncle’s direction.

Luckily, Clay didn’t take offense. “And that was the end of the compliments from Zach.”

“Your uncle isn’t the worst role model in the world.”

The teenager gave an exaggerated eye roll. “I think you may be biased.”

Lacey glanced over at Clay and purposely gave a dreamy smile. She spoke with a dramatic breathiness as she fluttered her eyes like a cartoon caricature. "Maybe you're right."

"Annnd that's my cue to exit." Zach headed toward the doorway. "*Sayonara*, folks. I'll be upstairs in the attic playing computer games."

"You might want to throw in some homework too," Clay said casually.

Zach pulled another Stevens shrug. "That's not really my thing."

Lacey debated whether she should step in and support Clay, but he spoke before she could decide. "But pissing off people is what you do."

Zach arched a golden eyebrow. "How exactly would I annoy people if I finished my assignments?"

"Because you're smart enough that even if you half-assed it, you could still pull As," Clay replied.

The teen tried to school his features, but Lacey could tell that his uncle's words both surprised and secretly pleased him. His tone, though, remained bored when he responded. "I'm still not seeing how this would irritate anyone."

Clay's smile stretched as wide as the Mississippi after heavy rains. "Just seeing a Stevens on the honor roll would tick off a lot of people. Imagine how irate they'd be if you actually were in the running for valedictorian."

Zach scoffed, but Lacey didn't miss the gleam of interest in his eyes. "Me, valedictorian? Maybe you're the one with the brain injury instead of Ms. Montgomery."

"Or maybe he sees you more clearly than anyone else,"

Lacey said quietly. Zach swallowed. For once, he didn't have a comeback, so she added, "If you want to become a zoologist or ecologist, you'll need to start studying sometime. You might as well begin now."

"Maybe. I'll see if I have time in my schedule," Zach said with a practiced nonchalance, but he didn't fool Lacey. She had a feeling the teen would open his textbooks tonight.

When he disappeared up the steps, an awkward silence descended. Clay cleared his throat as he started removing dishes. "Thanks for having my back with Zach."

"Anytime." Lacey rose to clean off the table. "You might be reaching him more than you think."

Clay nodded as he turned on the water in the sink. "You might be right. He's doing surprisingly well in the classes he has to take in connection with the diversion program. And like I mentioned at the zoo, we had a breakthrough of sorts after I gave him those books you recommended. Thanks for that."

"You're welcome."

They worked together in silence with her clearing plates and him rinsing and placing them in the dishwasher. Ace observed them with great interest, clearly hoping something would fall. The two of them gave the simple task almost the same laser focus as the dog. They both knew Clay hadn't asked her over for just a meal, and a new tension stretched between them. Energy zipped through the atmosphere, filling Lacey with a buoyant restlessness.

Wiping his hands on a towel, Clay turned to her, his

smile both hesitant and undeniably charming. "I'd offer an after-dinner walk along the river, but..."

The words hung uncompleted, neither wanting to finish the sentence and admit to the difficulties surrounding their new relationship. Instead, Lacey reached for Clay's hand, wrapping her fingers around his. "I don't need moonlit strolls."

His blue eyes softened into warm pools as he lifted their intertwined hands and kissed the back of her knuckles. He released her fingers, only to gently cup her face instead. "I'd still like to take you on them though."

A burst of joy ricocheted through Lacey, settling in her heart. She ran her fingers through his hair, and his expression turned so intense that she swore she felt a tug deep in her soul.

"Then why don't you tell me about it." She paused a beat before adding, "In your bedroom."

He kissed her, his lips hot and demanding. She met his hunger with her own. His hands slipped from her face, skimming lightly down her sides until they settled at her waist. He pulled her close, and her body, already liquid from the warm heat spreading through her, molded against his. The kiss deepened. The more they indulged, the more they craved.

Clay lifted his lips from hers. They stood under the overhead kitchen light, each breathing hard. This time, it was Clay who extended his hand. Lacey immediately took it and allowed him to lead her. Ace cocked his head as he watched them start up the stairs, but he didn't follow.

"First, we'd walk through the scrub to get to the river," Clay said, his voice low and soft. It seemed to have a current all its own, both peaceful and raging at the same time. "We'd hold hands just like this, and I'd rub my thumb over your skin."

A shiver ran through Lacey at the gentle brush of flesh against flesh. "I like this stroll."

He laughed, the sound a deep, rolling rumble. "So do I."

They reached the first landing, and he paused by a window. Moonlight bathed them, and his blond hair almost appeared silver. He drew her close, his lips mere inches from hers. She could feel the puff of his breath, but he didn't dip his head. Instead, he spoke in a husky whisper, this time using the present tense instead of what-ifs. "The water is below us now. It's like a glowing ribbon cutting through the land."

"I can hear it," Lacey said. "A rushing babble breaking the night's stillness."

Clay's mouth pressed against hers. A butterfly kiss. Then another. The next one landed on the corner of her mouth as he slowly worked his way across her cheek and jaw. When he reached her ear, he told her quietly, "We stop for a bit, enchanted by the beauty. But we don't stay. We head for the grove of cottonwoods. Normally, we'd hear Steller's jays scolding us, but they're asleep at this hour."

Clay stepped back and led her up the steps and down a hallway. They moved swiftly now, their breathing labored as if they'd actually taken a long hike. He paused at the end of the corridor. When he pushed open the door, Lacey said, "We startle a mountain cottontail."

Clay chuckled. "I can just make out a faint rustle as he hops away."

They entered his bedroom. He'd pulled the curtain nearly shut, but he'd left a big enough gap to allow bright moonlight to seep into the room. They walked inside, still hand in hand. The old wooden floorboards creaked beneath their feet.

"There's the splash of an otter fishing in the creek," Lacey said.

Clay stopped at the foot of the bed. "I lay out one of the old family quilts for us."

This time, their narration wasn't completely make-believe. A coverlet with a log-cabin design adorned the massive, mission-style bed. The room itself was bigger than most bedrooms for the time period of the house, but it had been designed after an English manor. It made for a cavernous space. Aside from a rope rug and basic furniture, Clay hadn't done much decorating. Nothing hung on the walls, except for a single, unembellished mirror and a couple of photos of the ranch, which she assumed he'd taken. The emptiness momentarily sucked away some of Lacey's joy, but she hid it. Clay hadn't brought her into his private space for sympathy, and offering any would do more harm than good.

Instead, she wrapped her arms around him and kissed him long and deep. He groaned against her mouth, the sound guttural. He picked her up, and she wrapped her legs around his torso. Without breaking their embrace, he carried her over to the bed. They tumbled onto the mattress, their lips locked, their limbs tangled. A desperate, urgent edge now drove their lovemaking. Lacey's blood thundered through her like a galloping mustang, wild and unfettered. She reached for Clay's Western shirt, her fingers fumbling at the buttons. His mouth moved from hers, trailing across her chin and then down her throat. When he hit a sensitive spot, she gasped. He paused, applying a gentle suction before his tongue darted out. Intense pleasure shot through her. She arched, yanking on the button still between her fingers. It ripped loose, and she felt his lips curve against her flesh.

"Why, Miss Montgomery, are you tearing off my clothes?"

"I'll sew it back on," she promised.

"I have more shirts. Feel free to continue. I want your hands on me. All of me."

A landslide of need collided in her. Without taking time to think, Lacey bunched the fabric in both hands and pulled sharply. The buttons flew off with satisfying pops.

Clay lifted his head to stare down at her. The moonlight glinted off the golden strands in his arched brow. "You are surprisingly good at that."

She smiled and ran her fingers over his defined pecs. "Beginner's luck and plenty of motivation. I've been wanting to touch you for weeks."

Clay responded with a long, hard kiss. Even with their jeans both still on, she could feel the heat of him against her. She pressed into the hard ridge, wanting, needing, craving more. He groaned, low and deep. "You're making it very hard to take it slow."

"Sorry," she said with a surprising giggle. Even as a teenager, she'd rarely tittered. If she was going to laugh, it was going to be a full one. But now. In this moment. The lighthearted sound seemed right, a delightful echo of the buoyancy Clay made her feel.

His fingers grazed the bottom of her T-shirt. "May I?"

She nodded. "I've been fantasizing about that too."

He chuckled, the sound a little raw. "Not nearly as much as I have."

Unlike her, he took his time dragging the shirt up. Then, he slowly unhooked her bra and slid the straps down her arms with one finger. His calluses gently brushed against Lacey's skin, triggering another eruption of delicious shivers.

Clay's eyes glinted in the silvery light, and Lacey had no trouble seeing his appreciation. His head lowered, and he took the tip of her breast into his mouth. Pure pleasure zipped through her like a shooting star. His tongue played against her flesh until she felt herself tremble. Unable to stop, she whimpered as she rubbed against him.

Her hands reached for the fly of his jeans. He shifted to accommodate her, but his mouth never left her body. She managed to get the zipper down, and she reached inside and felt his warm length. He paused, a harsh sound rushing from his lips. She felt his exhale against the moistened skin of her breast, and want speared her, sharp and beautifully incandescent.

"I need you," she whispered.

"Lace." Her name sounded reverent on his lips. She stroked him then, and he groaned.

"Can you help me get your jeans off?"

He nodded, the stubble from his chin rubbing over her already-sensitized skin. She sucked in her breath, and he kissed the other breast. As his lips closed over her nipple, he shifted to pull down his pants and boxers. Sheer pleasure ripped through her. Another cry tore from her as she reached up to tangle her fingers in his hair.

He lifted his head. Although she could no longer make out the color of his eyes in the low light, they still glowed with intensity. His fingers touched the waistband of her pants, and he arched a questioning eyebrow.

She swallowed, the motion surprisingly difficult. Her throat had gone thick with desire and anticipation. Mutely, she nodded, and his mouth stretched into a wolfish grin. He pressed his lips against her belly, right above her waistline. Then, his eyes watching hers, his mouth still on her body, he undid the button and pulled down the zipper. Pushing the exposed section of her panties downward, he left a trail of kisses in the fabric's wake. She gasped and wiggled. He used both hands to pull down her jeans to about mid-thigh. His mouth closed over her center. She cried out, feeling his tongue dart against her.

"Clay," she whispered.

He paused and raised his head. "Say it again."

“Clay?”

He nodded. “There’s something about how you said it. I want to hear it another time.”

“Clay,” she repeated in the same tone as before. “Clay.”

He kissed her lips. It was a deep, endless one. She could feel his hot length pressing against her with a need echoing her own.

“Are you ready for me, Lace?” he asked as he moved away from her just long enough to grab a condom from a drawer in his bedstand.

“Uh-huh.” The words came out half squeak and half moan. She’d never made such a sound in her life. She should have been embarrassed, and if she hadn’t been so saturated with pleasure and yearning, maybe she would have been. Instead, when she felt his lips curl against her mouth, she returned the grin.

“You’re like liquid sunshine, Lacey Montgomery,” Clay told her, his voice a low rumble that caused her nerve endings to resonate. He entered her then…slowly. The delicious friction caused sparks to ignite throughout her body. She felt alive with energy, but still it wasn’t enough. She pressed her fingers into the smooth skin of his back. She shifted her hips, demanding more. He groaned, and she bucked a second time. Finally, he began to move in earnest. Sensation shot through her. She didn’t try to fight it. She let herself explode as she clung to his broad shoulders, his lips pressed against the curve of her neck.

---

Clay almost lost himself when Lacey came undone, but he managed to pull back from the glorious brink. He hadn't been with a woman in a long time, and it had never felt this good. He wanted this to last, no matter how hard Lacey was making it.

He slowed his pace. Each time he plunged downward, Lacey rewarded him with a little gasp. She was not a quiet lover, and he loved her symphony of sounds. She made love like she did everything else—energetically, openly, fully. And he wanted to bask in the glory that was Lacey Montgomery. He hadn't been exaggerating when he'd called her liquid sunshine. It was as if something dark and lifeless inside him had unfurled, and he wanted to give it as much of her light as possible before it shriveled up again.

He felt her lips against the base of his neck, warm and sweet. She lingered, her tongue exploring the hollow of his throat. Sharp, white-hot pleasure sizzled through him. Her fingers glided over his back, leaving a wake of fire behind them. Her mouth moved to his lips, accepting him, welcoming him. His body slid rhythmically inside hers, his breath coming in short, harsh puffs. He felt as alive and as wild as a bare wire pressed against a metal plate.

He buried himself in her. Another cry tore from her throat. He went up like dry tinder in the fall. Squeezing his eyes shut, he held himself above her as his release tore through him. He collapsed, careful to keep his weight from smashing her into the mattress. Gently, she brushed her fingers through his hair before letting them trail down the back of his neck and then up again. The simple tenderness of the gesture caused his heart to swell until it damn near exploded too. He didn't know when he'd ever felt so relaxed, so content.

Gathering his energy, he brushed a kiss against her shoulder, her skin smooth beneath his lips. Then he turned them so they lay in each other's arms. Like in the hotel room, moonlight streamed across the counterpane, blanketing them in a silvery glow.

"That…that was amazing," Clay said, lacking better words to describe it.

She smiled and stretched. He could feel her body glide against his, her breasts brushing against his chest. He sucked in his breath as she nestled her head on his bicep and tangled her legs in his.

"I forgot about feeling light-headed, and that's saying something." Lacey affectionately nuzzled his neck.

He chuckled. "Hell, I forgot about everything. At some points, I don't think I could've even formed coherent words."

"I'm glad you invited me to dinner, Clay Stevens."

Some of the joy sucked out of the room as the past came creeping in. Her words, although meant lightheartedly, reminded him of how they had to sneak around… and why. "You don't regret sleeping with the Big Bad Wolf?"

Lacey's head popped up as she studied him. She must have seen something in his face, for her eyes went soft and her lips curved into a gentle smile. "Let me show you my answer." Then she leaned down and kissed him. He'd never tasted a kiss so sweet, so complete.

This time, it was Lacey who explored his body with her mouth. He groaned against the onslaught. She was thorough, his scientist, her lips examining every square inch. He'd never allowed a woman so much control during lovemaking, but ceding it to Lacey came naturally. Need and something stronger and sweeter swept through him, and he didn't fight the current. Didn't even try. It was like both floating down a gentle river and being rushed through the most thrilling rapids of his life.

When her lips closed over him, he groaned. She took him deeper into her mouth, and he gave himself over to her again. As he lay there, his body both limp and electrified, she appeared in his line of vision, a smile on her lips.

"How's that for a response to your question, Mr. Wolf?"

His voice sounded rough even to his ears as he spoke. "It's a pretty good one, Ms. Riding Hood."

A little furrow appeared between her brows. "I'm not sure if the moniker fits. Unlike her, I make friends with wolves."

He reached up and cupped the back of her head, running his hands through the smooth strands. "For once, I'm grateful about that." Then he proceeded to spend the rest of the evening showing her just exactly how much.

# Chapter 8

"So this is where you've been spending all your time?" Lacey's grandfather asked as they walked through the Sagebrush Zoo about two weeks later.

"Yup," she said. "Wait until you see the wolf pups. They're getting really active."

Her grandfather shot her a look. "Are you sure this is good for your noggin? You're off work to rest, kiddo."

Lacey laughed. "I know, I know, but I'm too much like you. I can't sit still. Plus, I have been improving since I started therapy."

He harrumphed, but Lacey could hear the affection underlying his grumbling. She'd always been close to him. When she was a little girl, he'd take her up on his horse and shown her the ranch. He'd passed his love for the land on to her father and then to her. Although she watched over wolves instead of wrangling cows, in some ways, she hadn't strayed too far from her family's roots.

"I wish you'd let me take you to your appointments," her grandfather said, his gravelly voice tinged with annoyance.

"It's okay, Grandpa," she said. "It would be a lot of driving and then sitting around waiting."

"I could find a coffee shop nearby."

She laughed. Up until ten years ago, her grandfather would have balked at the idea of setting foot in a dang-blasted establishment meant for yuppies and hippies.

Then June Winters had revitalized her grandmother's tea shop in Sagebrush. All the locals loved it…even the surliest old-timers like her grandfather and his best friend, Stanley. The two widowers went there every morning. It didn't hurt that the owner served up a sunny smile along with her hearty breakfast platters.

"The closest coffee shop is filled with hipsters, and there'd be no Stanley or June to keep you company."

"I'd make do," her grandfather said stubbornly as Lacey opened the door to the main building. "It would be better than letting that Clay Stevens fellow drive you."

Ah, Clay. The reason Lacey had invited her grandfather to the zoo. The past two weeks with Clay had been wonderful…well, as wonderful as they could be with the sneaking around. Lacey didn't enjoy hiding a major part of her life from her mother and grandfather, and she liked keeping Clay a secret even less. Some people might find clandestine affairs thrilling, but she didn't. The subterfuge drained her more than therapy for her concussion. She constantly worried her family would learn about her new relationship in the worst way possible.

Although Clay hadn't complained, she knew the secrecy weighed on him too. And he deserved better. The man drove her to every appointment. Lately, he'd even started bringing groceries to her house because he knew the lights in the stores aggravated her symptoms. On the nights when she slept over, he kept her company as she did her therapy exercises…and watching someone stare at letters pinned to the wall while moving her head slowly up and down and then left to right couldn't be scintillating. When she'd finally finished her assigned tasks and her mental fog seemed thicker than green chili stew, he'd hold her close until a semblance of steadiness returned.

Then there was the way he loved his herd and his land. Although they hadn't risked taking another ride on his property, he would talk to her about his progress with the ciénega restoration as they lay in each other's arms. He'd grown so excited when he told her he spotted beavers building a dam on one of the creek's smaller tributaries. Clay also kept her updated about his growing relationship with Zach. The two had started playing computer games together each night, and it was helping. They'd also visited the otters by the river on Clay's ranch.

For the first time in a long while, Lacey was excited about a man. She wanted more than anything to tell her mom. And she was tired of how everyone treated Clay. She hated the look in his eyes when they came up with an idea for a date only to realize they couldn't go out together. Not yet.

So today marked the beginning of her campaign. Although her grandfather wasn't a pushover, he wouldn't take her dating Clay personally. He might worry, even rail at her, but he wouldn't feel betrayed. The news wouldn't fester inside him either. If she could win him over, he'd help convince her mother.

"Clay's very considerate," Lacey said. "Not many people would take the time he does to help someone."

"Bah!" her grandfather spat out. "He's just avoiding a

lawsuit. That's all. You need to stay away from him, Lacey. He's a dangerous snake, worse than a rattler because he won't give any warning before he strikes."

Lacey debated the best way to rebut the accusation as she opened the door to the nursery. Luckily, she was spared from responding by a very high, very cute, but very emphatic howl.

"Someone has a set of lungs," her grandfather observed as he stepped into the room behind her.

With a broad grin on her petite face, Abby bounced up from her seat on the floor. "That's Perseus, Mr. Montgomery." She gestured enthusiastically at the wolf pup. The little guy had his head tipped back, his black lips pointing to the ceiling, his ears tilting downward. With eyes squeezed shut in concentration, he poured his considerable energy into the call. Not to be outdone by his brother, Theseus lifted his muzzle and added to the racket. Sylvia let out an atypical beleaguered sigh as she burrowed into the piles of blankets.

"They're practicing their howls. They've been attempting longer calls for a couple weeks now, but today is the first time they really got it." Abby beamed at the lobos. "Aren't they adorable?"

"They were...the first time," Zach said dryly from his seat in the corner of the room. Unlike Abby, he didn't rise to his feet to greet them. "They've been doing this for ten minutes."

Abby leaned toward Lacey, her gray eyes bright as she said sotto voce, "And yet he *stayed*."

Zach shrugged. "You get used to the sound."

Lacey hid a smile. She'd noticed that Zach picked jobs that happened to be near the zoo director's daughter whenever he could. She suspected that the boy nursed a huge crush, but Abby seemed oblivious. No matter his feelings for her, Zach clearly adored the wolf pups. Abby at least sensed that affection. Anytime the pups did something interesting, she immediately let the other teenager know.

Lacey's grandfather's eyes narrowed on Zach. He clearly didn't appreciate that the boy hadn't stood. Buck Montgomery had too much old cowboy in him to excuse rudeness. And he wasn't above taking youngsters to task. Lacey started to place her hand on her grandfather's arm, but she was too late.

"I see you're still lacking in manners, young man. The polite thing would be to stand, especially since you're the reason my granddaughter has a brain injury," he said, echoing the words his best friend Stanley had said when Clay and Zach had stopped by her bungalow to thank her for arranging his community service.

Zach froze, his blue eyes wide and startled before they went blank. His jaw clenched ominously, and his shoulders started to rise in a sullen shrug. An ice ball formed in the bottom of Lacey's stomach.

"Grandpa, we've already been over this. Like I've said before, Zach saved me from more serious injuries," she said quickly. "He stuck around and made sure I was rescued. And it was his friend who mostly triggered the cave-in, not him."

Zach's eyes flitted over to Abby. The girl stood as still as a jackrabbit sensing a predator. Her gray eyes formed large pools as she glanced around the room. Even the wolves had stopped howling. Their little ears perked in attention as they watched the humans with patent interest.

Lacey felt Zach's gaze on her next. His shoulders remained thrust into a fighting stance, his entire body unnaturally stiff. But he didn't go on the offensive. Not yet. Instead, he seemed in the middle of a debate. Then, to Lacey's amazement, he slowly rose to his feet. He didn't stomp out of the room angrily or even scuff his toe against the floor. Instead, he turned and faced the old cowboy.

"My uncle tells me I should accept more responsibility for my actions." Zach's eyes flitted to hers for a second before returning to address her grandpa.

Lacey's heart simply melted when she realized why he was cooperating. It wasn't just to impress Abby. He knew the trouble she and Clay faced, and he had a choice. He could either help the situation or toss lighter fluid into the flames. It touched her that he'd made this decision, and she knew how much his gesture would mean to Clay. Zach had finally started to learn that anger and bluster wouldn't win him anything.

He took a breath before he spoke again. "My prank hurt Ms. Montgomery, and I'm sorry about the trouble I caused her and the wolves."

Lacey's grandfather's face transformed from

cantankerous annoyance into surprise and then into something approaching grudging respect. "It isn't easy admitting something like that. I appreciate your honesty."

It was now Zach's turn to look shocked. He clearly hadn't expected praise. Although he flushed bright red, Lacey noticed his back straighten just a little bit, but this time with pride instead of defiance.

"Zach wasn't the main perpetrator," Lacey said, "and he's been a huge help at the zoo."

"I'm hoping to get a job here after my community service is done," Zach said, "which means I should probably get back to shoveling shi—I mean manure."

Lacey saw her grandfather's mustache twitch at Zach's aborted swear word. He kept his face solemn, though, and tipped his hat as he moved away from the nursery entrance to allow the teenager to exit.

"I'll go help him," Abby said. "It was my fault he got distracted, but I knew he'd want to hear the wolf pup chorus. He acts like he doesn't care, but he really does. Boys can be funny that way."

Neither Lacey nor her grandfather spoke as they waited until the two teenagers left the main zoo building. When they heard the exit door bang shut, her grandpa broke the silence.

"Zach isn't what I imagined. He's a straight shooter. Probably learned that from his ma's side of the family. Definitely didn't get it from the paternal line."

White-hot anger coursed through Lacey. Her grandfather had a knack for judging a man's character…except when it came to Clay. There, he had a blind spot as wide as the Platt River and as deep as Crater Lake.

"Do you have *any* idea what that boy has been through? Both his parents were addicted to drugs, his maternal grandmother too. Yes, she 'raised' him, if you can even call it that. The manning-up you just witnessed from Zach wasn't easy. He didn't witness stuff like that growing up. Not until Clay took him in last year. That maturity. That responsibility. Those were all Clay *Stevens's* doing. Zach even said so, but you're too dang stubborn to pay attention."

As if in sympathy, Theseus began to howl. Perseus immediately joined in. Their heads thrown back, they wailed with all their might. Ignoring the din, her grandfather scratched his head as he studied her, his golden-brown eyes serious.

"Ah hell, Lacey. *Him.* All the men in the world, and you choose a Stevens."

He *knew*, which was what Lacey wanted. But not like this. Not in anger. But there was no taking it back. No hiding.

"Grandpa, he's a good man."

Her grandfather pulled up a chair that Lou used when he recorded the wolves' weight and food consumption. He sank into it. He didn't say anything as his fingers worried the beat-up cowboy hat in his hand.

"Ah hell," he repeated. "Your mama isn't going to like this, Lacey Girl."

"That's a given," Lacey said softly. "But what about you?"

He leaned back and watched the pups. The little tykes had started wrestling. Their furry bodies were a blur of flailing limbs and wagging tails. Perseus had his jaw around Theseus's neck. Happy, playful squeaks echoed in the nursery, but even the wolves' joy couldn't dispel the cold hardness settling inside Lacey.

"You have a soft heart." Her grandfather kept his attention on the tussling animals as he spoke. "You always have. But some creatures, some people, are beyond saving."

Lacey tamped down the icy blast of anger his words triggered. Unleashing the bitter gale wouldn't help. Still, when she spoke, her words sounded clipped, even to her. "Clay Stevens doesn't need saving, Grandpa. He's a fine, decent person all on his own, and Sagebrush certainly hasn't made it easy for him to be."

"His father damn near gutted our town."

She tried to keep her voice calm despite the frustration burning inside her. "Grandpa, we have an outlaw in the family tree. He robbed trains, and he held up banks. People died during his crimes. Should I feel guilty about that?"

"Don't be ridiculous, Lacey Girl. That's not the same."

"Why? Clay wasn't involved in what his father did. What has Clay done?"

Her grandfather went quiet again. "He's not one of your wolves, Lacey."

"What do you mean by that?" Lacey asked. Before he could respond, the pups broke into excited yips. Despite Perseus's limp, the duo began chasing each other around the nursery. Sylvia rose from her nest of blankets to monitor them.

"Ever since you were a little girl, you had this need to champion the misunderstood. Like those two lobos over there. People in these parts viewed them as dangerous nuisances. Killers with no redeeming value. But you saw them differently. To you, they're always like this: the playful canine. And you made us see that too. But that doesn't mean that they're not predators and that they don't cause problems."

Lacey didn't like to admit it, but his words unsettled her. She did have the tendency to champion the underdog, but she wasn't being naive about Clay. "Grandpa, that isn't an answer to my question."

"If you'd asked me what Clay's father had done wrong before the investment scheme, I couldn't have told you a thing other than he seemed a bit arrogant and flashy. Most folks around here liked him. He had a way of putting people at ease and impressing them at the same time. People thought if they hung around him, his luck and business savvy would rub off onto them. But something about him never set right with me, and I feel the same about his son."

Lacey rubbed her forehead. Her wooziness had worsened. She noticed that it always did in stressful situations. She couldn't figure out the right response. Her grandfather's words buzzed in her head like a swarm of particularly angry horntail wasps.

"Lacey, when you first decided you wanted to make

a career of defending the unwanted, I was always afraid you'd get your hand bitten off. This might be the time when it happens. You're not responsible for the rehabilitation of every misjudged beast...or person."

"It's not like that," Lacey said, but she didn't like the doubt he'd stirred up. She was supposed to be convincing him, not the other way around. She had a knack for persuasion, but her grandfather was using her very skill to question her relationship.

"Lacey, the man has done nothing but cause you and the wolf program problems," her grandfather pointed out.

"It's true that our opinions differ, but he's not trying to just be a jerk. You should hear his plans for the Valhalla Ranch. And his land management strategy—"

"Which he asked *you* to help with, according to your mother," her grandfather said.

"You say that like an accusation."

"He's getting free advice, Lacey Girl. A Stevens is good at using people and then discarding them when he gets what he wants."

Lacey's head had now begun to throb, and she focused on the pups. They'd clambered over to Sylvia and had begun tussling with her. The capybara let out a long-suffering sigh as Theseus tugged on her short ear. When he got a little rough, the rodent bopped him with her big snout.

"Clay knows how much I love ecology. He wouldn't date me for my knowledge. He'd straight up ask for it."

"And what else does he want? He's been trying to

market Valhalla Beef all over town. I've even heard rumors he wants to turn his place into a fancy wedding venue. Now here you are trying to maneuver me into liking him. If I know you, it's the beginning of a multipronged plan to convince the whole town to warm up to him."

The little flickers of worry began to flame to life. Clay *had* asked for her help in getting Sagebrush Flats to accept his business. But he wouldn't seduce her just to market his ranch. For one thing, she'd already admitted that his land management strategy intrigued her. If anything, their relationship made it harder for her to help him since they had to keep everything under wraps. More importantly, Clay didn't act like a man only interested in his ranch.

"Grandpa," Lacey said, "you've always respected my instincts. You listened to my ideas to protect ranch animals from wolves long before anyone else. Lots of people would've dismissed a child, but you never did."

He grunted. "You were smart, Lacey. You researched things more than most kids do—hell, even more than most adults."

"Then why don't you trust me this time?"

He scratched his head again. "I don't want you getting hurt, Lacey, or your mother."

"But I am *happy*, Grandpa," Lacey said earnestly. "There's something about Clay and his plans for Valhalla. I don't know. We just fit, and I've never felt this way about anyone. What if I'm right and you're wrong? Then couldn't I get hurt your way too? I'm not a risk taker, Grandpa, at least not with my heart. And Clay is the first person who's ever made me want to take a chance on love."

Her grandfather emitted a soft chuckle and shook his head. "You always did know how to persuade a person. That might be a valid point, but that doesn't mean I trust or like him."

"I'm not asking you to do either of those things, at least not right away. I want you to give him a chance, Grandpa. He deserves that, and I do too."

"All right." He finally nodded. "I can give you that, but if I see, hear, or even sense anything that worries me, I won't hesitate to wallop him clear into the next county."

Lacey threw her arms around her grandfather, and he patted her shoulder.

"Thanks, Grandpa. I wouldn't expect anything else."

---

Theseus watched carefully as the Gray-Eyed One's fingers grazed Scamp's fur as the honey badger weaved between her legs. The sneaky creature moved backward, causing the biped to lose her balance. She fell straight on her rear. Anticipation built inside Theseus as he visually tracked the sleek animal clambering over the human's legs. The weasel scurried straight toward Theseus and his brother. Theseus crouched low, his muscles quivering. He tried not to spring too soon as he'd done in the past, but it was soooo hard. He wanted to pounce *now*.

Unable to contain his energy, Theseus squeaked.

Beside him, his brother did the same. Perseus moved, and Theseus could no longer hold back. He darted full speed at Scamp. Chasing the honey badger was even better than wrestling with his brother or tugging on a rope held by one of the bipeds.

The human swiveled to catch them, but Theseus and his brother easily darted around her. After a cry of frustration, she pulled out one of those rectangular objects all humans seemed to carry. Her fingers moved furiously across the device as Scamp darted under Theseus's paw. Theseus let out an excited yip, certain he would finally catch the taunting weasel. He pounced, but the rascal had already anticipated his move. Scamp skittered to the left, leaving Theseus to land awkwardly. The linoleum didn't provide the best traction, and the wolf's legs spread out. His sharp barks turned into surprised ones as his belly hit the floor and he spun 180 degrees.

Perseus quickly rose to Theseus's defense. With his limp, he moved more slowly. Observing the action from his undignified spread-eagle position, Theseus watched as Scamp allowed his brother to get close before the honey badger darted away. Despite his bad leg, Perseus gave a pretty good chase. Shaking himself off, Theseus joined in. Moving at full speed, Scamp flattened his long body and shimmied under a medicine cabinet. Theseus noticed the huge piece of furniture too late. He tried to stop, but he couldn't get a proper grip on the smooth floor. He yipped along with Perseus as they careened into the metal furnishing.

Scrambling to his feet, Theseus tried to squeeze under the small space, but he could only get his paws underneath. Beside him, Perseus did the same. Scamp pressed against the wall, and Theseus let out a frustrated whine that echoed his brother's. He had just managed to wedge his muzzle under the furniture when he heard the door open.

"I got your text. Where's Scamp?" It was the Blue-Eyed One's voice. Theseus swore the honey badger grinned at the sound.

Before Theseus could react, Scamp darted straight past him and charged at the Blue-Eyed One. He feinted left and then moved his body to the right...straight into the biped's hands. Amused pleasure shot through Theseus when the honey badger let out an undignified squealing cry. He pinwheeled his legs, swiping with his claws, but the human held him outward, so he sliced nothing but air.

"You're getting really good at that." The female's tone held admiration.

"Thanks." The Blue-Eyed One sounded how Theseus felt when he'd tasted meat for the first time.

"You should think about going into zoology."

"I've been hearing that a lot lately." The Blue-Eyed One's face turned an interesting shade of red, but his tone reminded Theseus of how he felt when he beat his brother at wrestling.

"Maybe there's a good reason for it." The noises from the Gray-Eyed One were quiet and soft but somehow strong.

"Maybe there is." The Blue-Eyed One's smile matched the cadence of his speech.

---

Clay had just drifted off to sleep beside Lacey when his phone rang. She made a sleepy grunt as he carefully slid his arm from under her body. Her hand reached for him, and his heart swelled at the sight. Gently, he brushed a kiss over her cheek. "I'll be right back."

Slipping from the room, he answered, "Yup."

"Tim Forrester just called," his foreman said, his tone sharp and clipped. "He saw the wolf pack head onto our land again."

"Shit."

"I'm heading up there with Hawkins and Stewart. Thought you should know."

"I'll ride along," Clay said.

"No need to disturb your sleep. We've got this handled." Although Pete Thompson's words were polite on the surface, the tone was dismissive. It was clear he didn't think Clay was disciplined enough to chase away wolves in the middle of the night.

"I'll meet you at the barn. Have my horse saddled up."

"Suit yourself," Thompson said, but the man sounded annoyed.

Clay shook his head and went back inside the bedroom. The room was still dark, but he could make out Lacey's outline as she sat on the edge of his bed.

"What's wrong?" she asked.

"There was another wolf sighting," Clay said. "Mind if I turn on a light? I need to get dressed."

Lacey flipped on the lamp beside the bed. Worry had replaced her sleepiness. "I want to come."

Clay paused in rooting through his drawer for a pair of jeans. He pivoted in her direction. This conversation needed eye contact. Wolves remained a strained subject, and he didn't want her thinking he was hiding something. "Are you sure you can handle riding the land with your concussion?"

She climbed from the bed. "I should come. I'll manage. My light-headedness has been lessening. Besides, it's dark, so there's no light to aggravate my symptoms."

"If I show up with you in tow, Pete and the rest of the men will know we're sleeping together. Thompson won't keep it silent," Clay pointed out. He knew her meeting with her grandfather hadn't gone as well as they'd hoped, and she hadn't even spoken to her mother yet.

"Clay, I need to make sure the pack is protected."

He walked over to her and cupped her cheek. "We won't do anything other than chase them away. I promise."

A mulish expression he recognized from their previous arguments fell over her face. "I need to be there."

A flash of hurt sizzled through him. After everything, she still didn't completely trust him. He dropped his hand, letting it fall limply against his thigh. "I still think it's a bad idea with your brain injury, but it's your choice, Lace. If you want, you can ride with me so you can keep your eyes closed. I'll call Pete and tell him to saddle up Charlie instead. The old gelding has the smoothest gait."

"Thanks," Lacey said. "That would help."

"Thompson isn't going to be happy to see you with me."

"I can handle Uncle Pete."

Clay wasn't so sure, but he didn't have time to argue. Lacey had made up her mind, and he knew she was implacable once she'd made a decision. After Clay called Pete back to tell him to ready Charlie instead, they dressed quickly and in silence. Clay first headed up to Zach's attic room to let him know what was going on. The teenager mumbled that he'd be fine before he rolled back over. Clay met Lacey on the porch. As they headed toward the stables, he squared his shoulders. As soon as they entered the circle of light by the barn, Pete stomped toward them.

"What the hell are you doing here?" he shouted at Lacey. Hawkins and Stewart turned at the sound of Thompson's voice. After taking quick stock of the situation, they immediately turned their attention toward the ground. Even though neither had started their ATVs, they pretended to fiddle with the controls. Clearly, the situation made them uncomfortable.

"I'm here to check on the wolves," Lacey said calmly, her voice cheerful and bright. It did nothing to mollify Pete. For once, her charm didn't appear to be working. If anything, her words only enflamed him further.

"You have no business being on this ranch." Thompson took a step toward her.

Protective rage roared inside Clay as he angled his body between Lacey and his foreman. "She's here on my invite," Clay told him evenly. "She's got every right to help chase away the wolves. I suggest we move quickly before we lose one of the herd."

Pete shoved him. If Clay hadn't been anticipating the strike, he would've stumbled back into Lacey.

"You're just like your father." Pete grabbed fistfuls of Clay's shirt and shoved his face into his. "Taking what doesn't belong to you. Hasn't your family stolen enough from the Montgomerys?"

"Last time I checked, I wasn't a piece of property." Lacey's voice no longer sounded sweet. Even though Clay didn't turn to look at her, he could hear her fury. "This is none of your business."

"I'm the foreman!" Thompson pushed at Clay again as he tried to shout in Lacey's face too. "Everything that happens on this ranch is my damn business."

"And I'm the owner." Clay worked hard to keep his voice regulated. It wouldn't help if he lost his temper too.

"Your grandfather was going senile when he left you this place. You're nothing but a lazy Easterner with a criminal for a daddy."

"His grandfather's brain was working just fine." Lacey stepped out from behind Clay. Her body seemed to vibrate with anger just like when she defended the wolf pack. Clay rested his hand on her shoulder, but the gesture did nothing to calm her. "My grandpa and Stanley had breakfast with John Frasier every Sunday, and they would've noticed if his mind was starting to slip. Clay belongs on this land, and he's worked hard to keep this spread alive despite your efforts to undermine him. His granddaddy left this place to the best person for the job."

Pete flushed, his whole body tensing like a bull before a charge. When he spoke, spittle flew from his mouth. "I didn't know head injuries could turn a woman into a whore. You're nothing but a modern-day Jezebel, spreading your legs and betraying your family for a pretty face."

Protective instinct slammed into Clay, and his tenuous grip on his temper slipped. He stepped up to Thompson, leaving only a couple of millimeters between them. He was just as tall as the older man, and he definitely had more muscle. Pete shifted as if finally realizing the city boy could actually pose a threat. Clay didn't back down. He leaned his face closer to his foreman's, taking satisfaction when the man flinched.

"Get off my land," Clay said quietly.

"What?" The intense red began to fade from Thompson's cheeks.

"I said, *Get off my land*," Clay repeated slowly. "You're fired. When you've cooled down, you can come back and pack your things. But you're out of here."

Pure shock flashed across Pete's features. "You can't do that."

Clay didn't speak. He just stared hard at Pete and watched as the man's temper crackled back into flames. Nothing hid his hatred now...not even a thin veil. It burned brightly, but it could no longer singe Clay. His own temper had ignited, and every rancher in the West knew nothing fought wildfire better than a controlled burn.

Pete spoke, his voice a low hiss. "My family has worked this fucking land almost as long as yours."

"And it is out of respect for that tradition that I've put up with you disobeying direct orders," Clay said, "but this time, you didn't just attack me. You went after Lacey."

"Valhalla will crumble without me. I'm the only one holding this place together."

Clay stared Pete down. "I think the other men would disagree. We *all* work hard to keep this ranch running."

"But it's in my fucking blood."

"Mine too," Clay said quietly, "yet you always conveniently forgot that. I'm not just a Stevens. I'm a Frasier as well."

"If you fire me, I'll see this ranch ruined. That's a promise." Pete's eyes burned. He balled his hands into fists, and Clay knew only their difference in bulk kept Pete from throwing a punch.

Clay would have preferred the blow. That, he could see coming. He could handle a physical fight, but he'd have trouble combatting a campaign to ruin him. Pete had the ability to persuade the ranch hands to leave, and the tales he would spread wouldn't help Clay build the Valhalla brand. But Clay couldn't and wouldn't ignore how Thompson had treated Lacey. No woman deserved to be treated like that, and any man who did had no place on Clay's land.

"You won't survive firing me," Pete continued. "You'll see."

Clay wouldn't allow this man to get in his head. Not anymore. Ignoring Thompson's second warning, he crossed his arms. "I asked you to leave, Pete. If you've forgotten the exit, I'm more than willing to escort you."

His former foreman stomped off in a storm of profanity and threats. Clay sucked in his breath as he faced Hawkins and Stewart. He had no idea how the two men would react, and as witnesses to the whole damn argument, they had the most power over how this would play out.

"Let's go chase off the wolves," Clay said.

Both men nodded. Joe Stewart spoke, his voice the same lazy twang as always. "You got it, Boss."

Relief flooded through Clay at the last word. The ranch hands rarely, if ever, called him *Boss*. They'd reserved that for Thompson. And Joe hadn't slung the word sarcastically either. In fact, Clay might even have detected a note of deference. As the most senior employee after Pete, Joe commanded a lot of respect. His support meant something.

Hawkins, who generally spoke little, added, "A man shouldn't treat a woman like that. It's not right. Sorry about that, miss. That kind of stupid should've died out years ago."

"Thanks, Carter," Lacey said. "I couldn't have said it better."

With a final nod, both men sped off on their four-wheelers. Clay mounted his gelding and then gave Lacey a hand up. He preferred taking the horse in case the wolves headed to the steeper parts of the ranch. He wanted to make sure they were completely gone from his land, not just chased into the hills. He'd have Hawkins and Stewart camp out the rest of the night with the cattle, just in case. He'd do it himself, but he had Zach back at the house and Lacey to get home.

He felt her slim arms wrap around his middle as she settled into the saddle behind him. She rested her cheek against his back, and a smile slid over his face. He could get used to riding like this. Being close to Lacey only made him crave her more. Everything about her intoxicated him, from the sound of her voice to the bounce of her chestnut-brown ponytail.

"Thanks," Clay told her as he set Charlie into a canter.

"For what?" Lacey asked, genuinely confused. "You're the one who defended me."

"But you let me," Clay told her quietly. "You were perfectly capable of taking Pete Thompson down yourself. Thanks for allowing me to do it. It's been a long time coming."

Her chin scraped against his shoulder as she held him just a little tighter, and for a moment, he felt lighter. Even after the confrontation with Pete and the fate of the ranch at risk, she could make him feel good with the tiniest of gestures. He'd needed someone like Lacey Montgomery in his life for a long, long time.

"What you said before, about keeping Pete because you didn't want your ranch hands to revolt? I don't think you need to worry. Thompson has been out of line for a long time. They'll support you, Clay."

He frowned as he stared at the stars dotting the sky near where the horizon would be. "I hope so. I can't afford to lose help, especially this time of year. I'd make Joe Stewart the foreman, but I doubt he'd want the job. He's thinking about retirement."

"Do you have anyone else in mind?" Lacey asked.

Clay shook his head. "I don't think any of my current ranch hands would be interested, plus I'd like someone new, someone who isn't going to have divided loyalty between Thompson and me. But I also need someone who the men and the town will respect. It's not going to be easy to find a replacement."

Lacey was quiet for a moment. "Do you want a recommendation?"

"Hell yes."

"What about Rick Hernandez?"

"Isn't he the son of your uncle's foreman?" Clay asked, surprised she'd offer up the name of someone who worked for her family. Lacey cared for him, that Clay didn't doubt, but her loyalty to her relatives went as deep as an old copper mine.

"I know he's young to be a foreman, but he's been helping out on my uncle's spread since before he could walk. And he's got a degree in ranch management. He'd love what you're trying to accomplish. He's smart, and you two think alike."

"Won't your uncle be mad? And what about Rick's dad? I don't want them gunning for me too."

"Both of them know Rick is planning to move on. His father is still relatively young, and Rick wants to be in charge. They'd be thrilled that he would be living so close to them. Our families have always been tight-knit."

"Do you think he'd work for me?"

Lacey nodded. "He was just a kid when the pyramid scheme imploded, and the Hernandez family didn't invest with your dad. You're going to be offering him a dream job that's next door to his folks."

"I'll talk to him later this morning," Clay said. "I should stop by your uncle's anyway and warn him about the wolves. He'll probably know already though. Tim Forrester is good about warning all the ranchers, and he's the best at spotting the lobos."

"That won't be the only news my uncle will have heard," Lacey said, and Clay could easily detect the whisper of worry in her voice. "I don't think there's any chance of keeping our relationship secret now."

Clay nodded, a heaviness settling over him like an eighty-pound weighted blanket. "How do you feel about that?"

"Concerned about my mom's reaction. I'm going to head over there first. Luckily, everyone knows she likes to sleep in since the Prairie Dog is open so late. Hopefully no one has bothered her. But other than that, I guess I'm relieved. I didn't like sneaking around."

If they hadn't been riding a horse, Clay would've swept her into his arms and kissed her right then and there. "I didn't enjoy the secrecy either, but I understand we still need to take things slow on the public front. I imagine it's going to take time for your mom to get used to us being together."

Lacey pressed her lips against the back of his neck, the kiss so soft and sweet that it caused an ache deep inside him. He wished like hell this wasn't so damn hard. He just wanted to be with Lacey, but he'd trudge through knee-deep manure if it meant spending even a few moments in her presence.

# Chapter 9

"I KNEW THERE WAS GOING TO BE TROUBLE AS SOON AS I learned *that no-good Stevens's spawn* was driving you back and forth from the zoo." Lacey's mother paced in the tiny living room of her house that sat directly behind the Prairie Dog Café.

Lacey rubbed her forehead. This was *not* the conversation she wanted to have with her head simultaneously pounding and swimming. Although her light-headedness had been gradually improving, she required more sleep than normal. Unfortunately, last night, she'd gotten practically none. She and Clay, along with Hawkins and Stewart, had spent most of the night and early morning searching for the wolf pack. They hadn't spotted anything.

All Lacey wanted to do was collapse. She'd even seriously considered returning to bed, but she couldn't. She didn't want her mother learning about her relationship with Clay from anyone else. She was surprised the incendiary gossip hadn't already sent the town up in flames.

"Mother," Lacey began.

"Don't *Mother* me. What has happened to my level-headed daughter? First, you tell me you're dating, *dating*, Clay Stevens. And then I hear he fired Pete Thompson! After all the years that man's family has worked—"

"Mom, Pete called me a whore who spreads my legs for a pretty face. I don't think you want to defend him."

Her mother's mouth fell open. "What? Pete said that? Pete *Thompson*?"

"Yes."

"But Pete would never say a thing like that. Especially to you!"

"Well, he did." Lacey tried to fight back her annoyance. She just wanted to find a dark room with a big comfy bed…preferably with Clay in it. Unfortunately, that didn't seem like it would be happening anytime soon.

"I know he lost big on Trent's scheme, but to attack you when you had nothing to do with it…" her mom began.

Lacey massaged her eyebrow. It didn't really alleviate her symptoms, but it made her feel like she was doing something. "Hmm, blaming people for events they had no control over. Now why does that sound so familiar?"

Her mother frowned. "Pete calling you a whore isn't the same as my concerns about *that Stevens boy*."

Lacey sighed. She felt weary of everything. "Mom, I know this is hard on you and Grandpa, but I really care for Clay. Could you try to give him a chance? For me?"

Tears welled up in her mom's eyes, and the sight sliced at Lacey. Her mom wasn't using them as a guilt tactic. Emotional manipulation wasn't her way. These…these were genuine, and they cut deep. But Lacey couldn't back down, not on this.

"I don't want to see you hurt, Lacey."

"Grandpa said that same thing, but, Mom, I've been protecting myself, my heart, for so long, I've been doing more harm than good. When I'm with him…I don't know,

I just *feel* again, and I like it. I like him. I'm not asking you to welcome him with open arms or even to accept him. I just want you not to dismiss him reflexively. Judge him on his own merits, not his father's."

Her mother pursed her lips together in a clear effort to stem her emotions. She gave a watery nod. "I'll try my best, honey."

Lacey sucked in her breath. She hated asking her mother for more, especially now, but she knew how rumors worked in Sagebrush. They could be as destructive and devastating as an invasive species to an isolated population.

"There's one more favor."

"What?"

"At the Prairie Dog this morning, can you make sure it's clear why Clay fired Pete?"

Horror flashed over her mother's face. "You want me to protect a *Stevens*?"

"Mom, he fired Pete to defend me," Lacey said. "Thompson has been undermining his authority for years, but Clay put up with it because he didn't want the town to eviscerate him. Now there's a good chance they will. Pete's going to try to paint himself as the hero who tried to save the silly female who got mixed up with bad company. Personally, that's not a very flattering picture of me either."

Her mother sighed. "Well, when you put it that way, I can see your point."

"I'm going to head over to June's tea shop for breakfast, but I'll be at the Prairie Dog when it opens for lunch. So hopefully you won't have to say much, but if the staff is talking in the kitchen, could you just make sure it's the correct version of events?"

"I will, sweetie, but you don't need to come yourself. You look dead on your feet, and I don't like how you're rubbing your head. You need to lie down. Your old bed is already made up, waiting for you."

Lacey managed a brilliant smile she didn't feel. She wanted nothing more than to accept her mother's offer, but running damage control was too important. "I'll see if June will let me crash in her apartment for a bit."

"Okay," her mom said, "but don't overdo it."

She was already overdoing it, but it wouldn't help to admit that. Instead, she gave her mom a quick peck on the cheek. "I won't do anything more than necessary."

When Lacey stepped out of her mother's house, she winced against the brightness. The brilliant desert sun had risen to its full glory during her visit with her mother, but she didn't pull her ball cap down further as she walked to the Primrose, Magnolia, and Thistle. She didn't want to look like she was hiding. Instead, she waved brightly whenever she passed a local.

As soon as she entered the tea shop, her grandfather's and his best friend's heads popped up like ground squirrels from their favorite table that served as a good vantage point of both the door and the large picture window. Although neither man would admit it, they were two of the biggest gossips in Sagebrush Flats, and they loved monitoring all the comings and goings around town.

"Thompson called me last night," her grandfather said. "Is it true Stevens fired him?"

Lacey pulled out a chair and gave him a kiss on his whiskered cheek before she sat down. "Yes, but only after Pete verbally attacked me. And Clay had every right to fire him before that. Pete constantly ignored direct orders with no reason other than spite. If your foreman had done that, you wouldn't have even given him a second chance. Pete had plenty."

Stanley tipped back in his chair. "Don't seem right not to have a Thompson riding the herd on the Frasier spread."

"It's a downright shame," her grandfather echoed.

Lacey fought the urge to press her fingers against her throbbing eyeball. The reveal of her relationship with Clay couldn't have gone worse.

"Clay's fighting to keep the ranch afloat," Lacey said, "and Pete stonewalled his improvements at every turn."

Stanley snorted. "What would a city slicker like him know about saving a spread?"

"Better land management for one," Lacey said. "That ranch has been overgrazed for more than a century, which I know is a pet peeve of yours."

Stanley let out a noncommittal grumble. He'd worked as a foreman on several ranches over the years, and one had folded when the owner didn't listen and expanded the herd beyond what the land could support. "My old boss was from back East too. He didn't know a cow's front end from back."

"Do you really think John Frasier would have left the land to Clay if that was the case?" Lacey asked.

Stanley turned to Lacey's grandfather. "Aw hell, it's the wolves all over again. She's not going to give up until we give in, is she?"

The other man sighed heavily as he took a long sip from his coffee. "'Fraid not. She's already convinced me to give the greenhorn a chance."

"Now if that don't beat all." Stanley turned back to Lacey. "How is it you can go on a fool's mission and still come out the victor?"

"Maybe 'cause the mission isn't so foolish." June's Southern drawl broke into the conversation. Although she didn't normally leave her station behind the counter during the breakfast rush, she stood beside Lacey, a pot of coffee in one hand and a sunny smile on her face. "Refill, gentlemen?"

As June poured Stanley a new cup, she turned her attention to Lacey. "Why don't you come up to the counter and order something, honey? You look as famished as a hibernating bear after a long, hard winter."

"I am starving." Lacey stood up and then addressed the older men. "I'll be back soon."

June grabbed her lightly by the upper arm and leaned close as they crossed the store. "The rumor mill is certainly churning this morning."

"And I'm the ground-up grain," Lacey said glumly.

June laughed, the sound as bright as her first name. She simply had a knack for putting people at ease. "Do I sense you're here to do a little damage control?"

"It's like trying to plug a tiny leak when the rest of the retaining wall has collapsed."

June gave her arm one last pat before she headed around the counter. She didn't attempt to take Lacey's order. Instead, she leaned both elbows on the glass and kept her voice to a conspiratorial whisper.

"Do you want a little bit of help with the cleanup?"

Lacey perked up. If there was anyone the town rallied around more than herself, it was June Winters. "Are you sure you want to take this on? There's a lot of buried resentment being stirred up."

"There's nothing I enjoy more than a good challenge," June said. She got out a dishrag and pretended to clean the glass. The woman spent so much time polishing, it was a wonder her display case didn't sparkle so much it hurt the eyes.

"And," June added, still keeping her voice low, "Clay came to me about a year ago, asking me to help him improve his reputation."

"Really?" Lacey forgot to keep her voice low. She'd known about Clay asking June to sell Valhalla Beef burgers but not this. Her grandfather's and Stanley's heads shot up again at her exclamation, this time like prairie dog sentries spotting a black-footed ferret.

June sent her a warning glance before continuing. "It was when Magnus and I had broken up for a spell," June said, mentioning her fiancé. "I'd sworn off meddling, so I turned Clay down. Then I couldn't even market his new beef like he wanted. I was in the middle of expanding my jam business, and I didn't want to take the risk of plastering the name of his ranch all over my tea shop."

"So what's changed your mind?"

"I'm getting better at not going overboard when I lend a helping hand," June said, "and if the two of us work together, we'd be stronger than a gale at full strength. Plus you're not just some greenhorn who breezed into town but my friend."

Lacey had to laugh at the transplanted Southern belle. "Clay and you have lived here almost the same amount of time."

June gave a cheese-eating grin. "But I don't carry a whiff of the East Coast."

"Clay doesn't either. People just think he does. If anything, he tries too hard to fit in."

"Yes, but my, oh my, can that man fill out a pair of cowboy jeans."

June was an incorrigible flirt, but everyone knew she only had eyes for her future husband. Playing along with her friend, Lacey pulled her face into an exaggerated frown. "I feel a little territorial over that particular backside right now."

June patted her arm. "And I'm otherwise engaged... in more ways than one, and even if I wasn't, I know better than to tangle with an ecologist, especially over something like territory."

Lacey couldn't stifle her whoop of laughter. June could coax a chuckle out of people even on the worst days.

"Now," June said, putting down her dishrag and resting

her arms on the counter again, "we need to strategize. I assume you have some sort of a plan."

Lacey nodded. "Well, a half-baked one since our strategy of taking it slow evaporated. I talked to my mom already. Then I came here for breakfast, and I'm headed to the Prairie Dog for lunch."

"I can run damage control here," June offered.

"You don't mind?"

June arched a golden eyebrow. "Spreading gossip with the consent of the main participants? Darlin', that's like an early birthday and Christmas present all wrapped into one. You can trust me to spin it right, so tell me exactly what happened."

Lacey did, not bothering to keep her voice low. She didn't mind if the whole town overheard them. After all, this was the story she'd come to tell. When she finished, June's green eyes had widened.

"Pete Thompson said *that*?"

Lacey shrugged helplessly. "Just don't make Uncle Pete into a complete villain. I'm not happy with him—at all—but I don't want the town gunning for him next."

"I can play it right," June said. "Don't you worry. Now, what's your long-term plan?"

"Slowly start being seen around town with Clay."

"You should bring him to my wedding."

Lacey shook her head. "I already RSVP'd for one. I don't want to saddle you with a last-minute addition."

June shook her head. "Nonsense. I can squeeze in another guest. In fact, have him bring his nephew too."

"You do realize inviting a teenage boy is like adding three adults when it comes to the meal?"

"We'll manage."

"Are you sure, June?" Lacey asked. "It's your wedding, and I don't want my scandal to overshadow it."

June patted her arm. "You are the sweetest, Lacey, but don't you worry about me. Magnus would be happier than a possum eating a sweet potato if all the attention wasn't on us."

"What if someone causes a scene?" Lacey asked. She had a feeling nothing would be easy about desensitizing the town to her relationship with Clay.

June delivered one of her huge, brilliant smiles. "Why, if that happens, then I'll just have the wedding people will talk about for years, won't I?"

"You honestly wouldn't mind a bit of drama on your big day?"

"Not in the least," June said. "Nor will Magnus. If he had his way, we'd be eloping and getting married on an ice floe in the Arctic so we wouldn't have to worry about guests."

"I'd go to that wedding in a heartbeat."

"Well, Magnus would still be pleased as punch if we had only one guest," June said.

"Are he and Nan in your upstairs apartment?" Lacey asked.

"Nan is in the sitting room off the tea shop's kitchen today, and Magnus is volunteering at the zoo this morning," June said. "Do you need to talk to one of them?"

Lacey shook her head carefully. "I've got a headache,

and I was wondering if I could lie down for a bit before I head over to the Prairie Dog."

June tilted her head. "You do look as white as a freshly laundered sheet."

"Gee, thanks for the compliment."

"Why don't you go to Nan's house around back?" June reached into her pocket and slipped her a key. "You won't hear any noise, and she won't mind. She's always had a soft spot for you. There's a spare bedroom up the stairs to the left."

"Thanks," Lacey said. For all their trouble, small towns did have their perks.

She stopped by her grandfather and Stanley's table briefly, but the two old cowboys didn't delay her long. Luckily, Mrs. Winters's former home abutted the tea shop. Lacey clambered up the stairs to the guest room, pulled the curtains tightly together, and promptly flopped on the bed. Unfortunately, she *didn't* promptly fall asleep. Her thoughts churned and spun like clothes in an overloaded washing machine. She hoped she'd made the right choice. She couldn't shake the feeling that taking this path with Clay would put them and her family on a course straight through hell. She just hoped what lay on the other side was worth it.

---

A clang disrupted Lulubelle's slumber. Although she could snooze standing up, she also enjoyed resting on the ground, her hump and one side of her body lolling to the left as she stretched her neck outward. She initially decided to ignore the sound, especially when she heard three sets of tiny scurrying feet. The honey badgers were tipping over garbage cans again. Although Lulubelle generally loved all creatures—four-legged and two-legged—the pesky weasels had rather mean personalities, and their nocturnal adventures disturbed her sleep.

But then Lulubelle heard something else…the tread of human footsteps. A biped, especially at this time in the evening, meant pats and lovely, lovely alfalfa pellets. With a huge sigh, Lulubelle hefted her body off the ground. Maneuvering a large hump could take a lot of effort, especially when getting up. Her calf Savannah, who'd been resting beside her, stirred slightly, but she did not awake. Hank, Lulubelle's mate, happily slept on, his loud snores causing his split upper lip to jiggle.

Lulubelle caught sight of the juvenile honey badger first. He was poised on the top of a pile of garbage right under a lamppost. The light also illuminated the overturned garbage can. Although the crunch of human feet on gravel sounded closer and closer, the rascal didn't attempt to hide. Instead, he triumphantly remained standing on his spoils for the evening.

The Blue-Eyed One stomped into sight. Lulubelle let out a rumbling greeting. She liked the young human. He sneaked her treats, and she noticed the sweet looks he gave the Gray-Eyed One. Tonight, however, the expression on his face looked like one a honey badger would make. Scamp chittered in triumph. The biped ignored both Lulubelle and Scamp. Instead, he just clomped over to the nearest pile and started shoveling the mess of garbage into a foul-smelling black bag.

The sounds emanating from the Blue-Eyed One reminded Lulubelle of how she felt when her daughter was younger and kept demanding attention. "Do you realize I have to clean this all up? Of course, you do. That's part of your sick fun."

"So you keep ditching your friends to pick up other people's trash and talk to weasels?" The new biped's vocal noises triggered Lulubelle's protective instincts. She did *not* like this voice. It was as grating and distressing as a hyena's cackle.

A figure appeared. The biped wore a dark-gray hoodie and blended in with the shadows. The hunch of his thin shoulders perturbed Lulubelle. There was something sinister and opportunistic about the male, like a white-backed vulture circling the skies looking for its next meal. Lulubelle curled her lip and got ready to spit.

The Blue-Eyed One didn't follow the normal human ritual and straighten to greet Gray-Hood. Instead, he continued cleaning up the debris. "Didn't expect to see you here. And you know I'm doing this community service shit and taking classes since I took the blame for everyone."

"Fuck, man. Just bail and sneak back right before your shift ends. The guy who runs this place will never notice."

"No." The sound from the Blue-Eyed One was short and emphatic.

Gray-Hood's face twisted. Lulubelle tensed. So did Scamp. Something about that look was off. Dangerous. "At least steal a key to the front gate. It would be so wild to party here. I just hid in a bathroom stall tonight, but it would be harder to sneak in booze and hide a lot of people."

"Do you want someone to get eaten by a mountain lion or a bear?"

Gray-Hood made a snort like one of the red river hogs. "I'm not planning on releasing the animals."

The Blue-Eyed One straightened. His eyes reminded Lulubelle of a honey badger defending its treat from another animal. "If we get drunk, one of us will dare someone to do something stupid."

"When did you become a boring fucktard?"

The Blue-Eyed One ignored him and bent back down. Gray-Hood's fists clenched, and he stalked toward Lulubelle's human. He yanked the Blue-Eyed One's shoulder, forcing him to stand. Scamp gave a warning cry. Lulubelle snorted. No one touched their biped.

"You don't ignore me." Gray-Hood made a few growl-like sounds.

The Blue-Eyed One shook off Gray-Hood's hand. "And *you* don't touch me."

"Don't fucking tell me what to do. You don't want to mess with me. I can make your life a living hell." Although Lulubelle did not understand the sounds the humans made, she recognized the threat in Gray-Hood's voice.

The Blue-Eyed One just shrugged with the insolence of a honey badger. "I'm done hanging out with you."

A guttural sound emerged from Gray-Hood as he swung his fist at the Blue-Eyed One's face. Lulubelle's human ducked, but he didn't avoid the stomach punch. He let out a pained grunt. Lulubelle blew air through her nostrils. Enraged, she did the only thing she could with a gate keeping her corralled. She spit. It landed on the side of Gray-Hood's face. He staggered back, away from the Blue-Eyed One.

"What the hell?" He raised his hand to his cheek and studied his wet fingers. Scamp, the clever little weasel, promptly sank his teeth into the attacker's ankle.

This time, Gray-Hood shrieked like a startled peahen. He shook his leg, but Scamp hung on, even as his body crashed against the garbage can.

"Stop!" The Blue-Eyed One sounded panicked. "I can get Scamp off you. Stop hurting him!"

"The fucker has to pay!"

Before the human could slam Scamp again, angry chitters filled the air. Lulubelle spotted both of Scamp's parents tearing in his direction.

Gray-Hood emitted more birdlike cries. "Shit! There's more of them!"

"Yeah." The Blue-Eyed One bent and tried to pick up Scamp. "And you just body-slammed their baby."

"They're nothing but fat weasels." Gray-Hood tried to sound tough like a honey badger, but even Lulubelle could sense his fear. Scamp must have too, because he released the human's leg and allowed the Blue-Eyed One to lift him into his arms.

"They attack adult lions...by going after their balls." The Blue-Eyed One sounded smug.

Gray-Hood spun around and tore down the path, his breath coming in short, frantic huffs. Scamp's parents followed. The trio disappeared, and shortly after, Lulubelle heard the fence at the zoo's perimeter rattle. The horrible biped had been chased off.

The Blue-Eyed One gently petted Scamp's fur before placing him on the ground. Lulubelle was surprised that the honey badger allowed it. He too must have sensed that the intruder had meant to seriously harm the Blue-Eyed One.

"Thanks." Lulubelle could sense the affection in the human's voice as he gazed down at Scamp. "I guess I don't mind cleaning up your shit after all."

Then the biped walked over to Lulubelle and scratched her neck. Her eyelids fluttered down. She loved being touched. It made her feel secure.

"That was some impressive spitting."

Although Lulubelle did not understand the juvenile human's exact words, she recognized praise when she heard it. She beamed.

The human produced an alfalfa treat from his pocket. "Here. You deserve it for distracting him."

Lulubelle carefully suctioned up the treat. Then, with a goodbye rumble, she lumbered back inside the barn and lay down, her mission complete.

---

"I wish I could have been by your side today," Clay told Lacey as they lay together in his bed listening to a rare spring rain beat against the windows as thunder cracked in the distance. He didn't like how exhausted she'd looked when he'd picked her up from the zoo earlier that evening. She'd texted him and told him she'd rested at June's, but her day would have been draining even without the complications of little sleep and her concussion. She'd barely made it through her therapy exercises tonight, and they'd ended up skipping the part where she watched videos of people walking down busy European streets. That task, which was supposed to rebuild her balance, always made her a little nauseated.

"We'll need to be seen in public soon," Lacey said sleepily. "We don't want to look like we're ashamed or hiding."

Clay leaned over and gently placed a tendril of hair behind her ear before giving her a soft kiss on the temple. "I wasn't talking about strategy. I just wish you didn't have to face everyone's disapproval alone."

She shifted to gaze at him, her eyes glittering in the low light of the moon. "It wasn't that bad, and bringing you along would've been like poking my family in the eye. They need time to prepare."

Clay wished this whole process wasn't so damn difficult. "You're probably right."

"June Winters is on our side."

"Really?" Clay had tried reaching out to the sunny Southerner before, thinking maybe fellow outsiders could stick together. It hadn't worked.

"Yep. You and Zach have been added to the invite list for her wedding."

"Oh, Zach is going to be beyond thrilled."

His sarcasm earned him a poke on the shoulder from Lacey. "First, June and Magnus's wedding is like a royal one for Sagebrush Flats."

"Oh, I know," Clay said, "but I don't think that will impress my nephew."

Another shoulder poke. When Lacey spoke, she added extra emphasis. "*Second*, she's holding it at the zoo just like Katie and Bowie did for theirs, so Zach will enjoy it. I'll check with Bowie and see if your nephew can help handle the animals participating in the ceremony."

"The *animals* are joining in?"

"Well, Lulubelle, Hank, and Savannah for sure. I doubt anyone could stop the honey badgers from showing up. June and Magnus wanted to take their vows near either the prairie dog or the polar bear enclosure, and there's more room in front of Sorcha's exhibit. The reception will be held throughout the zoo. I'm sure the cockatoo's cage will be situated near the dance floor. Rosie likes to boogie."

"Sometimes Sagebrush can be an odd town," Clay said.

A third poke from Lacey. "I prefer quirky and endearing."

Clay couldn't help the grin spreading across his face. "I definitely find one thing about Sagebrush quirky and endearing." Dipping his head, he captured her lips, taking his time as he explored her mouth. Even as need roared through him, so did a softer sense of peace. When he was with Lacey in the dark like this, things felt so comfortable and right, even if they weren't easy in the harsh light.

When he broke the kiss, she sighed and wiggled her body closer. He wrapped his arms about her as he buried his face in her hair, breathing in its slight citrus scent. "'Night, Lace."

She turned in his arms again. When she spoke, her voice sounded decidedly grumpy. "What do you mean, ''Night'? We've barely even kissed."

He brushed his lips against the back of her neck. "You're exhausted. Any idiot could see that. You need rest."

"What I need is to feel bliss." She flipped in his arms and pressed a kiss on his collarbone. "And you, mister, are very talented at making me experience it."

She'd said something similar before, and every time, it triggered a bolt of pure pleasure. It was novel being special to someone…to make that person happy by just being him, and he relished the feeling. Still, he worried about Lacey. She'd had a long day. Hell, he felt like crap after spending half the night chasing elusive wolves, and he hadn't faced an entire disappointed town wagging its collective finger at him.

"Lace, are you su—" His voice cut off as she kissed her way down his body.

"Oh, I'm sure," she said just before her lips closed around his cock.

---

Moonlight washed over the room as Lacey stared down at Clay. She'd brought him over the brink of pleasure a little while ago. To her delight, it hadn't taken long, and he'd rewarded her with more than one groan and hoarse cry. Clay constantly surprised her. She wouldn't have thought him a man to show his pleasure so easily. He had an openness that charmed and excited her.

His eyes fluttered open. In the low light, she couldn't see their brilliant blue-green, but their intensity remained. He looked glorious, all stretched out before her. He made no move to cover himself as he allowed her gaze to sweep over him. He just shifted to place his arms behind his head, which in Lacey's opinion only improved the view.

Anyone who claimed he stayed behind a desk all day should see him like this. Ranching gave men muscles, and Clay had plenty to spare. Even his thighs and calves were defined, but it was his biceps that really fascinated Lacey...and his chest, of course.

Bending over him, she caressed each intriguing contour, carefully observing his reaction to every light touch. His sated pleasure gave way to something hot and wicked that only fueled her own raging inferno. She wasn't a stranger to strong emotions. Even when she'd pulled away from close connections with humans, she'd always had her causes. People told her she had an extraordinary capacity for passion. But she'd never felt this much power...this much need. It roared inside her, and she wanted to feed it.

"Don't move," she whispered to Clay.

"I wouldn't dream of it." His voice sounded low and languid with just a tinge of amusement.

Climbing off Clay, she lit the candles he'd placed on each nightstand a few days ago. They'd discovered that the soft light didn't bother her as much as artificial.

"Better?" Clay asked as she returned to the bed. When she settled again, her knees on either side of him, he reached up and stroked her back. Even without the low glow revealing the affection in his face, she would've felt it in his touch.

"Much."

He captured her hand and brought it to his lips. As he brushed a kiss across her knuckles, he watched her, his irises a deep, endless blue-green. When he released her, she ran her fingers across his jawline and then down his body. The whole time she caressed him, she never broke their shared gaze. It was like watching the sea go dark and then light blue as the current changed.

"Did anyone ever tell you that you have the most beautiful blue eyes?"

Beneath her hand, his muscles stiffened. Her compliment clearly unsettled him. "The Stevens eyes, you mean," he corrected, his voice gruff.

She shook her head and placed her hands on either side of his face so he wouldn't look away. "No. I mean *your* eyes. I never knew blue ones could change like yours. They're like an aquamarine hot spring in Yellowstone now, but sometimes they're as clear as a mountain lake."

He brushed his thumb lightly over one of her cheekbones. "I love how you see me, Lace."

The tone of his voice triggered a swell of emotion that rushed over her. His hand skimmed her back as he lifted himself off the pillows. Leaning in her direction, he pressed his lips against hers. The kiss was softer than she'd expected but no less powerful. Like a golden sunrise over the desert, it slipped through her, warming every inch.

---

No one had ever made Clay feel the way Lacey Montgomery did. His whole life, he'd never truly belonged. But with her…he did. Which was all sorts of crazy considering how much they had to fight to be together. But in the candlelight with their past banished to the shadows, their differences vanished too. The connection he felt threatened to overwhelm him, but it made it no less intoxicating. He craved her, craved their closeness.

Breaking their kiss, he whispered in her ear, "You make me feel so good, Lace. I want to make you feel the same."

She turned her head slightly, pressing her lips against his neck as they curled upward. "You're very proficient at that."

"I'm just getting started," he said. Carefully, he flipped their bodies so she lay beneath him. She let out a surprised squeal that turned into a gasp as his mouth closed over her breast. Her nipple immediately pebbled. Her hands buried in his hair, pressing him closer. He flicked out his tongue, playing with the hardened tip. She rewarded him with a throaty sound that curled through him. Her hips began to lift, and he reached down with his hand, giving her the pressure and the friction she craved. Her cries came in sharp, beautiful, staccato notes. He watched as she tumbled gloriously over the edge, her body straining, her lips parting ever so slightly. When she went limp against the mattress, he kissed his way down her stomach to her damp center.

Her fingers threaded through his locks again, her touch light and tender. He teased her just as gently, relishing each little intake of her breath. He rubbed his thumbs against her inner thighs, her skin soft and smooth beneath his calluses. She shivered once. Then twice.

"I need you." Her whisper was throaty and full of decadent promise. Desire, stronger than any simple lust, pulsated through him. He swore his heart might fissure from the sheer force. But it didn't. It just pumped faster, sending his blood racing.

He felt Lacey gently guiding his head upward, and he followed her command, kissing a path along her body. When his lips reached hers, she wrapped her arms around him, holding him close. He didn't enter her right away. Instead, he pressed his length against her heat as he explored her mouth. She moaned, the sound almost causing him to lose himself. Then she began to rub against him. Squeezing his eyes shut, he focused on maintaining control.

Her hands slid to his butt, and he suppressed his own shudder. "Lace, I'm trying to take it slow."

"I'm all for slow as long as you're inside me."

Her words ripped away what little self-preservation he had remaining. He gathered her tightly as he breathed in her scent. Hell, he'd do anything for this woman, be anything for her. The Stevens men always had their weaknesses. His father's was money. His brother's was drugs. And Lacey was his. Luckily for him, she was his strength too. He'd never felt better than when he was with her.

Pressing his lips to hers, he explored her mouth as he slowly entered her. He swallowed each gasp and groan as he slid deeper and deeper. He retreated just as glacially, drawing out the pleasure...and the need. His arms shook from the effort, and even Lacey began to tremble. He went slightly faster the next time and then the next, increasing the tempo tantalizing beat by tantalizing beat. By the end, they were moving at a frantic pace, echoing the wild frenzy of emotions swirling through him. He held on long enough to feel her glorious climax, her muscles clenching around him, her body taut beneath his, her fingertips pressing against his rear. He erupted, somehow still managing to hold her close as he came.

His body near collapse, he rolled off her, thudding against the mattress. The seconds ticked away as they lay side by side, their breathing labored, their bodies slick with sweat. She recovered first, rolling against him. He managed to lift his arm and drape it limply over her.

"That...that was amazing. *You* were amazing," Lacey said.

He wanted to return the compliment, but he only had the energy to smile against her neck. She squeezed his hand. "I have a feeling we're both going to sleep well tonight."

"Mmm-hmm," Clay agreed sluggishly. Sure enough, it only took him a few more moments before he drifted off. Unfortunately, the rest of Lacey's prediction didn't come true.

---

The chime of Clay's smartphone startled Lacey from a deep sleep. Weighed down by tiredness, she couldn't fully wake up. She vaguely felt Clay slide from the bed as he answered. His words seemed to blend together until three particular ones.

"...fucking wolf attack!"

She bolted upright, ignoring her light-headedness. "What...what did you say?"

But Clay wasn't paying attention. He was already pulling on pants with one hand as he held the phone in another. "I'll be there as soon as I can."

Lacey flipped on a light and climbed from the bed, searching for the bag of fresh clothes she'd brought. The clock read four thirty in the morning, but she wasn't going back to sleep.

Clay shoved his phone into his pocket as he reached into the closet for a shirt. "That was Forrester. He was out early checking on his herd near my land. One of my cows was chased into a steep ravine last night."

"By wolves?"

Clay's gaze held hers, his eyes stark. So many emotions swirled there, making them darker than normal. They made her think not of warm seas but of stormy ones. She wasn't sure if she spotted accusation in those depths, but she definitely saw worry and frustration.

"Apparently. I should've had some of my men sleep with the herd again."

"I'm coming with you."

He rammed his hand into his hair. "I'd mention the brain injury and how tired you are, but I doubt that would stop you."

"You'd be right."

He gave a sharp nod. "We'll take the two-seat four-wheeler. I'll go wake up my guys. We can meet at the barn." He paused in the doorway, glancing back at her. "This is why I fought you so hard, Lace. This isn't the first cow I've lost this way, and it won't be the last."

He said the words matter-of-factly without blame, but they still smarted. She'd thought he finally understood, understood her. Her head swam uncomfortably as she swallowed in an attempt to rein in her sudden flare of anger. "Wolves have a right to exist, Clay."

"I've never argued that. I just don't want them on my land." With that statement, he disappeared from view.

She sank onto the bed as she fought against an unexpected wave of tears. Her concussion had brought her emotions too close to the surface. Resolutely, she pulled on her jeans and then yanked her sweatshirt over her head. The air would be cool this time of the morning.

Even with her body flushed with anger, she'd feel the chill.

When she reached the ranch yard, the men had the vehicles ready. She hopped on behind Clay. Neither of them spoke. She could feel tension in his body, a sharp contrast to the way they'd collapsed in each other's arms only a few hours before. He'd been so open then…so had she. Now they'd retreated into themselves. Even as she clung to Clay while the quad bumped along, she felt separated from him.

By the time they reached the scene, Lacey could feel her stomach start to sour. She hated seeing any animal distressed. Predators were a part of nature, even a part she loved. But that didn't mean it didn't bother her to see the results of their hunt. But it was part of the environment, the natural cycle of things.

Clay walked stiffly toward the ravine. Lacey debated about reaching for his hand, but she didn't know how he'd react. She didn't want to risk his men seeing any rift between them. She wasn't sure what was going to happen to their relationship after this, but she didn't want gossip before they'd had the chance to work this out privately.

She could hear the cow moving about, occasionally making lowing sounds. Fortunately, the animal sounded more panicked and frustrated than hurt. Although there was a path in and out of the deep dried-up arroyo bed, it wasn't a passage the animal would choose unless chased or herded. While Clay and his men climbed into the steep gully to rescue the cow, Lacey scanned the area for signs of wolves. She was surprised and grateful that the pack hadn't finished the kill after expending the energy to corner the animal. True, Tim Forrester had spotted the cow, so perhaps his presence had scared off the lobos. But something just didn't seem right to Lacey.

Using one of the lanterns stashed in the four-by-four, Lacey scanned the narrow entrance into the ravine. This would be so much quicker in the day, but the rain shower earlier in the evening made her job easier since the wet dirt meant better tracks. The ground was churned up due to the cow's hooves, but something made her pause and crouch down. She almost touched the print with her finger, wanting to test its realness before she called out to Clay. But no, her eyes weren't deceiving her.

"This wasn't a wolf attack."

The movement in the ravine paused. The men had been pushing the cow up the steep grade. Although the animal snorted, no one else made a sound. Tension swirled through the air. When Clay finally spoke, his voice was too carefully controlled. "Are you sure it wasn't? Or do you just want it not to be?"

Lacey took a calming breath. They were all under pressure, and it wouldn't do to snap back. "There's a human shoe print in the mud."

"Maybe it's Forrester's? He spotted the cow in the ravine," Stewart suggested, his tone languid despite having pushed a full-grown cow up a sharp incline.

"No." Clay took off his cowboy hat and shoved his hand into his hair. "He said he heard the cow lowing from his land. He didn't come onto mine."

"Did he specifically say he saw the lobos?" Lacey asked.

"No."

"Well, someone was here, and he certainly wasn't a wolf."

---

"It'll be a little bit before the anesthesia wears off," Lou Warrenton said as he clasped Clay's shoulder, "but luckily only a few wounds were deep enough to require stitching. Nothing appears to be broken either."

Clay swallowed and nodded. "Thanks for coming." They'd managed to get the injured cow out of the ravine and onto a trailer to bring her back to the barn. She had a couple of deep cuts from rushing headlong into the ravine that needed medical attention. He'd tried the local vet first, but the man was out of town visiting relatives in another state. Thankfully, Lou didn't mind taking an emergency or two.

"Not a problem." Lou finished returning his supplies to his medical bag before he faced Clay, his kind eyes serious in his lined face. "I know you've faced a lot of anger in these parts, but I've always measured a man by how he takes care of his animals. Many ranchers wouldn't have paid the vet bill for a cow beyond her calf-bearing years."

"Speckles is special," Clay said.

Lou nodded, automatically accepting without question that a rancher could have a favorite beef cow that he'd even named. "Give me a call if you spot any complications."

"Will do," Clay promised.

Lou bobbed his head a final time and walked stiffly from the barn. Fortunately, Bowie had accompanied the older man, so he wouldn't need to make the return drive to Sagebrush himself. Clay headed back into the stall to find Lacey waiting. Neither of them had spoken much, but she'd stayed by his side even though he knew she was exhausted.

"You should get some rest," Clay said.

She ignored his statement. "Why is Speckles special?"

Clay sank to the ground beside the cow and petted her wide neck. She was sedated, but he still felt the need to soothe. "I helped with her birth. It was a tough one—breech. Her mother didn't survive. One of my chores was bottle-feeding Speckles. She's the first animal I ever cared about. I think that was part of my grandfather's plan—to get me to love ranching."

Ace, who'd followed them into the barn when they'd returned with Speckles, laid his big head on Clay's thigh and heaved a huge doggie sigh. Clay scratched the mutt's broad forehead with the hand not petting the cow.

"I named her Speckles. My grandfather never knew. Hell, I don't think anyone did until Lou and you."

"My grandpa and uncle never let me name their calves, especially the bottle-fed ones." Lacey sat down on the side of him not occupied by a half-dozing dog.

A slight smile twisted Clay's lips. "It's a smart rule. You grow too damn attached otherwise."

"Is that why you've kept her even after she wasn't a breeder?"

Clay nodded. "My grandfather and I argued about it. It was one of the last conversations we had before his heart attack. He told me I treated the cow too much like a damn pet, and it was my city side showing. He wanted to send her to market since she was long past her prime, but I couldn't. She's a little over a decade old now, which is ancient for a beef cow."

Lacey reached for his hand. "It was just your compassionate side. You've got a big heart, Clay Stevens. It's bound to shine through."

"Well, don't spread that around. I've enough problems trying to convince people I'm a serious rancher without them knowing a cow comes running up to me whenever she catches sight of me."

"I think it's sweet."

He snorted. "You say the same about apex predators."

"True," she agreed.

He didn't know why he spoke the next words. Maybe because he wanted her to understand. Maybe because he was so damn tired of keeping things bottled up. He didn't even know if he was a naturally private person. He just hadn't had anyone who'd given a shit about his problems for a long time.

"It was one of Speckles's descendants who was my first calf killed by wolves. She looked just like her great-grandmother too. I'd even helped with the birth, although her mom had lived, unlike with Speckles, so she wasn't bottle-fed. That year, I lost five percent of the calves to the lobos."

"I'm sorry, Clay," Lacey said, her voice soft. "That must have been hard."

He jerked his head, the understanding in her voice washing over him like warm water against sore muscles. She kissed his cheek and rested her head against his shoulder. Neither of them spoke for a long time as they watched Speckles's measured breathing.

"Thanks for sticking by my side."

She nodded, the top of her head brushing against his chin. "If you want, I can work with you to think of more ways to protect your herd that won't interfere with the pack. You could get fladry fences like we talked about, but there are also motion detectors, which flash and make noise. Some alarms can even be triggered by the wolves' tracking collars. The park would be happy to help you with programming them."

"I'd like that," he said as he reached for her hand. Playing with her fingers, he added, "I still can't believe someone would attack one of my cows."

Lacey stayed silent for a long time. When she spoke, her voice was hesitant. "I'd hate to think he'd do this, but you did fire Pete Thompson yesterday."

Clay scratched the back of his head with his free hand. "There's no love lost between Thompson and me, but I can't see him purposely chasing an old cow into a ravine. Can you?"

Lacey made circles in his palm with her thumb. "I wouldn't have imagined him saying those words to me either. A bitterness has been eating at him for years.

It's like the anger has taken over the rational part of his brain."

"The man does hate my guts."

"Are you going to tell the police?"

Clay shook his head. "I'll report what happened, but I won't name Pete. Everyone knows I let him go. I don't expect this will be the police department's top priority either."

"Somebody was trespassing, and they could've seriously injured your cow."

"Considering it was my land and my animal, I don't think they'll take this too seriously. Besides, it was probably just kids messing around."

"I'm going to give my boss a call later this morning and give her a heads-up," Lacey said. "Something doesn't seem right to me. Even if it is just a bunch of teens, look how much damage a group of them did to the wolf den."

Before Clay could respond, the tread of boots on the wooden floorboards broke into their conversation. Considering the attack on Speckles and the idea Pete Thompson could be after revenge, unease trickled through Clay as he sprang to his feet. He waved at Lacey to stay seated as he quickly moved to the stall door. He doubted his old foreman would ambush him in broad daylight, but if Thompson had purposely herded a cow into a dangerous ravine, he wasn't acting sensibly.

To Clay's relief, it wasn't Pete's lanky form but Rick Hernandez's bulkier one. "Oh crap," Clay said. "I forgot all about our meeting."

"No problem," Rick said with a friendly smile on his face. "I heard you had trouble last night. June's tea shop is buzzing with rumors. Some people are saying wolves, and then others are claiming a human drove one of your cows into a dried-up arroyo."

Clay ran his hand through his hair and then jammed his hat back into place. "Lacey found a shoe print in the mud, so it looks like it was a person, not lobos."

Rick let out a whistle. "That doesn't sound good. Did you have to put the cow down?"

Lacey rose to her feet. "The wounds were mostly superficial, and Lou Warrenton was able to patch up the deeper ones."

Rick entered the stall, and Clay leaned on the door as he watched the other man inspect Speckles. His hands moved competently, and when Ace lifted his head and butted Rick's leg, he rubbed the dog behind his ears.

"She's not young." Rick tilted his chin in the cow's direction.

"No." Clay cleared his throat as he glanced at Lacey. She gave him a slight nod of encouragement. Maybe it was time he stopped cultivating his aloof personae.

"Speckles was the first calf I helped birth, and she's part of the reason I became a rancher."

Rick glanced at him in surprise. Clay didn't see any amusement or, worse, derision in his eyes. Instead, Rick said, "When you grow up on a ranch, there's always that special animal or two. Mine was my horse, Lightning. She died a couple years ago, but she used to come galloping over every time she saw me. It probably had something to do with the fact that I'd always slip her sugar cubes when my father wasn't looking."

"Lacey says ranching's in your blood."

"Yup," Rick said. "My mom calls us all horse and cow mad. Even on the longest days during calving season, I wouldn't trade the saddle for a desk job."

"Me either."

Clay didn't have any trouble detecting the shock in Rick's brown eyes. Evidently, neither did Lacey. She spoke quickly, her voice bright. "Clay, why don't you show Rick your plans for the ranch? I can stay here with your cow. I'll call you if anything goes wrong."

Clay frowned. He needed a new foreman, and Rick seemed like the best candidate and the only one with ties to Sagebrush Flats. He couldn't afford to blow this interview, but Lacey hadn't slept in days. He wanted her safely tucked into bed rather than sitting in a stall keeping watch over Speckles.

"Lacey, you need to lie down."

She waved away his concern with her smartphone. "I have to call my boss anyway. You two won't be gone long. I'll crash as soon as you get back."

"Lace—"

Rick made a clearing sound in the back of his throat. "I grew up with Lacey. She's as stubborn as they come."

Instead of looking insulted, she practically beamed. "See? I'm impossible to wear down. As June Winters would say, I'm as stubborn as good Georgian granite."

Still, Clay hesitated, but Lacey made a shooing motion. With a sigh, he left the stall with Rick following. As he and Rick saddled the horses, he called Hawkins to tell him to check in on Lacey.

Rick let Clay do most of the talking during the first part of the ride. He nodded occasionally, not giving a lot of his thoughts away. As soon as Clay mentioned ciénegas, the younger man came alive as he dismounted to inspect the work Clay had already done to reroute the water back to its natural course. Ace, who'd been following them, bounded headlong into the mud. He rolled around in pure doggy joy until his white coat looked reddish-brown.

"I can't get over how wet the soil is here." Rick lifted one of his boots to inspect the muck clinging to the sole. Water immediately seeped into the impression his foot had left.

Clay jammed his thumb in the direction of the source of the ciénega. "The water has really started to pool this year, especially with the spring melt. I'm hoping if we can add more dams, it'll spread out even more. I've noticed the quality of the soil is even starting to change. It's getting blacker."

Rick's eyes swept toward the shimmer of water. "Hell, this place even smells wet. I feel like I'm back East."

They moved closer, their boots making squelching sounds. Ace loped over to them, his tongue lolling from his mouth. Leopard frogs plopped into the water, while the sharp chirps of horned larks formed a pleasant chorus. The desert always boasted more life than the traditional image of a dry wasteland, but the Valhalla ciénega possessed its own special energy. Clay loved sneaking out here during the spring and summer and capturing pictures of the animals. He'd even snapped a shot of a great blue heron last year.

"I know I'm repeating myself, but I'm still in disbelief over how marshy the land is," Rick said.

"We're keeping the cattle off this section of the land to let it recover," Clay said. "But the plan is to allow them to graze."

As they started walking back to the horses, Rick bent to inspect a prickly pear. "You ever think about letting the cattle eat these?"

"We already do," Clay said. "The men aren't too fond of singeing off the spines, but they've gotten used to it."

"I've read about a university in Mexico doing a study on what supplements will help cattle better digest the cactus," Rick said. "I could look into it more if you wanted."

"Sounds good," Clay said. The words applied to more than just Rick's offer to research the consumption of nopals by cattle. Lacey's assessment of the young man was spot on. He was fascinated by holistic ranch management. Curious about Rick's ideas on protecting the livestock, Clay asked, "How would you improve the herd's safety given the local wolf populations?"

Rick shot him an assessing glance. Everyone knew Clay's opinion of the lobos.

"During college, I worked at a couple different ranches during the summer, so I could observe multiple ways of running an operation. At one of the spreads in Montana near Yellowstone National Park, the owner had a lot of success with low-stress herding. I showed my dad and Lacey's uncle, and it's worked out pretty well."

"Lacey mentioned something about that," Clay said. "She says it increases the cattle's natural herding instincts and makes them less vulnerable to wolves."

"Our losses to the lobos have decreased a lot," Rick said. "We've also experimented with fladry fences and motion detector alarms. There's a lot you could do here on Valhalla."

Clay nodded as both of them fell into silence. He mulled over their conversation, and he could tell Rick was doing the same. They turned their horses away from the ciénegas, and Clay ended their tour on the knoll overlooking the creek bank. Ace ran into the water with a large splash. He leaped into the air again, sending more water flying. At least the spray washed off his muddy fur.

Rick didn't say anything at first. He just leaned forward in the saddle, watching Ace play. Then he turned, his expression thoughtful. "You're not what I expected."

For the first time since firing Pete Thompson, a trickle of relief flowed through Clay. "You're exactly how Lacey described you."

A slow smile spread across Rick's face. "I hope that's a good thing."

Clay laughed. "She's the one who recommended you. Said you'd be perfect for the job, and she's rarely wrong."

Rick's grin grew wider. "I was surprised when you called me even though I'd heard about Pete being fired."

"I wasn't sure if you'd even agree to a meeting," Clay admitted.

"It's a good opportunity to become a foreman at my age."

"Even if it is Valhalla Ranch making the offer." Clay filled in Rick's unspoken words.

"I didn't say that," Rick said quickly.

"You didn't need to," Clay said. "I know what people think when they hear the name *Stevens*. If you come to work for me, some people might see it as siding with the enemy."

Rick's grin returned then. "I've never been a rebel before. This might be fun."

"Does that mean you're interested in the foreman position?"

"Hell yes. I like what you have planned for Valhalla."

"All right." Clay tried to mask the excitement roaring through him at the prospect of having a foreman who shared his vision. He hadn't thought Laçey's idea would work. Rick was taking a chance, but hell, Clay was accepting a risk too. The younger man might have lived on a ranch his whole life, but he'd never run one. And Clay wasn't that seasoned either. Thompson had called a lot of the shots, especially right after Clay's grandfather died.

Clay held out his hand, and Rick took it without any hesitation. By the way the younger man pumped the handshake, Clay knew he was just as enthusiastic about returning the ranch to its former glory. It was going to be hard, backbreaking work, but for the first time, Clay had people supporting him. That made the task a hell of a lot less daunting.

Despite the meeting's success, unease trickled through Clay as they rode back to the compound with Ace leading the way. Things never went easily, and he couldn't escape the feeling that a huge gaping hole was about to destroy his carefully laid plans.

---

"What do you mean there are wolves missing from the pack?" Lacey shouted into the phone, forgetting to modulate her voice. "Why didn't anyone tell me?"

"Because you need to rest," Lacey's boss said. "You're due back to work soon, and I planned to tell you then."

"But..." Lacey protested as her frustration swelled. The wolves were *her* babies, and if one of them went missing, she wanted to know about it. Immediately.

"Lacey, we're staying on top of this. I promise."

"Do you think they're being hunted?"

"They were younger males. We believe they've moved on, found new territory. That's what we want, right?"

"What do the trackers say?"

"We hadn't tagged any of the missing wolves."

Lacey bit off a swear word. No matter what her boss said, something didn't feel right.

"Lacey, I'm making sure Kylie is regularly checking on the pack. I promise they're in good hands."

"I know." Lacey forced a calm she didn't feel. "Kylie is a good ranger, and everyone cares about the wolf project, not just me."

Her boss's voice relaxed too. "We all know this forced time off is hard on you. That's why we didn't tell you. We didn't want to upset you when you're not up for long trips into the backcountry."

Lacey rested her head against the wooden slats of the barn and squeezed her eyes shut. As much as she enjoyed volunteering at the zoo, she needed to get back to the wilderness. "What are the wolves' identification numbers?"

Her boss told her. Lacey didn't need to pull up their database. She knew exactly which ones she meant. She visualized them now. M1350 was a lanky lobo who still hadn't packed on all of his adult muscle. He was playful and curious. She could easily envision him striking out to form his own pack, but she could also picture him wandering into a trap. M1371 was stealthier. He liked to keep to himself, and he was the best stalker. She also could imagine him leaving for better hunting grounds… or getting into trouble for shadowing livestock.

"Thanks." Lacey hung up the phone and closed her eyes again. She wished she'd insisted on tagging each animal, but she hadn't wanted to interfere more than necessary. Maybe she should've. The Mexican gray wolves were so critically endangered, losing even one was significant. To have two healthy males disappear concerned Lacey.

"Lace?" At the sound of Clay's voice, she glanced up.

He looked exhausted. Two sleepless nights were wearing on him too. The attack on his cow had hit him hard. He cared about his herd, about his animals. Lacey would never deny that. But did that love mean he would break the law to protect his cattle? Would he kill one of her wolves and not tell her? Even after they'd slept together?

"Is something wrong?" Clay glanced at her, his blue-green eyes soft with concern. He reached to cup her face, and she reflexively flinched away. He stepped back, his expression immediately guarded. When he spoke, his voice had roughened. "What is it, Lace?"

She watched him, part of her feeling guilty at suspecting him, the other wondering if she'd be a fool not to. "Would you take me on a hike?"

"A hike?" Clay asked, clearly confused.

"Some of the wolves are missing, and I want to check on the pack."

His bewilderment cleared, and he watched her with concern. "Lace, that's out in the backcountry."

"I know." She wished her voice didn't sound like a challenge.

He took a breath as if steadying himself. "Are you sure you're up to that?"

She crossed her arms. "Is there a reason you don't want me to go?"

Like thunderclouds moving over a lake, frustration darkened his aquamarine eyes. "Other than the fact that you're suffering from a brain injury and hiking for miles under the bright desert sun isn't the best idea?"

Lacey knew she shouldn't push, but she couldn't stop herself. She felt so damn tired of constantly battling lightheadedness, constantly working to *think*. She couldn't control the ball of hurt and anger forming inside her. Instead of answering Clay's question, she just stared at him. Hard.

"Shit, Lace, I didn't hurt your wolves."

"But you would if it was legal." It wasn't a question, but she'd retained enough self-control not to add *or if you thought you wouldn't get caught.*

Clay shoved his hand into his hair, making the blond ends stand up as he pushed his cowboy hat around his neck. "Hell, Lacey, I'm not sure what I'd do if the law changed now that we're together. I know how much those wolves mean to you. I certainly wouldn't kill one without telling you. That would be a breach of the trust you've given me...or at least I thought you'd given me."

She wanted to relax then, to accept his words. But that dark, ugly bubble wouldn't allow it. Not yet.

"Then why won't you take me to the lobos?"

Clay closed his eyes briefly, and Lacey could tell he was trying to maintain control. "First, I never said I wouldn't. I'm worried about your stamina. I care about you, Lace. A lot. Which is why I'm trying to be patient and why I'd never betray you by secretly killing one of the pack and then climbing into bed with you."

The fight left Lacey in a sudden whoosh. The doctor had warned that she could have abrupt shifts in her mood, and to her horror, tears pricked her eyes. She swiped at them, and the ice in Clay's blue irises immediately thawed.

"I'm sorry," she whispered. "I—I..." The tears spilled over and turned into a gushing waterfall that put Yosemite's to shame. Hell, she wasn't a crier. Ever.

Two strong male arms encircled her. Burying her face against Clay's warmth, she tried to squelch her tears. He felt so wonderfully solid. Gently, he rubbed her back as he rested his chin on her head. "It's okay to cry, Lace. It's been a long two days."

"I can't think," she admitted. "I'm just so worried about the pack. I haven't seen them in over a month, and now I learn this."

She felt him nod. "When you feel up to it, I swear we'll visit the wolves. We'll take plenty of breaks and bring along lots of water. But right now, you need rest. Neither of us has slept in two days, and you can't go without sleep."

"I know." Her voice sounded soggy even to her own ears.

"What do you say about taking a nap in my bed?" Clay said. "I'll make sure no one disturbs you."

"What about you?"

"I have work to do around the ranch, especially since you volunteered us to help set up June Winters's wedding at the zoo in a few days."

Lacey slowly rose to her feet. Clay needed a break too, but she knew better than to argue. She'd grown up around ranchers and understood the responsibilities they faced. That same work ethic had shaped her too, but she had no more energy left. She felt as drained as a long-dead car battery.

Taking Clay up on his offer, she wearily climbed the stairs to his room. When she collapsed on the mattress, she could smell his scent. Pulling the blanket up around her chin, she snuggled down…but she missed him. Missed his warmth. Missed his strength. Missed his ability to distract her.

# Chapter 10

"You sure you want me to give you a tour and not Lacey?" Zach asked Clay as they finished setting up tables for June and Magnus's wedding reception. The teenager had a knowing smirk on his face, which Clay ignored. He'd become better at navigating Zach's attitude. The kid had more layers than a giant jawbreaker, but Clay was beginning to recognize the kid's core personality.

"I'd like to see what you've been doing here as a volunteer. Bowie and Lacey keep telling me how much of a help you've been."

"I clean up crap. Literally."

"Then show me the crap."

Zach sent him a sidelong look. "Did anyone ever tell you that you're a weirdo?"

"You do. Constantly," Clay said.

"Well, if you want to see shit, come this way."

"Crap." Clay kept his tone easy and relaxed like Lacey did when she corrected the kid's language. He was trying to ease into a more parental role, and to his surprise, his nephew hadn't pushed back. He might roll his eyes or give him an exasperated look, but Clay sensed Zach ultimately wanted someone to show a consistent interest.

"You *do* know I've heard you speak?" Zach asked.

It was Clay's turn to lift his shoulder and then drop it. "Lacey might be on me about being a better role model in your presence."

That surprised a snort out of Zach as he led them to the camel enclosure. At their approach, the woolly animals raised their heads, pausing in their chewing. Lulubelle had a particularly large clump of hay in her gaped mouth. She shook it off with a mighty flourish before loping in their direction. Savannah, however, beat her mother to the fence.

"I see you've made a friend," Clay said as the juvenile camel rubbed her long cheek against Zach's hair, causing the blond strands to stand up.

His nephew couldn't completely hide his grin as the young camel continued to nuzzle him. He managed to keep his voice studiously nonchalant. "She knows I bring her favorite treats. Abby taught me that."

Clay wasn't sure, but he thought the teenager's face momentarily reddened when he mentioned the zookeeper's daughter. Clay didn't remark on it even if he did think Abby would make a much better friend than the troublemakers Zach normally hung out with.

Zach reached into his pocket and produced an alfalfa pellet. Savannah eagerly suctioned it from his hand. Lulubelle made a raspberry sound, sending spit flying. Zach ducked. Clay wasn't so lucky.

"Shit."

"Crap," Zach corrected, his voice strained from holding back his laughter.

Clay shot him a quelling look before he cracked up himself. Reaching into his pocket for the handkerchief he carried, he wiped off the saliva. "You're sure you prefer camels to horses?"

"And miss out on stuff like this?"

"Point taken." Clay reached out and rubbed Lulubelle's long neck. "No hard feelings."

The camel gave him a mournful stare with her huge brown eyes. Zach put a pellet into Clay's hand. "She wants this, not just pats."

After they finished giving the camels their treats, Zach led Clay toward a long, narrow building. "This is where Bowie keeps the snakes, the nocturnal animals, and a few birds."

"I haven't been in here before," Clay said when they paused to let their eyes adjust to the dimly lit building.

"It's pretty cool." Zach led them through a hallway lined with terrariums. A rattlesnake shook its tail as they passed, and a couple of green ball pythons lounged on branches. "Abby showed me how to handle the reptiles. None of the animals scare her, even the venomous ones. I mean, she respects them and all, but I've seen her walk around with a tarantula in her hand like it was a kitten."

Yep. His nephew was definitely nursing a crush, but Clay decided against teasing the teenager. He wanted Zach to feel comfortable talking about anything with him, and that wouldn't happen if he razzed him, especially when the kid hadn't even confided in him. Instead, Clay asked as an iguana eyed them with an aloof expression, "Is this one of your favorite exhibits?"

"Snakes and lizards are okay," Zach said. "But I like things with fur the most."

An offended squawk filled the air just as they passed

the chinchillas. A sulphur-crested cockatoo sat on her perch. When they finished rounding the corner, the bird let out another indignant cry.

"I think you offended this one," Clay told his nephew with a grin.

Zach gave the bird a surprisingly affectionate smile. The teen really had become close to the zoo's residents. "Nah, that's just Rosie. She loves attention almost as much as dancing."

"She really does dance?" Clay asked in surprise. "Lacey said the cockatoo loved to boogie, but I thought she meant it as a joke."

"She was serious. Mr. Wilson says a lot of parrots dance naturally. There've been studies on it. Rosie's also a drama queen."

Sure enough, as they continued through the building, the cockatoo flapped her wings and let out a string of complaints. Zach turned around before the cage was out of sight and said, "Don't worry, Rosie. There'll be plenty of dancing at the wedding reception."

The bird responded with another offended cry. Zach ignored the parrot as he led Clay past the main exit to a closed door.

"Where are we headed?" Clay asked.

"This is a new addition to the building. I helped Bowie with the finishing touches. It isn't open to the public, but he said I could bring you back here."

Zach unlocked the door and carefully pushed it to reveal a pitch-black room. Chattering filled the air, sounding even more disgusted than Rosie's squawks. Clay could hear the scampering of tiny clawed feet before his nephew flicked on a low, red light. About a dozen masked faces greeted them. Black eyes watched accusatorily, the animals' long bodies quivering in anticipation of flight or attack.

"Meet the black-footed ferrets," Zach said. "They look all cute and stuff, but you should see them when they go after prey. They can be tough and a little nasty."

As Clay moved closer to the exhibit, he noticed a few human-made burrows against the glass. Inside, he could see kits wiggling around. He crouched down to get a better look at the furry little tubes. They twisted and climbed over each other in their excitement.

"Mr. Wilson says they won't leave the burrow until about July, but their eyes are open now."

"I wouldn't mind a colony of these little guys on the ranch," Clay said.

"Really?" Zach's face was etched in such comical surprise that Clay stifled a laugh.

"You know I'm not opposed to living creatures on my land."

"Well, yeah, but I thought that just meant cows, horses, and dogs."

Clay glanced at his nephew. "We need to communicate better. I'm bringing more biodiversity back to the ranch. It used to be a wetland, and I'm in the process of restoring it. We've been overgrazing for years. Lacey and I are talking about reintroducing beavers. We already have a young male building a lodge near the ciénega."

Zach's eyes grew wide. "Really?"

Clay nodded. "Unfortunately, we have a prairie dog problem in the north pasture. They're the black-tailed ones and not the more threatened species."

"You know the difference between prairie dogs?" Zach was looking at him with newfound respect. If Clay had known his knowledge of animals would've impressed his nephew, he would have talked about this months ago.

"I majored in ecology along with ranch management," Clay said.

"I didn't know that."

Clay stood up. "Like I've said before, we're more alike than you think."

"You and me." Zach jerked his thumb between the two of them. "I'm still not seeing it. We're interested in animals, and Dad screwed us both over when he got hooked on drugs, but that's about it."

Clay took a breath before he spoke. He knew he was taking a risk. He wasn't sure if Zach was ready for a conversation like this. Hell, he didn't know if *he* was ready. But it felt right. And if he was going to become a father figure to his nephew, he needed to start relying on his gut instead of worrying that he'd push the kid away.

"We both spent years looking for a place to belong before we found it. Mine's the ranch, and your place is here at the zoo."

Shock rippled through Zach's gaze like fire. He glanced away quickly, as if not sure how to deal with the emotions. He rubbed at his upper arms, but he didn't walk away.

"I never fit in…unless I was making trouble." Clay cleared his throat before he continued. "I see a lot of me in you. Maybe that's why it's so easy to care about you."

Zach moved closer to the ferret exhibit. He didn't say anything for a long time. Clay quietly walked over beside him. In silence, the two of them watched the mustelids scurry back and forth. One of the long animals stopped to look at them, its little whiskers twitching inquisitively.

"You care about me?" Zach's voice was unusually deep, but it rose on the last word and almost cracked.

Clay tentatively laid his hand on the boy's shoulder. To his relief, the teen didn't shrug him off. "Yeah. I do."

"Even with all the shit I've pulled?" Zach still didn't turn, and neither did Clay. It was easier for both of them to have this conversation while staring ahead. The ferrets had lost interest in them again and chattered among themselves.

"Maybe even because of it," Clay said. "Life certainly isn't boring with you around."

Zach let out a huff of laughter, but he sobered fast. "I'm sorry about what happened at Rocky Ridge."

Clay gently squeezed his shoulder. "I know you never wanted to hurt those wolves."

Zach drummed his fingers against the railing meant to keep visitors back from the glass. "I'm also sorry about the crappy situation I dragged you into."

"It all worked out for the best," Clay said. "You've found your place here, and I found Lacey."

"She…" Zach paused and then rubbed his thumb against the railing. Stripped of his normal bravado, he looked nervous…and young. "She doesn't mind having me around, does she?"

Clay felt a rock-sized ache in his heart at the boy's question. Damn, he should have thought about that. "Naw," Clay said. "In fact, I think she might have a soft spot for reformed bad boys with the Stevens last name."

Clay heard Zach swallow. He finally hazarded a glance at his nephew and saw him bob his head. This was hard for the kid. A lot more than it was for Clay, and it wasn't easy for him either.

"And, Zach, if she did have a problem with your presence, that would be a nonstarter. You and I, we're a package deal now."

Zach looked at him then, and the kid's blue eyes blazed. Clay thought he might have even detected a sheen of tears, but he'd never embarrass his nephew by mentioning it.

"You mean that?"

Clay nodded. "I do, Zach. You and me, we're family."

He stepped forward and hugged his nephew. The embrace wasn't without its awkwardness. Both of them held themselves too stiffly. But the emotion was right, and Zach didn't shift away.

When they stepped away from each other, neither of them said anything more. But something had changed between them. Clay sensed it. They'd crossed some invisible barrier, and there was no going back. They'd formed more than just a truce or an understanding. There was a bond now.

"So this tour wouldn't be complete without a visit to the wolves," Clay said. The mention of the pups immediately put Zach at ease. It was amazing how much this place had broken through his surly husk. He almost seemed enthusiastic as he led them out of the reptile house and through the main part of the animal park.

"Perseus and Theseus look like mini wolves now," Zach said. "Lacey says they're starting to grow their guard hairs and stuff. They're always howling, and Bowie and I are working on getting an exhibit ready."

"He mentioned that you were a big help." Clay thought he saw a proud smile drift across his nephew's lips, but it was gone before he could be certain. But there was no doubt that the kid moved confidently through the deserted zoo. Working with animals could do that, even with people with pasts as troubled and complicated as theirs. In Clay's mind, he couldn't think of a greater lesson in humanity than caring for and protecting another living creature.

When Zach opened the nursery door, the pups looked up from their game of tug-of-war. The bigger of the two immediately scrambled in Zach's direction, making happy sounds.

"Which one is this?" he asked as his nephew bent to greet the animal.

"Theseus," Zach said. "He likes people. Bowie says maybe a little too much, but since he's not going to be released, it's okay."

Perseus loped more cautiously over to Zach and

sniffed his shoe. His limp was pronounced, but it didn't seem to bother him. Neither lobo would be a good candidate for life in the wild though. Lacey had made the right decision to bring the pups to the zoo rather than the rehabilitation center.

"I brought in a couple sticks earlier for them," Zach said. "Do you want to watch the lobos play?"

Clay nodded, suppressing a smile at the kid's obvious enthusiasm. Zach had completely forgotten to hide his emotions this time. He moved excitedly over to the cabinet and pulled out a couple of large twigs. Although he placed several on the ground, the wolves decided to fight over the largest one. Their play growls filled the room. Theseus spread his paws, trying to get more traction as he yanked. Perseus chose that moment to let go of his end, causing his brother to somersault backward. For a moment, Theseus's large black pads waved in the air before he managed to right himself. He blinked, a befuddled expression on his long face. His gold irises had just begun to clear when his brother barreled into him, knocking him right over again.

Zach laughed. "I miss their blue eyes, but they look so smart with their yellow ones."

"They grew up faster than I expected," Clay said.

Zach nodded. "They don't stay kids for long."

"No, they don't," Clay said, suddenly thinking no longer of the lobos but of Zach. His nephew would be college-bound in only a few short years, but this place, this zoo, had given the boy back some of his childhood.

And for the first time, Clay didn't feel uncomfortable in the role of guardian. Standing in this room, witnessing all that his nephew had accomplished…it felt natural.

It struck him that ever since Zach had arrived at the ranch, Clay had felt like an imposter. He hadn't known anything about raising a child, especially a kid with Zach's history. There'd also been an underlying guilt that he was trying to replace his brother…that by taking in Zach, he was acknowledging that Greg could never be a real father.

But finally those doubts had vanished as thoroughly as low-lying clouds burned away by the hot morning sun. Life with Zach wouldn't always be easy. They still had plenty of rough patches ahead, but they had started to put down their own ruts, forming a groove that worked.

Clay only wished he felt as certain about his relationship with Lacey. He knew she'd made his connection with Zach possible. Oh, they would've made it here eventually, but it would have taken longer. But even though she'd helped smooth things over with his nephew, Clay couldn't shake the feeling Lacey and he were headed for a tangled mess. Navigating the town's hatred of the Stevens family wasn't going to be easy, even if she fully trusted him. And Clay worried very much that she didn't…at least not completely. Something had broken between them when she'd learned about the wolves' disappearance. It bothered him that she'd believed he'd kill one of her wolves and then keep it a secret. And worse, he sensed she'd begun to doubt him again. She'd spent years considering him the enemy, and he feared she might once again.

It didn't help that their relationship would be forced into public display at the upcoming wedding. He just hoped their newly formed bond was strong enough to endure the increased pressure.

---

June and Magnus had taken a risk with an outdoor wedding in late spring. But the sun shone brightly over the huge tent the men had erected. Lacey knew June had rented heaters, but her friend wouldn't need them. The air carried a warmth that whispered of summer adventure.

Normally, on a day like this, Lacey would pull on hiking boots and head into the wilderness, but she wouldn't miss her friend's wedding day. Plus Clay had promised they'd check on the wolf pack tomorrow as long as she felt up to it.

But Lacey didn't want her worries to ruin her enjoyment of the ceremony, especially since the tent overlooked the bear exhibit. June had joked that Frida, the zoo's grumpy grizzly, should've been a groomswoman for Magnus since she'd been his confidant during some critical points in their relationship. The elderly bear, however, had no interest in the festivities. Instead, she snoozed happily, her head resting on her favorite rock. Once or twice, her nose would twitch or one brown eye would pop open, but she otherwise ignored the commotion.

The one-year-old Sorcha wasn't so cavalier. She'd moved to the edge of her exhibit to watch curiously. A couple of

# A COWBOY STATE OF MIND

---

The good folks of Creedence, Colorado get behind Creedence Horse Rescue in a brilliant new series from Jennie Marts

Scarred and battered loner Zane Taylor has a gift with animals, particularly horses, but he's at a total loss when it comes to knowing how to handle women. Bryn Callahan has a heart for strays, but she is through trying to save damaged men. But when a chance encounter with a horse headed for slaughter brings Zane and Bryn together, they find themselves given a chance to save not just the horse, but maybe each other…

*"Full of humor, heart, and hope...deliciously steamy."*

**—Joanne Kennedy, award-winning author, for *Wish Upon a Cowboy***

For more info about Sourcebooks's books and authors, visit:
**sourcebooks.com**

times, she'd grown bored and played with her rubber toys. The last time, she dragged one over so she could entertain herself and keep her eyes on the milling humans.

Beside Lacey, Clay shifted uncomfortably in his chair. She glanced at him, and although he kept his face impassive, she could sense his tension. To his left sat Zach, who'd just joined them after helping with the animals participating in the ceremony. The teenager looked as uneasy as his uncle. She didn't blame either of them. As people waited for the ceremony to begin, everyone's focus seemed locked on the two Stevenses. Ever since Clay had sat down, a low buzz had spread through the gathering. Lacey just hoped June hadn't miscalculated when she'd extended the invitation to them. Clay and Zach didn't need more town gossip, and June and Magnus deserved to be the center of attention.

Thankfully, when Abby appeared leading Savannah, the crowd collectively turned to watch her. Lacey didn't miss the way Zach's face reddened when he caught sight of the other teen. The girl's lavender-colored cocktail dress complemented her gray eyes and upswept black hair. Although the style was youthful, she looked elegant as she made her way to the front of the tent with a wide smile on her face.

The juvenile camel appeared just as happy as she practically pranced behind Abby. Her silly grin reminded Lacey of a pleased toddler's.

Katie appeared next. Everyone had expected her to lead Lulubelle, but instead, she pulled a red wagon festooned with hibiscuses, lavender, and pansies that matched the bouquets the bride and bridesmaids carried. Inside the Red Flyer under the careful watch of Sylvia the capybara were Katie and Bowie's twins. The girl wore a lavender dress that matched Abby's, and the boy sported a tiny tuxedo with a purple cummerbund. At the sight of the babies, the crowd gave a collective *awwww*.

Next, June's best friend from college, Josh, appeared herding two baby goats. The little kids bleated and bucked down the aisle. Laughter filled the tent, and even the solemn-faced groom cracked a wide smile. Though Lacey had known about the surprise, she couldn't stop her own grin. The cheerful, bucking goats fit with June's exuberant personality. Unfortunately, the sound of the chuckles overwhelmed the critters. Their breed had a tendency to "faint" when overexcited, and the poor little kids toppled over as their legs locked. Josh made a big display out of scooping them up and carrying one under each arm.

The "Wedding March" began to play, and June's father appeared leading Lulubelle, who was tethered to Hank. June rode on the male camel's back, her train draped over his large hump. She looked radiant as she waved to the onlookers. Lacey turned her attention to Magnus and saw him watching his bride with unbridled love. His spellbound expression was made extra special by the fact that he normally showed little outward emotion. Even with his ironclad control, he couldn't contain his affection for June. It just radiated from him.

Suddenly, in the midst of all the joy and laughter,

Lacey felt an unexpected punch of sadness. Not because she hadn't seen a similar expression in Clay's eyes when he gazed at her but because she didn't know if she could trust its staying power. They had an unpleasant past behind them and a difficult future ahead. Could they ever reach a point where they could stand before the town of Sagebrush Flats and pledge their love?

---

Scamp ran as quickly as he could with the flowers in his mouth. The Gray-Eyed One pelted after him. She'd kicked off the ridiculous things strapped to her feet. Scamp did not understand why female bipeds, even one this young, wore pointy spikes under their heels. It forced their feet into odd angles, and it looked very painful.

Scamp glanced behind him. The human had slowed, her hand on her waist. Her dress fluttered in the wind, and Scamp debated about grabbing it instead. But she seemed to want the collection of hibiscuses, lavender, and pansies that Scamp carried between his teeth. The Blond One, who had been dressed all in white with a sparkly object in her hair, had momentarily placed the collection of flowers on a bench while she stood in front of the fainting goat pen. Scamp had grabbed it, and the Gray-Eyed One had given chase. But the purple fabric of her dress *did* look so pretty and light. He could easily tear off a piece to bring back to his enclosure.

Scamp was so busy focusing on the tantalizing

material that he didn't hear the footsteps behind him. Strong hands wrapped around his midsection, hoisting him into the air. Scamp cried out in surprise, dropping his prize. The Gray-Eyed One quickly scooped up the bouquet as Scamp twisted helplessly in the Blue-Eyed One's grip.

"Thanks for coming so quickly." The Gray-Eyed One made breathy sounds as the bipeds walked in the direction of Scamp's enclosure.

The Blue-Eyed One jerked his head toward the limp, broken clump of posies in the female's hands. "I don't think the bride is going to want those anymore."

"Miss Winters—I mean Mrs. Gray—wants to throw her flowers into the goat pen instead of the traditional bouquet toss. I can add some flowers from my arrangement so it looks good in the photo."

"This is the weirdest wedding I've been to. Okay, it's the *only* wedding I've been to, but I don't think I'll ever be to another one like this."

The Gray-Eyed One laughed, the sound bright. The Blue-Eyed One's grip tightened slightly before he released Scamp into his home.

"You're a Sagebrushian now, so I'm sure you'll be to another crazy wedding."

"A Sagebrushian? You're willing to claim me as one of your own, huh?" The human's voice had a funny note to it. Scamp eyed him curiously. The Blue-Eyed One wore a broad, cheeky smile that matched his tone.

"Yup. Are you ready to be one of us?"

"You know..." The Blue-Eyed One drew out the sounds he made as the bipeds walked in the direction of the human gathering. "I think I just might be."

Something in the Blue-Eyed One's tone made Scamp grin his toothy smile. He liked seeing his biped happy.

---

Clay couldn't help but feel on display as he sat beside Lacey in the smaller tent he'd helped set up outside the prairie dog enclosure. He tried to focus on the little rodents scurrying frantically about as they flashed warning signals with their tails. Despite concentrating on their antics, he could still feel angry gazes boring into him like a swarm of enraged wood bees. The only reprieve from the stares had been during the ceremony.

The unseasonably warm day didn't help his mood either. Lacey looked like a wilted poppy beside him in her red-orange sundress. This morning when he'd picked her up, she'd been radiant. He'd only seen her in jeans or her ranger's uniform before, and the way the bright, soft fabric had clung to her curves had left him momentarily stunned. Between her excitement and the warm tones of her outfit, the gold in her topaz eyes had shimmered in the bright light.

Now, that glow had been replaced by a bleariness he immediately recognized. Although she'd been steadily improving, an event like a wedding was bound to be hard. The heat had always aggravated his brother's concussions, and the loud music and spinning dancers would be additional triggers. He leaned close, trying to ignore the death stares he received.

"How are you feeling?"

Her responding smile looked a little brittle. "Hanging in there."

"Do you want to go soon?"

She winced. "No. It would look too much like a retreat. We need to stick this out."

His eyes narrowed as he reached for her hand. "How bad is your headache?"

"Nothing a few aspirin won't fix."

He momentarily considered hoisting her into his arms and carrying her back to the truck. She wouldn't appreciate the gesture, and he didn't want to cause a disruption.

"Lacey, we've got plenty of time to get the good folks of Sagebrush acclimated to our relationship. It's not like people are speaking to me anyway."

A worried crease appeared between her brows, and he felt like an ass. He hadn't meant to make her worry more.

"We have to try, Clay." She squeezed his hand, but he didn't know if she meant to give him or herself encouragement. "We can't slink off at any sign of disapproval. We need to get used to the stares, and our relationship will just have to be strong enough to survive all the attention."

A raspy feeling scratched at Clay's chest. Her last statement sounded ominous...almost as if she doubted they could weather the scrutiny. Ever since Lacey had learned about the missing wolves, a slight tear had formed in their relationship. Lacey must have sensed the fissure too, and hell if he knew how to repair it.

"Lace—" he began before he heard the tinkling sound of a knife hitting crystal. Another guest had taken advantage of the slight lull between the songs to signal the couple to kiss. Since Magnus looked decidedly uncomfortable with the tradition, the townsfolk had gleefully taken every opportunity to clink glasses.

The groom gave a gusty, beleaguered sigh that reminded Clay of the zoo's grumpy grizzly. Just as he leaned over to give his laughing bride a kiss, a microphone screeched. Everyone jerked in the direction of the piercing squeal.

In the middle of the dance floor stood a sloppily drunk Pete Thompson. Clay's former foreman hadn't even dressed for the wedding. He wore a wrinkled T-shirt and a pair of mud-splattered jeans. His cowboy boots oozed muck onto the dance floor, and his hat was lopsided.

"Sorry to interrupt the festivities." Pete slurred his words as he watched the crowd with bloodshot eyes. "But this couldn't wait."

Clay shot to his feet with Lacey close behind him. Bowie, Josh, and June's brother, August, who was wearing his Air Force dress blues, all moved toward Pete. The former foreman swiveled in the other men's direction before his reddened eyes rested on Clay. His mouth instantly twisted in contempt.

"Thought you'd get away with it, didn't you?" Pete said. "Well, you don't fire me."

"Uncle Pete, please," Lacey said quietly, "this is June's wedding day. Don't do this to her when you're really angry at Clay and me."

"He shot one of your wolves." Pete's voice had a chill to it as he stalked toward Lacey. "Since you won't see reason, I gotta accuse him publicly before he poisons you with the snake-oil charm he inherited from his daddy."

Pete's accusations seeped through Clay like liquid nitrogen, freezing everything in its path. He swung toward Lacey, desperate for her not to believe the lies. But her face had already gone chalky white. The confusion in her topaz eyes sliced Clay.

"I didn't harm any of the lobos, Lace." Clay felt like someone had shoved a handful of gravel down his throat.

Before he could say more, Pete yanked out his smartphone. The former foreman triumphantly held it aloft like he'd won a grand prize. No one could make out the picture, but that didn't stop the murmurs. "I have proof of what I saw on your land. Land *my* family took care of for generations."

Lacey moved toward the older man. Clay wanted to reach out and stop her, but he didn't. He couldn't prevent her from looking at the doctored photos.

But he couldn't stay silent either. When he spoke, he tried to keep his voice steady when all he wanted was to outshout Thompson. "Lace, whatever is on that phone is a hoax. I'm telling you I didn't hurt any of the pack. You need to believe me."

People were talking loudly now. He heard several rounds

of "damn Stevenses" and even more of "she should've known better than to trust a Stevens." Despite the fact that Pete Thompson had drunkenly crashed a wedding, the crowd clearly viewed Clay as the villain in this drama.

---

Denial came first. Then the pain arrived. Like an out-of-control burn, it seared every inch of Lacey's heart. She'd *trusted* Clay. She'd shown him parts of herself that she'd kept closed off since her father's and brother's deaths. He'd told her, he'd *sworn* to her that he hadn't been responsible for the missing wolves. It didn't make sense that he'd lie and hurt her like this, but she couldn't argue with the image on the screen. There was no refuting that one of the female lobos lay sprawled on *his* land. She recognized the canyon in Pete's photo, the slope of the red cliffs as they reached for the sky, the ribbon of water snaking through the cottonwoods and aspens. And more importantly, she knew the wolf. Although she couldn't spot any obvious wounds in the picture, no lobo would sleep in that position.

Her brain buzzed, and she had trouble thinking. She could only feel. And in the firestorm of emotion, her mind had one single focus: the image of the motionless predator, its power and grace silenced forever.

"You're hunting them." Her throat had tightened so much, the words physically hurt, but she couldn't stop them.

"He said he didn't do it."

Lacey whirled in the direction of the new voice. She

found Zach standing next to his uncle, his face white except two flags of color over his cheekbones. He swallowed and glanced up at Clay. "I've grown up around adults who lie all the time. I know how to spot bullshitters, and my uncle isn't one of them."

The pressure in Lacey's head built. Clay had promised he hadn't killed the missing wolves, yet the photo seemed to prove otherwise. One thing was clear. She would not discover the truth with the whole town watching and her heart feeling like an eggshell crushed under the weight of a predator's foot. She needed to get out of the bright, relentless sun and away from the noise of the crowd. She needed to *think* clearly.

So she turned and left. She didn't stop until she reached Main Street. She shoved her fingers into her purse and pulled out her key to the Prairie Dog Café. Her mother had closed down the restaurant for the wedding, and no one was inside. After she locked the door behind her, she collapsed into the nearest booth. Burying her head in her arms, she burst into tears.

---

"Are we going to look for Ms. Montgomery?" Zach asked as they climbed into Clay's truck. After Lacey's abrupt exit, Clay had apologized to Magnus and June and then had retreated before the police officers in attendance got over their shock and arrested him.

"No," Clay said tersely.

"But she was really upset, and those photos were convincing, and—" Zach said, suddenly choosing to be chatty.

"Zach, I said *no*." The last word burst from Clay's lips in a brusque shout. His nephew instantly quieted and deflated into his seat. The sight punched through Clay's frustration, and he tried to force himself to calm. Too many adults had dumped on this kid when he hadn't deserved any of it. And Zach…Zach had just defended him. He'd believed Clay. He'd trusted his word. Clay didn't know if he could recall anyone else doing that. Ever. Even Lacey hadn't had enough faith in him.

Fresh pain ripped through Clay, but he ignored the fissures of heartache. He had to focus on Zach and on figuring out how a dead wolf had ended up on his land.

"I'm sorry," Clay said, pleased his voice sounded so damn normal. "I shouldn't have snapped at you."

Zach shrugged one shoulder, and another burst of frustration exploded inside Clay. Had he messed up his relationship with his nephew while trying to internalize the fallout from the one he'd shared with Lacey?

"I'm pissed off," Clay said. "I feel so damn helpless about this mess. I'm sorry I took it out on you."

Zach straightened a little. "I don't think you killed that lobo if that makes a difference."

Despite the dark emotions roaring inside him, Clay felt his lips quirk into a genuine smile. "It does, Zach. I should have thanked you for standing up for me back there. That was brave of you. It meant a lot."

Zach lifted his shoulder again and then dropped it, but

this time, the gesture didn't seem insolent. It was tinged with empathy instead. "Anytime. That was some crazy shi—stuff back there."

Clay nodded solemnly. He debated his next words and decided he needed to know. "Why do you believe me?"

Zach's blue eyes widened. Clearly, he hadn't expected that question. Clay realized how often Zach had been asked to blindly trust adults who'd failed him, yet people kept asking him to do it again.

His nephew was quiet as he gnawed on his lower lip. When he spoke, his voice was unusually thoughtful. "Because I think you may be the first person in my family who hasn't lied to me. When you say something, you do it, even when I don't make it easy."

Thickness banded around Clay's throat. Zach's words brought back a lot of his own childhood memories. The times his mother promised to take him into the city and then forgot to tell him she had a shopping trip with her friends planned instead. The endless summer days when his parents were off enjoying their separate vacations instead of taking him and Greg to the beach as they'd planned. The number of school holidays he spent with just Greg and their latest nanny.

"I always hated when my parents promised they'd do something and then they didn't," Clay said. "I didn't want to do that to you."

Zach nodded stiffly, and Clay could tell he was battling back his emotions. "I also don't think you'd do something that crappy to Lacey."

Clay felt his grip tighten on the steering wheel. "I wish she thought the same."

"The pictures were pretty bad."

"I know," Clay admitted. "But this has been building. She's been looking at me suspiciously ever since she found out a couple members of the pack had disappeared. Maybe part of her had already concluded that I was picking off the wolves one by one."

"You *were* pretty vocal about getting rid of them."

"I wanted them in a reputable zoo, not dead," Clay said. "I was always clear on that."

"One time when my mom was lucid, I remember her telling me people only hear what they want to hear. Funny thing was it described her perfectly. My father too," Zach said.

"Is that why you're not talkative?" Clay asked. "Because you don't think anyone's really listening?"

"Yeah," the teen admitted.

"I promise to pay attention to what you say, Zach."

"You do okay most of the time. But Ms. Montgomery really listens. That's why I think she'll come around. She was just shocked and worried about the lobos."

Clay rubbed a hand over his mouth before returning it to the steering wheel. "Don't get too upset if that doesn't happen." He hadn't considered Zach's feelings about his and Lacey's apparent breakup. The kid was close to her, and he'd had enough adults walk away from him. Hopefully, Lacey wouldn't lump him with Clay, and she'd maintain some sort of a friendship with Zach when they saw each other at the zoo.

Suddenly, another worry twisted through him. He hadn't thought through the full ramifications of Pete's accusations. As Zach's stand-in parent, he should've. If he ended up getting charged and convicted for killing the wolf, he didn't know how it would impact his guardianship. The rumors had a real possibility of jeopardizing his nephew's chances for getting a job at the zoo when his community service ended. If Bowie Wilson believed the accusation, he might not want to take his chances on Zach.

"This is a fucking mess," he said.

Despite the situation, Zach smirked. "And here I thought we were watching our vocabulary."

"I should've taken a better look at the photos." Clay ignored Zach's comment. "It was definitely my land, but maybe the pictures were photoshopped."

"Your tech-hating foreman doctored photos?" Zach asked. "Did he even own a computer?"

Clay sighed. Zach had a point. Pete detested anything digital. He was constantly riding Clay for how much time he spent in the office. The man probably wouldn't know the first thing about manipulating an image.

"Could Pete have shot the wolf himself?" Zach asked.

"Ah hell," Clay said as things started to click in his head. "Speckles."

"If that's a replacement cuss word, it sucks."

Clay shook his head as he started to see a pattern. "Speckles is the cow that was recently injured."

"The one that you thought was hurt by wolves?"

"Yeah, but Lacey found a human footprint at the scene. She and I considered whether Pete might've done it, but I didn't think he'd risk a cow's safety for a cheap trick. Maybe I was wrong."

"Purposely chasing a cow into a steep ravine is kind of demented," Zach said, his eyes wide.

"Yeah," Clay said. "It is. Pete's hatred of me must run even deeper than I thought."

"Are you going to tell the police?" Zach asked.

Clay shook his head. "They'd dismiss it as a crazy conspiracy, especially coming from me. I need proof."

"How are you going to get that?" Zach asked.

"I honestly don't know," Clay said. "The first thing I need to do is to check the wolf's body."

"I'll come with you."

Clay glanced at his nephew. "Pete might be a little unhinged, Zach. Accompanying me might not be a wise idea."

"He's back at the wedding reception," his nephew pointed out, "and he was drunk. There were lots of cops at the wedding. I don't think they'd let him climb into a vehicle."

"I still don't know, Zach."

"I might see something you don't."

All the sullenness had vanished from the teenager's face. He looked eager. It wasn't just the mystery either. The kid obviously wanted to help, and Clay needed it. After all, no one else would believe him. And in this shitstorm, it was good to have someone beside him who did.

Zach was right. It was extremely unlikely Pete Thompson would be up to hiking. Drunk as he was, he'd likely trip and get stuck in a dried-up arroyo. He'd been pretty unsteady on his feet, and Clay didn't think he could stay on a horse's back either, even with all the time the man had spent in the saddle. In fact, Clay was beginning to wonder how the man had managed to take down a wolf in his condition. Maybe he'd felt so guilty, he'd started drinking afterward, or he'd knocked back a few to screw up the courage to crash a wedding.

Either way, Pete wasn't going to make it to the back pasture now, especially not before Clay and Zach did. And Clay found he didn't want to be alone. If he rode out solo, he'd start thinking about Lacey. And then he'd have to deal with the pain of, once again, not being enough.

# Chapter 11

Lacey woke up when the bell on the front door of the Prairie Dog Café jangled. She raised her head from the scarred wooden surface of the table to find her mother standing beside her with a worried look. Neither of them said anything for a long moment. Lacey expected to see an "I told you so" expression on her mother's face, but she didn't. Peggy Montgomery only said, "I'll go make us something to drink. Do you want tea or coffee?"

"The second," Lacey said. She needed the extra caffeine. Her mother nodded and disappeared into the kitchen. Lacey sighed heavily and leaned her head on the upholstered bench.

She remembered the day she'd met the deceased female lobo. Lacey had been visiting the local wolf rescue center and looking for candidates to release in Rocky Ridge National Park. Her supervisor had been with her, but she'd let Lacey take the lead on selection. Lacey had liked the female immediately. Even as a pup, she'd had spunk as she'd tussled with her brothers and sisters. Lacey distinctly remembered the wolf barreling into two of the boys and simultaneously wiping them out before she pounced on them, her tiny tail wagging enthusiastically. She'd become a matriarch in the pack and an excellent hunter.

But had Clay hurt her?

Away from the heat, the gyrating dancers, and the constant noise, Lacey's brain could focus, and the image of Clay taking the lobo's life didn't fit. But was it because she didn't want it to…or because it really did not?

*I didn't harm any of the lobos, Lace.*

Clay's voice flashed through her mind. Deep. Earnest. Unwavering. He'd spoken with a quiet conviction. He'd stared at her, his eyes solemn and urgent. He'd wanted her to believe him, to trust him. But in that chaotic moment, she hadn't.

"Do you want to talk about it?" her mother asked as she sidled into the booth across from Lacey. She pushed a white mug in Lacey's direction before lifting the other one to her own lips. Both were emblazoned with the Prairie Dog Café logo that Katie Wilson had designed. Lacey just wrapped her fingers around the hot ceramic and stared into the dark liquid.

"You sure you want to hear about Clay?" she asked.

"I'm your mother, Lacey, and you're hurting."

Lacey sighed and finally took a sip. The bitter liquid slid down her throat. Her mother had always made her coffee strong. Folks in Sagebrush Flats liked it that way, and as Peggy said, if they wanted the fancier stuff, they could head over to June's tea shop.

"I'm confused, Mom, and my brain just won't let me think."

"So you need a sounding board. I make a good one."

Lacey stared across the table at her mother. Some people said they looked like twins. They both had the same chestnut-brown hair, although their eye color was different. They even possessed the same endless energy and drive. Although Lacey's dad had understood her the best, that didn't mean she and her mom weren't close.

"Mom, I already know what you're going to say."

A ghost of a smile touched her mother's lips. "Don't trust a Stevens."

Lacey knew her answering grin was even weaker. "Something like that."

"And you don't need a knee-jerk reaction right now?" Her mother took another sip of her drink.

Lacey nodded glumly.

Her mother was silent for a beat, and then she placed her cup deliberately down. "You're so much like me in every way, Lacey, but you have your daddy's heart. He could open it up to anybody and anything."

"That's what led to his death."

"The whole town was taken in by Clay's father. Cynical old cowboys and penny-pinching business owners fell for his scheme. He knew how to make a sales pitch that preyed on people's dreams, and your father had a lot of them, sweetheart. But in that respect, you're more like me. Practical. Steady. Clear-headed. You can smell bullshit from a mile away, and you didn't smell it on Clay."

Lacey stared hard at her mother. It almost sounded like she was defending him. "What do you mean?"

"I don't think you would be with a man who you thought was capable of hunting a wolf like that."

"He's capable of shooting a lobo to protect his herd,"

Lacey said slowly, "but you're right. He wouldn't just leave the body. Even if he didn't inform the authorities, he'd bury the animal respectfully."

"I agree that it doesn't make sense for him to leave the wolf out in the open. His land is remote, especially the part with the narrow canyons like the one in the photo, but it's also the closest to the park. A hiker could have easily stumbled upon it. Tourist season is picking up, especially with the college crowd."

Lacey pressed her fingers against her temple. "I just wish it wasn't so difficult to think. It's hard right now to trust my own conclusions."

"What do you feel, Lacey? That's what your dad would ask."

Lacey screwed up her face and told the truth. "I don't believe Clay did this, but I'm not sure if it's because I logically think he didn't or because I don't want it to be true. I also feel frustrated, like I'm missing something."

Her mother nodded slowly and drank more coffee before holding the cup in her hands. "Let's walk through this together."

"Really?" Lacey asked.

"Yup," her mom said. "In fact, I suggest we call your grandfather. He knows the land out there, and he's a rancher. He might understand how Clay would think."

A humorless laugh escaped Lacey. "Don't let him hear you make that comparison. He won't be happy about helping us."

"He'll behave, and he's addicted to detective shows. Stanley and he binge-watch them all the time."

"Maybe I shouldn't have gotten him that video-streaming subscription for Christmas."

"Are you kidding? He loved it once you got it set up. Let me give him a call. We'll help you work this out."

Lacey nodded, because she had to talk to someone. All she wanted was to go to Clay and lie with him in the dark. He'd hold her tightly as she spoke in the blackness and unraveled her messy jumble of thoughts. But that wasn't an option, no matter how much she wanted it to be.

Luckily, it didn't take long for her grandfather to arrive. He sat down next to her mother. "So you don't think Stevens killed that lobo?"

"If we're going to do this, can we please call him by his first name?" Lacey asked. "I want to work this out, not get more confused by bringing our family histories into the mix."

Her grandfather sighed heavily, but he didn't protest as he started again. "So you think Clay is innocent?"

"I *feel* he is," Lacey corrected, "but I'm not sure what to think. It's like I have all the puzzle pieces, but I can't get them to fit."

"Well," her grandfather said as he leaned back as far as the booth would allow, "why don't you start at the beginning?"

"There's been an increase of wolf sightings on his land," Lacey said. "We've never spotted one, but his neighbor Tim Forrester has."

"I didn't realized Tim rode his land that much," her

grandfather said. "He owns a few head of cattle, but not enough for a viable operation."

"He's more of a hobby rancher," her mother pointed out. "He made his money on Wall Street, and this is his retirement. He did say he liked to ride."

"I never thought of that," Lacey said slowly. "Some of his calls were in the middle of the night. It seems like an odd time for a retired investment banker to be out."

Neither her mother nor her grandfather seemed particularly comfortable with Lacey's knowledge of nocturnal activities on Clay's ranch, but they didn't comment. Instead, they stayed quiet as Lacey mulled over the information. A thought skittered around the edges of her mind, but she couldn't quite bring it into focus.

"When was the first incident?" Her grandfather finally broke the silence.

"That was during the day," Lacey said. "Clay was showing me his plans for restoring the ciénegas on his land—"

Her grandfather straightened. "Stevens is thinking about turning his property into wetlands? Clay Stevens?"

"Yes," Lacey said. "Why?"

"Seems like an awful lot of work for a city boy who just wants to live off his grandfather's legacy."

Lacey scowled irritably. "That's Pete Thompson talking. Sure, Clay wants to make a profit, but he cares about both the land and his cattle. He has good ideas for running the place."

"Pete sure as hell doesn't like that boy," his grandfather said. "I was surprised he didn't up and leave the ranch long before Clay fired him."

"Do you think Pete could've done this?" her mother asked, her voice excited.

"I don't know." Her grandfather placed his arm on top of the booth as he considered. "He has a temper, but I can't see him hurting an animal just to frame Clay—even if he was as drunk as a skunk. I wonder how he even got out to that part of Clay's ranch. He could barely walk straight."

"Shhh." Lacey sliced through the air with her hand to signal them into silence. "I'm just on the edge of a theory. I need to think, and you two are distracting me."

"Was it about Pete?" her mother asked. "If Clay didn't do it, my money is on him. He's grown into a very bitter man."

"No," Lacey said. "It's got everything to do with the first time Tim Forrester alerted Clay to the presence of wolves on his ranch. I remember thinking something was off at the time, but I had trouble focusing because of my head injury."

Lacey closed her eyes and imagined that day. Suddenly, a blazing moment of clarity burned through her mental fog, and she saw what she was looking for. All the other tidbits of information finally fell together in a clear narrative. Opening her eyes, she focused on her grandfather. "I think we need to make a visit to Pete Thompson."

---

Once at the ranch, Clay quickly grabbed his camera while his nephew saddled the horses. Riding hard across the land, he, Zach, and Ace reached the narrow canyon as the sun was beginning to set. Light still illuminated the land, but it had the golden glow of late day. The red hills provided a vibrant contrast to the pale sky as they rode into the area. The creek moved lazily along, the waning rays glinting off the surface. The whole landscape looked like the end scene of a Western where the good guy had defeated the bad guy and peace had been restored. Normally, Clay would take time to appreciate the sight. He'd stop his horse and just let himself steep in the beauty. Moments like this typically gave him a sense of pride and belonging.

But today, the serenity only mocked him. It wasn't just a cruel foil to the storm of pain and frustration raging inside him...it was a reminder that even if he felt a connection to Sagebrush Flats, its residents would never accept him. His roots on his mother's side of the family didn't count...only the poison on his father's.

"I don't see anything." Zach looked through the pair of binoculars they'd brought.

"Really?" Clay said. They'd stopped the horses on a promontory overlooking the narrow slit of land below. This section of his ranch and Tim Forrester's had a maze-like patchwork of small canyons carved by the river. The cliffs in this particular canyon were distinctive, and Clay had no doubt the wolf's body had been located here.

"I'm not spotting the lobo," Zach said as he handed the binoculars over to Clay. He scanned the area by the old cottonwoods where the animal had lain in the photograph. He observed nothing but grass, weeds, and a couple of ravens.

"That's odd," Clay said as he nudged his horse forward. Ace barked excitedly as if sensing his humans' confusion. Together, the three of them headed down the switchback trail with the dog in the lead. When they reached the gnarled old trees, Clay and Zach stopped as they surveyed the landscape. Ace began yapping, his tail moving furiously as he sniffed the ground. He moved in a zigzag pattern, fluctuating between prolonged snuffles, happy snorts, and enthusiastic woofs. Finally, he stopped in one spot. He pawed at the dirt, his nose practically buried in the soil.

"I guess we should look there," Clay said. They both dismounted. After tying the horses to the tree, they crouched low. The grass was compressed, and Clay noticed a strand or two of fur.

"Well, the wolf was here," Clay said.

"Do you think Mr. Thompson would've moved the animal?" Zach asked.

"It doesn't make much sense," Clay said. "He would've wanted to leave the lobo as evidence."

"Who would've done it?"

Clay shrugged in confusion. "I don't know. Even if Lacey called her supervisor, I don't think either a ranger or the game commission would've removed it already. It would've been hard for anyone to beat us here."

"Maybe the wolf isn't dead?"

Before Clay could consider Zach's theory, he heard the

rev of engines in the distance. His nephew also jerked his head in the direction of the sound. Clay walked forward, scanning the ridges with his binoculars. In the distance, he spotted a group of four-wheelers on Forrester's land. They appeared headed straight for the national park. Rocky Ridge specifically prohibited vehicles like those in the backcountry. With the arid climate and slow vegetation growth, the ATVs could do a lot of damage to the delicate ecosystem.

"Looks like your friend Linus is planning on joy-riding on federal land," Clay said.

His nephew scowled as he took the binoculars again and lifted them to his eyes. "Linus and I stopped being friends..." Zach stopped suddenly as he shot Clay a look.

"When he ditched you and let you take the fall for the wolf den cave-in?" Clay finished.

"You knew?"

Clay shrugged. "I had a good idea."

Zach scuffed the ground with his foot. "You never liked him."

Clay wisely didn't speak. No one appreciated a "told you so."

Zach lifted his eyes again. "I think you were right."

"He reminded me of a rattler," Clay said.

Zach gave a half smile. "You sound like you're from Sagebrush."

"I *am* from Sagebrush, whether folks around here want to admit it or not, and now so are you."

Zach grinned. "Abby just said something similar."

"She's a smart girl."

Zach nodded, but the smile on his face faded. "The photo Mr. Thompson showed made me start thinking back to that day. I…I think Linus knew the wolf pups were in that den. The others didn't. But there was something about the look on his face when he started the cave-in. Something mean. I'm starting to wonder if Linus killed the wolf in Mr. Thompson's picture—or at least shot the lobo."

Clay blinked. He didn't like Linus Forrester, and he didn't have any difficulty imagining the kid hurting an animal. But the scrawny, self-indulgent teen didn't seem the type to successfully stalk and kill an alpha predator like a Mexican gray wolf. At least not on his own.

"Do you think Linus would do something like this?"

Zach swallowed. "Yeah. He snuck into the zoo a couple days ago. Scamp bit down on his ankle, and I think Linus would have killed him if the adult honey badgers hadn't appeared."

Clay scrubbed his hand over his mouth as he tried to process what Zach was telling him. He wanted to ask more questions about what had happened between Linus and Zach to make Scamp attack the older teenager, but they didn't have the time at the moment. They needed to focus on the current problem. "Is Linus a good shot?"

"Very. We fooled around with his dad's guns a lot. Mr. Forrester is really, really into hunting. He's got all kinds of rifles and gear. There's a shooting range on the property. I've only been there once when Linus's dad went away for a long weekend. He doesn't like his son to bring friends onto his ranch. I think it has something to do with the dogs he raises. There were a lot of empty cages. I didn't see any, but I heard howling."

"Howling?" Clay asked sharply.

"Yeah. I thought it was a wolf or something, but Linus said it was a hunting dog."

"Zach, what exactly did you see on the property? You said hunting gear. What type?"

"The normal stuff and then some really weird rifles. Lots of my friends in Ohio were hunters, but they didn't have stuff like that. It almost looked like a fake gun with a really skinny barrel. One of my friends actually thought it was for paintball, but when he touched it, Linus freaked."

Clay whipped out his smartphone. If they'd been any closer to the national park, it would be useless, but the signal was just strong enough. Pulling up a picture of a tranq gun, he showed it to Zach.

"Is this it?"

Zach leaned close, studying the picture for a moment. "Yeah. It was. What would Mr. Forrester be doing with one of those?"

Clay pushed back his cowboy hat and jammed his hand in his hair. "At first, I thought you might be talking about an illegal hunting operation, but maybe Forrester is selling the lobos to people who want exotic pets. Gray wolf hybrids exist, but Mexican wolves are rare."

"Why would someone want an endangered species?" Zach asked.

"Power. Bragging rights. Exclusivity. For the same reasons someone would trophy hunt or buy a stolen painting he couldn't display. And Tim Forrester would have a lot of connections with people like that."

"Still seems pretty dumb and mean to me."

Clay began to pace as he arranged all the details in his mind. "It makes sense now."

Ace noticed his movements and started to prance around him, oblivious to the enfolding human drama. His tongue lolled out, his wide mouth stretched in perfect doggy bliss as he tried to weave his big body through Clay's legs.

"What makes sense?" Zach tugged on Ace's collar to keep him from tripping Clay.

"Every alleged wolf sighting was by Tim Forrester, but we never saw a single one. Hell, he purposely sent us on wild-goose chases."

"Why would he do that?" Zach asked.

"I was his fall guy," Clay said. "Everyone knew I didn't want the pack on my land. When the lobos started disappearing, people would naturally blame me. But then Lacey and I started to date, and his plan suddenly had problems. So he wanted to rile me up, rile her up."

"But it didn't work."

"No," Clay said. "He must have escalated by injuring my cow. When I didn't go nuclear on the wolf pack, he switched tactics and arranged for Lacey to distrust me."

"That kinda all makes sense," Zach said. "What are we going to do next?"

"*We* aren't going to do anything," Clay said. "You're going back to the ranch with Ace."

Zach's eyes narrowed in stubbornness. "What are you planning?"

Clay ran his hand through his hair. He didn't like this part of the scheme, but he didn't see how else he could convince the town of the truth. "I still need evidence. By the direction they're headed, it looks like they might be hunting tonight. Maybe the wolf in the photo escaped, and they're going after the lobo. If I can snap some pictures before it's too dark, hopefully that will convince folks."

"Your idea is sort of crazy, Uncle Clay," Zach said. "The Forresters have nasty tempers."

"That's why you're staying back. If I run into trouble, you can alert the authorities."

Zach crossed his arms. "You don't have to treat me like a little kid."

"One of us has to stay behind in case this goes south," Clay said. "This is my fight, Zach."

"I'm the one who's been working at the Sagebrush Zoo doing time that Linus should be."

Clay gave his nephew a dry look.

Zach shifted and scowled. "Okay, maybe I'm not completely blameless."

"Zach." Clay paused, choosing his words carefully. He doubted the Forresters would shoot him over an illegal animal trafficking operation, but his plan wasn't without danger. He needed to ensure that Zach didn't follow him. Although the teen might not want to be protected, Clay had every intention of making sure he stayed safe. "This is something I have to do. It's my reputation, my business, my world Tim Forrester is trying to destroy."

"Okay," Zach said reluctantly, "but if I don't hear from you within a couple hours, I'm calling the police."

"Fair enough," Clay said as he headed to his horse.

"And Uncle Clay?" Zach asked.

"What?"

"Be careful. It took me a long time to find someone who gave two shits about me and who I gave two shits about back. I don't want to have to try to find someone else."

Clay paused in getting up in the saddle. It was odd, not being completely alone in a crisis. Even though he'd never been a natural loner, through the years, he'd learned to live by himself. But now it looked like he needed to figure out how to be part of a real family. "I won't take any unnecessary risks, Zach. I promise."

---

Lacey and her grandfather found Pete Thompson at a dive bar just outside town. The place reeked of stale smoke, spilled beer, and the vague smell of horse. Pete was seated on a stool when they took one on either side of him. He glanced up belligerently before staring back down at his drink.

"Told you Clay Stevens was no good." Pete slurred his words.

"Clay didn't shoot that wolf," Lacey said. She was

certain of that now. She shouldn't have doubted him. Her distrust had hurt him, and she might have even irreparably damaged their relationship. The pain of that loss would come. It lurked inside her, ready to knock her down. But she couldn't allow that. Not yet. She needed the truth. For her sake. For Clay's. And for the wolves.

Pete snorted. "Are you really that naive, Lacey?"

It was her grandfather who spoke. "My granddaughter has her head screwed on a lot better than you."

Pete took a long drag on his beer. "Never thought I'd see the day you championed a Stevens, Buck."

Her grandfather shrugged off the statement. "Neither did I, but I also never thought I'd see you like this either."

Pete sloppily lifted his glass in a mock toast. Alcohol sloshed from the rim, landing on the wooden bar. "Getting fired will do that to a man."

"So will bitterness," Buck said, "and something tells me you're starting to rot with it."

Pete gave a mirthless laugh that ended in a sneer. "Don't mess with me, Montgomery. I'm not in the mood."

"Who sent you the pictures of the dead wolf?" Lacey asked.

Pete glared at her, his eyes streaked with red. "Who says I didn't take 'em myself?"

"The stench of beer. You smelled like a walking, talking brewery at June's wedding reception," Buck said. "There's no way you hiked to Stevens's back pasture."

"That land should've been mine," Buck growled. "Frasier should've left it to me, not to a whiny city boy."

"Clay's ancestors worked that land for just as long." Buck's gaze held Lacey's as he spoke. "According to my granddaughter, he's a good rancher. He cares about his cattle and the land too. Heard he's trying to make improvements."

"He wants to turn the spread into a damn swamp."

"It makes ecological sense to bring back the ciénegas," Lacey argued.

Pete snorted, but Buck said, "Something has to be done about the water shortage. The kid is trying something new. Maybe we should all give him a chance."

Pete's expression turned deadly. Clearly, he didn't agree with Buck. Lacey sighed. She'd respected this man, and she had to believe the old Pete Thompson lurked somewhere underneath a decade worth of resentment.

"Someone deliberately chased one of Clay's cows into a steep ravine," Lacey said. "It was reported as a wolf attack, but I found a shoe print, not paw prints, at the scene."

Pete jerked into a sitting position. His arm bumped his beer, but luckily, the glass didn't fall. His expression looked sharper and more aware as he crossed his arms over his chest. "I didn't hurt the animal."

"No," Lacey said, "I don't believe you'd attack a cow. But I think the person who sent you the photo would. Clay didn't shoot that wolf, Pete, but someone did. Someone who isn't afraid of forcing a defenseless animal into a potentially deadly situation. Do you really want to protect a person like that?"

Pete shifted awkwardly in his stool. "I don't like Clay Stevens."

"You don't have to," Lacey said. "I just want the name, Pete."

"Tim Forrester. Tim Forrester sent me that picture."

---

The purplish tones of dusk had just begun to mix with the golden evening light when Clay found Forrester and his son in a box canyon. The duo had cornered a snarling wolf, her lips pulled back, her ears flat against her head. When the lobo leaped toward the riders, the men revved the engine.

Clay stiffened. He didn't like how the men were toying with the animal. They'd been taunting the lobo so long that he'd had time to sneak into the canyon and snap pictures. The four-wheelers had drowned out the sound of his descent while the men's attention had been focused on their target. From what Clay could tell, the wolf's tranq had worn off, and she had escaped before the Forresters could cage her on their property…or they'd let her go to extend the chase.

Over the hum of the motor, he could hear their laughter—cruel and triumphant. It was clear this wasn't even about the challenge of the hunt. This was about the trophy…and power. And that caused a sick feeling to twist through Clay like a thrashing bull snake. None of this was right, but he had no idea how to stop them. He had no gun, and his cell phone didn't have reception. He doubted his mere presence would cause the men to retreat.

That was when he saw it—a flicker of movement on the opposite side of the canyon. The light had grown dim, but he could still make out the two people cautiously making their way to the edge. Even if he'd only spotted her silhouette, he would have recognized the energetic way her small form moved. Lacey. And the other figure with his uneven gait was her grandfather.

Clay sensed the exact moment Lacey witnessed what was happening. Her whole body went rigid, her hands clenched at her sides. He watched as her muscles began to coil. She reminded him of a mountain lion, ready to pounce.

The cliff on her side was steeper than the one Clay had descended. Most people wouldn't even consider climbing down the jumble of sandstone rocks and outcroppings. But Lacey had also rushed headlong into a collapsing cave to rescue wolves. And she'd grown up clambering over surfaces like these.

Just as Clay feared, Lacey started a rapid descent down the slope, heedlessly sending stones hurtling into the valley. The men on the ATVs didn't notice, but Clay did. Her grandfather rushed forward, but he had no hope of stopping her.

Clay didn't think. He just knew he couldn't let Lacey risk the dangerous cliff. He stepped from the rock sheltering him, right into the view of the Forresters...who were armed with more than just tranq guns.

---

Protective fury propelled Lacey over the edge of the cliff. She acted blindly, ignoring her grandfather's cusses. Her foot slipped a couple of inches before she grabbed a tree root. She turned her head to check on the scene below, and every organ in her body petrified. Clay walked calmly out in front of the line of ATVs blocking the narrow entrance to the canyon. Behind him, the miraculously still-alive female wolf made a low, threatening sound deep in her chest. Only the noise of the vehicles kept the frightened predator in her crouched position.

"What the hell are you doing here, Stevens?" Tim shouted.

"Trying to stop you from committing a federal offense on government land," Clay said, his voice steady and easy as he walked toward the four-wheelers. Linus reached down and pulled out a rifle, leveling it on Clay. Mindless rage suffused the younger man's face, twisting it into an ugly mask. A chill tore through Lacey as she realized she hadn't put all the pieces together properly. Tim Forrester hadn't attacked Clay's cow. His son had.

As she stared at him in his gray hoodie, another horrible realization struck. He was the one who had intentionally collapsed the unstable wolf den. It hadn't been an awful, youthful mistake. Possessed with a cruel streak, he'd intended to bury the mother and pups. And now he had a gun pointed at Clay.

Lacey's muscles moved before her brain even formed a

plan. She scrambled up the cliff and rushed to her mount. Both she and her grandfather had rifles on the backs of their horses, but his eyesight wasn't great in low light. Although she didn't particularly like guns, she was an excellent shot.

"Put the weapon down, Linus," Tim said, his voice tight. "We can't shoot him."

The sound of the rifle cocking bounced off the tight canyon walls, funneling it up to Lacey.

"Why not? Nobody likes him. The police wouldn't look too hard." Linus had taken up a hunter's stance as he looked straight down the barrel.

Lacey exchanged a look with her grandfather. He gave a slight nod, and she fired off a warning shot that buzzed over the men's heads. A new chorus of profanity ricocheted off the cliffs. Clay used the distraction to drop to the ground and roll toward the canyon wall.

"Linus," Lacey said, trying to infuse her voice with calm authority while also shouting to be heard, "put your weapon down. Now."

The eighteen-year-old wavered, his eyes flicking from side to side as he tried to locate her. It was clear he didn't completely view her as a threat.

She fired at the ground near them. "That was another warning. If you keep holding the gun, I'll adjust my aim."

"You couldn't hit me if you wanted," the boy said, but his bravado sounded hollow now. His father's gaze swept the canyon nervously.

Lacey's grandfather spoke next. Despite the fact that

he had to raise his voice to be heard, he still managed to sound like he did when he quieted a spooked horse. "Tim, my granddaughter's a crack shot, and your boy is threatening to kill the man she loves. I suggest you do something about your son."

Tim bit off some more colorful language as he yanked the rifle from his kid's hands. A bullet went into the dirt, which thankfully didn't land anywhere close to either Clay or the wolf. With Linus disarmed, Clay began to scramble up the cliff to escape both the Forresters and the cornered lobo. His feet slipped a couple of times, but he didn't slow down.

"Tim, it would be a good idea for you to leave now," Lacey said.

As if to punctuate her words, the wolf emerged from the crevice where the animal had managed to wedge herself. Her snarl turned into a full-fledged growl.

"Linus, we better go."

"But—"

"*Now*, Linus." Either the parental command in Tim's voice or the low rumble coming from the lobo finally got through to the eighteen-year-old. He made a disgusted sound in the back of his throat, but he spun his four-wheeler around and sped from the canyon with his father close behind. The wolf bounded away, her body a dark blur in the gathering shadows.

From her vantage point on the opposite cliff, Lacey watched as Clay finished making his way up the side of the canyon. He moved carefully now, but then he hadn't grown up scurrying around the rocks out here like she had. She doubted he had much climbing experience. He slipped a few more times, and each time she saw him fumble, pain seized her heart, threatening to tear her apart from the inside out. Finally, he pulled himself onto solid ground. He sat there for a moment, his head resting on his knees. By the way his shoulders heaved up and down, she could tell he was breathing heavily. She wanted to run to him, but there wasn't an easy path to the other side of the ravine, and it would take time to reach Clay. Before she climbed on her horse, she needed to make sure he was all right.

Using his hands to push himself from the ground, Clay stood stiffly. The incident had clearly left him shaken. Lacey understood completely. If her knees weren't locked in place, she might have collapsed too. Ever since he'd reached safety, her body had begun to quake. She'd managed to keep the tremors outwardly in check, but that didn't mean she didn't feel more unstable than an active fault line under pressure.

Clay gave her a wave, and tears sprang to her eyes. He was okay. The man she loved was okay.

---

Evidently, standing between a loaded rifle and an irate wolf took all the stuffing out of a man. Clay felt as eviscerated as one of Ace's plush chew toys. Despite his legs feeling like a gelatin salad at a picnic on a hot summer's day, he managed to pick his way back to his horse. When he swung his legs over Midnight, he just sat there for a moment, patting the gelding's neck. The horse whickered softly, and Clay forced himself to relax. He'd made it out of that canyon alive thanks to Lacey.

The thought of her brought another rush of adrenaline. He didn't know exactly how she'd ended up at that box canyon, but he intended to find out. Had she meant to confront him? Or Forrester? Did her presence mean she'd trusted him enough to reconsider all the facts, or had she been trying to track him down to prove he was behind the wolf disappearances?

He knew one thing. He loved her—completely and utterly. Although his mind hadn't processed that fact until now, his soul had realized it the moment he'd watched her skitter down the canyon wall. He couldn't afford to lose her...even if in some sense he might have already. Because he couldn't be with someone who could never fully trust him. He'd spent his whole life trying to seek people's approval, and he couldn't do that with Lacey.

Sucking in his breath, he gently tapped Midnight with his heels, and the gelding began to move. Although the day had been unseasonably warm, a night chill had descended over the desert. The cold gave him another infusion of energy, but it didn't help his shaking muscles.

It took a good ten minutes before he spotted the shadowy outline of two riders headed in his direction. The smaller of the pair jumped off her horse after throwing the reins to the other. Clay dismounted, hoping it didn't look as awkward as it felt. He didn't mind showing weakness around Lacey, but he didn't want to add evidence to her grandfather's belief that he was nothing but a greenhorn.

She was in his arms in a second. He wrapped them tightly about her as he lifted her into the air. The heat from her body spread through him like a brilliant sunrise over the arid land. The cold permeating him finally lifted, burned off by her warmth. He buried his nose against her neck and breathed in her familiar scent.

"You could've gotten shot!" Lacey's scolding tone managed to be both watery and steely at the same time. It wasn't hard to detect the lingering panic tingeing her exclamation. Despite everything, he felt his lips curl upward at her fierceness. She was ever the protectress, his Lacey.

"And you could've tumbled down the cliff and then been hit with a bullet," Clay countered.

She made a snorting sound as her hands clutched his T-shirt. "I know these canyons. I would've been fine."

"You're no more bulletproof than I am," Clay pointed out as he kissed the side of her cheek.

"When Linus aimed his—"

"I know," Clay said softly. "I got the same gut punch when you started to slip down the canyon wall."

"I love you, Clay," Lacey said. "It shouldn't have taken me so long to say it, but I do love you. The forever, earth-shattering, this-is-the-one type of love."

Emotion clobbered him. He couldn't even speak for a moment. His grip on her tightened even more as he held her against him. Closing his eyes, he forced himself to find the willpower to talk.

"I love you too, Lace."

She pulled back, tracing his face with her fingers. The last rays of light had vanished from the horizon, but the silvery light of the moon gave enough illumination. "You do such a better job of showing it. I'm sorry, so sorry for doubting you. I should've listened to you like Zach did."

"Thanks," Clay said.

"It's no excuse, but I couldn't think properly. It was so hot at June and Magnus's wedding, and there was so much movement and sound. I felt like I was drowning from dizziness, and then Pete showed up with those pictures."

Clay held himself still as he asked, "What made you realize it wasn't me?" He felt like he was climbing the cliff again with two predators—one human and one canine—below.

"I ended up at the Prairie Dog after I fled the reception," Lacey said. "All these emotions were pumping through me, and I didn't know how to handle them. I collapsed into one of the booths and sobbed myself to sleep."

Clay kissed her temple as he stroked her hair. "Pete Thompson is a bastard. He shouldn't have sprung those pictures on you in public."

"He wanted to hurt you, and I allowed him. I realized that as soon as I woke up, when I could think again. But I—I was still afraid to trust myself. Not you, Clay, myself."

"I don't understand."

"With my concussion, it is so hard to process things when I'm upset." Lacey hugged him tightly. "I *knew* you wouldn't treat a dead animal like that...or hide something so important. But I didn't know if I could believe my own brain. Then I talked through my conclusions with my mother and grandfather. At first, I thought it was Pete, but then I realized all the stuff that's been bothering me about the alleged wolf sightings on your land."

"And you figured out it was Forrester?" Clay asked as relief rushed through him.

"Yup."

"And your family agreed?"

"They trusted me even when I didn't," Lacey said. "You're a good man, Clay Stevens, and you belong here in Sagebrush Flats and on this land. I'm done with letting our histories interfere."

He kissed her then—deep and hard. It was a kiss of homecoming with a promise of a future. It focused the frenetic energy bouncing inside him, making it strong and steady. He'd never felt so complete, so content. He would've made the embrace longer, but he hadn't completely forgotten about the presence of her grandfather or the need to get back to Zach.

They broke apart, but Clay couldn't let Lacey go completely. Snagging her hand, he wrapped his fingers about hers, resting his thumb against the pulse on her wrist.

"You kids done affirming you're both alive?" Buck asked. "I'm getting tired of looking at the inside of my cowboy hat. Didn't seem to be any other way to give you privacy. Moon's damn bright tonight."

"You can look now, Grandpa," Lacey said. "And it's a good thing we have this much illumination."

Just then, Clay heard the sound of four-wheelers. Lacey's fingers dug into his hand as another burst of adrenaline pumped through him. Quickly, he jumped on his horse and then hoisted Lacey up behind him. He set off in the direction of Buck, who'd started moving toward them. When they reached each other, they positioned their horses to protect Lacey as she dismounted and got on her bay.

Buck extended his rifle to Clay, the glow from the moon highlighting the worried creases in his already leathery face. "You good with a firearm, son? My eyesight isn't what it used to be in the dark."

"I'm not as good as Lacey," Clay said as he accepted the gun, "but I can hold my own."

The buzz of engines drew closer, and it dawned on Clay that the noise came not from Forrester's property but his own. Lights appeared on one of the ridges to his land, and a voice called out through the darkness.

"Is that you, Clay?" It was his new foreman's voice.

"Yeah, Rick. I'm here with Lacey and Buck Montgomery," Clay hollered back.

"Your nephew was worried you might be in trouble. He said you didn't want to call the police without proof, but we figured we better lend you a hand just in case."

"Thanks," Clay shouted back as the three of them started riding again. "The situation is under control, but I appreciate the assist." The would-be rescue party waited on the ridge, clearly not wanting to enter the national park unless necessary. A strange feeling swept over Clay as he approached the line of men, and not just because it felt like an updated version of an old-fashioned Western. He hadn't expected anyone to believe his wild theory against Forrester, even with the trouble on the ranch. But his men had come for him. They wouldn't have known Buck and Lacey had also decided to investigate. For the first time since he'd inherited the property, he didn't feel at odds with his ranch hands. Maybe with Pete gone and Hernandez in charge, they'd finally form a real team.

"How's it feel to have a bunch of people concerned about your safety?" Lacey asked quietly.

"Like I might finally start to belong."

He could hear the smile in her voice when she spoke. "You already do. We just all needed to stop being so doggone stubborn and realize it. And, Clay?"

"What?"

"We're a clannish bunch here in Sagebrush Flats."

He snorted. "I'm well aware of that."

"But once we claim you as ours, we don't let go."

"I'm counting on that." Clay wished he could pull her onto his horse again and just hold her tightly. "Especially with one resident in particular."

---

It was close to midnight before Lacey finally collapsed onto Clay's bed. Once they'd all made it back to his ranch and Lacey had contacted her boss about the Forresters' illegal animal trade, everyone had wanted to hear their story. Buck had relished every minute of it. He'd beamed from ear to ear, and the embellishments grew with each retelling. Her mother had driven out to check on the three of them. She'd even hugged Clay. It had been an awkward embrace but a start. The police arrived and took statements from everyone. The Forresters had tried to flee the area, but county law enforcement had spotted their truck and arrested them. Animal control had found one of the missing male wolves on Tim's property and had a solid lead on the whereabouts of the second. The recovered animal was thankfully in good health.

Lacey felt the bed dip, and Clay settled down beside her. They'd left the drapes open, and the silvery light of the moon filtered through the curtains. Memories of their first night together drifted through her mind like a familiar song as she snuggled against him. He gently kissed her cheek before drawing her even closer.

"I love you." She relished saying the words. They came easily, bringing a buoyant joy.

He pressed his lips against the back of her ear and gave her lobe a little nibble before whispering, "Same here, Lace."

She turned in his arms, needing to see his face. They'd spoken about this already, but they'd been high on adrenaline, their bodies still prepped for a danger that no longer existed. But the charged energy had drained away, leaving nothing but raw honesty.

"I'm sorry I doubted you," she said again. "I let my old prejudices define you."

Clay traced her shoulder lightly with his finger. He hadn't stopped touching her since they'd dismounted from their horses. She'd also needed the constant connection. Watching Clay challenge the Forresters with an angry wolf at his back hadn't been easy, and she needed physical reassurance that she hadn't lost him.

"You believed me in the end," Clay said. "There's nothing to forgive. You're human, Lace. Those pictures were damning, and your head was throbbing. I just...I just need to know that deep down, you see me as worthy."

"Oh, Clay!" She cupped his face in both her hands as his word choice caused a sizzle of pain deep inside her. It spoke of the loneliness he'd faced during the years—the hopelessness of never quite fitting in. "You *are* worthy. More than worthy."

He kissed her, his lips soft. Liquid pleasure pooled through her, her limbs going deliciously lax at the slow, sweet assault. He lifted his head a few inches, his eyes glittering with intensity in the low light. "I've never felt so right as I do with you, Lacey."

She pushed her hands under his soft cotton T-shirt so she could spread her fingers over his warm skin. In this moment, she needed to feel him with no barrier. "It's the same for me, Clay. After my dad's and brother's deaths, I shut part of myself off. I was afraid to love and lose again."

"And now?" he asked, his husky voice catching ever so slightly. She could see a nervous flicker in his eyes.

"I think," she said significantly, "that in the end, it's much worse living an armored existence. It's a half life, and I don't want that anymore."

"Good." He pressed his lips against hers for a quick kiss.

"Because I don't want just part of you, Lacey. I want it all. The ugly, the beauty, the pain, the joy, the dark, and the light."

Tears burned in her eyes from the sheer intensity of the moment. She blinked, and when she spoke, her voice sounded hoarse. "And I'm planning to give it to you, Clay. Because I want to, need to. I could build a million walls between us, and I swear you could dynamite each of them down without even trying. What I feel for you, the connection between us, it's that powerful. You're an incredible man, Clay Stevens, and so easy to love."

"Lace." His rough voice injected her name with layer and layer of meaning. He crushed her to him, his mouth hungry and demanding on hers. Power rippled through both of them. They'd come together in a blaze of passion before, but this...this eclipsed anything she'd ever felt. It didn't consume her, it fueled her. Every cell inside her felt energized.

He rolled her under him, and she thrilled at the press of his body. Despite propping himself up on his elbows, he managed to frame her face with his hands as his lips slid hungrily against hers. For a long while, they did nothing but explore each other's mouths. Slowly. Thoroughly. Completely.

His fingers moved first, trailing down her sides, stopping to sweep over her breasts and then skimming down to grip the hem of her shirt. His mouth headed downward, his lips and tongue tasting each bit of skin he exposed. He watched her as he did so, his eyes gleaming in the low light.

Need tightened her chest, momentarily trapping her breath. She felt wonderfully powerful and cherished.

Love swamped her as she reached up to bury her hands in his soft locks. His gaze never left hers as his mouth closed over her nipple. She gasped, her back arching. He used the opportunity to pull her shirt up to her shoulders. Then he lifted her, his lips still around her breast. Supporting her back with one hand, he pulled the shirt over her head with the other. She wanted to remove his, but then his tongue started doing wicked things to her already-sensitized body. He blew gently across her wet skin, the sensation causing her to shiver. His whiskers scraped against her flesh as he moved to the right, his free hand now massaging where he'd kissed. Unable to stop herself, she pressed against him, heedless of the layers between them.

Listening to her unspoken command, he gently laid her down on the bed. He pulled off her loose pants. He kissed the back of each knee before gazing down at her, the expression in his eyes just as enticing as the weight of his body. "You're so beautiful, Lace."

She smiled, finally gathering enough sense to tug his T-shirt over his head. He obliged, shifting his body. The moonlight washed over him, once again making his blond hair appear almost silver and his skin marble. She felt the corners of his lips turn up as she skimmed her fingertips over his chest. He certainly didn't feel cold. His heat permeated her as she reached lower. Dipping her hand into his boxers, she watched as his eyes fluttered shut. She stroked him as pleasure washed over his face. He held nothing back as the emotions freely played over his features. His lips parted ever so slightly as he groaned softly.

Leaning forward, she pushed his underwear down and kissed his tip. His eyes opened, searing hers.

Gently, he lifted her, bringing her mouth back up to his. Together, they managed to undress him while still maintaining contact. This time, he lay down on his back, her legs straddling him, her torso flat against his. His hands brushed down her spine, sending sparks everywhere. She wiggled her hips, and his moan poured through her.

"Did you like that?" she asked against his mouth.

"Hell yes." His fingers gripped her rear, positioning her. Then he framed her face, his eyes earnest. "I don't want anything between us anymore. Can you trust me?"

She understood instantly what he wanted. Just as he'd given her all his emotions, he wanted the same. This was as much about mental nakedness as it was about the physical.

She smiled and nodded. He gently stroked her breasts, and she gasped at the whisper of contact.

"You know what I've always admired about you, Lace?" he asked, his voice tight.

She shook her head helplessly as his calluses swept along her sensitive skin. Her body had begun to glide against his, unable to withstand the sweet pressure building inside her.

"Your energy," he said. "You're like a star, burning and spinning so brightly you have your own gravitational pull. And I've been helpless against it from the beginning."

She moaned as he thrust deep inside her.

"Can you shine for me, Lace?"

She smiled at him, somehow finding her voice despite

the love swamping her. He understood her so well. How could she not feel hopelessly entangled with him?

"I think that can be arranged," she told him, her voice low, "since you make me feel like I could glow forever."

And then, smiling down at him with all the affection bubbling up in her, she began to move.

---

Clay almost lost control when he saw the golden sparkle in Lacey's topaz eyes. But he held on, determined not to miss out on watching her. She rested her hands against his temples as she stared down at him, her lips curled into a magical grin. Then, with their gazes firmly locked, she began to slide slowly up and then slowly down. Lust clouded her brown irises, but her eyelids didn't flutter down. Neither did his despite the urgent need rushing through him.

He held himself still, allowing her to set the pace—to take her pleasure first. Her lips slowly parted as the rest of her muscles tensed. Her breathing changed, becoming more and more unsteady. She moved faster, need and pleasure flitting across her face, permitting him to see and feel everything she experienced. This, this was the vulnerability he'd asked for, and it practically undid him.

When she came, her eyes finally drifted closed. He lifted his hips, prolonging her climax as long as he could. Her eyes opened, lazy and satisfied.

"Your turn," she said, her voice just as smoky as the deep-brown accents in her irises.

He thrust as she moved downward. Like her, he turned himself over to pleasure, withholding nothing. His groans mixed with hers. He stopped thinking. Hell, he might have even stopped breathing. But he didn't stop feeling. He allowed the sensations to roll through him unchecked, leaving nothing of himself protected. He held her gaze for as long as he could. When he came, his eyes shut, and his body trembled from the force of it. She collapsed on top of him, pressing a kiss against his jugular.

They lay there, both gasping, their bodies slick with sweat. He'd never felt so drained and energized at the same time.

"That…that was incredible," she whispered against his ear.

"No," he said hoarsely as he traced the delicate ridge of her spine. "*We're* incredible. Together."

She wiggled up his body to rest her head on his shoulder. He had no idea where she'd found the energy to even move that much. He listened as her hard, short breaths slowly softened into shallow little snores. Smiling at the sound, he lay still in the darkness. Sleep beckoned, but he wanted to enjoy the peace flooding through him just a little more. There'd be other nights like this. Years of contentment stretched before them like untouched prairie lands. But tonight…tonight was special. Because it marked the beginning of something he'd looked for his entire life—belonging.

# Epilogue

"So Bowie's planning to introduce some female wolves soon?" Buck Montgomery asked as Clay stood with him, Lacey, her mother, and Zach at the edge of the wolf exhibit the teenager had helped build. The kid hadn't even tried to hide his enthusiasm as he'd shown Buck and Peggy Montgomery the zoo. Over the past few months, the two families had been spending more and more time together. Although Zach sometimes pretended the get-togethers annoyed him, Clay could tell his nephew was secretly pleased to have so many adults interested in him. The entire staff at the Prairie Dog Café had practically adopted him. He hadn't had to pay for a single lunch the entire summer.

The townsfolk had become surprisingly accustomed to seeing the Stevens boys at the restaurant. Ever since word had spread about Clay stepping in front of a loaded rifle to protect Lacey and a wolf, he'd lost his greenhorn status. The Prairie Dog Café proudly advertised that its burgers were made with Valhalla Beef, and June Winters had started offering cured cuts at her tea shop. She'd also started selling the jerky on her website in addition to her jams, and Clay and she were in discussion with Rocky Ridge National Park to stock some at its gift shop.

"Yeah," Zach said in answer to Buck's question about Perseus and Theseus. "Bowie says he wants to create a pack here at the zoo."

"He received grant money to set up a breeding program," Lacey said. "He's going to work in conjunction with the wolf rescue center and Rocky Ridge."

"Ah, just what we need. More lobos." Clay's sardonic response earned him a poke in the ribs from Lacey. They'd reached a détente about the canines. Clay had invested in some fladry fences to use next spring. With Lacey's input, he'd bought a couple of Karakachan dogs already trained as livestock guardians. Rick had started assigning men to sleep with the herd at night. Clay had put himself in the rotation, and Lacey had joined him under the stars a couple of times. Rick was also teaching them all to use the low-stress herding techniques he'd mentioned during his interview. Clay planned on using some of the funds from his increased beef sales to buy motion-activated alarms to scare off the wolves too.

"It's hard to think of Theseus and Perseus being founders of a new pack," Zach said. "They still act like giant puppies."

As if to prove Zach's point, Theseus began to howl, and his brother threw back his head to join him. They'd grown comfortable with the exhibit. Bowie and Zach had added a lot of trees for shade and a number of boulders for entertainment. Since the zoo owned acres of undeveloped land and Bowie had received more grant money, they'd been able to make a large enclosure with plenty of room for additional wolves. Theseus was already showing signs of leadership, with Perseus eager to follow his brother's lead. Although the wolves were still juveniles, Bowie and Lou wanted to introduce the females when the boys were still young to avoid conflict. They hoped it would increase the chances of the animals forming strong familial bonds. A wolf conservation center back East had a few females that weren't suitable candidates for release and that would add good genetic diversity.

Suddenly, Theseus's howl turned into more of a bay. His ears flattened as he crouched low. His brother followed suit as the two predators began a coordinated stalk toward a large log. Just as they reached the felled tree, a black-and-white head popped into view.

"Scamp," Zach said, his voice a mixture of frustration, worry, and a little admiration.

"Is that the baby honey badger?" Peggy Montgomery asked.

"Not exactly a baby," Lacey said. "He's bigger than his mom now. He hasn't quite reached his dad's size, but we think he'll eventually overtake Fluffy."

"What in tarnation is he doing in there?" her grandfather asked. Both wolves took a swipe at Scamp, but the little mustelid was too fast. He darted away, barely avoiding the scrape of Theseus's claw.

"He likes to live dangerously." Zach frowned as he watched the chase. When the wolves got too close to the honey badger, the teenager banged on the fence to distract the lobos. Clay swore the little weasel shot Zach a dirty look for interfering.

"Scamp reminds me of someone I used to know," Clay said.

"Har har," his nephew said dryly, his gaze never leaving the mustelid's darting form. "He's been playing with the wolves since they were little, but I always worry."

Scamp paused by the fence. He made a chittering sound, causing Clay to laugh. "Is he mocking the two wolves?"

"Apparently so," Zach said crossly.

Lacey laid her hand on the teen's shoulder. "They do this all the time, Zach. I don't think any of them would hurt the other. Scamp's father, Fluffy, and Frida the grizzly have played together for years. It's not ideal, but at least it gives the animals exercise and a little excitement."

Both wolves dive-bombed Scamp, but once again, he was quicker. With a flick of his tail, he slipped under a small hole in the fencing and darted onto the path. He paused a moment to scold them before disappearing through a bush.

"Yep. He definitely reminds me of someone I used to know," Clay said.

Zach crossed his arms over his chest. "I was never that bad."

Clay shook his head. "Oh no. You were worse."

"I still can't believe you didn't kick me out."

"We're a pack." Clay slung his arm over Zach's shoulders. "We stick together."

---

"That was nice," Lacey said as she buckled her seat belt. "I enjoyed hanging out at the zoo together. I still don't know why we needed to do it so early in the morning though."

She swore Clay looked a little nervous as he shrugged. "I wanted to take a hike with you today. You keep saying you want to check on the wolves now that all the lobos captured by the Forresters have been released back into the park."

Lacey nodded. Although she'd returned to her job and her symptoms had begun to fade, her brain still wasn't a hundred percent healed. Long walks, especially in the sun, could make her head swim. She'd been stuck with visitor-center duty all summer. Luckily, Clay would take her for short hikes on her days off. They'd started slowly, going a little farther and moving a little faster each time. At his insistence, she'd even talked with her therapist about how to properly push herself without causing a setback.

"Zach's surprisingly pumped about spending the day with my grandfather at my uncle's ranch," Lacey said. "I couldn't believe he talked so much during the car ride to the zoo."

"Each week that passes, he's relaxing more and more," Clay said. "He's a good kid."

"And you're a good father figure," Lacey said.

"Thanks," Clay said. "Your family has done a lot for him too. He feels part of something. We both do."

"My grandfather's taken a special shine to him. From the stories Stanley tells about their days on the rodeo circuit, Grandpa was more than a little wild before he met Grandma. I think he sees a part of himself in Zach."

"Heaven help us all," Clay groaned as he pulled his truck into the trailhead's parking lot.

"They're good for each other," Lacey said with a smile as she climbed out of the cab. She hoisted her knapsack.

"Zach is more interested in the ranch since this summer's restoration work on the ciénegas," Clay said. "The group from your alma mater helped move it along."

"Dr. Juarez was really impressed," Lacey said.

Clay nodded. "She emailed me yesterday about setting something up for next summer. I meant to talk to you about it last night, but it slipped my mind."

Lacey smiled wickedly. It had been Clay's turn to watch the herd, and she'd joined him. Suffice it to say, she found "sleeping" under the stars an inspirational aphrodisiac.

"When are you on night duty again?" Lacey asked.

She watched as Clay tried to smother a smile and feign nonchalance as they started to hike along the trail. "I don't know. I'll have to check with Rick. Is there any reason you're asking?"

"Oh, I think you know my reasons," she said casually. "There's just something about the night air and me."

"I'd say," he told her with a smile.

She sobered. "It's great how much your ranch hands respect you now."

Clay nodded. "I thought they'd grumble at the night watch, but Rick's a good foreman."

They fell into silence as they wound through the landscape. Lacey loved these moments with Clay. Even in the quiet, she felt a hum of connection between them. She'd always enjoyed the outdoors, but sharing it with him meant so much more. He was an observer like her, his eyes catching things other people overlooked. He embraced this land, this place, just as much as she did.

When they reached the wolves, Lacey stifled her gasp of delight. The recovered males lounged in the sun with the rest of the pack as the young pups tussled each other. In this heat, the adults wouldn't begin the hunt until dusk.

"I can't believe we're here, together, watching this," Lacey breathed, not taking her eyes off the majestic animals. Back when they'd been arguing at town hall meetings, she never would've imagined that one day, they'd hike to see the wolves together…or that she'd want him by her side. But he'd become just as critical as the canines in front of her.

She heard a rustle and turned to see Clay on one knee in the red dirt. It didn't escape her notice that he'd purposely avoided disturbing the cryptobiotic crust growing on the soil. In his hands, he held an open ring box, the diamond glinting in the sun. The setting was old, and she knew at once he'd used a Frasier heirloom.

"Lacey, my whole life, I've yearned to belong," Clay said. "Then I fell in love with my grandfather's ranch. I wanted to live where my ancestors did. To be connected to something. But it never felt real until the night after our confrontation with the Forresters. I finally found my home. With you. In my arms. Like I told Zach earlier, we're a pack. You. Me. Him. Your mom and grandpa. There's nothing I want more than to make it official. Will you marry me?"

She couldn't speak. Tears sprang into her eyes as she nodded fervently. Laughing and crying, she sank to the dirt beside him and flung her arms around him. Their lips tangled together. They broke apart to stare at each other, their eyes bright. He chuckled then, low and deep. The sound curled inside her belly, filling her with joy. Their mouths met again, and in their kiss, she could taste the promise of their future.

# Author's Note and Acknowledgments

Lacey's concussion is partially based on my own experiences with mild traumatic brain injury. In 2011, I bumped my head on a heavy chandelier. As newlyweds in our first home, my husband and I had yet to put a table under it, and I walked right into it. It took me nine months to realize the symptoms that I was feeling (headaches, lightheadedness, nausea, visual issues, light sensitivity, etc.) were related to what I thought had been a minor event. Due to the wonderful care I received through the UPMC Concussion Clinic and PAVC Vision Therapy, I fully recovered after another nine months.

Fast-forward to Christmas 2018 when my overenthusiastic, bouncing toddler cracked her head against my nose. Suddenly, in the middle of writing a book about a heroine with a concussion, I once again found myself battling one of my own. This time, I received excellent care through the Allegheny Health Network, UPMC, and PAVC Vision Therapy.

I have had a wonderful support system during both my recovery periods. My husband has twice—without any complaint—taken over additional household responsibilities, allowing me time to both heal and meet work deadlines. My mother has also been a huge help, making meals and helping watch my daughter. Their assistance enabled me to write and complete this book while dealing with the aftereffects of a brain injury. Writing about a concussion while suffering from one proved difficult at times. My friend and fellow writer Sarah Morgenthaler, who has also dealt with a concussion, kindly volunteered to read through my manuscript. A former barrel racer, she provided insight on what steps Clay could take to make horseback riding easier for Lacey. (If I included any inaccuracies in my description of riding with a concussion, they are solely my own.)

I also want to thank my friend Laura McVay for helping a thoroughly corporate attorney better understand the mechanics of the criminal justice system. Ms. McVay has worked both as a prosecutor and as a public defender, and I am profoundly grateful for her and the other lawyers who are instrumental in making our court system function as it was intended. Public defenders provide an important service to our country, often with low pay and little recognition. They are also statistically more at risk than prosecutors for being a victim of a violent crime in connection with their job.

Any mistakes that I made in regard to Zach's arrest, charges, and experiences with the diversion program are solely my own. As alluded to by defense attorney Marisol Lopez, many youths, especially those of color, do not get the opportunity to avoid juvenile detention through a diversion program. It is also less common in the federal court system than at the state level.

Once again, I would like to thank my editor, Deb Werksman, and the entire team at the Casablanca imprint for helping me bring my stories to life. Ms. Werksman's advice pushes me to make sure the characters—both human and animal—are vibrant and real to the reader. Using the right name for a juvenile animal (i.e., *kit* for honey badger, *cub* for bear, *pup* for wolf) can get confusing, but the copy editors make sure I keep it all straight. The art department provides beautiful covers, while the marketing department ensures that the books reach readers' hands.

I want to express my gratitude for my readers. Thank you so much for taking a chance on a beginning author by reading my books, leaving reviews, recommending to a friend, interacting with me on social media, or otherwise supporting my work. I very much enjoy hearing from all of you, and you can find me at facebook.com/laurelkerrauthor, instagram.com/laurel_kerr, and twitter.com/laurelkerrbooks.

## About the Author

Erin Marsh fell in love with the American West at the age of nine when she rode a slow, stubborn mule named Minnie Pearl down the cliffs of Bryce Canyon in Utah. The vibrantly colored rock formations and the nearby wide-open spaces spurred her imagination. Now she enjoys setting her stories in the untamed landscape that meant so much to her growing up.

A suburban girl who married a farm boy, she has proudly clipped a sheep's hooves (although not proficiently), helped herd the flock (with limited success), and witnessed the birth of a lamb (from a respectful distance). She lives in the rolling hills of Western Pennsylvania with her husband, daughter, and a very sleepy Cavalier King Charles Spaniel called Selkie.